LIFE

A Novel by

Derek Hunter

ISBN: 1480269255

ISBN-13: 978-1480269255

DEDICATION

To Ray Phoenix Hunter, my son and Light in the Dark, 2005 – present; and John Wisdom Dancer, my father, best friend and guide through life, 1941 – 2005.

What is Life?

A Murder Mystery or Tragedy or Comedy?

ACKNOWLEDGMENTS

This book could not have been written without the inspirational work of Francis Bacon, D.H. Lawrence, James Joyce, Henrik Ibsen, August Strindberg, Charles Baudelaire, Fyodor Dostoevsky, Anton Chekhov, Sylvia Plath, Ernest Hemingway, Jack Kerouac, and many more.

Read and ...

... find out what life is.

LIFE

A Murder Mystery(?) in Nine Parts
With Prologue and Epilogue

Written For His Son and Humanity

By
Derek Hunter

PROLOGUE.

DEATH.

A big, dark, black, deep, cruel, cruel, bellowing, boisterous laugh on Thomas Timons. How ridiculous was it to imagine Charlotte would've shown up? On this cold beach in-between Santa Monica and Malibu, in the middle of the night, years after Thomas saw her last, years after things went so sour, bad, and rotten. The whole thing had been a tragic farce, a sad, demeaning horror show.

But then why did she write the letter to him? Why did she pull his chain, yank his curiosity, toy with him after all this time, if she wasn't going to show up? He had no clue. He felt like a bum, a horrible, stupid bum, then reminded himself to think clearly, don't simplify. Self-sympathy was important. Understand why he was there, sitting on cold sand, waiting for an unlikely lover. Remind himself of everything, the hanging on, last ditch attempt this act was.

Still, he thought he was a little nutty for being out there on the beach, for a number of reasons. He got news about four months ago that Maya was pregnant with his child, a baby boy. He was excited, thrilled, joyful, truly, deeply happy. He moved in with Maya, not quite sure if he wanted to commit to her, though, because of their past.

They loved each other but verbal communication was never at its best between them. Misunderstandings came out with his move-in. After a few fights, she kicked him out only a month later. Each had reasons for positions they held. One thing was for sure, they both loved the coming child in her womb. Thomas dedicated himself to his son in his heart and was going to back it up with action, everything but commit to Maya. Fatherhood was the biggest thing to happen to him in his life. It was a beautiful, nervous expectancy.

And now here was Thomas, in the middle of the night, on a cold beach, waiting for Charlotte. He'd been sitting on the ice-like sand for two hours now. The moon was dimly shining, the reflection on the water, peeking through the waves. The ocean hurled itself onto the shore, breaking apart, crashing, roaring in its thunder claps on the earth.

An unexpected impulse rushed up inside him, urging him to jump into the water, to kill himself ... then he thought of his future son ... he couldn't do it, even after everything ... his son was the new light in his life ... as his own father was a constant, so would Thomas be for his child ...

He took a deep breath, soaking in his lungs the damp sea air. He wondered what it would've been like if Charlotte showed up and they made hot, steamy love on the beach. Then he remembered the past, all the pain, all the things he went through in his head a hundred times before. It was a short, troubled, unrequited passion on his part that resulted in hurtful lunacy. What should have been simply an unrequited love turned into a vicious conundrum.

Thomas felt Charlotte never understood what he expressed to her. Perhaps she did. If so, it was the night he gave the letter to her and not later. Also, besides her own comprehension or way of dealing with his love, there were others. Conspirators who influenced her and ganged up on him, lurked in the shadows, out of his sight, and stabbed him in the back through Iagoistic persuasiveness. There were so many, Thomas thought, who could've played the Iago to Charlotte's Othello, perhaps Charlotte herself.

However it happened back then, for right now Thomas started to believe it would've done neither Charlotte nor himself any good to see each other. He should once and for all forget about her, go home and get some sleep. She wasn't showing up. Either it was a prank by her or someone else, or something made her change her mind. But he couldn't leave. He had to hold on for a little longer. ... Who knows? ... Ten minutes and then he would leave.

Suddenly, he began hearing someone running up behind him over the sand. He turned around and before he could see who it was, the person threw a canvass bag over his face. Kicks and punches quickly started to pummel him. One hit after another, after another ... Who was this? Whoever it was, they were fast and strong, he couldn't see them, and he was getting beaten to a pulp ... it was horrendous ... blow after blow after blow ... sharp, sharp pain ... again and again ... all over his body ...

Thomas was completely helpless as he tried to fight back. He was simply a punching bag. Then something tight, thin, and hard, like a steel wire, went around his neck and began strangling him. ... This was it, he thought ... He couldn't fight back, he was losing energy, the will to struggle ... This person was set on killing him ...

... This was his death ... Thomas would never see his son ... he'd never see him born, grow up, he'd never have the opportunity to love his son, go through life with him. He'd never see Maya, never see his dad, his mom, his grandmothers, no one at all. He was heading towards the Big Nothing, Death ... He would never see this fever, this horror, this terror, this beautiful, lovely thing called life again ...

Soon, Thomas lost consciousness and was dead ... The person strangling him let go and quickly ran away ...

At least he wrote the manuscript ... at least, Thomas' son could read it and know who he was ... perhaps his son would even find out, somehow, who killed him ...

LIFE:

A PERSONAL DIARY. A RECOLLECTION OF THINGS PAST. A JOURNAL. A PACK OF LIES, EXCUSES, DISTORTIONS, SOME MAY SAY. LET THEM SAY WHAT THEY WANT. THIS IS MY LIFE. NOT THEIRS.

By Thomas Timons, for his son, Daniel Phoenix Timons.

A NOTE FOR YOU, DANIEL,

I've written this as way to document the last few years ... I could've gone back further, back to when I was born, but that would've been another thing altogether ... what I need to express most urgently to you are the last few years ...

If I'm not alive when you read this, please keep in mind that I loved you when I was ... and through this manuscript, in case there is no after-life, I will still love you through these words ... I hope this will help you understand who I was ... and perhaps you can use it to help yourself ... because, unfortunately, in life you will need all the help you can get ...

All my Love,

Your Father,

Thomas

PART ONE. CINDY.

CHAPTER ONE. RUNAWAYS.

"A couple of runaways." Rick, the tall, overweight General Manager of Canvass Directors for C.W.F.P.S.J.N. (California Workers For Peace and Social Justice – Now!) said with glee.

Rick traveled down to the Los Angeles office now and then to check in with Cassandra, the L.A. Canvass Director, and everyone else of Importance. A strange looking fellow, with a long, skinny neck connected upwards to a bald, spectacled head, and downwards to a large, wide body. There was something strict and authoritarian about him, albeit liberally, Correctly.

He wasn't especially humorless, either, as he displayed when talking about the new hires. Kurt and Cindy were the newbies. They were hired a couple days before I came back from my cross-training trip up in Berkeley. I hadn't met them yet except for a quick hello.

Stately, plump Rick etched out an imposing presence in the cumbersome Culver City office. Cassandra, Charlotte, Siango, Sharon, Max, and myself were all working on files, paperwork, and other things before going out to the Hollywood Hills to canvass. I didn't think Rick's remark was especially harmful, but the superiority-complex he and many of the others had irritated me. Around this time was when I was beginning to despise the condescending tone which the majority of activists had, at California Workers for blah blah blah and other places as well.

California Workers For Peace and Social Justice – Now! was one state affiliate of a nation-wide grassroots lobby of the same name without the California. The organization had been around for decades, under different names. It was a non-profit that began at the height of the cold war in reaction to the nuclear proliferation between the United States and the Soviet Union. Several celebrities backed the cause for nuclear disarmament and pieces of legislation were claimed the responsibility of the organization's actions.

Over the years, C.W.F.P.S.J-Now! saw ups and downs but kept itself going somehow through the down times. The early '90's saw the emergence of the current name once the Cold War ended. The reach of the organization went beyond nuclear disarmament and into human rights abuses and weapons sales, of which the latter issue the U.S. led the world.

During the mid to late '90's, the Los Angeles office saw a large drop in interest and closed shop. With the World Trade Organization protests in the late '90's, the shady dealings of the 2000 elections, the 9/11 tragedy, politics became more popular than it had in years. The L.A. office reopened months after 9/11, with Cassandra as the canvass director coming down from the Berkeley state headquarters.

Charlotte was soon hired, then Siango, and others who came and went. Six months later, I was on-board. Five months later from then, Kurt and Cindy were hired. Now at this moment they were waiting outside for me to give them their second week's training.

What the organization actually did was gather memberships from constituents (people) in various districts across the country. California was one of about twelve states that had offices. Through membership gathering (called canvassing, going door-to-door in neighborhoods city-wide or by phone drives), the organization could get money and "people power."

Each member should technically be connected to thousands of others to influence legislation by writing letters to congress, contributing to newspaper ads, going to town hall meetings, passing out literature at protests, and more. It was all done grassroots.

The effectiveness of the organization was vague and hard to pin-point, though. There was no real way to see if they influenced legislation or the way people felt on issues. By going door-to-door, at least the canvassers could interact with people to stimulate and inform on a one-to-one basis. This aspect of the job was what interested me the most.

Everyone in the office was busy with various things so no one noticed Cindy standing in the doorway, looking at everyone and smiling. I soon caught her and acknowledged her presence.

"Hey, Cindy. I'll be right there." I said.

"Okay." she replied and walked away, feeling a little unimportant with everyone acting so important and busy.

Cassandra stood writing notes on the white board, preparing the day's briefing she'd be giving soon. She was a quiet, oblique, short East Indian American woman in her late 20's, adorned with various New Age garb. She had a retro '60's hippie-dippie look meets "you control your destiny" '90's spiritualist vibe. Normally she wore long, flowing, thin, smooth material in a variety of colors.

She had a strict refusal to shave her arm-pits and legs. Whenever I caught a glimpse of these parts of her body, I saw huge clumps of thick, black hair. She flaunted her hairy armpits and legs. I have to admit my politically incorrect feelings of not getting aroused by this hairiness. Cassandra also had beautiful, large, dark eyes that were forceful in an intriguing way. Her skin was gorgeously bronze, smooth, to go along with bushy, wild, black, dread-locked hair.

The young canvass-directing woman was born and grew up in a small town near Ontario, California, east of Los Angeles. Spending a few months as a teenager in Canada and England made her convince herself to convince everyone else she was born in Toronto and went to school in London. Of course, she didn't have either accent, which she never explained to anyone.

Charlotte sat at her desk preparing files. She was more of a new arrival at Feminism, still shaving her armpits and legs, still washing herself daily. She almost looked like Paris Hilton a bit, she was that eye-catching. Better than Paris Hilton, since she looked real. She was a "Lipstick Feminist" so to speak. She came to California from the land of Minnesota, where her father was a wealthy stock-broker, her mentally unstable sister going in and out of institutions and her younger brother coming and going from Spain, living off their dad.

She stood about an inch shorter than me, about 5'9", and had the same hair color - dark, dusty blond – and same color eyes - hazel brown. We were both 25 and both had to wear glasses, although my eyes were far worse and she had contacts on most of the time. There were enough similarities between us to make people joke we were brother and sister.

From her voice came a high pitched, squeelly Minnesota accent that stood out loudly. She tried to cover it up at times but to little effect. Her body movements were fast, gangly, awkward, but beautiful. She moved as if a dancer, although she wasn't and at times went off-balance, another similarity to me. She was athletic, having spent most of her teenage years as a soccer player and continuing to stay in shape.

Charlotte's body was long, lean, firm, strong, full, angelic, and lusty. She was almost always the center of attention for men and women's eyes. She also changed her look constantly. Some days she'd dress like a masculine, butch, tough girl, with jeans, a wife beater, and hair pulled back. Other days, she wore the same retro-hippie/New Age long, flowing dresses Cassandra wore, and yet other days, yuppie, gentrified brand name apparel.

Contrasts in clothing styles was one expression of her identity crisis and mood changes. As with her clothes, some days she was stern, stoic, solemn, other days hyper active, bubbly, bouncing around like a child, and other days melancholy and depressed. It was hard to know which persona one would get from her, day to day, or even hour to hour.

Siango was on the phone at his desk, talking quietly and gently to a person inquiring about the C.W.F.P.S.J.-Now! LA Weekly ad. The main way the organization advertised job openings (which was every week), was through the weekly publication. "Want to work for Peace and Social Justice?" or "Want to get paid to stop President Bush' policies?" was usually what the ad said. It was often Siango's responsibility to field these calls.

Dark haired, dark eyed, with a medium build and height, Siango was a 22 year old half German, half Brazilian American from Cleveland, Ohio. He had Dennis Kucinich, the congressional Rep. and former mayor of Cleveland, as a local hero and role model. Plain and Midwestern, with a friendly, college style intellectual, Latin warmth. He was a nice guy who, at Ohio State University just a couple years before, discovered tons of political writers, from Noam Chomsky and Howard Zin to more obscure ones. It was one of those new discoveries that made a young person slightly defensive about the political positions they held.

Siango was highly logical, almost to a fault, and had a streak of dark sarcasm which conflicted oddly – but happily for someone like me – with the political correctness he learned in college. He had another contrast. One side of him desired to do nothing more than play his guitar, and listen to Rage Against the Machine. The other side a committed, crusading male feminist and peace activist.

Max – the part Russian, part African American six-foot three, heavy, dark red haired, bearded, mustached 29 year old father – sat at the main table, putting some political literature in a box. He was involved in a conversation with Rick. Max was expressive and emotional, talking quickly and always on top of previous sentences. People felt he talked too much, to the detriment of their ears, which was true. But there was also a sensitivity to him as well, which was for the most part ignored at C.W.F.P.S.J-Now!

Max grew up most of his life in Inglewood, California, amidst the joys and sad realities of Black American street life. Like a lot of African Americans, he lost friends from gang warfare, police brutality, familial abuse, and hip-hop machismo. He stayed away from the violence and became an Inglewood semi-Casanova and trance/electro/dance/hip-hop DJ.

The guy with the more commonly female name was Sharon, at the main table as well, putting away literature and listening to Rick and Max. Sharon spent his entire life growing up in Hollywood, with his overly talkative, former heroin and opium-addicted, currently not very practicing Orthodox Jewish mother.

Sharon's father was a "lower class" Jewish truck driver going back and forth across America. He divorced from Sharon's mother years before, shortly after the birth of Sharon's youngest brother. Like his oldest brother, Sharon played guitar and recorded music in a studio behind his mother's house.

Long, brown haired, thin, feminine by nature (the "daughter" out of the three boys) but consciously behaved like a surfer or skater more than a homosexual, Sharon was a 26 year old Hollywood area Jew. With his long hair and casual California demeanor, he seemed like a retro '70's Classic Rock white guy who surfed or skateboarded (neither of which he did, but he did ride a motorcycle). He talked in short, affected, calculating, reserved, cautious sentences. He was the last person to wear his heart on his sleeve, although the calculating appeared more shy than ill-intentioned to most people, which, of course, worked to his benefit.

I stood near Charlotte's desk, helping her prepare files for the day's turf. Charlotte and Siango were assistant canvass directors to Cassandra, while I was a field manager, and Sharon and Max were lead staff. As a field manager, I had more authority than Max or Sharon, but less than Charlotte, Siango, and Cassandra. When Charlotte, Siango, and Cassandra were at the office the entire night, I was in charge of the canvassers. Sharon and Max would help.

Now to tell you what kind of person I was, Daniel. Well, I'd have to say I was a kind, contained, and independent young man of 25, also capable of awkwardness, arrogance, and moodiness. There was an inner intensity about me deflected by a mellow, sardonic, and casual tone of voice. When I spoke, I seemed to waver between sincerity and insincerity. The insincerity came from an ironical sarcasm, and the sincerity from a diabolical penchant for truth. I sought to balance the two as much as possible.

There was a softness to my face, as if the boy would never leave me. With blond, wavy hair, sometimes a "somewhere else" look, to go along with an unpredictable inner violence at times, I was told I resembled Arthur Rimbaud a bit. Take a look at the French poet's picture and see what you think. Enjoy his poetry while you're at it. His writings, along with others - I should tell you, so you know, who my favorite writers are: James Joyce, Dostoevsky, Shakespeare (who was actually Francis Bacon but that is a whole other story), Celine, Baudelaire, Lautreamont, Chekhov, Flaubert, Strindberg, Proust, Ibsen, Moliere, and of course Rimbaud, to name all those I can think of - were a big influence on me.

Most of the time, when I didn't turn too far inward and become overly serious, melancholy, self-absorbed or lose my temper, I was friendly and giving, probably to a fault. I could be both slow to react socially and quick on my feet clever and witty, depending how far into my head I was. My wit could be a bit too flippant, sarcastic, or intellectual for some, though. I found this to be true with the people at C.W.F.P.S.J-Now!

I received my dark, intellectual sarcasm, and anti-authoritarian individualism from my biological father Jean, and also from a diversity of experiences. I was born in Venice Beach, California and grew up there (along with stops in Canada, Colorado, and New Jersey) until I was eight. I moved to Seattle, Washington with my mom and step-father at eight, then to a boarding high school in Switzerland at the age of sixteen, then back to Los Angeles at 18. I befriended a variety of people in all places, preferring to be with mixed crowds and not any one group. I had a searching nature, partly due to all the moving around. I had to adapt to new environments. This created my independence and my isolation.

“Runaways, huh?” I said to Rick as I put papers into the box on Charlotte's table. Charlotte rolled her eyes at me after my brief remark.

“Yup.” Rick replied with a Berkeley tone of authority.

“That's cool, Richie-Rick.” Max said casually. No one would ever call Rick 'Richie-Rick'. Max could kind of get away with it because he was quick. “Everybody's runnin' away from somethin', yo.”

“I'm not.” Rick said sternly, dignified.

"Neither am I." Charlotte said in calm defiance.

Minutes before, Rick and Max were chatting about materialism in hip-hop music, how from the early 90's onwards "bling bling" had taken over the art form. Max agreed, then added the gay and lesbian community had become enamored with materialism the decade before (the 80's). This offended Rick and Charlotte, and well, everyone except me, while Sharon played it safe and kept quiet. Each person was so busy that they decided now was not the time to debate Max.

Cassandra brought up the fact the new hires were waiting for me outside. I responded by saying I'd be out there as soon as I was done helping Charlotte. Charlotte played a little power game with Cassandra by asking me to help her a bit more. She then asked Rick what he thought of Kurt and Cindy. That's when he called them "runaways."

"I'm not running from anything, bub." Charlotte said to Max, continuing from her defiant, "Neither am I."

"Runnin' from myself ... oh-oh-oh-oh ..." I sang in imitation of Billy Idol's 'Dancin' With Myself'. "... I'm just Runnin' from Myself ... Runnin' from Myself ... oh-oh-oh-oh ..."

"Be quiet, Tom." Charlotte snapped.

"You go, Billy Idol." Max chuckled to me, then spoke more generally to everyone in the room, "I guess I should crystallize what I said earlier, 'Everyone's runnin' away from themselves in some shape or form, some peoples more than others."

"So true, so true, my man. Materialism is a disease spreading to all corners of the Universe." I said as I walked from Charlotte's desk past Max, then said with Utter Seriousness, which I detected in the room, "But what I want to know is, who's running the fastest from themselves? Oh-oh-oh-oh?"

Max and I laughed. No one else did.

"Come on, you guys, shut up." Charlotte said.

"Yes, Ma'am." I snipped with a smile.

"Don't call me, 'Ma'am'." Charlotte came back.

"Yes, Charlotte Sometimes." I smiled to her.

Charlotte didn't get The Cure reference and gave me a 'I could kill you' gleam in her eyes. She breathed heavily and stared at me for several seconds, as she often did when irritated, then turned back to her paperwork.

"You need to go outside to Cindy and Kurt now, Tom." Cassandra shot at me.

"Yes, on my way." I answered as I walked out of the office.

I went to the landing leading to the stairs, which Cindy and Kurt waited patiently on. I quickly lit a cigarette as they looked up innocently at me.

"Hello." Cindy said with a shy but friendly smile as she puffed on a cigarette as well.

"Hi." Kurt waived in greeting, shyly, as well, not being as smoker, he had no cigarette.

Cindy and Kurt were indeed "runaways," but with a quiet pride and dignity not given them in Rick's snide remark. There was a decency about them that was missing from most people at C.W.F.P.S.J.

Kurt and Cindy "fled" - as young adults, fully capable of going anywhere they wanted – upstate New York. Cindy came from a tiny prison town called Dana Mora and Kurt from the larger nearby town, Plattsburgh. "Fleeing" mainly the uptight boredom of the small towns they were born and grew up in.

Also, out in L.A. there was Kurt's band. Back home in Plattsburgh they had tons of friends but their existence was still limited and repetitive. They couldn't do much more than get drunk and high at somebody's house day after day. No where to go publicly at night, as they were too young for local dive bars, which they didn't want to go to anyway.

In Dana Mora, the central, all encompassing entity was the enormous maximum-security prison where dangerous criminals were locked up. The prison had high, high walls, making it seem like a fortress, and next to the prison were the most upscale homes of Dana Mora: the prison guards' houses.

Plattsburgh, the town Cindy told most people where she was from, was a twenty minute drive from Dana Mora. It was famous for a Tech and Arts college and a lake away from Vermont. Montreal, Quebec, in Canada was a couple hours drive north. Locals in Plattsburgh talked like Anglo-Canadians, even saying “eh” at the end of their sentences.

Cindy and Kurt had a large network of friends in Plattsburgh that were into sex, drugs, and rock n' roll, turn of the 21st century, post-grunge, nu-metal music, violent video games included, small town hick style. Narrowness, a restricting feeling of little to choose from – that was what Kurt and Cindy were running from.

Cindy was strong-willed, impulsive, kind-hearted, considerate, and generous. She chose to please herself while putting other people's needs just as often. Rarely did she just go with the flow. It was always directly intentioned, either to please herself or others.

Kurt was not as gregarious as Cindy, preferring to keep quiet, especially amongst people he didn't know. He loved playing music and whatever hampered his communicating verbally, he made up for it in guitar playing. His talents went beyond the nu-metal and death metal influences, but he was also limited because of a faithfulness to those bands.

Cindy was relatively tall, around 5'9", a little heavy and thick, but with a sweet, beautiful face. She had a gloriously charming smile, sensitive, sexy, intelligent eyes. She, like Kurt, had pale white skin and natural brown hair. Kurt, though, did his hair up in dreadlocks. He wore glasses and was thin, almost fragile. He stood about the same height as Cindy and they both spoke in that upstate New York, Canadian-sounding accent.

"How you guys doing?" I asked as I stood on the stairs with them.

"Okay." Cindy replied.

"Not bad." Kurt added.

"Let's go somewhere to do your training, like around the corner on the grass." I said as I walked down the stairs.

Cindy and Kurt followed me down the stairs, through the small parking lot, out to the sidewalk next to La Cienega blvd., then around the corner to the grassy area. C.W.F.P.S.J- Now! had its office in a plain two-story '80's style office building that had in it a real estate office, a casting agency, a call-girl service (where the dispatcher and other "office" personal worked from) and an office for a New Age church, as well.

"So you two are from upstate New York?" I asked as we came to the grass.

The three of us began to chat about ourselves, where we were from, what we were up to. I asked Cindy if she was a musician as well, and she replied that she was only his cheerleader. She liked to write stories and poetry, and take pictures. She wanted to make a movie some day, too.

I was intrigued by her interest in film making since I was a filmmaker myself. I'd been writing and directing short films, writing screenplays, acting in my own and other people's projects for ten years, ever since I was 15. Now, I was preparing for my first feature film, "Loveincrazy," a psychological family drama about a 9/11 survivor and his two sons.

I could tell Cindy and Kurt liked and respected me, maybe seeing me as some kind of "cool elder." Perhaps I came across to them as a knowledgeable, easy going, and down to earth guy. Everyone else at C.W.F.P.S.J-Now! made them feel less than they were. While I may like to talk about myself and my interests a fair amount, I was also sincerely interested in them as people, not just as two new hires to go and collect money.

Because of my personal involvement with them, though, our conversation took a 30 minute chunk of time from their training. There was about 15 minutes left before the briefing.

"Shit, I'm sorry, guys, but we've been talking for so long I forgot your training." I said as I looked at my watch.

"That's okay. We don't have to do the training." Cindy said slyly.

"No, no, we have to." I laughed, acknowledging their unease with the organization's formalities.

"How come everyone here besides you seems to have a stick up their ass?" Cindy said in her usual casual directness.

"I don't know." I replied with a chuckle. I liked her forthrightness. "But no, it's good to give you some training, besides whatever Cassandra or the others want."

I went on to give them their 15 minutes worth of training. As quickly as I could, I went over the skeletal structure of a canvasser's "rap." The rap was the pitch a worker gave to a person who passed the intro/qualifier question. The question could vary but usually it was something like, "Are you against the development of new nuclear weapons?," or "Do you want to see a safer U.S. Foreign policy?," or "Would you like to see your tax dollars go to schools, hospitals, and other social programs instead of building more bombs?"

One issue the organization was working on was stopping the funding for "Bunker Busters" (with nuclear tips) to be used primarily in Iraq and the Middle East. The funny thing was the Bunker Busters didn't even work properly. They wouldn't reach a bunker or other underground military sites. They'd go about about 5 to 10 feet into the ground before exploding, releasing nuclear fall-out in the air from the tip of the bomb. It was ridiculous but somehow considered by many government officials a "legitimate weapon for the War on Terror."

So if the person the canvasser was speaking to answered 'yes' to that first question, the rap would proceed. First, would be the "Problem" section, in which the canvasser explained the what, the how, and the result of the problem connected to the opening question. Second, came the "Solution," where the answer to the problem was briefly fleshed out in grassroots terms. Third, was the organization's history and past "success" on legislation and other actions. Fourth and lastly was the "Ask," the point where the canvasser asked for membership, letter-writing, and most importantly of all: money.

Cindy and Kurt told me they felt uncomfortable asking for money from people, especially $120 or $250. They never worked at a job where they had to ask for money. I explained to them, still relatively idealistic about C.W.F.P.S.J (despite having done a petition against the organization a few weeks before), that they should remind themselves how important the information they were providing to people was. It wasn't as if they were conning old ladies into buying vacuum cleaners or joining a religion. Cindy and Kurt smiled as it made sense to them like that. Little did I know, though, how wrong I was in the comparison ...

CHAPTER TWO.

THE FRIENDSHIP BEGINS.

Cindy and Kurt never truly liked working for C.W.F.P.S.J. The organization was too stiff for them. They were looser, freer spirits, especially Cindy. It was easier for Kurt to stay because he was more interested in the issues. Ironically, Cindy raised more money, just because she was more outgoing and a better salesperson. As far as the agenda was concerned, she didn't care much at all.

Another week went by and Cindy and Kurt struggled to make staff. They were still "trainees." They had to average $120 a night over a five day period to make staff. The Womens Day Retreat came up, obligatory for all women in the California organization to go to. Essentially it was a camping trip for two days, where the women bonded intellectually, socially, and emotionally (and for some, physically) in the mountains near the Bay Area.

Cindy hated it there. She despised all the women's whining. It seemed so stereotypical she told me afterwards. The whole thing seemed just an excuse for them to complain about men and the world in general. There wasn't true bonding going on. It was pretense for an agenda. Cindy spent most of the time hanging out with Charlotte's ex-girlfriend, Ali. Ali was a slightly butch but beautiful African American/Native American/French 20 year old lesbian feminist. She was even militant, to a degree.

But Ali had an earthiness and sense of humor the other women there lacked. Ali used to work at the L.A. canvass but quit and went on to help the Political Strategy Department at the L.A. office now and then while going to UCLA. A couple months before Kurt and Cindy started working for C.W.F.P.S.J., Charlotte broke up with Ali when she found out Ali was sleeping with another girl.

Cindy was ecstatic to come back to Los Angeles and see Kurt. There hadn't been two days where she missed him more. When the van came from picking up the L.A. women at the airport (driven by the upstanding male feminist, Siango) and arrived at the Culver City office, Kurt was waiting for Cindy on the steps. Cindy bolted out of the van and ran to Kurt, nearly jumping on him in excitement.

"Hey, babe!" Cindy exclaimed with her arms wrapped around him.

"Hey." Kurt replied quietly, as usual, but with a little extra warmth. He missed her, too.

Charlotte, Cassandra, and some other women were getting things out of the van when they looked up resentfully at Cindy and Kurt. The other women didn't appreciate Cindy's lack of interest in the Retreat and now as soon as she got back home, what did she do? Go running into the arms of a man in excitement.

"Excuse me." Charlotte said as she walked up the steps past Cindy and Kurt.

"We need your help, Cindy." Cassandra said to her from the van below, as if she were scolding a child.

"Okay, I'll be there in a minute." she shouted, then went back to kissing Kurt.

"We need your help now." Cassandra insisted.

"Okay!" Cindy came back irritated. "What a bitch." she whispered to Kurt.

A few days later, Charlotte and I were sitting outside the office on the landing, smoking cigarettes, looking at La Cienega blvd.

"It's disrespectful, Tom." Charlotte said after a puff.

"They're a little spacey sometimes but I don't think they're being intentional." I replied.

"Intentionally what?"

"Disrespectful."

"By being late? Again?"

"They try hard."

"Kurt's thirty minutes late to a training you're supposed to give him. That's not cool and it's not trying hard."

"Okay then, why don't we write him up and give him a warning when he gets here?" I said to please her while being annoyed with her strict moods like the one she was in now. It seemed as if she had a personal grudge against them, maybe because of Cindy's behavior at the Retreat, perhaps because Cindy spent most of her time with Ali, Charlotte's ex.

"You know the rules, Tommy." she responded in a demure voice, quickly changing to sound more sympathetic. "You get sent home if you're more than twenty minutes late to a training."

"They do take two buses to get here from Olympic and Union. Why don't we tell him not to come in tomorrow?"

"The rules are the rules. He's gotta go home today. I know it sucks but ... well, looks like that's them."

Charlotte nodded to Cindy and Kurt's direction as they walked from the sidewalk to the office through the parking lot. Cindy and Kurt waived to me and Charlotte, smiling innocently.

"Hey, kids, how's it goin'?" Charlotte asked in her squeaky, motherly tone of voice, as if preparing herself.

"Fine. Sorry we're late but the first bus took forever to get to our second stop, so we missed the second bus, and the next one was late, so, that's why we're late." Cindy said, breathing heavily as she and Kurt came to the steps.

"That's too bad. I'm sorry that happened but you guys know Kurt's more than thirty minutes late for his training, which means you know what." Charlotte said as she took on the Boss mantle, with or without much pleasure, it was hard to tell.

"What?" Cindy asked.

"Kurt has to go home. He can't work today." Charlotte said bluntly.

"No way! You can't do that! We came all this way just to be here!" Cindy shouted.

"Fuck this." Kurt got out under his breath as he turned and walked away.

"Sorry, Kurt." I tried to reach him, but didn't really help.

"Wait, babe." Cindy said as she followed Kurt, while he kept walking away.

"No, hold on, Cindy, you don't have to go! You didn't have training today, you're early!" Charlotte yelled.

"I don't care! If he goes, I go!" Cindy retaliated triumphantly, as she and Kurt left the parking lot, going around the corner on La Cienega.

"Well, there goes both of them. Shucks." Charlotte said in frustration. "I just wished they hadn't taken it so badly."

"That's dedication for you." I said as soon as they were out of sight. I felt they over-reacted a bit, even if I admired their spirit.

"What?" Charlotte asked me.

"Cindy. She loves Kurt with everything she's got. It's admirable, that kind of love she has for him."

"Yeah." she responded ambiguously.

I wasn't sure if Charlotte agreed with me or not, nor if she understood what I meant. She turned and smiled at me, then went inside the office.

I wanted to make it up to Kurt and Cindy, so the next day I came to their apartment to pick them up and go to work. I called them on the phone before and asked if I could give them a ride. Earlier, they thought about quitting C.W.F.P.S.J., then realized it was better than most minimum-wage jobs, so why not stay? I waited for a while in my car, knowing to come early. I listened to Dave Ball's song "Sincerity," on the car stereo.

"You like those 'Fast Fags', Tom?" Cindy laughed good naturedly as she and Kurt hopped into the car.

"'Depeche Mode' means 'Fast Fashion' in French, babe." Kurt added with a smile.

"Oui, monsieur, but dis iz Genezis P. Orridge and Dave Ball's zong, 'Sincerity', not 'Depeche Mode'." I said in a cheesy French accent.

"Genezis P. Orridge? Dave Ball? Who is dat?" Cindy laughed, replying with her own French cheese.

"Ball waz ze guy who did ze muzik for 'Soft Cell', you know, ze band who did 'Where Did Our Love Go?' Dis song, zo, is a zolo album song. The other guy Genzis P. Orridge worked with Throbbing Gristles, Zychic TV, ok?"

"Zounds cool. Zuper cool." Cindy continued. "It sounds as if he's sincere and making fun of sincerity at the same time. This is the kinda music the people at California Whores for Peace and blah blah blah don't get." She finished with a delightful chuckle.

"You're right. It's a little too complicated. I mean, where does he stand on SINCERITY?" I continued to joke. "Is he for it, or against it?"

We all laughed.

"And they probably would insist this was Depeche-Mode." Kurt chimed in.

"Right!"

"'People are People so why should it be, you and I should get along so aw-fully?'" Kurt sang in a deep voice, in caricature of David Gahan, with a big smile afterwards.

"'Ba-do-m-do-do-m." Cindy added the synthesizer effect.

I continued to laugh with the two of them. We all sincerely enjoyed each other's company as we joked our way to work. Before we arrived at the office, I was worrying about my film behind the jokes and singing. I obsessed over my movie. It was my creation, my baby, and I was secretly panicking over a number of things as the production was nearing the actual shoot. One, I needed crew people. Then it dawned on me.

"Hey, would you guys be interested in helping out with my film?" I asked.

"Sure. What would you want us to do?" Cindy lit up.

"The cinematographer and sound man need help with the equipment. One of you could help with the sound by holding the boom, the other could help with the camera and lights. There might be other things I'll need you for, too."

"That sounds cool." Kurt acknowledged.

"Yay! We'll be working on a movie, babe!" Cindy jumped in excitement in the back of the car. She was beautiful, bouncing enthusiasm.

"I'm glad you're both happy about it." I said with some surprise. I wasn't used to hearing someone say "yes" to me so easily, especially with what I'd been through with the movie so far.

"Just promise me, though, Tom," Cindy began to say.

"What?"

“Promise you'll go to Kurt's show this Sunday.”

“Of course. Where's it going to be?”

“At the Dragonfly. I think it's on Santa Monica blvd., somewhere in Hollywood. Seems like a pretty cool venue.” Kurt said enthusiastically monotone.

“I've been wanting to hear your band anyway, so now I will. It should be cool.” I said.

I was looking forward to having Cindy and Kurt on the shoot. I needed people to be enthusiastic and interested. I made so many attempts before to get others on board, including good friends, and was shut down, turned down, thwarted, or rejected in one way or another. To hear “yes” so easily, so enthusiastically, almost seemed like a joke.

CHAPTER THREE.

CINEMA.

Since a child, even at 3, I was around movies. World cinema – visceral images of life, death, sex, drama, comedy, men, women, romance, fantasy, realism, black and white, color, period pieces, thrillers, horror movies, existential foreign films and more – bombarded my early, unformed psyche. Bunuel, Fellini, Cassavetes, Renoir, Ozu, Truffuat, Godard, Ophuls, Kubrick, Welles, Bertolucci, and more, all had an influence on my mind. My biological father and mother met while working at a movie theater and when my mother was at work, she brought me with her sometimes. As I became a toddler, I ate lots of popcorn, swept the floors, had customers (including Sean Connery) pat me on the head and I watched Italian movies with sexy Italian women walk around naked on-screen.

My father and mother didn't get along despite genuine love between them. They just weren't compatible. They were on two very different life roads. She ended up meeting another man who happened to be connected to movies as well, an out of work actor who used to produce a t.v. sports show (even though he had no interest in sports). This down and out middle-aged actor had two sons from a previous marriage but they were pushed away from him by their mother. He intended to take on the father role for me and the husband role to my mom.

As I got older, growing up with two fathers, I became estranged from my more favored biological father. I moved to Seattle with my mother and step-dad while my real dad Jean lived in LA. Movies came back into my life in high school by way of a film class, where I found my inspiration at 15 to be a filmmaker. Talented in writing and drawing, as well, I had teachers hoping I'd become a writer or painter. In the end, it was the more glamorous art of film making that won me over. Many young men and women were the same: having talents in other fields but choosing film because it was considered by modern perspectives to be the most important, most relevant, most seen, most prestigious, most popular art form in the world.

Cinema was the art which could make you the most famous. It was captivating, alluring on its own artistic merits but it also ensured a person to be heard by the greatest number of people, as well. One's voice seemed to matter more through cinema. I bought into this allure, fell in love with the form more sincerely than the majority of young people. I didn't realize just how little an art form it was and how much of a business machine until years later.

And even though I had creative integrity, what I would never admit to myself was one of the main sources for my creative and professional drive: I wanted to be a success. I didn't want to repeat the “failures” of my step-father nor biological father. They were artists themselves - my step dad an actor, my real dad a writer – and neither found success in their endeavors. I wanted to prove to myself I would be different, my dreams were real and not fantasies.

I started early, making short films, writing screenplays, and acting in stage plays and shorts as a teenager. Into my twenties I continued with screen-writing and making short films. Now, at the age of 25, I was making my first feature length movie. Just like Orson Welles - who did “Citizen Kane” at the age of 26 - I acted in my film, directed it, wrote it, and produced it. Unlike Orson Welles, though, I was a nobody, not riding any fame from a radio broadcast of aliens attacking New York, nor did I have the resources at my disposal to make a masterpiece. Still, I was in love with my movie and it mattered everything to me.

While pursuing my selfish artistic passions with “Loveincrazy,” working at C.W.F.P.S.J was a means to act out my conscience. Was my life making a difference in the big picture, in the grand scheme of things? I wanted it to and felt in my own small way was doing so by working for C.W.F.P.S.J. Not able to make a living as a filmmaker, it was better to save the world while paying for rent, anyway. C.W.F.P.S.J. fit the bill.

CHAPTER FOUR.

A REPRESENTATIVE OF THE PEOPLE.

Not too many days after Kurt's bands show, I had to go to my grandmother's in San Pedro, help her with groceries and other chores. In the mail was a letter from my representative in congress, Herbert Weinckoff. A self-declared "Moderate Democrat," he voted for the Iraq War Resolution in 2002, the vote which gave President Bush full authority to invade Iraq.

Weinckoff was head of the L.A.P.D. in the late '80's, early 90's, ran for L.A. Mayor and lost, then ran for the 36th congressional district seat and won. He represented Venice, Marina Del Rey, El Segundo, Hawthorne, Manhattan Beach, Hermosa Beach, Redondo Beach, all the way down to San Pedro. One of the biggest districts in Los Angeles county.

Often called "Tough Guy Herbert," he was involved in some scandals as L.A.P.D Police Chief, including allegations officers from his department murdered innocent civilians for unknown reasons. He was a 50-something masculine Polish American ex-cop who eventually wanted to flex political muscles as well as biceps. Born into a wealthy stock-broker family, he felt he owed it to the community to "protect and to serve." Policing was his protecting, politics his serving. He sold himself as a pro-business (yet somehow - but of course, being a Democrat – pro-labor, as well), pro-military, pro-prison system, tough on crime Democrat. He became popular with many.

Weinckoff was a big pusher for the Three Strikes law in California, justified the death penalty, and had support from the Defense Industry, of which the majors – Boeing, Lockheed Martin, Raytheon, Northrop Grumman – were all located in his district. He was also one of the louder Democrat Bush supporters – post 9/11 – on foreign policy.

Weinckoff compared Bush's "courageous actions" against Osama Bin Laden and Saddam Hussein, to Winston Churchill's standing up to Hitler. No one in the mainstream media – nor his colleagues in congress – laughed at this ridiculous comment like they should have. As big and moronic and empty headed Weinckoff should've appeared to everyone in D.C. and the media, he was taken seriously. Everyone in D.C. and the media basically thought the same way as he did so of course they wouldn't criticize. 2002 was a Great Patriotic Year.

So this was my representative. The guy who represented my interests, my well being, my goals, my life, my very soul! What a great guy that Weinckoff. And now I got something in the mail from him, well, his office, probably one of his staff members. A plain, generic flier and letter. A few pictures of him, his wife, daughter, and son; one picture of him playing touch football with them on Manhattan Beach; another one posing under the American Flag.

The letter stated proudly Weinckoff was leading the way in congress for the crusade against pornography. Weinckoff was "distraught" to see the easy access and availability to Internet porn when his 12 year old daughter found porn websites while looking for a Britney Spears site. From there Weinckoff realized he had a Mission to fulfill.

Disparaged to see that few representatives were tackling the evil of pornography, Weinckoff took charge, made it his issue. He was quick to act by introducing legislation to crack down on the porno industry, even willing to "take to the streets" if need be. In an L.A. Times interview the week before, Weinckoff declared, "We must acknowledge there are terrorists of Morality in our society, just as deadly, just as dangerous, as Al-Qaeda and Osama Bin Laden, and that these moral evil-doers must be stopped, by any means necessary."

The Times interviewer surprisingly asked what Weinckoff meant by "any means necessary." Weinckoff replied that he was insulted by the question, as if the interviewer was insinuating something unsavory, and insisted the reporter ask him more responsible questions. Thus was the way of post-9/11 politicians: bully the media to make them feel insecure about their patriotism. And it worked, especially in 2002.

I decided I should write to my representative, let him know how I felt about him, say what I thought was the real pornography in today's society. After all, it was Weinckoff's job to hear his people out, even if I knew it was probably an exercise in futility.

CHAPTER FIVE.

SUICIDE.

A few weeks later, Cindy and Kurt got into the canvassing groove, meaning, started making money. They were doing pretty well, despite Cassandra's opinion they needed to inform themselves on the issues more. But however well they were doing, Cindy began to get bored of the job.

Cindy and I were canvassing in the wealthy homes of Westwood one day, after transporting everyone else to their drop-offs. We were putting our clipboards together with literature when I looked at her and sensed an unease. She looked back with a deep, penetrating glance. Her glances were amazing, and this time it caught me off-guard.

"How's it going?" I asked her.

"Okay." she answered with a quick smile. Something was wrong.

"Nothings bothering you?"

"Nope."

She couldn't let on her attraction to me. I was oblivious.

"You getting bored of the job?" I asked.

"Kinda." she decided to open up a bit, then quickly opened up even more. "It's just we do the same thing every night. We go to a different neighborhood, knock on people's doors, they either slam the door in our face, or if they talk to us, we give our rap, tell them how bad the Bush administration is, how bad nuclear weapons are, then try to get as much money out of them as we can, then walk away like we don't care about them, and then go talk to thirty more people the exact same way! And every night! It's boring! Ugh! I wish we could do something else tonight. Come on, Tom, screw canvassing. Just for once. One night. Let's go to a liquor store and get a 40. I know you wanna get drunk! Come on!"

"Of course I'd like to do that ..." I said with a smile. I loved her spirit and she was right in a way. But I still believed in the Cause at that point. I wanted to be a responsible field manager. "But we gotta go out there and get some money. If we zero out tonight and come back to the office with no money, that's going to bring both our averages down this week. It'll look suspicious as well."

"You're such a Workers For Peace whore, Tom!" she laughed and exclaimed dramatically, all in tenderness.

"How about this. Let's go canvass for a couple hours and make a little bit of money, then go to a liquor store, get a couple of 40's, then stop drinking an hour before the end of the night and chew gum and smoke so they wouldn't tell we were drinking." I suggested, hoping to be persuasive. I would've rather have done what she wanted, but I just couldn't do it.

"Okay. I only compromise for you, though." she said with a telling smile, then checked herself. "And Kurt, of course."

We proceeded to finish putting our clipboards and bags together when she stopped and looked at me.

"Do you ever think about suicide?" she asked in her typical casual, quick bluntness.

"Suicide?"

"Yeah, suicide."

"I used to ... a couple times when I was in my early twenties." I replied with hesitation. She caught me off-guard again. My mind was set to get out of the van and go knocking on people's doors. Now we were on suicide. Based on the look she had and how much I liked her as a human being, I couldn't dismiss this. It was suicide after all. "Why, what made you think about it?"

"It's just everyone makes such a big deal about it. All it is is someone decides to stop living. They're not killing anyone else, are they?"

"No."

"So, if someone feels it's, like, their time to go, why should anyone try to stop them?"

"Is someone you know thinking of killing themself?"

"No, not now. But back in Plattsburgh there was a girl I knew who actually did it, went all the way."

"How long ago was that?"

"About three years ago."

"Were you close?"

"Yeah."

"I'm sorry ..."

"She really wanted to do it, and it was sad seeing her the way she was, so at least now she's at peace."

"What was wrong with her?"

"All kinds of things. She had a fucked up relationship with her parents. Her dad hit her a lot when she was younger then acted like it never happened. Her mom was a creep and always told her she was worthless. Her brother raped her when she was 12, and both her mom and dad thought she was lying to get attention and make her brother look bad. They thought she was jealous of him. When she was 16, she got pregnant and her boyfriend left her for one of her friends and never helped with the baby. When we were all, our group of friends, first experimenting with drugs, at around 14, 15, mostly just pot, she wouldn't do it. But later she started getting into H, heroin you know, and some other stuff. She got really bad, really addicted to H especially. It was the only thing that made her feel good, she said, nothing else did. Not coke, not speed, not pot, just H ... Most of her friends acted like they didn't give a shit about her, and I don't know why, but they didn't. She didn't have anyone she could turn to."

"But you?"

"We were friends and I tried to be there for her but the worse she got, the less she wanted to be around me and the more she wanted to be around the friends who were mean to her, who, of course, either shot up H with her or got her the shit or whatever."

"Damn ..."

"Committing suicide was the last place she could go ... after a while, it seemed everything she did was going in that direction ... I remember her telling me she thought death was probably a lot like H … everything just seemed to float away …"

"Did she OD on heroin?"

"No, actually … she slit her wrists. In the bathroom sink at her parents house."

"How old was she when she killed herself?"

"18. She was a year older than me."

How many young women were like this? It was an all too common story. The fact that this poor girls life sounded like millions of other women's stories made it even more tragic. The commonality of it, almost a normalcy, the way Cindy talked about her friend so matter of fact, as if it was accepted this happened all the time, was heartbreaking. This story may have been shocking to most people in the 1950's, 60's, or heck in the 80's, but now, in 2002, it was no longer shocking. It was simply sad.

What could I say? The girl should've stuck it out, should've stayed alive for her baby, should've stayed away from drugs, stayed away from the cruel people in her life? Of course, she should've done all those things, but knowing what she should do is a completely other thing than the living of her life. All the weight, the hurt, the baggage of her past must've always been in her present. She had no secure place to go within or outside herself.

"What do you think? Should she have tried to stay alive?" Cindy asked me after a moment of silence.

"I don't know." I replied. I didn't want to moralize. "My first response is yeah, she should've ... but then I didn't go through what she did. She was tortured by her life ... what her brother did to her, how her parents treated her, her boyfriend, her friends ... she had a long list of cruelties ... it's too bad she didn't turn to you more ... it's too bad she couldn't get out of that town ... every town has its shit problems, but I think it would've helped her to get out of there, get away from her family and people she knew, start a new life with her child somewhere else ..."

"You would've liked her. She was a cool person. It's too bad she didn't meet you ... you would've been a good boyfriend for her." she said with another intent look and smile.

"You think?" I said with surprise. Cindy could make me uncomfortable in a good way.

"Yeah. ... I still feel sad about her, you know ..."

"... I don't blame you ..." I started to cry … I felt this deep pain for Cindy's friend … as if I knew her myself … perhaps in my own way I could empathize with the girl … I didn't go through what she did, but I understood … I understood pain very well. Cindy looked at me and was surprised and moved by my tears but felt embarrassed to say anything. I continued, trying to minimalize my crying as much as possible. "Death is unfortunately something that's always there ... at every corner we turn, it's there ... whether it's someone we knew like your friend, or something that happens in our life ... death never seems to leave us ... the attitude we take towards it and towards life, is important ..." I began to smile as I turned to Cindy.

"Just laugh at life and death?" She responded to my smile with her own.

"Yeah ...we have to ... besides try to understand it, life. If we lived in a more humanistic society, one which actually cared about being human, all those horrible things that happened to your friend would not have happened. I guarantee you. But since we don't live in a society like that, you're right, we do have to laugh. Look at the people we canvass. They make us laugh. Look at everyone on the planet. It's like that old French saying – 'If you look for the Ridiculous in everything, you'll find it.'"

"Ha, that's a cool saying."

"I know, I like it, too."

"Well, anyway, enough about suicide!" she changed moods immediately, smiling and laughing. "Let's go canvass!"

We went out and canvassed the neighborhood for the whole night, checking in with each other, enjoying ourselves, the trees, the houses, people's odd behaviors. By the end, neither of us made a cent. The rich Westwood families weren't biting that night. Somehow it didn't bother us. We made fun of the people, laughed, took pleasure in the sheer experience of those four hours, knocking on people's doors. Without the perspective we reached through our conversation on suicide, it would've seemed just another boring four hours of canvassing. Instead, we found The Ridiculous, and we loved it.

CHAPTER SIX.

THE QUIET MAN.

No one did well in Westwood that week. There was a lot of support from students on the west side of the UCLA campus. The dorms and other student living quarters were there. Unfortunately, the way canvassing worked, getting support from young, idealistic, rebellious students didn't equal success. They just never gave big chunks of money.

Students wrote letters, gave moral support, and many were inspired by the canvassers, but if they did give money, it usually never exceeded $20. I liked canvassing the students because they were fresh to the issues, open-minded, and actually inspired by what the organization did. In terms of motivating the populace, students seemed one of the most important aspects to building a peace movement. It was obvious: the youth were the future.

For the people running C.W.F.P.S.J.-Now!, the bottom line was collecting enough money to keep the ship going. They said all kinds of things about "Building the Peace Movement" but the actions didn't follow the words. Money was where their hearts were at.

Going to a snobby rich neighborhood, , like just east of the UCLA campus, the opposite side of the dorms, and getting two people to give $120 each (pocket change for them, really), was a great night. It was $240 after all. It meant, though, out of going to 40 houses, only two were supportive. Going to students one could get between 20 to 30 supportive kids and in the end make no more than $80 to $90. A canvasser may get 15 to 20 letters, but little money. Bottom line was money, again and again and again ...

This bothered Cindy and Kurt – ardent anti-materialists they were – and, really, it bothered me as well. I understood as a non-profit peace organization, C.W.F.P.S.J needed money to keep going. To cover all the costs – paying employees, overhead for all the offices, transportation, political literature, advertisements in the LA Times and other papers – money had to come from somewhere. And it did.

With so many people disgusted with the Bush Administration, C.W.F.P.S.J was getting more money than ever before. Instead, though, of putting less emphasis on collecting money and more on reaching out to people to get them involved in the issues, the organization created new departments to collect even more money, as well as make uninspired attempts for "coalition building" with other groups. Nothing was ever brought up in terms of reaching individual human beings.

The next couple of weeks we the LA canvassers went to Pasadena, which brought more fruits for almost everyone's labors. Cindy did well in Pasadena but Kurt struggled. Cassandra, Charlotte, and Siango decided Cindy and Kurt trusted me the most. I should be the one to help Kurt, which I was glad to.

Kurt and I were dropped off in the more affluent west side of Pasadena, with big, big trees, and big, big houses. Standing on the side of a hill, clipboards in our hands, backpacks on our backs, I looked at Kurt, who seemed bummed.

"I hope I do okay tonight." he said quietly.

"I'm sure you will." I replied.

"Sometimes I think I just naturally suck at canvassing."

One of the many bad things about canvassing was it brought out a competitiveness between peace activists, and over a stupid thing like money, too. Kurt was made to feel bad quite often. He was quiet and passive, so he was picked on almost every night.

"Kurt, you only raised $40 tonight, and last night you raised only $25."

"Last week, Kurt, you raised a total of $200. That's an average of $40 a night over five days. $80 below our quota average."

"Is everything okay, Kurt? You seem to be having a tough week."

"Kurt, you need to stand up straight. Don't hunch over."

"Kurt, you need to make eye contact. You're looking down at the ground all the time."

"We need you to talk louder, Kurt, it's hard for people to hear you."

"Don't mumble when you talk, Kurt, and don't say, 'uh, ah, um,' especially when you get to the Ask section of the rap. We don't want to hear you say, 'can you become a member tonight?' or, 'would you be interested in being a member tonight?', or, 'is that something you would, um, like to do?' Just say, loud and clear, but calmly, 'Will you be a member tonight?' Stand up straight, shoulders squared, chin up, feet spread, knees straight, breath calmly, look them directly in the eyes, then wait for their response. Exude confidence. SELL yourself."

Kurt was barraged with all this every night by Cassandra, Charlotte, Siango, Sharon, and others. When I first started I got a taste of that myself. It made Kurt feel like shit. It only made his insecurities worse, especially when he saw Cindy do well.

"Nobody naturally sucks. You just need to focus on your strengths. Everybody's different so what works for you isn't the same as what works for Cassandra, Charlotte, Siango, Sharon, and the others." I insisted.

"It just seems like I've been doing this for a while now and I'm not much better than when I started."

"The problem's been that everyone's telling you what to do based on what works for them and what they think works for everyone. Everybody who's criticized you for mumbling, saying 'uh, um, ah ..." or looking at the ground, or being too quiet, or saying 'could you possibly be a member tonight?' instead of 'WILL YOU be a member tonight?', Cassandra, Charlotte, Siango, all of them, have done that, too."

"They have?"

"Yeah, and so have I. They used to get on my case just like they have with you and the same with Sharon. They like to go after us soft-spoken men." I said with a smile. "Once I started making money, though, suddenly the criticism stopped."

"Well, unfortunately I haven't been making much money recently."

"When you've done well, what was the interactions like with the people who gave you money?"

After breaking down details in techniques of social interactions, I then pried out of Kurt an over-arching vision of the world, found out what his deep down personal point of view was. Once he verbally clarified how he felt about the big picture, I told him never to forget that when talking to people. That vision was his and no one else's. Something happened to Kurt after that, a light clicked on inside.

Kurt went on to canvass well that night and through the week. He gained a confidence, a driving force as he began to trust himself better. He told me later our conversation on the side of that hill in Pasadena was crucial. It seeped into his music, as well, when about eight months later he recorded amazing guitar work for the soundtrack to "Loveincrazy." I was sincerely touched. I had to admit I never met a couple more open-minded and warm than Cindy and Kurt. They were like my kids before having kids, before having you, Daniel. They trusted me faster and more willingly than anyone ever before.

CHAPTER SEVEN.

"LOVEINCRAZY"

The first weekend of production for my movie soon arrived. "Loveincrazy," after an up and down roller coaster ride, was now set to go. Kristianna, Jonathan, and myself got all the equipment, locations, people and other logistics ready. No one from the original cast was in the film.

Two friends of mine – Bernardo and Gus – dropped out at the last minute, as did Charlotte and three other professional actors. Even the crew and locations were different. Kristianna wasn't the original cinematographer, and several crew people I hired dropped out, as well.

Originally wary of casting my step-father Frazier in the role of Jack Henry – the estranged father in the drama – the old man ended up playing the role. The original actor didn't show up for a rehearsal so I asked Frazier if he could read just for that night. Frazier showed up, Charlotte preferred him, while Bernardo and Gus did not.

The original actor was an interesting but gruff (especially for Charlotte's tastes) Vietnam veteran turned actor. Bernardo liked his off-the cuff gregarious sarcasm and I did, too. But I thought with my step-father in the film, playing the lead, he would create a different tone. He'd be less raucous, more mellow, which might make Jack Henry, despite his problems and alienation with his children, more sympathetic. So with that I decided to keep Frazier in the production.

Frazier had been in three of my short films before. I felt "Loveincrazy" would be a good opportunity for him to give that one last great performance. This was so even if there were mixed feelings on my part towards him personally. This movie was in many ways a last ditch attempt to resolve our problems. Not only would I direct Frazier, but play opposite him as his son after Gus dropped out.

My step-father became the main object of coming to terms with my demons ... and the other casting changes created other personal projects within the project as well. Your mother, Daniel, Maya, replaced, ironically, Charlotte as the girlfriend. Benny – a friend of mine who had cerebral palsy – replaced Bernardo as the brother. For me, the personal and the professional lines often blurred, and as fate would have it, for "Loveincrazy" this ended up being especially so.

The locations also changed. Two friends – Lara and Gerald – promised I could use their house in Venice for the shoot. Two months before production, Gerald left for Hawaii to help his brother. While there, Lara broke up with him over the phone. Because of the break-up, Lara told me Gerald would be uncomfortable with everyone making a movie at their house. I had to find another house. Later, though, I ended up using Gerald and Lara's house, after Gerald told me he never had a problem with the shoot. I became suspicious of Lara until later I realized that the whole thing was about the two of them using me as a tool against each other. One day, I'd be used by Lara as a ploy against Gerald, and another day by Gerald against Lara. After a while, I gave up on trusting either of them.

There were other problems in the search for Jack Henry's house. Sharon from C.W.F.P.S.J offered his mother's house when I considered casting him in the film next to Charlotte. Sharon seemed to take a liking to her at the time. When I casted my friend Bernardo instead of Sharon, Sharon felt snubbed, and since I saw this, I looked elsewhere for a house.

My mother's husband also offered his old house in Pasadena. When he found out my step-father Frazier – my mother's ex-husband – was in the movie, he had noticeable reservations. I told him I'd find another house, as to not step on anyone's toes. Lastly, my biological father – Jean – had a friend in Northridge who had a house we could use. That was it, that was to be Jack Henry's house. I had the cast, the crew, the locations, the equipment. The project, close to falling apart before, was now rolling.

I picked Kurt and Cindy up early Saturday morning, then drove to Kristianna and Jason's apartment right on the Santa Monica beach, near the pier. Jonathan's family had money, which allowed him to afford an apartment there. The first location was at his place, to film the opening scene of Maya's character and mine getting up in the morning, making love, then receiving a call from Jack Henry.

I wanted to get the sex scene out of the way and break the ice, for myself and for everyone. Kristianna and I set up the DV-CAM camera and lights for a stationary shot. Maya and I could make love in private while everyone in the crew waited outside.

After the scene finished, along with some other shots, we all drove to Gus' apartment in Silverlake. It was Benny's characters place, another quick introductory scene. We had lunch at a taco stand afterwards, then drove over to Jack Henry's house in Northridge. Benny's mom, Samantha, was a sweet, overly talkative older lady who'd been through one drama after another. She was totally fine with having a low-budget film getting made in her house, even thinking it was kinda cool. She ended up, along with her daughter and grandchild, having cameo roles in the movie as Jack Henry's girlfriend who leaves his house at the beginning.

Towards the end of the day's shoot, the cast and crew arrived at Samantha's house, where she and Frazier waited for everyone. We were a couple hours late but Samantha and Frazier were patient. A few establishing shots of the house, then of Jack waiting, smoking, and drinking with the bleached sun coming through the windows. Then the scenes with my character – Colin – and Benny's – Roland – arriving at our father's home. All the characters were pensive, awkward, smiling, but tense.

Kurt and Cindy had a blast. They loved Kristianna and Jonathan, constantly joking with them the whole time. Occasionally they lost focus because of the horsing around, but for the most part they respected the shoot and were immensely reliable, supportive, and enthusiastic.

Kurt and Cindy never had anything to do with making a movie before. It was fresh and exciting to them, like a new adventure. I was driving them home in the early evening, listening to Cat Power on the car stereo, when something about them struck me.

“Kurt and I just wanted to thank you, Tom, for asking us to help with your movie.” Cindy said with a happy gleam in her face.

“Yeah, it's been rad, man.” Kurt said with his own, more introverted smile.

“'Rad', babe.” Cindy teased.

“Yeah, rad.” he smiled back.

"I'm really glad you guys could help, you know ..." I said to them from the driver's seat, looking at them through the rear view mirror. "It means a lot to me to see how supportive you guys have been. I'm not exactly used to that ..."

"No prob, Tom." Cindy said happily.

As I saw Kurt and Cindy in the backseat, seemingly so innocent, joyful, pure, my gut swelled up in emotion. I'd get like that at times, like during that conversation with Cindy about her friend's suicide, tenderly overwhelmed by feeling, touched by something I'd see in someone else or in some situation.

It often would be a simple, sentimental event, unhinged by anything that complicated, such as seeing a couple I admired like Cindy and Kurt, holding each other; or watching dogs playfully, jubilantly wrestle in the grass; or a mother caressing her baby's cheeks as the child giggled; or two friends, even strangers, joke with each other in good humor. It moved me because for some reason, when I saw such moments, however sentimental, I was reminded of Death. Nothing lasted forever, sentiment especially ...

I was becoming attached to Kurt and Cindy. I even started to idealize them as the perfect young couple, capable of growing into a more satisfying, more developed, sophisticated, and nuanced male/female pairing. This idealization on my part kept me from seeing their problems sometimes. Cindy complained Kurt was not adventurous enough, wasn't a free bird like her. Kurt complained that Cindy was a spendthrift and prone to irresponsible moodiness. And they both could be a little flighty at times.

However much of their conflicts I minimized, the fact was a lot of the positives I saw were true. And in comparison with most people I ran across, they were a breath of fresh air. Especially at the time I met them, when I was becoming more and more displeased with C.W.F.P.S.J.-Now!

Even if there were times I couldn't connect with them intellectually, it didn't seem to matter. Cindy and Kurt didn't have the morose, self-serving, cunning, protective, mean-spirited "maturity" most people had. They weren't "hip," nor had that knowing "I've got my shit together and you don't" attitude. They had the instincts to give up on the social pretensions everyone else was scrambling to hold onto.

Kurt and Cindy were considered, especially by the people at C.W.F.P.S.J.-Now! too naive, too simple, too open, too unguarded, too careless. They laid themselves out on the table, and in modern society, with all the great freedoms, rights of mankind, Democracy, Business ambitions, shopping malls, brand names, wealth of information, scientific knowledge, and technological advances, a person just didn't do that. To me, they were beautiful because of that. As I continued to drive Kurt and Cindy home, the sentimental gut feeling took hold of me, and a tear slipped from my eye.

CHAPTER EIGHT.

OFF WITH KURT'S CANVASSING HEAD.

After production for "Loveincrazy" wrapped two weeks later, Kurt was getting into trouble at C.W.F.P.S.J.-Now! He'd been put on fund-raising probation the week before. From the management meetings I was in, I knew Kurt was not a favorite at the office, despite his humility, work ethic, and sincere interests in the issues.

One night Cindy and I were waiting outside the Workers For Peace office, smoking cigarettes on the landing, and not at ease. All the canvassers had come back from canvassing, and either were doing paperwork inside or had left already. Cindy and I were waiting for Kurt – who was talking to Cassandra privately in a separate room – so I could take them home.

"What do you think she's telling him right now?" Cindy asked me after she took a quick puff on her cigarette.

"We'll find out when we see him." I replied somberly. At the management meetings, I argued to keep Kurt. I was fighting a one-man battle. Everyone else wanted Kurt to go.

"They better not fucking fire him." Cindy said quietly.

We remained quietly smoking our cigarettes on the landing when we heard one of the office doors open. Kurt came out. Cindy jumped up and immediately rushed to him. I got up, and could see Kurt wasn't well.

"What happened, babe?" Cindy asked him.

"I got fired." Kurt said with a sad, matter of fact exhaustion.

"So they went and did it." I said, disappointed but not surprised.

"Those fucking bastards." Cindy flared, her eyes angrily looking down the hall at the closed office. She knew Cassandra was behind the door. “Cassandra's such a bitch.”

“They should've given you more of a chance. I've seen other people do worse hang around much, much longer. There was this one Japanese guy Cassandra liked – a nice but totally harmless and unquestioning kind of dude – who was horrible at canvassing, far worse than you, Kurt, but stayed around a month longer. Go figure.”

“Why didn't they fire me? I've been making the same amount of money a day as Kurt.” Cindy spat in disgust.

“According to Cassandra and Charlotte, you've been averaging just enough to get by. They think you have more potential than Kurt, too, because they say you're more outgoing than him. They say Kurt's too shy.” I put in sympathetically. I knew it was hot air. They simply didn't like Kurt for some reason.

“That's bullshit. It's just because I'm a girl and Kurt's a guy and they're all a bunch of uptight feminists in there. Fucking haters is what they are.” Cindy said as she abruptly turned away and went down the stairs. “Come on, babe.”

Kurt and I followed Cindy to my car. While driving them home, continuing to complain about C.W.F.P.S.J, I realized I had to help Kurt find another job. Kurt was insistent Cindy stay at C.W.F.P.S.J, even though she thought they were full of shit. Kurt said it was better than most jobs they could find for minimum wage. At least she could talk politics instead of flipping burgers. Cindy would stay, but only grudgingly.

A couple days later, I got Kurt a job working at an independent art house movie theater, one of a chain owned by an old Hollywood Jewish family I used to work for. Kurt loved the job, preferring the laid back environment where he could work on writing music. It was a nice change from the high tension at C.W.F.P.S.J.-Now!

CHAPTER NINE.

AN AX TO THE HEART.

On a bleaching sunny day, Cindy walked up the stairs to the C.W.F.P.S.J office, still unsettled going to work without Kurt. As she went inside, she saw Cassandra, Charlotte, Sharon, and Siango, all silent, all busy doing something. There was an odd, unnerving ambiance in the air.

"Hey, everybody." Cindy said, vulnerable, open. For all her bitterness against the organization, she couldn't help her kind nature. And, it was her way to be on guard as well. No one responded, except Siango looked up and smiled awkwardly. Something troubled him, Cindy noticed. "Where's Tom? I haven't seen him for a couple days."

"Thomas is no longer with us." Cassandra said with little humanity, not even looking at Cindy.

"What do you mean he's no longer with us? Did he die?" a crack in Cindy's voice broke out. She said it in slight jest, poking at the ridiculous mystery Cassandra wanted in the room. Cindy was also worried about me. Where was I?

"No, he didn't die, Cindy." Cassandra rebutted as if someone scratched nails on a chalkboard. "Thomas no longer works with us at California Workers For Peace and Social Justice." she continued like a condescending textbook. "That's what I meant by him not being with us anymore. I'm sorry I wasn't clearer."

Deadly, penetrating ice was what Cindy felt in the room. A few weeks after Kurt was fired, so now, too, was I. A paranoia crept inside Cindy as she felt trapped in the room. What was going on? What happened to me? She continued to wonder as she looked at everyone. She trusted Sharon before, but now with his silence, no more. Sharon didn't even look at her the whole time as he worked on files next to Charlotte.

"What happened? Why isn't he working here anymore?" Cindy inquired indignantly but afraid.

"No one is at liberty to discuss why Thomas left." Cassandra continued with the same ice.

"So he left? He wasn't fired?" Cindy responded directly.

"Cindy," Cassandra finally looked up at the young woman, a thousand hateful screams inside her. "I told you no one is at liberty to discuss why Thomas is no longer with us."

What the hell was going on? Cindy continued to panic, inwardly. Everyone acted like robots, silent, strange, stiff. Was she working for a cult? The government? Aliens? What was with these people?

The next day, Cindy and Kurt called me to find out what was going on. I wanted to tell them but couldn't, not yet. The drama hadn't come to its tidy little conclusion yet. Cindy insisted and insisted, curious as hell. What was the big deal, she kept asking me. Why was the office so awkward, quiet, and uptight, more than usual, now that I was no longer there? I remained unopened on the phone, for the moment.

Two nights later, I was told the final goods. I was officially fired. I met with Cassandra at the Cuban restaurant Versailles across the street from the office, ordered garlic chicken while she ordered nothing but water. She told me she backed Charlotte's decision to fire me for sexual harassment. I couldn't eat anything. I was devastated. I couldn't believe they were doing this, after everything, and for what I actually did. It was one of the worst blows I'd ever been hit with.

Sharon came in to the restaurant to ask Cassandra for the office key as everyone came back from canvassing. Of course, Sharon forgot the key, and he happened to arrive just after I received the final execution, and of course, Sharon, Charlotte's boyfriend, had to be the one coming in at that moment. Of all people. It almost seemed planned. Sharon couldn't look at me, shaking, trembling in tension, as I could feel his hatred from the side of his face. I could've said, "Et tu, Brute?" to

Sharon, but he was never a Brutus to me, more of a Cassius the last few months.

The following week I met with Siango after picking up my letter of recommendation. If they were sticking it to me like they were, so be it. I'd force congeniality on them to help me find another job. Fire me, disgrace me, slander me, bring me down, beat me up? Fine. I was a push-over because of my love for Charlotte. I couldn't enact revenge on her. They knew that and that's why they could kick me around.

The only options the organization gave me was to go after Charlotte. Somehow, I knew she wasn't the only culprit. I wanted to get back at others I cared less about, and perhaps even Charlotte, but only once I found out the whole story. There was something missing from the carnival of hate. I didn't know who did or said what to influence Charlotte, if anyone at all. I felt helpless, but at least I could force them to sign a letter of recommendation.

Siango signed the letter of recommendation I wrote myself, while Cassandra did not. Not surprising. From the beginning of the melodrama, Siango rose up to defend me, acting as a self-appointed lawyer on the case, while Cassandra clearly had an ax to grind.

"I'm unable to sign this document, Thomas." Cassandra told me as I stood in the office with her and Siango and no one else. The others were out canvassing that night.

"You promised me a letter of recommendation last week." I responded.

"And you'll get it. I'm just not able to sign my name to this. I'll work on my own letter of recommendation. Okay?" she politely spat back.

"When can I expect to see it?"

"Next week."

"Fine."

Siango and I went around the corner and had some coffee before the others came back from canvassing. Cassandra went home early. Siango explained as much as he felt he could. Some things became clearer, while the overall picture was still hazy. Siango believed, however sympathetic he was for me, he was not at liberty to discuss certain things. He was, after all, still working with the organization. He didn't want to ruffle too many feathers.

I asked if I could see my friends, meaning Cindy and Max, once they arrived at the office. Siango hesitated, then said it was okay. Charlotte wasn't working that night. Siango went with me back to the office and showed me how the organization was doing. He stressed certain legislative "success'," which I was suspicious of. C.W.F.P.S.J always took credit for things that were unlikely but couldn't be disproved, either.

Soon, the canvassers came back to the office. Cindy rushed up and gave me a hug.

"Tom! I missed you!" Cindy said while hugging me, then let go. "Are you gonna work with us again?"

"Nope ... I'm not." I responded quietly, moved by her, as I always was.

"Hey, what's up, man? Where you been?" Max slapped then shook my hand, then gave me a hug.

"I've been busy with some things." I said simply.

There were some other people I didn't know – new hires – and of course, Sharon, who was completely caught off guard seeing me. Sharon's face turned red, and his body began to shake. I decided to go up to him.

"Hey, Sharon, how's it going?" I said with a cynical smile as I extended my arm out for a handshake.

For all the cynical sarcasm in my voice, I honestly couldn't understand Sharon's hatred for me. He never came across as a maniacally jealous boyfriend, always showing everyone how accepting he was, how hippie dippie and progressive he was. The two of us also used to get along in the beginning. Now, the look in Sharon's eyes expressed nothing more than the wish for my death. My sarcastic smile made it even worse, with my hand extended for a handshake. I knew Sharon must've had something to do with the firing squad.

Sharon was unable to shake my hand, nor even say anything, but did, finally, move. He put his bag on the table. Resentment continued to seep out of his pores while he trembled. He walked away as if busy doing something. Several minutes later when I went outside on the landing to have a Winchester little cigar, Siango asked me to stay outside. Sharon had told Siango he didn't want me in the office. It was as if Sharon was Siango's superior and not vice versa. Not wanting to seem overly supportive of me, Siango obliged Sharon. I laughed when Siango told me the jealous, shaking boyfriend's demand.

Soon, Sharon left the office, obviously in turmoil, quickly walking by. I smiled as I saw Sharon pass me on the landing.

“I'll catch you later, Sharon.” I said with a smirk, wanting to get a response from him.

“Fuck you, man!” Sharon blasted, turning around from the staircase, raising up his middle finger in frustrated animosity.

“I thought you knew me!” I shouted to him as he walked away.

I said it again, half-sincerely, half in taunt. Sharon didn't respond as he went to his motorcycle. Siango came from around the corner, watching the whole mini-drama. He scolded me for taunting Sharon. What did Siango expect me to do, I thought to myself, give Sharon a kiss? As much as I liked Siango standing up for me, I didn't like how he tried to control everything. A couple minutes later, Cindy came outside and I took her home.

In my car, Cindy poked and poked until finally the truth came out. She had the right to know, and now that I was officially fired, I felt no obligations to the organization. I stopped the car outside her and Kurt's apartment.

“Charlotte fired you for sexual harassment?” Cindy exclaimed. “That's insane! What happened?” she continued with anger and curiosity.

“About two months ago I realized I was in love with her ...” I said, not really sure of where to start or where to end.

“Charlotte? You were in love with her?” she asked, hesitant, bewildered. She did notice I seemed closer to Charlotte recently for some reason. Still, this was a shock. “Why?” she stumbled innocently. She was not only shocked but unnerved and hurt.

Charlotte may be sexy, may give guys hard-ons, but she by no means deserved to have someone in love with her. Sharon was one thing, but me? I was too good for her. Why waste my emotions on a snobby, rich, Daddy's Girl, obnoxious, Femi-Nazi bitch from Minnesota? Cindy couldn't understand it. How could I be so stupid? But she couldn't show her anger. She loved me too much.

“It's crazy, I know ...” I said, laughing at myself uncomfortably.

“I just don't understand how you could fall in love with her ... I mean I know she's got a nice ass and tits, but ...” Cindy said, hiding her frustration with me as much as she could. She still couldn't stop from it leaking out.

“I guess I thought there was another side to her ...”

“So, what'd you do? Tell her you were in love with her and then she freaked out and screamed 'Rape! Rape! Rape!'” she said with an odd nervous laugh.

"Almost ..." I smiled painfully. "After about a month, I was really pent up and troubled over my feelings for her, and stressed about other things. I was falling more and more in love with her as time went on until I couldn't hold it inside anymore ..."

CHAPTER TEN.

FAREWELL.

Not too long after I was fired from C.W.F.P.S.J.-Now!, Cindy finally quit the organization. She wondered to herself why it took her so long. The arrival of a good friend from Plattsburgh convinced her to do the obvious and quit. The friend – Andy – was a tall, big-boned, goofy, nice guy who did a lot of coke and speed and worked on electronic music. He was more outgoing than Kurt (though not as trustworthy) and when he moved in with the young couple, Cindy spent more time with Andy than Kurt.

Right after Andy persuaded Cindy to quit C.W.F.P.S.J., he also convinced her to take a trip to Mexico, and invited Kurt and I. Kurt chose not to go because he wanted to work to pay the bills and felt Cindy should do the same. Cindy told Kurt he was a party pooper. After the pain I just went through at C.W.F.P.S.J., I saw a trip to Mexico as exactly what I needed. Especially with Cindy, and Andy, too, who I befriended after a few nights of boozing it up with him, Kurt, and Cindy.

Cindy, Andy, and I had a ton of adventures on our trip to Mexico, from the drive down listening to Andy's techno music while making one joke after another; to frolicking and riding donkeys on the beach at sunset; to doing a couple lines of coke at our cheap motel room; to feasting on cheap tacos at one restaurant after another; to drinking margaritas, beers, shots of tequila one after another at bars; to dancing on the streets in the middle of some Mexican parade; to going to strip clubs and watching Mexican women dance as erotically as possible; to smoking Cuban cigars; to going to dance clubs until 2 a.m.

After 2 in the morning, Cindy and Andy decided to call it a night and went back to the motel room. I wanted to keep going. At one dance club, I met a group of young Mexicans who had me tag along on their adventures. I struck up a romance with one of the girls, who had her brother translate for her and I. By 5:30 a.m., I spent all my money. When they dropped me off in front of an ATM machine, I freaked out and realized they wanted me to keep spending money. I'd been buying them drinks all night. I was completely wasted.

I found enough energy to fight them off as one of the butch women tried to force me to the ATM. The woman I'd been making out with the whole time looked at me from the car. She had sad eyes as I walked away, back to the motel.

Once the Mexican adventure was done and Los Angeles was our home again, I decided to work full-time on editing my movie. Living frugally off my unemployment checks, I spent twelve to fourteen hour days working on "Loveincrazy." After six months of arduous fine-tuning and cutting, I finished the job, then got Andy and Kurt to do the music.

While Andy's electronic music at times had a certain Angelo Badalementi feel to it, it was Kurt's beautiful delay pedal guitar work that shined through. "Loveincrazy" came together really in the editing and the soundtrack. Without the hard work put into both aspects, the film would've come across as just another boring slice of life drama. I loved the month and a half of hours and hours of working with Kurt and Andy (but mostly Kurt).

Soon after I finished the movie, I showed it to everyone involved in the production, and friends and family. I continued to spend time with Cindy and Kurt, while Andy moved back to Plattsburgh. With Andy gone, Cindy yearned to go back to the small upstate New York town. Besides Andy, there were other friends waiting for her. Los Angeles offered Cindy and Kurt very little. They didn't like the majority of people they met and all their friends ended up being unreliable and shallow. I was the only one who sincerely liked them. It wasn't enough.

I dropped Kurt and Cindy off at the Greyhound station in Downtown L.A. early one Sunday. The emotions had been swelling up inside me all morning ... I didn't want them to leave. I was losing my innocent and pure couple. When we said our goodbyes, I couldn't help myself and broke down in an unbearable rush of tears ... It was so bad, I had to leave ... I waived goodbye quickly, then went to my car, where I broke out into an even more painful cry in the driver's seat ... for a good five, ten minutes, right there in the car, in the Greyhound station parking lot ... Cindy and Kurt were surprised and a little heartbroken as well ... They knew they meant a lot to me, but not this much ...

Kurt and Cindy stayed in touch with me through e-mails now and then. Later that year, I met up with them in New York for a screening of "Loveincrazy." We had fun, but after that trip, I sent them e-mails and occasionally got responses. For the most part, though, we lost touch. I would hear from them less and less. One day I found out they broke up for good, and Cindy was pregnant with her new boyfriend's child, while Kurt was in a new band. The physical distance got in the way and created an emotional distance as well. I had lost my innocent couple for good.

PART TWO. BENNY.

CHAPTER ONE. A BUSINESS MEETING.

I was wary about the meeting with Benny's friend. I didn't know much about the guy or what he really wanted. Jean – my biological father – thought it'd be a good idea to work with him and Benny. It'd be a way to get our philosophical movie zine on the Internet, create a website, maybe get involved in some on-line business the guy was doing.

Jean was to me very loving as a father and as a close friend. He invested so much time and energy into my life, even if initially when my mother wanted a baby, Jean disapproved. He felt incompatible with my mother and in many ways he was right. Still, my mother was hurt and felt rejected, so she chose to be with another man: Frazier. Between the ages of 8 and 17, Frazier was my main father figure. But when I came back to Los Angeles at 18, I struck up a closer bond with Jean than with Frazier. Blood won out over environment.

Now, when I was 22, Jean and I started working on an underground publication on movies, society, relationships, philosophy, and politics. The zine was called The Hollywood Absurd. At this point - meeting with Benny and his friend, Stan - Jean and I had just done the first two issues only.

Jean and I sat outside a coffee shop near Cal State Northridge, with Benny and Stan, having just met them moments ago. I'd seen Benny once or twice before, but didn't know him that well.

Jean wore a black baseball hat that said, “No Problem,” a cheap brown jacket with a fur neck and gloves. He covered himself to protect his sensitive skin. Ten years before his doctor told him he contracted a mild form of skin cancer. Fortunately, it never became serious. Jean was careful not to stay in the sun too long.

The loving and unconventional father stood about 5'8" and for most of his life was pretty thin. In the last few years, though, he gained a relatively large gut. Since he was a young man, he had a bare head, only the very back and sides having black hair. He had large, childlike, dark, sarcastic, sensitive, penetrating eyes on a youthful and goateed face. The hint of sorrow in his wrinkles pointed to heartbreak in his life. Jean considered himself introverted, a lone wolf, even though he was extremely open, direct, talkative, and sociable. He could get people to open up and trust him as a close confidante on a first meeting.

"So, you guys did a magazine before? How was that?" Jean inquired.

"It was more of a silly kinda comic strip, about this pot-head who goes on adventures." Benny replied, laughing. Stan cracked a smile, but didn't laugh.

Benny was born with type-3 cerebral palsy, the least damaging of the disease. Still, the effect on his life could not be over-stated. He would have, for the rest of his life, a difficult time walking or standing for long periods, let alone the social and psychological troubles gained from how others saw him and how he saw himself.

His legs, with not a lot of strength nor agility, could at times give way, causing him to fall. By now, 32 years old, he had long ago figured out a routine for the falls. When at the moment he knew he was going down he made his body fall forward, then stop from getting hurt with his strong hands, and soon push himself back up. It was amazing to see this display of dexterity in his upper body.

Because of the disease, his stamina was limited, though, but mentally speaking he was as sharp as anyone else. And since he had type-3 and not worse, his speech was not impaired. Benny's face and eyes were distinguished. He had a sculpted jaw, cheekbones, forehead, nose, and mouth.

Benny looked like, with his black beard and thick mustache, a cross between Jesus Christ and Rasputin. Even with his cerebral palsy and his lack of interest in personal hygiene (out of laziness), Benny was a handsome guy. Despite his cerebral-palsy, I felt he could actually get an attractive gal as a girlfriend. But Benny had a tendency to choose people around him, friends or his girlfriend, that weren't all that deserving. Growing up in the San Fernando valley his whole life, most of the people he associated with were on the white trailer trash edge of society, always fixing cars, bikes, computers, playing video games, lounging around, not doing much.

A lot of friends took advantage of his kindness, his people-pleasing. It was important for him to be liked, because he always had in the back of his mind someone might not like him. Mainly, for his cerebral palsy.

Samantha – Benny's mom – was also a people-pleaser, kind, generous, pleasant, but also, more than her son, could talk a person's ear off. Benny's adopted sister was the opposite in terms of kindness. She lied, cheated, stole from her giving mother, justifying it for one self-pitying idea after another. While Benny was the one born with a disability, she triumphed far more in feeling sorry for herself.

Benny had an American tough guy stiff upper lip when it came to his disease, never allowing people to feel sorry for him. He was, though, more than eager to have his mother take care of him as much as possible. Unfortunately, to please his friends and girlfriend, he allowed them to take advantage of Samantha, too.

"We were just goofing around then." Stan said quietly, guarded, almost under his breath.

Heavy set, wide, tall, mustached, Stan leaned back in his chair, in a methodically calculating pose. He looked at me and Jean, then his attention went elsewhere, his eyes rarely coming back to the table. He wasn't shy or awkward, but coolly distant, hippishly uninterested.

I didn't know what Stan thought of us, or what the detached young man's agenda was, but superior posing didn't interest me at all. If he felt that was the business-like thing to do, he could take it somewhere else. I wasn't a business man, and only stayed at the table out of politeness.

"Sounds like you guys had fun." Jean put out simply, hoping to pull

Stan out more.

"It wasn't as serious as what you and your son do, with your zine." Stan said, his eyes looking elsewhere, his attention elsewhere.

"Did you read one of our issues?" I asked him.

"I glanced at it for a sec. Read the intro. Very nice. Deep."

"You think so?" I asked cynically, trying to get Stan's eyes back to the table.

"Definitely. So, I have to ask you guys – Thomas, Jean," Stan started as he leaned further back into his chair, his eyes still not connecting with us. "What do you plan to do with your zine?"

"Well ..." I started to say awkwardly, still irritated with Stan's aloofness. "My main interest, our main interest, is to provoke readers on the things we talk about in the articles. By dealing with movies as a context, we can dive into a variety of subject matters that interest us, mean something to us, philosophical questions that relate to everyone. Personal experiences, political or social issues, existential dilemmas, relationships, love, sex, and more. We want to get people to think about their lives in a more profound way than any of us normally get a chance to." I said with enthusiasm, surprising myself, considering my lack of interest in the meeting after the first few minutes.

"Like I said before, I think what you're doing is deep, guys. But what I want to know before we become business partners, is what do you want, business-wise?" Stan said.

"Business partners?" I asked as my heart sank with anger.

Even though I was expecting the worst based on Stan's earlier behavior, somehow Stan saying that made me infuriated. Perhaps it was just simply more chalk being scratched against the chalkboard, more of the same agony. But I said nothing, just sat there quietly, pensively. Jean noticed this and knew how I was, so he tried to help things.

"What Tom is hoping for is if someone in the entertainment industry will pick up an issue of the Hollywood Absurd and want to give him money to make a movie." Jean said.

"Wouldn't we all?" Stan said as if it was poetry, then laughed stiffly.

"Yeah, well ..." I said, wishing I could just get up and leave.

"You know, the name of your zine is pretty good." Stan said in a weird, put on earnestness.

I silently jolted. What was Stan thinking? Was he going to steal our zine's name? I gave myself away with a split second freeze.

"Don't worry, man, I wouldn't steal your name. Benny can show you how to copyright it on the Internet later." Stan said to calm me down. At least for once he seemed to pay attention to us.

"Yeah, it's real easy." Benny said as he lit his second cigarette. He seemed to be quietly in awe of Stan the Business Man.

The conversation continued in the same manner. I gave up a long time before but Jean kept on trying to see if anything could come from the meeting. Jean didn't wanted it to go to waste but I felt, why bother? I didn't come there to strike up a business deal with someone who was from another planet. If money or business had a part to play in our zine, it was only a necessity, a secondary or third or fourth factor, not the first. Stan was obviously not interested in the personal nor the philosophical, not even a little bit.

By the end, Stan told us about his on-line business, how it helped other businesses, how we could hook up with him, basically pay him to be one of his web-links. Then came some vague ideas about how Benny would design the on-line website for the zine, and we'd get a ton of people looking at our site. Stan said, "who knows? Maybe a famous producer would see the site and want to give you a million bucks for your first feature." Then, finally, the conversation was over.

Somehow, Jean and I agreed to some kind of interest. I didn't know how it happened. The next week, I e-mailed Stan I was planning to move to Chicago, so I couldn't work with him on the "business deal." I didn't know why I just couldn't tell him the truth – I wasn't interested.

CHAPTER TWO.

REHEARSING FOR "LOVEINCRAZY."

A couple years past and I didn't see Benny much at all. We didn't have much in common, even though I liked him. I would see Benny's mom, Samantha now and then since she was a friend of Jean's. Samantha wanted to be Jean's lover but he only wanted the friend angle. They liked some of the same movies and discussed politics, but she was a little shallow in her understanding, and spoke in not very interesting monologues. She'd go on and on about the most trivial of things. This irritated people, including Jean, so much that it unfortunately detracted from her sweetness and generosity.

When Jean mentioned to me Samantha offered her house to shoot "Loveincrazy" in, I wasn't sure if it'd work out. After all, the other choices in locations fell through, why wouldn't this one? But because of Samantha's kindness, her house was to be the one.

While I rehearsed with the semi-original cast, Benny was around the house, along with Samantha, her adopted daughter, and grandchild. They all lived there but didn't seem to mind a low-budget film was taking over. Only one weekend's worth of rehearsals went by when Bernardo and the last remaining professional actor quit. Frazier and Maya were all that was left. I decided to cast myself as one of Jack Henry's sons.

The cinematographer, Kristianna, and sound man, Jonathan, came by the location to check out the rehearsals, and talk things over with me. Jean came by often, as well, and suggested I use Benny as the brother in the film. To me, it was a stroke of genius. Benny's face was strikingly cinematic and unique, again that cross between Christ and Rasputin.

Benny never acted before but in many ways I preferred non-professional actors. There was more openness, freshness, originality about them. Professional actors, including the ones I cast, had a difficult time with the improvisational, loose structure I wanted. Professional actors needed rigid outlets to express themselves. If in the "Loveincrazy" shoot we were ambling, finding our way in the dark, it became confusing, unsettling, awkward, too personal.

For non-professionals, taking in the moment, instinctive direction, and following through with rehearsed and rehearsed but still impulsive acting, was more natural to them. There were no formula behaviors they could rely on – no Tom Cruise tricks, no Matt Damon tricks, no Robert DeNiro tricks – so the responses given were completely their own.

Benny had no problem being himself. That was part of it, but being oneself wasn't all one had to do. The non-professional couldn't make it work just by being a non-professional. The person had to have a personality in front of the camera, one that fit the role and the story. Or, like what I did, change the story to fit the actor.

My opinion was that anyone could be a good actor. One just had to mold the film for them and not vice versa. Actors were off the mark – professional or non – if they were forced, by themselves or by the director, to say a line, do a movement, not natural to them.

I noticed after the first set of rehearsals with Benny, he had a hard time memorizing lines. But this was not the only reason I ended up breaking down the script into scene blocks on cue cards. Besides my own problem with memorization, I didn't want to memorize the lines and direct and produce and do all the little things a low budget filmmaker had to do at the same time.

Frazier had a hard time remembering lines as well, despite his numerous years of experience. Maya was also unfamiliar with the process of memorizing. Finally, though, I just didn't like the dialogue. Why not just write down what happens in the scene, what I wanted the actors to talk about and that's it? The story structure remained intact, and what each scene dealt with thematically remained the same.

Now, though, as actors we had the freedom to say the lines in our own separate ways. I would tell everyone what was important to communicate, then let it rip. It was a true collaboration with me leading the way. Since we spent several weekends rehearsing every scene, everyone was familiar enough during the production to have the necessary confidence to make improvising work.

The third week of rehearsals, Kristianna's friend Celebrity (a name she gave herself), dropped out as the sister of my character and Benny's. Originally, Jack Henry had four sons, then three, then two sons and one daughter, and then, finally just two sons. I cast Celebrity after the first week's drop-outs, Bernardo and the last professional actor.

I met Celebrity while working with Kristianna on pre-production to see if she'd do the art design. That was her main interest, with acting more of a side thing. The art design wasn't necessary, as I pretty much did it myself with all the on-location sites. I asked her if she could play the sister role, and she accepted. After rehearsing only one day, she didn't like my style, so she quit, saying she got an offer as a production designer on a paying studio gig.

That was fine for me. She wasn't a very good actress and I was annoyed by her giving Frazier so much attention about astrology. Frazier was distracted by all the charts he was doing for everyone in the cast and crew. The production seemed far off, not close to him. There was the threat of a half-assed performance by Frazier. He felt, after all, he was just doing his step-son a favor. He didn't take it that seriously. But with Celebrity gone – since she was the only one who really cared about the charts – that threat to Frazier's acting was much less real.

Benny especially didn't care about astrology, though didn't have my contempt for it. I grew up with those god-forsaken charts. A lot of the time, Benny was an attentive actor. Other times he'd get tired, lazy, or a little clownish, or caught up in telling stories. The physical weariness was understandable. The poor guy had cerebral palsy. He also smoked weed a lot, which I smelled one Saturday morning as I went to Benny's bedroom to get him.

"Hey, Benny," I said as I knocked on his door, "it's time for rehearsal."

"I'll be right out!" he replied behind the closed door. The alluring stench of pot poured underneath the crack.

"Okay."

I went back to the living room where Frazier and Maya were waiting patiently. Frazier sat on the couch as he often did during rehearsals while Maya stood near a window, looking out, then turned to me as I came in.

"Was he asleep?" she asked.

"I think he was doing something else ..." I said with a hand gesture to my mouth as if pretending to smoke.

"Pot head." she shot back with a smile.

For all of Maya's toughness, she'd often look at me attentively like a child. A glance, sometimes almost unnoticeable. It could be unbearable for me, mostly because that look was a reminder of past moments, many, many moments ... One particularly heart-breaking drama was horrible anguish ... her and I sitting side by side on the floor in my old apartment in Silverlake ...

The vulnerable glance of love she gave reminded me of that emotional turmoil on the floor. She loved me so much but always denied it. She shoved it into her gut, repressed it, making the feelings come out in possessive, unhealthy ways ... Still, she had one of the largest, genuine hearts in the world ... your mother has the capacity for true beauty, Daniel ... She was, after all, acting in "Loveincrazy" out of love for me.

Pretty much everyone working on the movie was doing it out of love, in different degrees and reasons. Even Frazier, after the sour drama of the divorce with my mother, after other bitter things, was playing Jack Henry out of love, however insincere or troubled by the past.

Perhaps Frazier was trying to prove something out of bitterness or it was the continuation of his life-long con-game with me and my mother. He had spent 20 years taking advantage of my mother, until eventually she had enough. Whatever ulterior motives he had, Frazier was still there, while others, including friends, quit. Charlotte didn't quite quit, as she wanted to do the movie, only a month or two later, when Kristianna wouldn't be available. Gus and Bernardo, though, flat out quit, justified or not.

Frazier came from a well-off Scottish Canadian family which owned a large 60 acre island in Georgian Bay, a southeastern section of the Great Lakes. Frazier considered himself a kind of rebel in the family because he became an actor in his youth. In reality, though, he was no threat to the family unit.

As Frazier got older especially, he was no where near the black sheep he might've considered himself, only mildly quirky and eccentric in behavior but in attitude the same. He sang show tunes all the time, obsessed about astrology, lost his temper, and discussed politics now and then. He never became financially successful as an actor (nor in anything else), so in this way he was odd compared to the others. Almost everyone in the family did well for themselves financially. Despite his lack of success, he bought into materialism and the upper-middle class values of his family. Money was God.

Frazier had a relatively regal bearing, standing about 6 feet tall, big boned, charming, jovial but also nervous and uncomfortable with himself. He wore thick glasses, his dark brown hair being overwhelmed by gray, his regal bearing withering away with wrinkles, and his smiles becoming more and more insincere.

Maya, on the other hand, did not have a problem with sincerity. She had a hard time getting something off her chest, or admit to something, or she'd hide something through harsh sarcasm. But, she'd never pretend to be something she wasn't, unlike someone such as Frazier. When she was kind she was kind, when she wasn't, she wasn't.

Her rough experiences growing up in El Salvador – from having her father murdered when she was six years old, to losing her right arm in an automobile accident at nine, to living on the streets when her mother hit her too often, to the civil war of the 1980's, to the oppressive Catholic Church, to the poverty of a lower income family in a third world country – molded her into a proud, sometimes stand-offish, independent, tough cookie. She didn't take shit from anybody. After her twins were born, she allowed herself a certain amount of softness, but still not a great deal.

Maya had gleaming jet black hair, wide, beautiful, dark brown eyes, gloriously smooth and lush dark bronze skin, large breasts, long, luscious legs and a body I just adored. She wasn't ashamed of only having one arm and carried herself confidently. If she had insecurities about her missing arm (which I believed she did, catching her at times), she hid it well. Like Benny, she had a stiff upper lip and didn't allow self-pitying for the disability. She may have had a lingering subconscious resentment against the world when she was younger, but now in her mid-30's, she mellowed a bit. By no means all the way, though.

"So you know what's going on in this scene?" I said to Maya as I came up to her near the window.

"No, I have no idea. You haven't said anything to me." she snapped back, even while having that innocent, child-like look in her eyes.

"We talked about it in the car." I snapped back, as well.

"I didn't understand what you said."

"So you do admit we talked about this scene in the car?"

"Thomas ... just tell me what you want me to do. I've never done this before. I've never acted before. I don't know what you want from me. Just tell me." she said heatedly in her thick Spanish accent.

I went on to explain the scene we were about to rehearse and what I wanted from her character. Part of my directorial technique with actors was to bring their energy level up by way of creating various kinds of tension between me and them. Sometimes I'd do this by irritating them or throwing zingers, or sometimes, as I just did, be on edge and snippy.

A little later, Benny came out of his bedroom and joined us. I finished talking to Maya while Frazier sat on the couch, quietly reading the script. I stood silently, paused in thought as I looked around the living room.

“What's up, Tom? Why're you lookin' around as if ya lost yer underwear?” Benny joked with a chortle and smile.

“I'm just thinking about this room. It's no good.” I responded, only slightly smiling, still lost in thought. “You know what? Let's rehearse this scene outside, next to the pool.”

“Do you need me, Tom?” Frazier asked from the couch.

“No, no that's okay.” I answered, still thinking.

“Okay, I'm going to make a quick phone call.” Frazier said as he got up, took out his cell phone, then left the room.

I opened the sliding glass door to the back patio and swimming pool area, going outside, with Maya and Benny following. Maya and Benny often didn't know what to expect from me but they trusted me somehow.

Samantha's dog, Gertie, ran up to Benny from around the house, excited, nervous as the dog sniffed, licked, and nudged Benny's hand. As Benny tried to follow me and Maya to the swimming pool area, the dog wouldn't get out of Benny's way.

“Girl, get on. Get outta here.” Benny said, shooing the dog away.

Eventually, the dog got the message and split. I walked around one end of the swimming pool, lost in thought. Maya stood next to me, not sure what was going on. Benny came up to us.

“Alright cap'in', what's next?” Benny said as he sat on one of the patio beach chairs.

“Okay, the scene we're rehearsing right now is ... after Naomi – your character, Maya – is able to get into the house, after my character,

Colin, tries to stop her from getting involved in the family get-together for the second time, then she comes in and meets Jack Henry, the dad, who lets her in. She sees that no one is communicating with anyone else and even Jack, after being polite with her initially, doesn't say anything to her. She gets up, wondering where Colin disappeared to and goes looking for him. She comes outside here to the back patio area and finds Colin with Benny's character, Roland. You guys see that in your scripts?" I said, looking at Benny, who didn't have a script, which is why I asked.

"Um, as you can tell, I don't got one ..." Benny said uncomfortably.

"That's okay, I'll get you one." I said as I went back into the house, sympathetic and irritated with him at the same time.

"What page is it on?" Maya asked as she flipped through her script.

"46 or 47, I think." I said as I went inside the house.

Soon I came back outside with a script in one hand and the scene index cards in the other.

"Okay, so page 46." I said as I handed the script to Benny.

The three of us went on to do the scene. My character, Colin, was pensive, didn't want Maya's character, Naomi, at the house and so clammed up with her there. Naomi introduced herself to Roland, Benny's character, and the two strike up a friendliness while Colin (me) sat volcanically quiet.

Soon, Colin grabbed a basketball and began dribbling it, smashing it against the ground while Naomi and Roland tried to have a conversation. All of my real life pent up frustrations came out through Colin; the tension in making my first feature length film, being the producer, director, actor, writer (re-writing scenes as we went along), at the age of 25, the disappointments and changes in the cast, crew, locations; the insecurity in knowing whether I knew what the hell I was doing, whether my film would be any good or not, whether I could get decent performances out of anyone, including myself, whether the cinematography, the lighting, the sound would be any good; to all my personal frustrations with friends, with Maya, with women, with work at C.W.F.P.S.J.Now!

All these things came to the surface as I smashed the basketball against the concrete patio near the swimming pool. I was like a child screaming for attention and yet wanting to be alone. After a while of loud pounding, Maya and Benny became annoyed and got out of character, asking me to stop. I kept pounding the ball, looking at them maniacally, intensely, sadistically smiling. They told me to stop firmly and I still wouldn't. They asked again and again and I kept bouncing the ball. At this point, Maya and Benny didn't know what to do. What was wrong with me?

Eventually, I stopped and Maya and Benny could breath again. But from that point on, they didn't know what to expect from me, when I'd be in character, when I'd be directing, or when I'd just be Thomas. This uncertainty, this insecurity, created a dynamic wherein the camera would record the action, and the cast and crew didn't know the line between the actors performing and human beings just being themselves. The drama seemed to be present amongst everyone there, so no one could truly feel comfortable or detached. That was exactly what I wanted.

CHAPTER THREE.

BENNY IN THE LIMELIGHT.

"Let's do it again!" I yelled from outside the back house.

The production for "Loveincrazy" was into its second weekend, the fourth day. I decided to change the script so that Jack Henry had a second house. It was done partly because the best visual aspects to the house had been used up, and partly because I had an idea to change the narrative.

The first house was the one Jack Henry had more recently bought and was using as his home. The second house was the place where Colin and Roland grew up in, and which their father was planning to sell. Right as Colin is about to leave the family get-together, Jack mentions that he's soon selling the old house and would like Colin and Roland to see it for sentimental reasons. Colin ends up agreeing to go, despite the lack of sentiment.

Minutes after their arrival at the old house, Jack Henry had thrown a huff and threw a glass of whiskey in Colin's face. Colin went on a tirade on the reasons why 9/11 happened in a very anti-U.S. Foreign policy fashion. Jack Henry was a 9/11 survivor, a conservative to boot, and not only that, he invited his two sons home for an act of reconciliation on the first anniversary of 9/11.

Jack assumed his two sons would automatically welcome him with open arms because of the obvious 9/11 sympathy. For Roland this could happen, at least initially, but for Colin, who had an unresolved deep-seeded bitterness, this was possible only on his terms. Jack had done something unforgivable to Colin as a child. Colin would actually forgive his father for the harm done, but only if Jack would communicate openly with his sons. These were the angry young son's terms, although it was difficult to clarify. Thus, the conflict.

After the outburst over 9/11, Jack stormed into the back house, while Colin convinced Roland to go searching through the property for something that belonged to Colin's mother. During the search, Colin persuaded his older brother how their father was never emotionally available to them. Once Colin found the little statue, Roland went inside to the back house kitchen and Jack was there. He was caught off-guard when Roland suggested he be easier on Colin. Jack insisted Colin needed to grow up, and that no one should feel sorry for him since he did that so well for himself.

This was where the scene began. We started filming early that Sunday morning, at the house I originally wanted, Lara and Gerald's house in Venice Beach.

"How many times you want us to do it, Tom?" Benny joked, laughing with an undertone of irritation.

I was pushing Benny that morning, past his usual physical and emotional boundaries. It was difficult not only because of Benny's condition, but for personal reasons as well. His mother was rushed to the hospital for one of her nervous breakdowns after an argument with her boyfriend. While Samantha had been rushed to the hospital several times before under the same circumstances, it still worried Benny. And here I was demanding the best possible performance out of him. When in film making mode, Daniel, directors can be the most self-absorbed people.

The other reason why I pushed Benny besides being a dictator, was this was Roland's climax. This was his most important scene, where Roland finally confronts Jack. After years of cordiality and getting along superficially, the subtext between them bursted out: the father's shame of Roland's disability. Roland comes at Jack in the same aggressive way that Colin did earlier - refusing their father's business be passed down to them. It was one of the more important scenes, and I had to get Benny and Frazier to hit the right notes.

"You're not working with Clint Eastwood here, Benny. Don't be lazy." Kristianna affectionately goaded him. She then realized that probably only Jonathan and I knew the reference: Eastwood's rule of two takes only. I was on take ten.

Kristianna and Jonathan were running the technical aspect of the film while I focused on the acting and staging. In pre-production, I outlined the specifics to my ideas on the cinematography, locations, production design, and sound. During the shoot, I gave them a good deal of freedom, approving or disapproving of takes on the replay monitor, or from the sidelines.

Kristianna was an intelligent, talented, and professionally ambitious twenty-two year old Bulgarian woman. Her father was an established and highly respected cinematographer in Bulgaria, and her mother was the first female cinematographer in Bulgaria. Her parents urged her to stay away from cinema, warning that as a woman, it would be a struggle to succeed as a director of photography. Her mother may have worked on a few films, but nothing more reliable than her teaching job. Even in Hollywood, they felt, it would still be difficult. There just weren't many female cinematographers anywhere in the world.

Initially, at a college in Chicago, Kristianna majored in political science. Her parents were pleased – she stayed away from their profession. Then after befriending a group of film students (that included Jonathan), her desire for film making sprung up again. She changed her major to cinema, soaking in all the new films from the Scandinavian movement, Dogma, and Hong Kong director Wong Kar Wai's cinematographer – Christopher Doyle. There was of course many other influences, but those two forces were the main ones.

Kristianna stood about 5'4", had grayish blue eyes, dirty blond hair, and had a soft, tender presence about her which hid a fierce determination to succeed. She talked for the most part gently and tenderly, but now and again a stern, angular, commanding voice would come forth. She was quite good looking but she didn't show it off, thinking herself too short, her hips too round, and her nose too big. There was a mysterious air about her, a taking things in and weighing her options. It was hard to know where she placed her bets.

Jonathan was a decent, generous, goofy, tall guy who also seemed hard to pinpoint. Having a paranoia I'd get now and then, sometimes I felt the two were hiding something from me, that something was up their sleeve. Coming from a well-off San Francisco family, Jonathan had the knowledge that all privileged children have: whatever he wanted in life, he'd get the financial backing to do it. Being an aspiring filmmaker, he knew that whenever the day came to make a movie, the resources would be there.

Not only to make a movie, but ensure a respectable low budget production (at least $250,000, compared to "Loveincrazy"'s $7,000), and also a distributor to get at least a straight to video deal. Jonathan's relationship to Kristianna was hard to figure. They worked from project to project, on bigger budget B-movies, and on low-budget indies like my film. That much was for sure. But were they lovers? Friends? Their behavior didn't make it obvious either way.

"Gee, I never knew Tom wasn't Clint Eastwood. He had me fooled 'til now." Benny said affectionately sarcastic to Kristianna. It appeared he might've had a little crush on the cinematographer, but because he was always joking with everyone, he didn't seem that serious about it.

"I think it's ridiculous to have a two-take rule like that." I said to Kristianna. "Can we take a look at that one?" he asked her.

"Sure." she said as she went into the back part of the house with the camera.

Kristianna turned on the monitor and plugged the camera in. I sat next to her on the floor as we watched the playback. Just then, Benny came up behind us.

"No, no, Benny." I said as I caught him. "Actors aren't allowed to watch the dallies."

"You're one of the actors." Benny shot back with a smile.

"I'm also the director, the producer, the writer - " I smiled back.

" - and the goffer, make-up artist, script girl, and coffee boy." Benny said with his valley hark of a laugh.

"Okay, Olivier, we have to do it again. Don't lose your focus and don't forget what I said to you and Frazier earlier."

"Okay, boss." Benny followed the orders humbly and walked outside.

Soon, everyone went back to their positions – cast and crew. Cindy, Kurt, Kristianna, Jonathan, Frazier, Benny, and myself. Gerald hung around to help as well, while he made sure the house was okay. It was a close knit, fun-loving bunch, with things going swiftly.

Frazier sat in the front living room to the back house, looking at a picture of Colin (in real life, me, when I was a child, swinging on jungle gyms). The lights were set outside through a couple of windows, but mostly natural light was used. Kristianna held the camera on her shoulder, getting ready for the steady cam shot with Cindy behind her. Jonathan had the headsets on, holding the sound mixer, with Kurt holding the boom mic over Benny's head.

"Okay ..." I said as I stood near Kristianna, watching Benny. " ... Action ..."

Benny began walking up the three steps to the front door, entering the back house. Frazier, on cue, looked up from the picture in his hand to Benny, who just walked through the door. As rehearsed, there was a moment of silence at first, a tension, as they acknowledged each other. Benny had a different look on his face than before, and Jack picked up on this. The father was worried Colin turned Roland against him.

"You know ..." Benny said hesitantly. "... you shouldn't be so hard on Colin." he continued, referring to Jack throwing the whiskey in Colin's face, and the over-all antagonism between Jack and Colin. Initially, Roland laughed at Colin getting the whiskey in the face. Roland was on Jack's side from the start of the visit. But now, after Colin's persuasion, it was different. "I know Colin can be a little stubborn sometimes, but he's doing the best he can ... in this situation." Benny said hesitantly, continuing from before.

"I shouldn't be so hard on him? After the way he's been acting? After that shit he said about 9/11 and all his politics crap?" Frazier said, quick to defend, a look of worry in his eyes. "Colin needs to stop feeling sorry for himself. Maybe he shouldn't be so hard on me. After all, he has a lot less to feel sorry for himself than you do."

With that, something dropped into Roland's mind, a triggering of memories. One was that he had some knowledge of what Jack did to Colin as a child. Colin actually had something to feel sorry for himself. Roland became defensive with Jack's defensiveness. Why did he say Colin has less to feel sorry for himself than he does, Roland asked. Jack came back with Roland's handicap.

This then brought back Roland's feelings Jack was ashamed of his cerebral-palsy. It was as if Jack avoided him in some way all his life, said his hello's and how you doings, then not much else. The shame was never on the surface, but Roland felt it. Now, at this moment, he wanted to bring it to the surface.

"Why should I feel sorry for myself? Because I've got a handicap? Come on now, don't put that shit on me." Benny shot back, as he walked into the kitchen, as if the swelling up of emotion was too much for him to stay in the front living room with Frazier.

"All the suffering you've gone through because of your disease isn't enough to make you feel sorry for yourself?" Frazier said as he followed Benny into the kitchen. "Colin never had to go through that."

"You always talk about my disability as if I was some other guy's son. You never wanted to get to know me, know me as a person. It's like you always avoided me, something to have pity for, like a dog who's missing a leg." Roland came back defiantly, but moving around, nervous.

"What're you talking about? I've always liked you." Jack returned in his own defiance, but also now pleading, nervous, and uncomfortable.

Roland was right.

“'Liked' is a nice way to put it. You never gave a damn. When was the last time you ever met a girlfriend of mine? Do you even know my girlfriend's name, the one I'm going out with now?”

“I've been busy with the family business my whole life, Roland. You know that. But let me tell you something. Whenever I try to get in touch with you, I always feel you're ashamed of me , like you don't want anything to do with your old dad.”

With that, a fire struck up inside Roland. And, in the real Benny. He had become personally invested in the scene. Jack Henry became the object of all his frustrations in life. He could punch him.

“Me ashamed of you? ... How can you say that?! You've been the one ashamed of me my whole life!” Benny shouted in outrage.

“I have never been ashamed of you!”

“Then why've I felt that way? Why did I always get this feeling you never wanted to be around me more than a couple minutes, like I remind you of something bad?”

“You know what I think? I don't think you've felt this way at all. I think Colin has been putting ideas into your head just now. He's gotten you to imagine this is how you feel and it's not the way it really is.”

“So now I can't think for myself, huh?”

“No, it's not that, it's just you've allowed your brother too much sympathy.”

“Well, maybe he's right. Maybe you are full of shit.”

“Come on now, stop this! You're not Colin!”

“And I'm not you, either.”

“Look, Roland, let's forget about this right now. If you have some bad feelings towards me, I'll accept that. I'm sure you'll get over it soon enough. The most important thing at the moment is the family business. At least you're going to keep that going. The business transcends whatever personal problems we may have. Remember that."

"I'm not taking on the family business anymore. I've decided."

"You're what? You can't do that!"

"Not anymore."

The argument continued, building and building until it got to a bitter climax. Roland flat out refused to take on the responsibility of continuing the family boat-making business. He was going to stay a musician. Jack couldn't accept it. In his eyes, Jack was a failure if he couldn't pass on his father's business to his sons. He spat in disgust at Roland, erupting in bitterness, telling him in so many words he was a loser and a failure in life. Roland stood quietly, but defiantly. He resisted Jack Henry, the most ominous, dominate, yet distant figure in his life.

I decided to do a couple more takes, but in terms of Benny's performance, that was the best one. When I put the film together in the editing room, I inter-cut other takes now and then for Frazier or reactions from Benny, but for the most part, that take was the center of that scene. There was some great cinematographic moments in that take as well, where Kristianna caught a beautiful light coming through the window and wonderful angles of both Benny and Frazier's faces. I was proud of Benny's acting and everyone congratulated him on his performance. I told Benny that this should show him what he was capable of. He had never acted a day in his life and look at what he did.

CHAPTER FOUR.

THE PRODUCTION ENDS.

"I don't want any goofing around right now!" I violently snapped to everyone near the back house from the gate. "You're not supposed to be fucking smiling in this shot!"

Benny and Maya were chuckling at me as I came up to them towards the back. Even Kristianna, Jonathan, Kurt, Cindy, and Gerald were laughing. Once I was obviously in a serious mood, Kristianna quickly stopped being amused, respecting me as her director. Jonathan did, as well. But everyone else, while trying to hide their laughter, let some giggling trickle out.

I had allowed a certain amount of goofing around on the set, as long as it didn't break up everyone's concentration. Now, towards the end of the shoot, people were getting more restless and fooling around more. I was becoming more and more irritated with it. Funny enough, after I praised and encouraged Benny with his acting, he began to get a wee bit haughty. I made it clear "Loveincrazy" was an ensemble piece but Benny started to think the film was about him. I didn't mind this too much, but Benny began undercutting me as a director, as well, with joking continuously through the shoot.

I felt this was maybe because I was so demanding as a director, asking for take after take, and for everyone to be Marlon Brando. Whatever the reason, Benny's goofing around irked me after a while. Benny's habit of going on and on about some trivial story or other was another annoyance.

"I forgot we're supposed to be depressed through this whole thing." Benny cracked with a smile and a laugh.

"We're about to shoot the very end of the movie, you guys," I said to everyone, not wanting to single out Benny, although I stood closest to him. "I know everyone likes to joke around and it's been a long day and we're almost done with the shoot, but in case you haven't noticed, when you're shooting, you don't act like how you all were just now, goofing and all that, you act according to what is demanded by the scene. This is the very end of the movie. We just had a huge blow-up between Colin and Jack - "

"Yeah and you were screaming your head off, waking up the neighbors -" Benny continued to joke. He just couldn't take me seriously.

"You don't need to get so angry, Thomas. Don't yell at us like that." Maya said sternly to me.

I stood silently, looking at Maya, pensive, then looked away. I then walked up to her and Benny, who were standing next to each other.

"I'm making a movie, Maya, and its something thats important to me personally, not only as a professional project. I don't want a shit film." I said heatedly, unfortunately like an asshole, coming into Benny and Maya's faces. I was becoming maniacal. "If you guys want to fuck this up and turn in half-assed performances, go right ahead. Turn this into a shit production. But if you want me to ever talk to you again, stop jacking off here, and fucking do your best."

With that, everyone became thunderingly silent. Everyone was afraid of the violence in me. I seemed as unpredictable as an animal, as if with the wrong word I could snap and eat someone alive. It was an impulse, a shot, volcanic, something that would build and build inside me until it exploded. Once the rush of feeling subsided, it was difficult for me to sustain the tone. The gentle Thomas would kick back in.

The next take we did after my outburst was phenomenal. It was one of the best takes in the production, which was great since it was also the very last shot in the film. Kristianna started with a wide shot of the back of the house, placing the camera right behind Jack Henry, sitting dejectedly and worn out. Then she swung the camera to the left, catching Naomi (Maya) standing by, then Roland sitting on the steps. They both had great, solemn looks on their faces, no smiles.

The timing was right on in this shot. As soon as Kristianna panned left to Maya and Roland, Roland, on cue, stood up and began walking to the front gate. Maya soon followed him, with Kristianna and her camera walking behind. Once past the gate, they got to Colin's car. As Kristianna arrived, Colin opened his door in front of Naomi and Roland, making the car door stop them. The camera caught Colin's look as he stared Naomi down. As Colin got out of the car, Kristianna moved the camera and herself to the right. Moving at the same time was Colin, getting out of the car.

The camera captured a beautiful three shot with Roland standing screen left as Colin grabbed Naomi, looking intently at her as she looked away from him but allowed to be held. Colin leaned forward to kiss her as she turned to the side. He continued forward anyway, holding her in his arms like he might die tomorrow, kissing the side of her head passionately.

Roland stood by, letting the two lovers play out the romantic and dramatic moment between them. Naomi allowed Colin to hold and kiss her, but didn't return the kisses, holding back emotionally from him. Eventually, Colin stopped kissing her and looked up at Naomi and Roland, not saying a word, but recognizing the emotions of the moment. There was uncertainty in Colin as he turned fully to Roland. He looked fixedly at his older brother. The screen then would cut to black. The movie would be over. End title credits would roll.

The production continued for another day, the following Saturday, only to do some make-up shots at the first house, Samantha's home. The primary reason was because the camera we used (on the second weekend) was not the one we used for the rest of the shoot. With that camera we ended up recording in cinema scope format, making everyone abnormally tall and skinny. Also, some of the acting was off. Other than that, the production was over. A day and a half ahead of schedule.

Before jumping into the post-production editing obsession, I wanted to take a break and hang out with Benny. We hadn't really hung out before and I wanted to reward him for his hard work. It was a Friday and I decided I needed to go out. I gave Benny a call and asked if he wanted to join me for a few drinks at a strip club. There was one in the eastern part of Hollywood that I liked.

The strip joint had a dive bar feel to it, with the typical strip club down and outers, along with a fair amount of hipster couples. Courtney Love apparently had stripped there before she became famous, and the place was known as a hole in the wall that appealed to Los Feliz and Silverlake hipsters.

I'd been introduced to Ginko's Clown Room – as it was called – by Gus, a couple years before when the two of us started hanging out more. Benny was a little hesitant on the phone, worried that his girlfriend might find out. I consoled him by insisting only the two of us would know. Benny gave in, excited about seeing almost naked women dance erotically right in front of him.

I drove over to the valley and picked Benny up at his mom's house in Northridge. Benny was all smiles as he came into my car. Samantha waived goodbye to the two of us, thinking we were going to a local bar to watch a Lakers game. I felt we could trust Samantha, but Benny thought, why bother? There'd be a chance she could let it slip out in a conversation with Benny's girlfriend.

On the way over the hill to Hollywood, I questioned Benny's fears about his girlfriend.

"It's not as if I'm taking you to have sex with a hooker or something. You're just watching some strippers dance on stage. Why should she care?" I insisted. "I mean, you wouldn't care if she went to a place like Chip 'N Dales and watched some guys dance for her, would you?"

"Uh, yeah." Benny said with a smile and a laugh. "Of course, dude."

"Why?"

"I don't want her getting all horny because of some naked guy on a stage."

"But it's not really some other guy, it's a professional dancer. He gets paid to turn her on, just as the women we're going to see will get our money to turn us on. It's innocent fun."

"It's innocent fun if she doesn't know about it."

"So if she were to go to Chip 'N Dale's and you never found out about it, that'd be okay?"

"No." Benny said with another laugh. "I wouldn't know if she did something more."

As much as many people would think Benny was very different from them based on his cerebral-palsy, in mentality he was exactly the same. The views he just expressed to me in the car were commonly accepted ideas by the majority of modern day people. A great number of Americans, especially, held onto monogamy as a conceptual institution. As Benny just showed for himself and how many people would reply, when asked about specifics in human behavior, the answers were often contradictory, hypocritical, and vague.

We soon got to Ginko's Clown Room and had a blast. The place was a decent dive bar with relatively down to earth customers, and a couple sexy dancers. I was able to secure a lap dance for Benny from the best dancer in the club, making Benny blush in excitement. Benny loved it and seemed to really appreciate me taking him there. We hung out a few more times but mostly Benny preferred to spend time with his usual Valley mates while I hung out with others.

I came by Samantha's house once to see Benny after spending time with my dad, Jean. The day before, Charlotte had fired me from C.W.F.P.S.J.-Now! I went to Jean to talk about the situation, and as always, I depended on my father for guidance in difficult times. Jean was always there for me, the one consistent guide-post in my life. I always felt perhaps Benny wished Jean was his father. Benny's dad died years ago.

I decided to stop by and say hello to Samantha and Benny and give something to Samantha from Maya. Maya and Samantha were good friends. Although I liked and trusted Benny's mom for the most part, I thought it'd be better to only tell Benny about my troubles at C.W.F.P.S.J.

Eventually, if I was to be officially fired – because at that point the decision had to be made by Cassandra later – then I would tell Maya about my love letter and what happened. But I wanted to be delicate in the matter and not let her know, for now. Maya was still in love with me. I certainly didn't want someone else telling her. Telling Samantha, it might get back to Maya.

"I can't believe it happened, you know?" I said dejectedly in the garage while Benny was working on a broken computer. "I didn't see it coming at all."

"So when you gave her the letter, she didn't get pissed off or anything?" Benny said as he continued to work on a computer.

"Not at all. She said she was touched and she actually cried ... she seemed moved ..."

"'Touched'?" Benny said with a laugh. "So did ya touch her?"

"No, no, not what you think." I said, laughing half-heartedly, not being able to help but be amused by Benny's humor. I was also still saddened by the whole thing, which just happened the day before. "We held hands."

"You held hands?" Benny laughed at me again. "That's funny."

"... Funny?" I said defensively, trying to read Benny. Was he really mocking me in a mean-spirited way, or a light-hearted way? I decided to not get too defensive "It was an intense moment. I was in a desperate place, emotionally speaking. I needed her hand."

Benny didn't know how to respond. He was uncomfortable with personal, intimate feelings. He tried to make a joke out of the situation but could tell I wasn't in the mood. I tried to not always be so intense or serious around Benny, since I knew I came across as such to people. But then I shifted moods. I didn't feel like staying on a jovial, joking, silly mood anymore with Benny. The vicious came out of me.

"Have you ever written a love letter to a beautiful girl before?" I said with a dark smile.

"Nope." Benny said quietly, with a hidden, hurt feeling.

"It wasn't fun to write, full of a bunch of angst and pain ... then for her to fire me for it ..." I switched moods again, regretting my last questions tone.

"I'm sorry to hear it." Benny said, his attention more on fixing his computer than me.

I looked at Benny, knowing why there was that part of him which couldn't care less. At least for me, I could have the possibility of being with a beautiful woman like Charlotte. For Benny, in his own mind and in the likely-hood of reality, given his disability, he could never even allow himself to begin with the feeling. It was an impossibility.

A couple weeks later, I was driving Maya and Gerald to a diner in Venice where we were meeting some friends. Gerald asked me why I was fired for sexual harassment at C.W.F.P.S.J. over a love letter. I jolted, completely caught off-guard. I wasn't ready to tell Maya, and how did Gerald find out? Both Gerald and Maya had sinister, gossipy smiles on their faces, awaiting my response.

"How do you know about that?" I asked, vulnerable, paranoid, defensive. My mind was racing.

"Maya told me." Gerald responded simply.

While Gerald seemed to like me over the years, it was, for the most part, superficial. There was a time when he was jealous of me being too close to his ex-girlfriend, Lara. He had an element of revenge in putting me on the spot like this.

"How the hell did you find out, Maya?" my heart beated faster as anger pulsed through me. The animal in me wanted to beat up whoever told her.

Maya and Gerald refused to tell me who it was, torturing me, making it worse. Thomas, "The Playboy," was finally caught. Thomas, the unfaithful object of Maya's affections, was found out. I couldn't "hide" anymore. I explained myself, told Gerald and Maya what happened, as many details as I could. I mentioned at the end, when I saw their mocking smiles, that, anyway, Maya and I weren't romantically involved now. When I wrote the love letter to Charlotte, Maya and I weren't together then either. They replied that's why I should've had no problem telling Maya. We were just friends. I smiled back, insisting they tell me who told Maya. I didn't want to say I knew Maya was still in love with me, that I didn't want to hurt her feelings, and that's why I wanted the love letter to be a secret. More important than honesty at that moment was finding out who did it.

Eventually, they gave up. Maya said it was Benny. I was shocked. Benny? I thought I could trust Benny, of all people. ... Right? It was odd. I couldn't understand it ... Why would Benny do that? I knew we weren't super close, but still, there was no reason for Benny to tell Maya ... And besides, I felt I did a lot for Benny. ... It stuck a nail into my gut for the rest of the night.

After that night, whenever I came by Samantha's house, Benny avoided me as much as possible. I never wanted to be anything else but friendly with Benny, even if inside I was ticked off. There would be nothing but a minute's worth of "hello's" between us until one day I decided to confront him.

"Benny ..." I said as he just came outside from the house to see a friend. I was in their driveway playing basketball with Benny's 10 year old sister. "I just wanted to tell you that I know you told Maya about my love letter to that girl I worked with ... and that I'm also not angry at you for doing it ..." I said sincerely, even though I still had a residue of anger. Most importantly, I wanted to forgive. "Recently, I've been feeling like you've been avoiding me, expecting me to be angry, and so - "

"It's cool." Benny said with an unease. He felt I was putting him on the spot, which, of course, I was. All Benny wanted to do right then was go hang out with some friends. He'd rather avoid me, as usual. "I'm glad you're not angry." Benny said with a smirk, then proceeded to walk to his friend's car on the street. "I'll catch ya later, Tommy." There was an element of ridicule in his voice as he walked away. It seemed to me in that moment he consciously told Maya ... to get revenge? But no, he couldn't possibly ... right?

Months past and I was looking for a place to live. Samantha was going to sell the house and was wanting to move into a mobile home in the same mobile home park as Jean. Meanwhile, she needed to find a place for Benny and her adopted daughter to live. Samantha thought of buying an affordable mobile home for Benny. Jean thought why don't Benny and I move in together? The mobile home would be bought by Samantha meant for Benny. I would help pay for rent and stay in one of the rooms.

I thought it was a good idea and came around to see Benny, hoping to bring back the closer friendship we had during the making of "Loveincrazy." I drove Benny to several mobile home parks in the valley after doing some research with Samantha. Benny showed little enthusiasm for moving in with me. He wasn't unfriendly but he acted like before: avoiding. A couple times Benny just outright stood me up. I came by – after driving thirty miles to Northridge – and would find Benny not there when we had set to look for mobile homes.

Eventually, I gave up on Benny. I found my own apartment in the Pico/Union area near downtown Los Angeles, close to the Convention Center and Staples center. It worked out because I continued to take care of my grandmother in San Pedro and the 110 freeway was close. I'd see Benny now and again after Samantha bought a mobile home for him.

Benny didn't pursue acting, even though I continued to encourage him. Benny kept toying around with mechanical things, kept his same white trash circle of friends who continued to take advantage of him, and kept his not very bright and overweight girlfriend.

Life was still the same and would continue to be for Benny. Whether it was that way out of choice, habit, or circumstances, he didn't know. Benny, like most people, never asked himself those kinds of questions.

PART THREE. KRISTIANNA.

CHAPTER ONE. THE REALIZATION OF A DREAM.

In the editor's introduction to "The Hollywood Absurd," I explained why my dad Jean and I were ending the publication after two years. I thanked the readership – however many they actually were, considering the zine's 300 copies circulation per issue, coming out every three or four months – for their interest. I was sorry to stop doing the "H.A." but there were other projects to do. I set out to make my first feature film, "Loveincrazy" and Jean was going to do a play, "Feminine/Masculine," a philosophical dark comedy set in a fantastical other world. Jean was inclined to continue the "H.A." but film making demanded all of my creative energy. There just wasn't the time.

When I decided to make my first feature, I had to figure out a story which I'd personally be interested in, and that'd also be logistically and financially realistic. My biggest creative influences were John Cassavetes, Fyodor Dostoevsky, and Bertolt Brecht. I also recently watched a German film from the '70's called "The Bitter Tears of Petra Von Kant," directed by Rainer Werner Fassbinder.

"The Bitter Tears ..." was an extremely economic film and was also satisfying on a creative level. The story took place all in one location: the lead character's bedroom. Sure the bedroom was fairly large, but still, it was one room. Fassbinder wrote the screenplay like a play (he'd done lots of theater as well as films), making it dialogue heavy. But it was by no means a "talking heads" picture. The film was very cinematic by the use of inventive camera angles, dynamic stage direction, and interesting lighting and production design. Depending on where the camera was the background would create an altogether different mood from the other walls.

Jean felt this film should be taught in film schools. I agreed, but of course it wasn't. Hitchcock, Ford, Capra, Hawks, etc. were "The Masters." But all those filmmakers had the resources and money Hollywood could provide, and were pretty conventional in their styles, as well. Most aspiring filmmakers wouldn't have Hollywood at their disposal. It was unrealistic to teach those "Masters." Fassbinder, with "Bitter Tears ..." showed how a young filmmaker could be economical and creative at the same time.

The "The Bitter Tears ..." idea would be a jumping off point. I'd make my movie take place in one location: a house. Then I'd come up with a story. I just finished reading Dostoevsky's "The Brothers Karamazov" and liked the idea of a story that dealt with a father and his sons. Each son would represent a different aspect to my own personality. I also wanted to do a kind of modern day "King Lear," in which the father would try to bring his children together by giving them all that he owned before he died.

I started the story, writing the general outline and character histories. While figuring out the details of the story and characters, I introduced the Cassavetes and Brecht influences. For the former, a pragmatic, emotional life force instilled through the acting. For the latter, social and political awareness through the dialogue, title cards, and other techniques which disassociated the audience from the story. I felt it may be somewhat difficult to mold all these different influences into one cohesive vision of my own. As I wrote and re-wrote the script, going over the conceptualization in my mind, the film began to crystallize and take shape.

The hard part for me, though, wasn't so much on the artistic end. I spent years working on and honing my own vision and sensibilities. The biggest bump on my road to film making success were: 1) I was a nobody with no connections to the industry, and 2) I didn't have tons of money to throw at any obstacles that came my way. I was starting from scratch, and moving forward, for the most part, alone. I knew from the beginning it was going to be tough.

Perhaps I should've tried to go about it from a different angle. Try to work my way into the industry in one field or other, and when I made more connections, then I'd go ahead and make my first feature. That's how most filmmakers did it. But I couldn't do that. The movie was inside my gut then at that exact time, and I had to get it out of my system immediately. It couldn't wait.

I had to find all the elements to put the movie together – the actors, the crew, the equipment, the money, the locations. Before Lara and Gerald offered the use of their house in Venice I seriously considered finding a stranger's home. I drove around Silverlake, Echo Park, Mt. Washington, looking at houses from the outside, soon realizing most people would say no or ask for too much money.

I looked at various video equipment rental stores in Los Angeles before running into a guy who lived in a condo below my mom in Hermosa Beach. The guy had done so well as a business man that he actually retired in his 30's, now devoting his time to the stock market and whatever else he wanted to. I told him about my film and he nicely offered a big discount on a camera/lights/sound equipment package. I thought the guy was always nice and his explanation for the discount was wanting to be a nice neighbor. I also felt the guy had a little crush on my mother, as well, which was fine by me. He was nice to her.

Then I had to find my cast and crew. I didn't know any professional working actors nor crew people, so I went ahead and advertised for them. I placed an ad for actors in the industry weekly, Backstage West, for two weeks, expecting a modest response. My film was, after all, a low budget movie shot on digital video where the actors received no pay, getting only food and copy (a tape of the film). Instead, I received around 400 head shots and resumes.

It was a huge task to sift through all the Tom Cruise and Brad Pitt wannabes, and find quality actors just based on their pictures and past credits. Since there were originally four brothers, all in their twenties and thirties, hundreds of young struggling actors pounced on my film. It didn't matter if I was a nobody, they were nobodies, too. They all hoped that I, or someone like me, would go from nobody to somebody and they could ride on my coattails to fame. One just never knew. So actors sent out their head shots and resumes to everyone who advertised in Backstage West.

The parts for the father and one of the brother's African American girlfriend was harder to find but there was still enough to choose from. I was genuinely shocked at such a response to my ad. I thought there might not be enough interest, so maybe I'd go to some plays and see if there were any good actors to find there.

For the crew, I put up ads at film schools: USC, UCLA, AFI, LACC, the LA Film School, and others. Surprisingly again, people responded. Not nearly as much as for the actors, but enough. Positions which I later deleted – assistant director, line producer and script girl – I got replies for and met the people. Some were more interesting than others. A working camera operator called me for the cinematographer job and we met a couple times in Venice and Marina Del Rey. The guy was professional, reserved, and cordial, and seemed to respect my cinematic vision, even if he didn't understand it.

Then I got a message from Kristianna on my answering machine for the assistant camera position. I liked the gentle intelligence in her voice, with her Bulgarian accent, and slightly thick nasal tone. The next day I got a call from the cinematographer letting me know he got a paying gig to be a camera operator and couldn't do "Loveincrazy." When I called Kristianna back, she was surprised to be offered the cinematographer mantle. We set a time to meet in a couple days.

I wasn't sure at first if I'd replace the original cinematographer with Kristianna or someone else. I wanted to find out, for one thing, if she'd be interested, and two, if she'd be the right person. We met at the Coffee Bean on 2nd street and Santa Monica, half a block away from where I was arrested for kicking a parking vehicle years ago. I'll tell you more about that later, Daniel. Initially, Kristianna seemed an attractive, intriguing, elfish young Eastern European, wearing a blue and white striped beach shirt, and having a cute, shapely little body.

There was electricity between us, not all physical, but definitely the erotic attraction was there. We both expected to meet less appealing people. The energy created by the two of us was balanced. Both of us were sensitive and aware of our environment, conscious of others in a good way, in being able to soak things in. Neither of us were overbearing, but she wanted me to be the more aggressive. She was comfortable with letting me guide the conversation, since after several minutes of talking, she sensed my intelligence. She liked me and inwardly was excited by the possibility of working together. That was where most of the electricity was: in the discovery of a mutually creative person.

"So that's the story, the characters, and the ideas behind the film. Again, the main thing is that the audience is to be thrown into the situation of Jack Henry and his sons, trying to make the reconciliation work out. I want to go for a small emotional epic, an opera of the commonplace, so that the smallest of tensions will seem to be played out on a grand scale. The conflict and resolution will come off both tragic and every day ..." I continued the conversation while people walked by us every second. Despite the busy commotion of the street, we were zoned in on each other.

"And so the acting will be larger than life while the camera will be more restrained?" Kristianna inquired, my enthusiasm rubbing off on her.

"No, actually, almost the opposite." I said, continuing as before, sensing that she knew where I was coming from and was just asking questions. "The acting will be naturalistic. I want everyone in front of the camera to behave as if the camera wasn't there."

"Okay."

"And how we'll get that is to rehearse for a month to get everyone comfortable with the script, the story, situations, characters, feelings, ideas, everything. Then some of that rehearsal time will be with you as the camera woman filming us to get the actors comfortable with you."

"Great. Perfect."

"Then with the camera, the majority of it will be hand-held. The framing will be tight, lots of close-ups. But we don't want it to seem too reality t.v.ish, or too much like a documentary."

“Good.”

“As much as possible, there should be smooth movements with the camera, very, very little jerky moves and none of that quick pan to the left, quick pan to the right stuff. You know what I mean?”

“I know exactly what you mean. I love hand-held but I hate it when the camera moves like that.”

“It's tacky.” I smiled.

“It is.” she smiled back.

“It's one of the lamest attempts at being 'edgy' we could do. And we have to be careful because hand-held digital video can easily come across as unprofessional.”

“Yes, very much so. What kind of camera will we use?”

“At this point I think it's gonna be a Sony PD-500, professional broadcast color.”

“Nice.”

“It's kind of big and heavy for digital video but the quality is really good. The image has more depth than most video.”

“And the tapes are DV-CAM?”

“Yeah. And one more thing about the camera work is that, in a conceptual sense, the camera should fall in love with the surface of whatever you're recording. Every little detail on a person's face, for example, should be eaten up, tasted, licked almost, every pore, every pimple, every hair follicle should show up - ”

“So lots of extreme close-ups - ” she said while laughing at my obsessiveness. She liked that.

“Yeah, and move along the surface of the person or the objects sensually. The cups the actors drink from, their fingers, to the cigarettes they'll smoke, to say, something on the table, to their faces. We'll have to work on it, but if we orchestrate the actor's movements with the camera placement and camera movements, and then later in the editing, with the cuts, there should be a rhythm, a musical pacing to everything visual. The emphasis of the camera almost sexually analyzing every object is important." I said with a smile. She smiled back. "A combination of sensuality and nausea, like Sartre's 'Nausea'."

"Cool. I love that book.'

"Me, too."

We met again several times to go over the shooting schedule, the budget, the equipment, and other logistics. We also met to watch movies from which I could show her examples of what I was asking for visually. We watched Cassavetes' "A Woman Under the Influence," Bergman's "The Passion of Anna," the Dogme director Vinterberg's "Celebration," and some others. Kristianna was excited about my interests in Dogme's style of film making. She was just as happy that I also didn't want to follow the tenets too strictly (no artificial light, no props, no clothes other than the actor's own, no post-production sounds or music, no pay for anyone, no credits, and some other rules).

The spirit of Dogme film making was more important. The idea was to rely on one's creativity with a shoe-string budget, make sure the acting was good, the story didn't need action scenes nor special-effects to hide behind, and the visual style wouldn't fall back on expensive camera tricks.

The second time we met was at the small apartment her friend Jonathan was renting, a place literally on the beach in Santa Monica. While the place was small, one still needed lots of money to be living there.

"When you said you lived on the beach, you meant on the beach." I said to Kristianna as I walked onto the patio area with her. About 20 yards out was the bike path, then about 40 yards passed that was the ocean. There were no other houses in-between, and the Santa Monica pier was just to the left.

"Yeah." Kristianna responded with a light laugh. "Jonathan's parents have a lot of money."

"So you guys just moved in, huh? It's a nice place, that's for sure."

I looked at the glorious view, relishing the ocean. I thought about my attraction to Kristianna, then figured to give up on that. One, if she was living with this guy Jonathan and as I saw there was only one bed in the apartment, then she was already taken. And two, I didn't want to complicate my working relationship with her, which offered a lot of possibilities.

"It is a nice place. I guess I don't spend enough time here to appreciate it." she said gently. "Did you want some of that white wine?"

"Of course." I said as I turned to her.

She brought out the Bulgarian bottle of white wine and poured it into two glasses. We started to talk about more personal things, which town she was from, her parents, her time in Chicago, going to school. I told her about my life, my past, family, friends, creative interests and ambitions. We gelled together nicely.

She told me about the small Korean-owned production company she was working for. At the moment she and Jonathan were editing the latest straight to video B-movie action flick the company was doing. From Chicago Jonathan contacted the producer of the film – who happened to be one of the company's owners – and got Kristianna and himself a paying post-production deal.

Back at their college in Chicago, Jonathan and Kristianna decided to become film making partners. In the beginning, they'd take any work they could find, but eventually they wanted to be a director (Jonathan) and cinematographer (Kristianna) duo. Jonathan knew a lot about the technical aspect to film production, as did Kristianna, so they could do editing, sound, lighting, and camera jobs in the meantime.

Kristianna hesitated to talk much about Jonathan, preferring to focus on me or herself. But I was confused. Was Jonathan planning to work on "Loveincrazy"?

"Well, he was the one who found your ad posted on the wall at AFI." Kristianna said ambiguously.

"So ... is he interested in working with you on the project?" I asked, thinking maybe it'd be a good idea since I needed someone in charge of the sound recording anyway. And Jonathan had already worked with Kristianna before. But I could tell she had reservations for some reason. "Don't you two have a working partnership?"

"In a way, yes. Do you have a sound recordist already or do you need one?"

"I have a couple people interested. But if you're doing the camera and lights, I'd prefer the person in charge of sound was someone you already worked with."

"Okay, I'll let him know." she said with some detachment. There was a hidden air about her with the subject of Jonathan and herself.

I got a phone call the next day from Kristianna saying Jonathan was excited to work on the project. By the end of the conversation, Kristianna mentioned that she and Jonathan wanted to get paid. I thought about it, figured that while I wasn't paying anyone else – cast or crew – for Kristianna and Jonathan I'd do it.

By that point, I decided to act in one of the major parts. I'd be relying on the two of them to run the technical aspect of the production quite a bit. Better to pay them what I could - $1,500 each, for the whole thing – and keep them happy and motivated. After so many people had bailed on me before, I didn't want to risk losing Kristianna's talents. She mentioned that it was Jonathan's idea to get paid and not hers, to help the rent at the apartment on the beach. I thought it strange, since

Jonathan came from a wealthy family, but oh well.

I went to meet Kristianna at the place she was doing the editing and Jonathan was there. The production company had a suite on the 12th floor to a commercial building on Vermont and Wilshire, in Korea Town. All the businesses were Korean-owned as I went through the lobby, past the strong smelling hair salon, then up the elevator. I realized I was the only non-Korean person in the building so far.

On the 12th floor, I went down the hall to the editing suite where Kristianna and Jonathan were.

"Hello." I said as I knocked on the door that was slightly open.

"Hi." Jonathan said with his big nervous, wide-eyed smile as he opened the door, his hand extended to shake mine.

"You must be Jonathan?" I said as he shook my hand.

"Yup." Jonathan said nicely, nervously, but standing ominously at 6'4" or so.

"Hey, Thomas, come in." Kristianna said from behind Jonathan in the suite.

I chatted with the two for several hours as they worked on editing. They took "breaks" now and then - usually just a cigarette on a window landing on the next floor upstairs. They showed me the movie they were working on, and laughingly acknowledged the poor artistic quality and production value.

Jonathan held onto a love for Godard, although couldn't explain in much detail why he liked the New Wave auteur except for talking about jump-cuts. Jonathan knew the techi stuff to film making but the conceptual eluded him. When Kristianna and I hit it off on the creative side, he'd feel left out. He was even a little jealous, I could tell for a minute or two, usually cutting in with something off-subject.

But I liked Jonathan. He was a nice guy. I felt comfortable with

Kristianna and Jonathan and was looking forward to working with them.

I met with them several more times before the actual shoot. One time was to watch those movies – by Cassavetes, Bergman, Vinterberg, and others – to use as reference points. We went to Kristianna's friend's – Celebrity – house in Topanga Canyon for that night. This was before I asked Celebrity to act in the film. The house belonged to her and her Bulgarian husband. The Topanga home was up in the hills, nice and big and Western style, with a few acres of property surrounding the house. Someone had money, but I decided not to be nosy and ask.

While watching the movies, only Kristianna seemed interested. I discussed with her what I wanted visually, then Kristianna responded with what she liked. For one, she had never seen a Cassavetes film and besides the obvious quality in acting, she got into the lighting and camera work, too. Celebrity and Jonathan seemed to observe jealously at our conversations, not really liking the movies.

I wondered if they both had the hots for Kristianna. I noticed Kristianna and Celebrity sitting next to each other, touching their hands, while eating food earlier at the house. Was Kristianna a lesbian? I actually thought Jonathan was gay, to be honest. Then that'd make sense for them to be living and working together if they were both into the same sex. Maybe I was just imagining things. One thing I noticed that night was that Celebrity's husband was pretty much oblivious to everything except the alcohol.

Many times when I met with Kristianna and Jonathan, I felt something was being held back from me. They seemed to be sincerely committed to working on "Loveincrazy," so that was what mattered most. My sights were set on making my first feature film, no matter what. Kristianna and Jonathan were to help me realize that goal.

CHAPTER TWO.

THE DIRECTOR IS ALWAYS ALONE.

"I just think I'm shit, Kristianna ...." I said to her on my cell phone while sitting in my car in Silverlake.

I just got a part for my car from a Ford dealer. I knew the dealer jipped me and I knew I let it happen, which added to the insecurities I was already stressing about.

"Everyone else's performances are good, but I suck, I really, really suck. Benny's good, Frazier's good, Maya's good, hell even the dog's better than me, in that one shot ..." I continued to complain, after sipping a small Jack Daniels whiskey bottle. I tended to drink any time of the day, anywhere. "It's just watching the dailies again today ... God, I hate how I look ... I hate my voice, I hate the way I sound ... maybe I'm not being objective, I don't know ..."

"Well, were there any takes which you liked of yourself?" Kristianna said on the other side of the cell-phone.

She was reserved, detached, a little worried about her director. Was I freaking out and losing serious confidence in myself? She was also a little concerned because it sounded like I'd been drinking. But she didn't express the concern. She left me hanging a bit. Perhaps I was losing it, perhaps I was reaching out to her in need, seeing how she'd react. I was disappointed by her distance ... then felt I should maybe snap out of it, pull myself together.

"Maybe I'm being nutty, too self-critical. They say a person can't stand to look at themselves on camera, let alone be a good judge of their own acting. Maybe that's what's happening. I mean, Orson Welles was throwing up every day while he was making 'Citizen Kane' and couldn't stand to look at himself in the dailies ... Marlon Brando walked out of a screening of 'On the Waterfront' because he thought he was horrible ... I'm not either one of them, but ... "

“That really happened? I didn't know that about them.” she responded over the phone with more enthusiasm than before, as if she preferred talking about that than my insecurities. I couldn't blame her I guess.

“You know what, Kristianna?” I said with a little slur from my drinking.

“What?” she replied simply but detached.

“It's okay. Things'll work out. Don't worry. I'll take another look at the dailies tomorrow, then reconsider things more objectively before next weekend, before our second week of shooting.”

“Okay. Sounds good, Thomas.”

It seemed as if she was patronizing me or maybe she really cared. Maybe she was doing both. However it was, I snapped out of my morose self-criticism and realized my performance was actually pretty good, once I looked at the footage again.

Alcohol and Red Bull energy drinks were readily available to cast and crew during the shoot. I brought the alcohol – whiskey, gin and vodka – and, along with Kurt and Cindy, was the only one partaking in it. Everyone else was getting high on Red Bull. Right at the beginning of the day, I had someone, usually Kurt or Cindy, get some Red Bull, coffee, and some muffins for breakfast. That got us going pretty good.

On the fourth day of the shoot, Kristianna tried to sneak past my rule of never discussing something without involving me. Everything, every detail had to be run by me. After talking with Benny and Frazier about their acting, I looked for Kristianna and Jonathan to watch the last take we just did.

“Where's Kristianna and Jonathan?” I asked.

Kurt, Cindy, Benny, and Frazier all shrugged their shoulders. I went outside to the courtyard area of Gerald's house, where Gerald was working on the garden.

"Have you seen Kristianna or Jonathan?" I asked him.

"I think they're out on the sidewalk." he replied.

I went and opened the gate, going past the cars in the driveway, and finding Kristianna and Jonathan talking.

"Hey, guys, what's up?" I said, a little nervous, a little drunk, but somehow still intensely focused on the movie and worried what they were talking about.

"Oh, we were just smoking." Kristianna said with some hidden guilt as she put out her Camel Lights butt.

"You know if there's something you guys're talking about related to the movie, I'd like to be a part of it." I said as politely as possible, attempting to hide my need for directorial dictatorship.

"No, no, we were just talking about what we have to finish tonight with the editing." she quickly put out.

"Okay." I responded with a smile, reacting to their nervous smiles.

I knew they were working hard on editing the B-movie for that Korean production company. They had just two more days to come up with a final cut. But why was that something they had to go way out to the sidewalk for? No, there was something else. I felt it might be my drinking too heavily while directing and acting. My drinking made me hypersensitive and paranoid, as well. Well, damn it, I thought, who cares what they think. My critical skills were still in high-gear. Even if I was a drunk, I was still an in-control drunk. And really, I had no idea what they were talking about.

No similar situations came up for the rest of the shoot. Kristianna and Jonathan never seemed to mind my drinking, as they could tell I was able to keep the ship going. Anyway, they were having a good time and goofed off themselves. Towards the end when I snapped at everyone, they respected me and stopped the goofing around. The Red Bull and alcohol were necessary, I felt, to keep chugging along, focused and yet loose, to play the parts of director, producer, actor, re-writer, script-girl, etc. ...

On the last day of the production – back at Samantha's house to do some re-shoots – I found Kristianna in tears. It caught me off-guard, as I never saw her in a bad mood. She was on her cell phone outside in the driveway, talking to someone in Bulgarian as she cried. She let Jonathan organize all the equipment with the help of Kurt and Cindy. Occasionally Jonathan would come over to Kristianna sympathetically and just stand near her for a few moments, then go back to setting things up. I asked him if she was okay.

"Yeah, she's fine. Just some family troubles." Jonathan replied.

"What happened?" I insisted gently.

"Her dad's not feeling well."

"Over in Bulgaria?"

"Yeah."

"I'm sorry."

"It's okay."

"What's wrong with him?"

"I'm not sure really." he said with his nervous, odd smile and big, wide eyes. "We haven't got much sleep so I think that's part of it. So would you like the light where it was the last time?"

"On the right side of the door, yeah."

When Kristianna stopped her phone conversation, she turned around and was surprised to find me in front of her. Her eyes were red and swelling, and she looked at me almost ashamed.

“Are you okay?” I asked her.

“Yeah, I'm fine ... Sorry ... Very unprofessional of me.” she said as she brought herself together.

“Don't worry about it. It seemed like something important.” I said intently, my eyes piercing into hers.

“No, not really.” she said, touched by my concern, but still withdrawn. “So is everything set up?”

“Almost ...” I said, gazing at her, pausing, weighing the pause. “This is the last scene.”

“I know.” she responded, smiling warmly at me. Our bodies were almost pulling to each other.

“Of course, we already shot it, but ...”

“In Cinema scope!” she laughed.

“Wacky camera.” I smiled back.

Jonathan came outside, behind me, then hesitated as he saw the two of us together. Kristianna immediately became uncomfortable and I turned around.

“How's it going? We're almost ready?” I asked him, unaware of the awkwardness between Jonathan and Kristianna.

“Yeah, it's all set. I think Maya needs to talk to you.” he said with a strange smile.

“Okay.” I responded, now picking up on something but still not knowing what. Jonathan went into the house.

During the shoot, the creative back and forth between me and Kristianna was a pleasure for both of us. Kristianna knew exactly what I wanted from her and I knew exactly what she would give me. After almost every take, we went together and replayed it on the monitor.

Sometimes Jonathan would participate, but rarely. The monitor replay became only our domain. Everyone else was not included, as if she and I were speaking another language.

We would sit in front of the monitor, I'd tell her what I liked, and more often than not she would completely agree. I loved the way she moved the camera, the choices she made in which direction it would go, where it would stop, on whose face and when, at the right moments and the right angles. And when something wasn't right, we both would quickly acknowledge it, often at the same time.

It got to the point between us that Kristianna would even pick up on a weak moment in the acting. After a couple observations were made by her and I saw her point, I began to trust her judgments for the performances at times, asking what she thought. It was smooth and it was beautiful. Because we worked so well together, and because we spent so much time in preparation, the shoot was ahead of schedule.

There were times in the shoot when Kristianna and I enjoyed working together so much that it seemed it became erotic. We would stand near each other, looking at something, discussing a scene, and our bodies would lean into each other's, her breasts coming close to my chest, her hips coming close to mine.

My favorite was when Kristianna squatted or kneeled in front of me, with the camera or without, and I'd either stand behind her or kneeled behind her, too. I'd look at her, her back, her hips, her ass, and get an erection. Sometimes I'd get a glimpse of her underwear, usually red panties. I loved that. Other times we talked, laughed, then would put our hands on the other's shoulder or chest. One time when I was a little more drunk than usual, I accidentally put my hand on one of her breasts. She looked up at me and smiled, acknowledged the sexual attraction, but then she'd withdraw and so would I. That was as far as it went.

These moments were not ignored nor missed by the others. Jonathan and Maya especially took notice. Kurt, Cindy, and Gerald joked to me about it afterwards, poking at me with the fact the director wanted to fuck his cinematographer. Benny was a bit jealous, who enjoyed the attention Kristianna paid him. She loved to photograph Benny's face, and laughed at his jokes and stories. Even Frazier played for Kristianna's attention, getting her away from his step-son, attempting to contradict my psychological realism with traditional acting techniques, stage actor stories, and astrological charts.

But Maya and Jonathan were the most intent on interrupting Kristianna's creative closeness and sexual tension with me. Maya would come nearby and say something loud, make a joke to someone else in front of us, or just awkwardly interrupt to ask me something. Jonathan would usually do the interruption by way of asking a professional question about the shoot. How I wanted something done, where the mic and lights should go, if I liked one take or another, and so on.

And that's how Jonathan came into my moment with Kristianna's crying in Samantha's driveway.

"So where did you want those lights again?" Jonathan asked, again with that odd, wide smile of his.

"Uh yeah, the same place." I responded, not understanding why he was asking the same question again.

I realized there was some kind of subtext going on but what was it? If Jonathan was jealous, and he and Kristianna were really together in a relationship, then why didn't they just come out and say it? It seemed simple enough.

"Oh yeah, right. Duh! Sorry. Maya still needs to talk to you by the way. She forgets what the scene is about, I think, since it's been a few weeks."

"Okay. I'll be right there." I turned to Kristianna "You'll be okay?"

"Yeah, I'm fine. Let's shoot this. Go inside and talk to Maya." she responded with a smile.

I smiled back at her. I loved my cinematographer. We finished shooting the scene in about two hours and with the last take, I yelled, "That's a wrap!" Everyone exclaimed in excitement, but my heart was heavy ... I didn't want the shoot to end.

Kristianna and Jonathan mentioned to me that they hoped we could have the wrap party that day, since they still weren't done with editing the B-movie. On Monday, in two days, they had to fly out to Atlanta, as well. Production would start on the Korean-owned company's next film, where Kristianna would be assistant camera operator on a 35mm film shoot in Georgia. She couldn't miss the opportunity. I agreed and soon the food and festivities were rolling.

I got thoroughly and happily drunk. My first feature film was in the can. I was complete and yet empty. Maya made her excellent bow-tie El Salvadorian pasta for everyone and Samantha cooked up some lasagna, as well. While I was smoking and drinking, talking with my father Jean, the others decided to play a prank on the director. Maya and Gerald came up behind me and pushed me into the swimming pool, in my full black, long sleeved shirt, and red jumper pants Colin attire.

Cindy decided to join me in the swimming pool, with Kurt following soon afterwards, both with their clothes on, too. Jean caught this all on tape with a video camera. During the shoot, Jean had been shooting a making-of documentary, interviewing everyone involved in the production. When Jean turned the camera on Jonathan, he turned red in embarrassment and jokingly but nervously yelled at Jean to turn the camera on someone else. Everyone teased Jonathan until he finally said a couple words to the camera, then ran away.

Everyone continued with the fun for several more hours at Samantha's. I was still in the swimming pool for a while, smoking my Winchesters, looking at everyone, soaking in the good times ... and my heart sank. I knew this was the end to it all. Tomorrow the production would be over and Monday Kristianna would be on an airplane to Atlanta.

CHAPTER THREE.

POST-PRODUCTION.

Kristianna promised she'd help out with editing "Loveincrazy," if not edit it herself, if I wanted her to. She planned to come back to L.A. in a couple months, probably in January. We kept in touch over the phone now and then. Meanwhile, she pushed back the time when she'd come to L.A., from two months to three to four. Eventually, she got back to L.A. by March. I was already half-way done with the editing. She did help with some troubleshooting problems over the phone, which helped a bit, but not much. It was all on my shoulders, and, I missed her.

I drove out to Mt. Washington to pick Kristianna up at the house she was staying at. I then got a call from Jonathan. He was going to drive her down to a coffee shop in Mt. Washington to meet me. I said it was fine, although wondered to myself, 'why?' Was I forbidden to come get her myself?

Jonathan and Kristianna waited outside the cafe, both with their 'nice to see you after a while' smiles, along with some odd tension between them. I didn't acknowledge the latter feeling, happy to see them both. A few minutes into their 'how are you's', Kristianna got me to take her in my car. Jonathan seemed bothered by us leaving together, so I asked if he wanted to go, too.

"No, actually, I have to get back to work." he replied.

"Oh? I thought you guys were done." I responded.

"I still gotta finish editing a scene from the movie we worked on in Atlanta."

"Okay."

Then the discomfort came more prominently to the surface as no one said anything for a while. I didn't want to be rude so I waited for Kristianna to say something, which she did and we left.

As I drove Kristianna in my car to get a bite to eat in Pasadena, Kristianna opened up to me more than ever before, at least on the subject of Jonathan and her.

"I noticed something was odd when I came to pick you up." I started. "I mean, first of all, why did he call me and then drive you down to the coffee shop? Why couldn't I just pick you up at the house?"

"Oh, God ..." she laughed, out of stress more than anything.

"What is it?" I smiled back at her as I continued to drive.

"You have no idea what I've been going through with him ..."

"Tell me!" I laughed in relief and frustration. "I've been wondering ever since I met you two what the hell was going on."

"What do you think it is? I'm curious to hear what you've thought all this time."

"Well ... I don't know ... I guess he's really into you, isn't he?"

"That's putting it mildly!" she laughed again.

"You know, for a while I thought Jonathan was gay, and that's why the two of you could live together and work together on projects as well."

"That's funny! Maybe he is!" she continued to laugh.

"But he can't be gay and into you at the same time, can he?"

"Maybe he's confused."

"So, you two have been in a relationship this whole time?"

"Not really. We never had sex."

"What? Then ..."

"Yeah. Never. We've slept in the same bed but nothing every

happened."

"I don't get it."

"Didn't you notice on the first day of the shoot, at the apartment on the beach, when you and Maya did the sex scene on our bed, that he was acting weird?"

"I just figured he was kinda goofy or nervous."

"He's that, too." she said with another laugh.

"I still don't understand ... he's ... what? In love with you but you've never had sex with him, and you've slept in the same bed, and he gets jealous of you being with me, but really nothing romantic has ever happened between you?"

"Right. Kind of."

"It doesn't make sense." I had to smile.

She then went on to explain her relationship with Jonathan. They met at the film school in Chicago, hanging out and doing projects with the circle of friends they had there, which included Celebrity. Shortly before they all graduated, Jonathan convinced Kristianna they'd make good collaborating on film work in Los Angeles, as he'd just gotten a positive response from the Korean-owned production company.

From the beginning, the tone that had been set was friendship, and then on their way to Los Angeles, a professional and creative collaboration. Once in Los Angeles, they stayed at friends' houses or at motels until Jonathan got the small one-bedroom on the Santa Monica beach. A month into Los Angeles and this, apparently, was when Jonathan started to fall in love with Kristianna.

In one drunken night at a motel room, right before the move to the Santa Monica apartment, Jonathan declared his love for her. He made it clear, though, his love was not sexual. He didn't need to make love to her and he was completely devoted to her with an undying love without sex. So when they moved into the apartment, they decided to sleep in the same bed, but would never do anything physical. There wasn't enough room for a second bed and so since their relationship was platonic, it seemed to work out.

But it was confusing. If Jonathan had this powerful love for Kristianna, why didn't he want their relationship to be physical? Kristianna explained to me she made it clear she wasn't interested in anything more than friendship. So Jonathan wanted Kristianna to feel comfortable with her knowing all he wanted was friendship. And he'd prove it to her by not ever touching her in a suggestive way.

This was why, Kristianna explained, when I was so touchy-feely with her during the shoot, Jonathan acted weird. If he couldn't touch her, no one should. I never felt Jonathan was supremely jealous nor stand-offish the whole time we were worked together. She said, though, Jonathan instigated a lot of the goofing around with cast and crew as a way to throw my concentration off. I had no idea.

The real troubles between Jonathan and Kristianna came about in the last few months while working on the movie in Atlanta. One time while the two of them were driving alone from L.A. to Atlanta, once again in a motel room, Jonathan let his bleeding heart be more revealed than usual. This time, unfortunately, his 'undying love' for her got ugly. He threw a major fit, violently smashing things in the room, cursing her, threatening her.

Jonathan screamed and screamed, saying he wanted to marry her, have children with her, and if she didn't want that he'd kill himself. The rest of the drive she was in a constant state of fear, not knowing if at any moment he might snap and kill them both.

I was perplexed to the extreme. If he was acting this way, why was she staying around him? She explained that she needed to stay with the production company in order to get a permanent working visa and unfortunately the company wouldn't let Jonathan go. She was also concerned not only for her own safety but for Jonathan's, if she were to cut all ties to him. I felt, though, the more she stayed around Jonathan, the more it'd feed into his desperation. And, really, she should put her life before his. He'd get over it in time.

I thought of the inevitable next. I asked if the main thing for her was getting the working visa to stay in the country, then why not marry me to get citizenship? She turned to me, not expecting that. At first, she said it was okay, that it wasn't necessary, but as I insisted she seemed to like the idea. Then doubts came into her mind. What if she liked me more than as a friend? What if I liked her more, too? Was she attracted to me? Was I to her? What would happen if we got married just so she could get her citizenship then later something sexual happened? That would complicate things, obviously. Or what if I got romantically into her, but she wasn't inclined to reciprocate?

The situation seemed too risky. She decided – mulling over the questions only to herself – not to go for it. She would not marry me. After everything that happened with Jonathan she didn't want to take any chances. Just to be safe, she would keep her distance from me. Of course, she didn't tell me this as we had a friendly conversation over lunch in Pasadena. I had no idea what she must've been thinking about at that time. Now, though, I realize this must've been what she was running through her mind.

Month after month and Kristianna wouldn't respond to my e-mails. Soon after our lunch in Pasadena, she told me she was going to Bulgaria to see her parents. Months after the screenings of "Loveincrazy" in Los Angeles and New York, my repeated phone calls and e-mails went unanswered. I then got a message from her almost a full year since we had that lunch in Pasadena.

She came back into town to look for work and decided to give me a call. I was excited to hear from her and wondered why she disappeared so completely from my life. Part of me was worried about her, based on what she told me that day about Jonathan. Another part of me was disappointed in her. We seemed to have a lot going on between us as creative collaborators and as friends. We decided to go catch a movie in

Pasadena.

I picked her up the next day and we drove to the theater. Kristianna explained why she was out of touch for so long. One, was that she had family troubles, with her dad getting sick, and her not getting along with her mom. Another major thing was that she worked as the cinematographer on Jonathan's first feature film.

This blew my mind. After what she told me a year before with Jonathan's behavior, she went and made a movie with him? She ignored all of my calls and e-mails, and during that time she made a movie with someone who threatened her life and his own if she wouldn't love him? I had to ask – did Jonathan improve or something?

"Not really." she said somewhat vaguelly as the two of us got out of my car.

I didn't know what next to say so we walked quietly down the street to the Laemmle's Pasadena Playhouse movie theater. We were going to see "Young Adam," a dark British indie film about a frustrated young writer, starring Ewan McGregor. How appropriate. Here I was, a frustrated young filmmaker, walking with a smooth operator (hey, a camera operator) from Bulgaria. I began to realize Kristianna was slick ... but I didn't want to accept that, not then. There had to be something genuine between us ... right?

"He never had another violent outburst or anything?" I asked her in front of the box office.

"Well, no, not really, nothing as bad as before but he was still weird. But I don't see him anymore. He moved back with his parents and is working on the post-production."

"So you're safe now?" I asked with a smile.

"Yes, I'm safe." she replied with a smile of her own.

"You know, I wish you were around for the premiere of

'Loveincrazy'."

"I know. Me, too. When you left the messages I was in Bulgaria shooting Jonathan's movie."

I was still amazed. Kristianna tried to explain herself, saying that Jonathan's budget was $300,000 and she could shoot on a 35mm camera. Her dream had always been to shoot on 35. Since there were no other offers coming from elsewhere, at least with Jonathan's B-movie horror flick (with Godardian jump cuts) she could put 35mm footage on her reel. Her father helped Jonathan out with professional crews, getting nice locations in Bulgaria, and great local Bulgarian equipment, even though Jonathan already had a $300,000 budget.

I thought to myself – where was Kristianna's father when I was making "Loveincrazy"? I could've used the help, could've used a 35mm camera, a professional crew, nice locations. My budget was only $7,000, and I also didn't threaten to kill Kristianna or myself! And, I felt, I made a better film, just from hearing Kristianna explain Jonathan's movie. She thought so herself.

"I really don't get it." I said as we walked together down the sidewalk. The movie wasn't starting for another twenty minutes.

"I know ..." Kristianna nervously laughed, almost embarrassed.

"Why would your dad help Jonathan out if he knew about all the weird, abusive shit he did to you?"

"I asked him to."

"You what?" That blew me away.

"Because it would be helping me out. It was my first 35mm shoot as cinematographer."

"Okay ..." I said with a skeptical smile at her. I could tell she didn't like that.

“Probably if Jonathan didn't have such a big budget and such a nice camera to work with, I would've told him to get lost a long time ago.”

Ouch. I was stung.

“I mean, maybe that's just the way the world works. If you had lots of money and had a bigger budget, maybe my dad would've helped you out more, thought you had more of a chance to succeed ...” she continued with her gentle tone of voice, but words of stones. “Maybe that girl you worked with who fired you would've picked you instead of that other guy if you had lots of money. Isn't that how you felt yourself, when you told me what happened in the e-mail a long time ago? She felt more comfortable with the other guy because he came from a wealthy family like her?”

I'd forgotten I told Kristianna about being fired by Charlotte from C.W.F.P.S.J.-Now! Was telling her that happened another reason she never responded to my calls and e-mails? I looked at her, uncertain, uncomfortable. She seemed to have a deadly, penetrating ice coming from her ... I was hurt, and she intended to do so ... she then picked up on this and felt bad ...

“I'm sorry, I didn't mean to bring that up ...” she said with half compassion, half calculating distance.

“It's okay.” I replied with a similar ambivalence.

“Are you still with Maya?” she said, as she came closer to me, suddenly changing, becoming warmer.

“No.” I replied, not knowing if she was showing interest in me or not by her movement. “We would be together for maybe a few months then break up and be separated for a few months more, then get back together and repeat ourselves. A broken record drama. This time, though, we're definitely not getting back as lovers.”

“Just friends?”

"Just friends."

There was then a pause between us as she looked away and I looked at her, eyeing her body, reminding myself of the film shoot, of the connection we seemed to have at that time. I began putting questions to myself. Should I make a move? Should I let her know I was attracted to her? Should I pursue a romantic interest in her, even though I told her of my troubles at C.W.F.P.S.J, even though it may disrupt our friendship and possible creative collaboration on my next film?

Did she call me after all this time just to check in and see if I had any success with my film? Perhaps she was hoping I might help her with her career? I did notice a disappointment when hearing my difficulties in getting into film festivals, getting recognized by people in the industry, and my inability to secure a distributor. I couldn't decide whether I should do or say anything about my attraction to her, so I'd let it play out and see if there was an opportunity at some point later.

We went into the theater and sat down together, talking about movies and our lives. Five minutes before the coming attractions, I leaned over to her and awkwardly asked if I could kiss her ... I knew the second the words came out of my mouth I was acting like a complete idiot ... If I was going to make a move, at least do it right.

Oh well, I thought, now that I knew I probably blew it altogether with her – romantically, as friends, as professional collaborators – I'd just wait and see what my blunder would do. I smiled while waiting for her response.

"Thomas, come on ... don't do that to me ..." she nervously laughed. "After what happened with Jonathan ..."

"I know. I'm sorry ..." I sincerely felt bad then my smile came back. "Are you sure? Just a little one?" I said with awkwardness again, hoping to pass it by with a smile.

"Come on. Don't be like that." she said with her own smile just as the lights faded and the coming attractions came on. "Let's watch the movie."

We sat and watched the movie together. The whole time the insecure little school boy in me was wondering if I should attempt to kiss her or put my hand on her leg. I decided I'd just sit back and enjoy the show with her. It was a good film, anyway.

The movie ended and we left the theater. I didn't bring up anymore romanticism and told her about watching "Loveincrazy" projected at a movie theater one morning. A projectionist I knew said he could run it for me one day and so I took him up on the offer. After all, as the cinematographer, Kristianna should see it on the big screen.

We met at the theater and watched the movie. Kristianna seemed to be impressed. After the movie we talked for a couple minutes, and she promised to stay in touch this time.

While in the beginning of pre-production for my next film, I tried to contact Kristianna over and over again. I wanted her to be the cinematographer on the next one. She never replied to my messages and I never saw her again.

PART FOUR. BERNARDO.

CHAPTER ONE. DRINKING BUDDIES.

Despite not wearing my glasses, my wandering eyes put the breaks on a beautiful, short, young Asian woman standing half-way down the bar with her group of friends. Of course, my vision being blurry, I couldn't tell for sure if she was truly attractive or not. I didn't like to wear glasses at clubs. One, if I decided to dance, as I usually did, the glasses would get sticky from sweat and slide down my nose, sometimes falling off. Two, I thought I was more attractive without glasses.

Bernardo stood near me at the corner of the bar, the two of us drinking for several hours, starting at our apartment in Silverlake and continuing at Myagi's. Myagi's was a four-story night club/Japanese restaurant with six full bars, four patios, three dance floors, and four dining areas. It was on the Sunset strip, in Hollywood, drew the wannabe Hollywood hipster and inner city hip-hop crowds, and played rap music mostly. Leonardo DiCaprio and Dr. Dre had been spotted there.

Bernardo and I were definitely outsiders at Myagi's, but really, pretty much any club or bar we went to, that was case. We were better at fitting in and finding our way, though, if we'd been consuming alcohol. There was also a fair amount of UCLA, USC, or other college students there who weren't a part of either the Hollywood wannabe crowd, nor the hip-hop crowd. The group of females Bernardo and I were scouting out were the student kind.

Probably because I had so much drink in me, I stood fixedly with my eyes on the young Asian girl, even though I couldn't see her that well. Bernardo looked at all the other girls but didn't stay fixed on one like I did. There was one that appealed to him but she kept looking around. I was lucky since the one I was staring at was looking straight back at me.

Bernardo was a couple years older than me (I was 23 here), and preferred to be the one who acted older, as well. He was a 25 year old who felt 45. Bernardo didn't have a lot of experience with women, nor did he exactly have a roller coaster ride through life, it was just his soul felt 45. There was a tiredness about him, of feeling worn out, a lot of the time.

I didn't fully realize just how worn out he could be until he moved in with me a few months before. He usually slept until one in the afternoon. I knew for myself, when I was an 8 year old kid I'd be like that, sleeping all the time, and that was because I'd been diagnosed with mononucleosis. I asked Bernardo if he had some kind of sleeping disorder like that, but he said he didn't.

As I acknowledged later, my excessive sleeping for 6 months at the age of 8 came on as a way to deal with a childhood depression. Bernardo admitted the main source for his sleeping all the time was because of depression, as well. I inquired why he was depressed and he'd say he didn't know.

Bernardo stood the same height as me – 5'10" – weighed about the same – 160 pounds – but had black hair, dark brown eyes, a darker complexion, and larger head. His body and head weren't overly disproportionate, just noticeable. His parents were upper middle class Mexicans who moved to Santa Monica, where Bernardo was born.

Bernardo went to visit Mexico now and then and knew Spanish well, but spending his entire life in Santa Monica made him seem more like a white kid from the west side. His skin wasn't all that dark and his features were more European Spanish, coming from his father, who was very white looking.

"Go talk to them." Bernardo urged, standing next to me with a Heineken bottle in his hand. I had a Guinness.

"If I'm going, you're going with me." I responded, my eyes still stuck on the one girl.

"Okay, let's go."

The two of us walked over to the group of young Asian girls, proceeding to introduce ourselves. The girl I was staring at was, indeed, beautiful. It went smoother than usual for us. I especially seemed to be in a zone with the one who put me under a spell. As Bernardo was talking to the other girls, I blocked everyone else out and asked my lady if she wanted to go somewhere.

"Sure." she replied.

I seemed to put her under a spell, as well, as I took her hand confidently and walked with her, guiding her to another section of the club. We went from one spot to the next until finally we went to the top floor and found a dark corner exit with no one there. I put my back to the wall and held her shoulders.

"This okay?" I asked with a smile.

"Yeah." she said with a shy but seductive smile.

"What's your name?"

"Aileen. Yours?"

"Thomas. You're beautiful, Aileen."

"Thank you." she blushed. "I like the way you look, too."

Our eyes were intent on each other the whole time and now we couldn't hold back. We plunged forward impulsively and fell into each other's arms in a passionate kiss. We moaned immediately once our mouths locked, our tongues twirled, and our hands gripped and caressed our bodies furiously. We rubbed against each other with horny enthusiasm.

"Where you from?" I asked as we continued kissing.

"UCLA. I mean, I go there ..." she responded, moaning while smiling at herself. "I'm Vietnamese but I was born ... mmmmmm ..." she tried to speak through the kissing. " ... but I was born in L.A. ... mmmmm ... oh god I like you ..."

We kept kissing and kissing and kissing, the sensuality building, becoming more and more in pure animalism. Aileen was 20 years old, smooth jet black hair, black ruby-like eyes, stood about 5'2", her build thin but also full, slightly curvaceous. She wore a shimmering, gold, tight-fitted, high-cut dress. My hands caressed her thighs, then moved up underneath her dress, gripping her lower hips.

"Mmmmmm ..." we moaned together.

Aileen's hands glided through my hair then moved down to my face, neck, shoulders, and back until she gripped my ass.

"I like that." I said with a smile then put my hands firmly on her ass, feeling the hard mesh of her skirt.

"You want to feel the skin on my ass?" she asked as we continued to kiss.

"Yeah ..." I said with utter delight as I slipped my hands underneath her skirt, gliding my fingers upwards, and clenching her ass cheeks.

I loved the flesh of her ass. I wanted to strip her dress off entirely, rip off my own clothes, and make love to her right there. She began licking and sucking my ears, then my neck as her hands explored my shoulders and chest. She opened up my shirt and began kissing my hair and skin madly. I lifted her entire body off the ground, with her arms and legs wrapped around me. We started dry humping, our crotches rubbing into each other's, and moaning uncontrollably, wanting to fuck on the spot.

I looked below and noticed how plump her relatively small breasts were. I bent my head down and kissed her chest, going to her tits. She moaned again. I gripped through her mesh with my hands as I licked her skin. I got so horny I crossed the barrier, pulling out her breasts and started sucking and licking on her nipples. She moaned, her body jarred, not expecting me to go that far. She was thrilled, not wanting this to stop, telling me she wanted me to fuck her ...

Just then a large black man came into the dark corridor. His wide, muscular build, 6'6" frame, and staring eyes stood over us. For a good three minutes, Aileen and I continued kissing (but we put her tits back behind her dress). We acted as if the man wasn't there, continuing with our intense make-out session. The man came closer and was literally standing over us, still staring and not saying a thing. I stopped kissing Aileen and turned to the guy.

"What's up? What do you want?" I asked, irritated.

The man said nothing, but took a step closer, standing even more intimidatingly over me. Then he stood on top of my foot.

"What the fuck?" I yelled, jumping back. "I'm sorry, man, if you're having a bad night, but the exit's right over there." I said calmly at first, not wanting to start anything. The man didn't move an inch, nor said anything. Aileen covered herself and walked to the corner. "Do you have a problem? Don't you see we're in the middle of something? Fuck off."

Suddenly, without saying a word, the big guy grabbed me and picked me up.

"What the hell're you doing?! Get your hands off me, motherfucker!" I shouted as the man carried me towards the staircase. "You can't stand to see a white guy making out with a cute girl or something? Why don't you fucking say something! Get your hands off me, asshole!" I yelled at the guy while trying to break free. "You feeling insecure with your big, dumb ass? Couldn't get any lady to talk to you so you're taking it out on me? Let go of me, you piece of shit!"

Soon, Bernardo, Aileen's friends, and group of black guys came to the doorway in the dark corridor.

"Throw that motherfucker's ass down the stairs, Big D!" one of the black men yelled.

"What's your problem, man?! Let him go!" Bernardo yelled to the big guy, who was ready to throw me down the stairs.

I continued to yell and struggle with the big black man at the top of the stairs, flaying my arms and legs wildly, then ramming my feet against the wall and pushing my back against the big man. Bernardo continued to yell and argue with the group of black guys over my innocence and for them to calm down. Aileen rushed to her friends back inside the club, disappearing from my sight.

The big black man decided not to throw me down the stairs but instead carried me all the way down to the bottom floor, and outside the front exit. The whole time I struggled and battled and screamed expletives. Bernardo followed, trying to convince the big guy to leave me alone and not kick my ass in front of everyone on Sunset blvd.

"This big motherfucker is security! You don't mess with security!" one of the black men screamed in my face.

"He didn't know he was fucking security! There's nothing on him that says he is!" Bernardo yelled at the guy, coming between us

"It don't matter! It don't matter!" the black guy replied.

"Just leave him the fuck alone and we'll go!" Bernardo yelled at them.

The big security guy kept pushing and standing over me, keeping me away from the club. Everyone at Myagi's, waiting in line or inside the club, and people walking by or cruising down the Sunset strip in their cars, were watching the whole event. All the Hollywood wannabes and hip-hop crowd were confounded and wondering what the hell was going on.

"You didn't say one god damn word the whole time," I yelled at the security guy. "you just stood over us like you wanted to start something, cause some trouble, upset the beautiful moment me and the girl were having! Why? Because of the jealousy in your little fucking heart! You had to stop two people from having a good time, two people who weren't bothering anybody, all because of your god-damn inferiority complex! You want me to say I'm sorry about slavery? I'm fucking sorry! I'm god damn sorry my ancestors were assholes! But you wanna know what? I'm not one of them! I 'm not fucking cracking any whip at you!"

"You best shut the fuck up, motherfucker!" one of the other black men said.

"All you had to do was say, 'Excuse me, but I have to ask you to stop, I'm security and we don't allow people making out'. Of course, it'd be bullshit anyway, since there's nothing wrong with two people making out." I continued to rage at the big security guy. "You didn't say anything to other people kissing and hugging in the main part of the club, in front of everyone else. But with us, way far away from everyone, out of everyone's sight, we were enjoying ourselves too much, we weren't fucking posing like you and your dumb ass friends, we weren't a couple of hollow, boring pieces of crap who throw stupid ass Gangsta Rap clothes on and fucking act like you actually got a brain!"

"Tom, come on, forget it, let's go." Bernardo said as he stood in between me and the big guy, trying to push me away.

It was ironic that I was the one raging against black men. So many times before I criticized Bernardo for making black jokes. But I wasn't raging against these guys' race. I was raging against their attitudes.

"Alright, I don't fucking care, let's go." I said as I started to walk away from the entrance. "Where's Aileen? Where is she?"

"I don't know. She's up there with her friends." Bernardo said as the big security guy followed us, still not saying anything, as if he was mute, but looking at us with anger. "We're fucking going, man, leave him alone."

"What the hell's your problem? My little fucking words hit a sore spot? You not used to people using words as fucking daggers against your low self-esteem? Don't worry, I'm leaving. You won't be hearing me say anything any more. We won't mess up your scene anymore."

Then a tall, 30-something, blond lady dressed expensively and with tons of make-up on, came from the club and towards us. I didn't notice her from all the other people as I realized I didn't have my jacket.

“I left my jacket. I have to go get it.” I told Bernardo.

“No, no, let me get it.”

“He's not going anywhere.” the big security guy said, referring to me. He finally said something.

“He's not going back in there, I am.” Bernardo said defiantly. “He left his jacket.”

“I'm the Manager here and I'm telling you to get the fuck off this property!” the tall, well dressed blond lady screamed at me and Bernardo. “If you don't leave my fucking club right now, I'm calling the cops!”

“We're leaving for Christ's sake! Let him get my jacket! That's all!” I yelled at the lady. “And besides, I'm not on your property anymore, I'm on the sidewalk in front of this other bar here.”

“You're still in front of the club -” the Myagi manager said.

“I'm not! I'm fucking over here and you're empty headed club is over there!” I barked at her.

“He's going to stay over here while I get his jacket, okay?” Bernardo said as the security guy stepped closer. “And tell this guy to leave him alone.”

Neither the Myagi manager nor the security guy moved. I then told them they had no right making demands on me, being as I could sue the club for the actions the bouncer took. There was nothing I did wrong and was almost thrown down a flight of stairs. Bernardo and I were going to leave and all we wanted was to get my jacket. It seemed simple enough.

The Myagi manager and the security guard said they would let Bernardo go up there but they wanted me to shut up and walk away. I was disturbing the customers. Bernardo went back into the club to get the jacket.

"Before this guy's jealous ass tried to throw me down the stairs for kissing a girl, hey, guess what? I was a customer." I said defiantly to them.

"Well, I'm sorry you pathetic loser, but because of the way you've acted, don't consider yourself a customer ever again." the Manager said with dismissive authority.

"Good!" I laughed darkly. "I don't need to come to a place where the bouncer feels intimidated by someone who makes out with a girl. Nor do I need to come to a place with a manager who's a sad old lady in her mid forties with a really bad lip job -"

"I'm 35 and -"

"- who not only has a shitty lip job but has to throw shit loads of make-up on her face and buy expensive clothes to impress the flat and boring Hollywood wannabes and stupid ass hip-hop customers that come and go to her pathetic Sunset strip club -" I continued, interrupting her, then being interrupted by her, as we were yelling over each other.

"You've said quite enough -"

" - and the biggest loss any kind of loser could have, lady, is to have an empty fucking heart behind a wrinkly, flat chest."

"You asshole." she said, hurt by my words and the violence behind them, then backed away. Big Darell the security guard stepped up to me again.

"You wanna kick my ass?" I screamed at him, then took an orange parking cone from the Myagi parking lot and threw it onto Sunset blvd., missing a car just barely. There was complete insanity in my eyes, as if I was really ready to get into a fight with someone who could kill me with his fists. "Come on! Do it in front of all the other sorry, empty-ass people driving by and in your club! Show them the only thing you're capable of! Be the good little bouncer you are!"

Big Darrell was so taken aback by my insanity he didn't know what to do. Bernardo came back with my jacket and quickly tried to bring me away from the club. Fortunately, the manager and bouncer chose not to do anything and just let me and Bernardo go.

As Bernardo drove us back to our apartment in Silverlake, I explained to him the reasons for why I exploded the way I did. All the times the two of us went clubbing, all the times I ever went out, I always felt I was entering cold, stand-offish, and pretentious territory. It didn't matter which club I'd go to – a place like Myagi's or Dublin's or some other club on the strip, or to the college bars in Westwood, to dive bars in Hollywood, Downtown, or the west side, to other dance clubs, to concerts, shows, and even to my favorite goth, industrial, dark wave or 80's clubs – people didn't go there to have fun. They went there to protect themselves. Of all places in society, night clubs should be sanctuaries of hedonistic and open release. During everyone's 9 to 5 jobs in the week, social uptightness and game playing was sad but expected. It was the corporate workplace.

But at clubs? That's where everyone should drop their masks, be themselves, stop with the social one-upmanship, and have a good time. After repeated disappointing experiences, I finally found a pure, sexual, beautiful moment with that girl Aileen, only to have some big, stupid bouncer interrupt and try to throw me down a flight of stairs. And why? Simply because the guy didn't like me.

When Bernardo first met me years before when I was going out with a girl we both knew, he didn't like me. There was something arrogant in a goofy, too nice sort of way about me then, according to him. At the time I felt he was trying too hard to be cool and stood aloof from everyone. He liked to start shit with people and saw me as too easy going, not serious about life enough. The years went by and we would run into each other here or there since we shared a lot of the same friends, but we never interacted much.

We then began hanging out with one particular mutual friend a bunch of times. A few months afterwards, we both had a falling out with that mutual friend. We soon became closer friends, finding out we had a fair amount in common. We both liked a lot of the same music music – The Cure, Depeche Mode, The Smiths, Cocteau Twins, Joy Division, and other bands – so we went to the clubs in Hollywood that played that music.

Several months later we decided to move into an apartment together, where we'd use our two-bedroom pad as a home base for nights of carousing. We joked we'd be the deep-thinking drinking buddy Casanovas of Los Angeles.

CHAPTER TWO.

WINNING THE HEARTS OF GOTH GIRLS.

It took Bernardo and I a couple months before we found an apartment. We looked all over. Hollywood, West Los Angeles, Santa Monica, Culver City, Mar Vista, various blobs of Los Angeles, Korea town, Echo Park, and, of course, Silverlake. A lot of these areas were under rent control until a few years before, then landlords - like everyone in positions of power in society – had their way and rents skyrocketed.

When I came back to Los Angeles in 1996, a person could find a two bedroom for $550 a month or so in a decent low-end area. By the time Bernardo and I moved into our two-bedroom – really a one bedroom with a large living room – in 2001, that $550 was impossible to find. It took us a while to get the $775 one-bedroom. Most two-bedrooms had at least doubled since the turn of the century.

Bills went up, as well. Gas, water, power, and phone bills, along with car insurance, car registration, and oil prices. Costs of living went up while minimum-wage stand down. Living-wage jobs for low-income people was a joke. It was a necessity obviously, but it was laughed at. Business apparently couldn't stay afloat if they raised minimum-wage to a living-wage. It'd mean cutting into the CEO's paychecks. Couldn't do that.

At the time I worked for an independent movie theater on Crescent Heights and Sunset blvd., I was making $7.35 an hour, about $1.60 over minimum-wage in early 2001. It was only because I worked for the family-owned business for over four years and gotten tiny raises now and then. Bernardo worked at an Italian restaurant across the street from the West side Pavilion mall on Pico. Our combined income got us barely by the $775 a month, plus all the other bills. Being poor did not help our party -going prospects in Los Angeles.

The two of us essentially became friends not only because of the mutual friend who we both fell out with but also other pals on both sides.

It was a new phase in both our lives in terms of how we viewed our friendships.

For me, it was getting away from the people I met at film school. For Bernardo it was getting away from guys he tried and failed to make music with. My friends from film school weren't into clubbing, drinking heavily, trying illegal drugs, nor picking up girls as if it was an adventure. For however unlucky me and Bernardo were in dating women, we both saw the pursuit of them as one of the great dramas (or comedies) in life.

We were romantics each in our own way. Neither of us could get over our social stiffness or awkwardness altogether, but both of us were capable of being charming and funny. I had more experiences with women but I'd tell Bernardo the only reason was I tried more often. I'd been shut down far more than Bernardo as well. Also, though, I was relaxed, open, and witty at times, qualities which were harder for Bernardo to come by.

The romantic in Bernardo was moody and, self-admittedly, self-pitying. He knew he felt sorry for himself. It was a vicious cycle. He wasn't hugely successful with women, which made him feel sorry for himself. The feeling sorry for himself made him less confident and therefore made him less successful with women. It went round and round. Added to that, Bernardo wasn't sure what he wanted. If he met a woman, did he really like her? Did he just want to have sex with her or was this the woman he'd one day marry?

Deep down – and once again, admitting to others – Bernardo was simply looking for the Ideal Woman. Coming from his Catholic upbringing with its emphasis on the Virgin Mary – the Pure, Comforting Mother – Bernardo was looking for that Perfect, Consoling woman to take care of him. On the other side of the coin, he was looking for the woman to take care of, too. After his father left his mom early on in childhood, Bernardo took on the father role, since his mother and sister were incapable of doing so. His mother continued to do all the practical things for him – doing his laundry, cooking his food, many other things – while he was there for her in some kind of "manly" guidance way.

Really, he was telling her what she should do with certain personal or moral situations in her life.

I didn't exactly care about finding the ideal woman, nor was I looking for a wife. I would pretty much indiscriminately throw my attentions one direction or another, then get let down when my expectations weren't matched by the person. Usually, I'd find myself coming on to attractive but shallow women, then at some point in the conversation lose interest because they were intellectually lacking. I'd become bitter and say cruel things in retaliation when I realized they were bored.

I was good at being charming up to a certain point. If I was in the mood, I'd be Cary Grant. Witty, clever lines I could throw out with a nice smile. But then I'd hit a stump, get stuck on a pause, and lose momentum. My insecurities would kick in and I'd get down on myself, becoming dark, stiff, and closed off. To my credit, a lot of the women were just not that interesting. They expected me to do all the work in the conversation, entertain, entertain, entertain, and I just couldn't do it. I was the man, it was expected of me.

So many men hit on women that women generally picked the guys who were good at first impressions, not moody young awkward men like me or Bernardo. A fair amount of women found us interesting, but interesting wasn't enough and we were hard to figure out. We just didn't have the spontaneous confidence women required of men who were hitting on them.

A Friday night came around and neither myself nor Bernardo had to work. We had to go out. But where? We'd been going to a lot of the New Wave, Dark Wave, '80's clubs in Hollywood. There was Violane, an '80's club on the east side of Hollywood on Sunset blvd., in a sushi restaurant by day. Then there was Clockwork Orange, Bang!, Perversion, Dungeon, Helter Skelter, and others but we wanted to try something different. We flipped through the LA Weekly while drinking whiskey and coke and listening to The Cure's “Faith” album. We were both big Cure fans but neither of us made attempts to look like Robert

Smith.

The one-bedroom Silverlake apartment sat in a large, 38 unit, three-stories high, building on Westmoreland and Fountain. Bernardo wasn't that pleased with the pick. He deferred to me, though, since I was the one paying more rent. It was also closer to my job than the pad in Korea Town Bernardo liked more.

The building had a tacky early '80's brown, orange, and white thing going on, and a security gate at the front which lead to a hallway down to the "courtyard." The elevator often didn't work and usually the floors where littered with trash. Our apartment was at the back on the first floor with lights over the doorway that barely flickered on and off.

Inside the apartment the large living room was straight ahead – where Bernardo slept on an inflatable mattress and the t.v. and stereo were. To the left was the kitchen and beyond that was the tight "dining area," which opened up to the living room. There was only a small wall dividing the kitchen from the living room, no doors. To the right was the sink and beyond that the shower and toilet. Turning to the left from there was my small bedroom, also with no door.

"How about Club London? Downtown?" Bernardo asked while sitting at a chair in the living room, looking at the LA Weekly club section.

"I thought that was only Sundays." I responded while reading the "Faith" liner notes and drinking my whiskey.

"I guess this weekend it's Friday."

"Didn't we go there a few months ago with my dad?"

"Yeah. He was the one who told us about it."

Bernardo had a weird tension between genuinely liking people, such as my father, and spitefully mocking them. He would do odd things, such as patting Jean's bald head with his hand while saying hello at the club, then laughing at him awkwardly, condescendingly (with only Bernardo thinking there was something funny). Other times, Bernardo would show my dad a lot of respect and engage in an intellectual conversation.

“It was a good club. I liked it.” I said. “Let's go.”

Fifteen minutes later, our whiskeys done, and a new set of clothes on, we jumped into Bernardo's car. Bernardo smelled of musk cologne, which didn't always cover up his bad breath. I asked why some days his breath was god awful, and other times, like tonight, it was fine. He didn't know. He said he brushed his teeth every day, which I don't think was true.

I wore all black as I often did when I went clubbing, especially to a place like Club London. A long sleeve, collared, black dress shirt, black slacks, and black shoes. Bernardo dressed simply like me, with black slacks and shoes, but a beige dress shirt.

Driving east on Sunset blvd. from Vermont towards downtown, we continued our Cure listening groove in the car, putting on “Carnage Visars.” After all, it was The Cure night at Club London. The album was all instrumental and took The Cure's early preoccupation with stark mood pieces to the extreme. No Robert Smith vocals but plenty of long, intricate guitar and bass riffs.

“You can tell these guys took their music seriously. Even though they may have been completely wasted on drugs, their riffs are really focused.” I said.

“Almost all the melodies, from 'Seventeen Seconds' on, all their albums, once Simon Gallup was their bass player, all the songs built around the bass.” Bernardo, a bass player himself, said. “Robert Smith just plays around the bass.”

“Well, Smith's the architect of the band anyway, even if he builds around the bass line sometimes. He just so happens to have a really good bass player.”

“That's bullshit.” Bernardo said defiantly. “All he does is have everyone play off the base.”

“You seem so anti-Robert Smith for a Cure fan.” I said with a sarcastic, teasing smile.

“He gets too much fucking credit.” Bernardo said with an odd outrage. When he got drunk he'd often shoot out defiant, angry opinions about something which really wasn't that important. “His voice sucks most of the time and his lyrics are almost always bullshit. Fuck him, man.”

“I like Robert Smith.” I kept taunting Bernardo with a sarcastic smile. “I think he's cool.”

“You would. He's a fucking poser like you.” Bernardo said with some seriousness, angered by my flippancy. It was strange how he could mock other people, but now and then he couldn't stand to be mocked. “He's pretentious.”

“Like me.” I added with a smile.

“Like you.”

Bernardo's car soon came to Figueroa, we turned right, and quickly found parking a block before Club London on Temple. There was a line to get in, filled with young Latino guys and girls dressed in black attire. Mesh shirts with black sleeves on some guys, mesh black panty hoes on girls' legs, black leather pants on most of the guys, black leather boots and tight, high cut black skirts on the girls, black lipstick, eyeliner and nail polish on both the girls and guys.

Some of the guys dressed like women, and some of the women dressed in S+M outfits, all leather, exposing gorgeous bodies, only the obvious places covered while the rest was bare. While Latinos seemed to dominate Club London because of it being an East side club, there were people of all races and backgrounds there.

I liked going to Goth clubs because even if the people still tried to be fashionably hip and coolly detached and boring, and the Goths still had their snobbish clicks like every other scene did, at least the people were creative with their outfits. And I liked the music. And the women in their sexy outfits. At this stage in my life, though, I couldn't go to clubs only with the expectations of enjoying the music, dancing, and the eye candy. I still felt the necessity of getting laid. Bernardo was the same way. Unfortunately, this made the two of us wound up a bit, and therefore not as successful in getting what we wanted.

"There's a lot of Hispanics tonight, but I guess that's to be expected." I said to Bernardo as we waited in line.

"Yeah, the club's closer to where they all live than the places in Hollywood." Bernardo replied as if he himself wasn't a Latino. He had a weird relationship with Latin culture. Because he looked white, grew up in Santa Monica and didn't act "Latino," he felt not quite a part of it. At the same time he had an emotional attachment and pride in Latino culture. This was mostly because of his admiration for his uncles – his mother's brothers – who were traditional, upper middle-class Mexicans, and more role models to him than his own father.

"It seems a lot of Latin American kids are into the dark wave bands like The Cure, The Smiths, Depeche Mode, Joy Division, and all them."

"It's because Latinos are into death and romanticism and all those bands deal with those two things in their music." Bernardo said calmly. He was capable of making accurate and interesting observations, even profound ones now and then. "Tonight I feel like somethings going to happen."

"Like what?"

"Like we're going to meet two girls and they're going home with us."

"That'd be nice."

"Let's split up when we go in there."

“Okay. Most likely, you'll find the girls. It's hard for me to read women without my glasses.”

“You did at Myagi's that one time.”

“Look at what happened.”

A few minutes later and we got into the club. There were two rooms: one below to the right that was smaller than the large main room straight ahead. There was a bar to the left, which both of us went to. After getting our beers, we went our separate ways to explore the club and hopefully find those two women Bernardo expected to take home.

I went to the main room and waded through the mass of dancing flesh. The place was packed and warm. The fan blowing in the corner wasn't able to reach more than a few feet in front of it. There were so many sexy young Latin goth girls, mostly dancing with guys, but several dancing in groups of girls. I wasn't comfortable dancing yet so I walked outside to the patio area where everyone was smoking, drank my beer, and looked around. As I finished the beer, I went back inside and left the bottle on the bar counter. Enough alcohol was in my body so I started dancing.

The way I danced was completely my own. My love for dance came from both my mother and father but it was my dad Jean who truly and sincerely invested himself in dance. I wasn't nearly as individualistic as my father, but I still had a style that was unique. My shoulders were a little stiff, so to make up for it I moved my whole body.

I'd drop one knee while straightening the other, pulling the bent knee back, then dropped the opposite shoulder forward while sticking my elbows out, one arm forward, the other back, rotating legs and arms and shoulders back and forth. Meanwhile, my body would lean this way, then that way then another and another, allowing myself to sway and shift, moving smoothly at times and other times jerkily. My head would roll and move, sometimes with eyes closed, sometimes open, looking at people or into space. I listened patiently for the music, letting myself absorb the tempo and rhythm before moving my feet, which was a combination of tap dancing, marching, and an Indian rain dance.

Since I wasn't too concerned how others saw me, especially when I was drunk, I'd often get people checking my dance style out. As I wasn't dancing only to scope the scene, as most guys did, but actually enjoyed myself, I let loose and seemed almost more comfortable dancing than if I wasn't. It was pure, physical release.

Twenty minutes into it – sometimes with girls, sometimes by myself – a group of young Latina women began dancing near me, giving me the eye. Two tall and voluptuous women who seemed to be sisters danced the closest to me. "Let's Go To Bed" just so happened to come on as one of them moved even closer, turning her back to me so her large ass wiggled near my crotch. The other sister came and danced behind me. I smiled as I was now sandwiched. Two songs later and the three of us were grinding into each other provocatively, one girl's behind into my crotch, the other girl's crotch into my butt. I loved it.

Just as I was about to ask them their names, Bernardo came up and tapped my shoulder.

"Hey, Tom," Bernardo said with a quick, drunken nervousness.

"Yeah?" I responded as I turned around, a little surprised.

"I have to talk to you."

"Now?"

"Yeah."

I smiled awkwardly to the two women who were dancing with me. They seemed disappointed as I walked away with Bernardo.

"What is it?" I asked, with my own disappointment. "I liked those two." We were now in the hallway between the two rooms.

"They were fat." Bernardo replied with a sarcastic smile. He seemed more confident than normal.

"You may think they were fat, but a few extra pounds is not fat to me. They were just right. Shapely. Don't you like something to hold onto? Couldn't you see yourself doing one of them doggystyle, slapping their big ass, gripping their hips as you fucked them from behind?" I said with excitement. I really was disappointed Bernardo interrupted.

"No." he laughed, completely amused. "I don't like doggystyle."

"And you don't like chubby girls. You better have something important to tell me."

"Fuck those girls you were dancing with. I -"

"I wanted to."

"Forget them. I met these other two who're a hundred pounds less and cute."

"What are they, twelve years old?"

"I was dancing in the middle of the other room when they began dancing next to me."

"Uh-huh."

"We started talking and then I took them to the liquor store and I bought us some gin and coke -"

"Yay? Cocaine?"

"No, you idiot, coca-cola. The girls are 18. One's 18 and the other's 19."

"I thought this place was 21 and over."

"One of them is a friend to the bouncer."

"So where are they now?"

"Waiting in my car. That's why I pulled you from the fat chicks."

“I see. Let's go then.” I said with surprised excitement, following Bernardo out of the club. “So where're we taking them?” I said with an expectant smile.

“Back to our place.”

“Ho-ho! Casanova Bernardo! Bernardo Casanova!” I exclaimed as we walked down the sidewalk, away from the club. “So tell me, which one do you like? I don't want to butt into something you started.”

“That's the problem. I don't know.”

“What do you mean you don't know?”

“I like them both.”

“Wait a second.” I said as I stopped walking, making Bernardo stop. “If you want to be alone with them, don't feel guilty about it. I can go back to the club or you can drop me off at Gus'.”

“No, no, I want you to go with me. I just don't know which one I like more.” Bernardo said with a smile, amused at his own indecisiveness, as he started walking again down the sidewalk.

“Alright then. We'll just see how it goes, I guess.” I said as I followed.

“Don't fuck things up, though.” he said with an odd smile.

“Okay.” I looked at him uncertainly.

“Because sometimes you talk about things no one wants to listen to and you don't notice. It's like you're not present.

I didn't know why he was telling me this. Bernardo would get this nervous, high pressure feeling where he wouldn't be himself, as if he felt he had to be a certain way or fail. The pressure was self-imposed but extended even more to others. It was an angry, uptight, awkward, nervous need to make sure someone like me wouldn't “fuck things up.”

It was as if to Bernardo there was some kind of divine rule to behave in the "right way," with a slightly macho attitude to go along with it. I could fall into this at times, though with less of the machismo Bernardo had.

"Of course you're always in the moment. That's why you're such a charmer." I replied, then looked up ahead. "There they are."

"And by the way, don't make fun of their names."

"Why? What're their names?" I asked with a smile, to which he didn't reply.

Half a block down the street and the two girls waited outside Bernardo's car, smoking cigarettes. Both were short – 5'2" or so – thin, long black hair, Hispanic, black clothes. They had an overall grungy goth look. They weren't able to afford the more refined or more exotic goth attire. They didn't have much in the way of make-up, just black lipstick, and a little eye shadow.

One of them (Chaos – yes what a name, right?) was the smaller one, wore a black dress that went to her ankles, had high top sneakers, a black hooded sweater, and a black tank top that barely showed her nice, round, but not too large breasts. She had a cute, small face, with a tiny nose, and daintier figure than her friend. She stood there waiting more closed off, less trusting.

The other girl's name was Sax (yes, again) and she seemed to be the older one. She had a tight-fitted black skirt, black mesh tights covering her smooth legs, wore heeled black shoes, a black lingerie bra and a black leather jacket. She had a wider, less attractive face but a fuller, lustier body, and seemed more open with her sexuality. Neither of them were all that friendly as they waited, though, neither smiling nor even looking at me nor Bernardo.

"Hello." I said, as Bernardo and I walked up to them.

"Didn't the music suck tonight? They played all the worst Cure songs, except 'Charlotte Sometimes'." Sax said, foregoing any introduction to me. "Now that's a rad song."

"That is a rad song. The video's pretty rad, too, with the young girl walking through the old school or church or something." I said.

"Are you making fun of her?" Chaos shot out seriously.

"No, I'm not." I responded with a smile.

"This is Thomas and this is Sax and Chaos." Bernardo said with an attempt at a gentleman's introduction.

"Nice to meet you both." I said with a large smile. So these were their names?

"Hi." Chaos said unenthusiastically as she finished her cigarette, noticing my reaction to their names.

"So you guys have some Coronas at home?" Sax said with a surprising enthusiasm.

"We do, right?" I asked Bernardo.

"Yeah, of course." he said, annoyed with my question. He shot me a glare. I think he thought I was acting as if we didn't know what we were doing.

"So ..." I said, still smiling. "Are those your real names?"

Bernardo hated me right then.

"Yeah. You have a problem with it?" Chaos said seriously.

"Not really." I said, still smiling. Bernardo continued to shoot me a death glance.

"Sorry, but Tom is only used to white people's names like Dick and Jane." Bernardo joked.

Ha ha. Chaos and Sax laughed. I smiled. At least Bernardo seemed more charming than he usually was.

As we all got into Bernardo's car, me and Bernardo were kind of oblivious to what was the girls' main intention in hanging out with us. They wanted to find two guys that could give them free alcohol and a ride home. There was also an element of risk and adventure in hanging out with some strangers.

Neither girl had a car nor had friends who wanted to go to Club London, and neither girl wanted to take the bus. Sax lived in Echo Park which was not too far, but Chaos lived in Glendale. Bernardo and I sensed we were being used, but we also felt the girls were actually attracted to us. They probably were, to a degree, but most likely not as much as we thought.

At the apartment things got a little warmer as Bernardo and I were able to amuse them with jokes, coronas, and music. They liked our collection, and constantly kept putting on a new CD, playing only one or two songs before changing the album. Sax continued to be more open, but there still was the lack of kindness from both her and Chaos. After all, they just met these two guys and who knows if we were freaks or not.

Around 2am Chaos said she had to leave, so as Bernardo promised, he took both her and Sax home. I sat in the back of the car with Sax while Bernardo drove and Chaos was in the front seat. We all seemed to get along and amuse each other. There wasn't much still air the entire night so that was good. There was the possibility of something but the dynamics hadn't been worked out yet. After we dropped Chaos home in Glendale and began driving home, I wanted to find out if Bernardo had now preferred one or the other.

“I can't tell yet. There was a couple times I felt like me and Chaos ...” Bernardo started to say, then cracked up over her name.

“Are we going to have keep calling her that? And Sax? Why not just call her Sex? Or Saxophone?” I chuckled.

"I don't know ..." he said, laughing. "I have to tell you I think I had something, a moment, with Chaos, when she opened up to me, you know ... but I'm more attracted to Sax, I think."

"Sax is sexier – I think we should call her Sex. But there is something about Chaos. She didn't open up to me like she did with you, though."

"It doesn't matter."

"You know what ... I'm gonna go for Sax and you go for Chaos. Yeah, that'll be better. I like to have order in my life."

"Why don't you just wait and see how things go?" Bernardo said while we both continued to laugh.

"Yeah, maybe you're right. No, you know what? Let's decide. Fuck it. It'll make it easier the next time."

"We've only hung out with them once."

"You're right." I said as I smiled, amused still.

"Fucking names." Bernardo said with another chuckle.

As the week went on, Bernardo and I continued to talk about Chaos and Sax. Bernardo had talked with them both over the phone but had much longer and more interesting conversations with Chaos. He told me he liked her more. He decided. I thought we should somehow make it clear to the girls who liked who. After a few shots of vodka one night, I told Bernardo to tell Chaos I had a crush on Sax. Bernardo laughed, but then went along and did it, which caused some awkwardness with Chaos over the phone.

"Sometimes it's good to be direct." I said with a smile to Bernardo, after the phone call.

"Maybe you're right. You better be." Bernardo said, smiling but also worried I did a dumb move. In this case, Bernardo was probably right about my knack for 'messing things up'. It was hard to tell. Sometimes something silly like that worked.

The second 'date' the girls wanted to go to a 'club' out in Pomona. Bernardo and I laughed at not only the distance needed to travel but that the place was in someone's house. The girls tried to make it clear it was a happening thing and not a dud. They'd been out there before and had a blast. It was an all night deal, lots of people, and lots of free drinks.

Bernardo was hesitant, realizing Chaos and Sax were using us simply as chauffeurs. I was, as always, just excited about the prospects of getting laid, and also whatever the club in Pomona had to offer. I urged Bernardo to do it. The lingering possibility of hooking up with one of the girls, especially Chaos, eventually won Bernardo over. He called them back and soon we picked the girls up.

In the car, while we continued joking and chatting, underlying Bernardo's joviality sat his romantic depression. He invested a lot of emotional energy in those few moments of friendly tenderness between him and Chaos. Now, watching Chaos behave as we got out of the car – so preoccupied with how everyone at the 'club' was going to perceive her, if her ex-boyfriend was there, if friends from high school were there, others, etc., etc. - suddenly, she seemed as shallow as could be.

"Hey, man, you wanna split?" Bernardo asked me as the two girls walked up ahead, going to the house on the side of the hill, oblivious to me and Bernardo.

"What, and leave them behind?" I replied. "How would they get back home?"

"They said a bunch of their friends were here. Someone could drive them back to L.A."

"That'd be kinda cold." I said with a smile at Bernardo. "Besides, we're already way the hell out here. We might as well stay. Maybe we'll meet two other girls. Chaos and Sax made it clear they were doing their own thing. We can do ours."

"I don't know ..." Bernardo really felt like leaving, then changed his mind. "Fuck it. Let's check it out."

So we walked to the house and down the steps to the front door, where a bunch of goth kids smoked cigarettes and drank beer in plastic cups. Music was heard from the backyard and a ton of people could be seen inside the house. A large, goofy looking guy stood near the door and asked for our IDs. Once in the house, we waded through the crowd of young guys and girls towards the back.

At the backyard was a large concrete area with two levels. The lower level had people packed near bushes and trees dancing to the booming goth music. The higher level had the DJ mixing songs, the outdoor bar, and people drinking and talking. Chaos and Sax were amongst the crowd, chatting with their friends and ignoring their chauffeurs.

It was literally a club at someone's big three story house. Chaos and Sax didn't bother to tell me and Bernardo whose house it was, if they knew the person, nor introduce us to their friends. This was a separate adventure.

"Well, let's just enjoy ourselves." I said, standing next to Bernardo, both of us quickly looking at Chaos and Sax before turning to the bar.

"You want a drink?" Bernardo asked. "I'll get it."

"No, I'll get mine."

"No, no, don't worry. Tonight I'll buy." Bernardo insisted in an aggravated tone.

"You sure? You drove all the way out here."

"Yeah, come on. What do you want?"

"Just a Bud, for starters."

As we went to the bar to get our drinks, Chaos and Sax glanced at us, then made sure no one noticed them looking. Bernardo and I decided to go through the club on separate voyages. I went to the lower level where everyone was dancing while Bernardo went to the house to talk to people.

There was an intimacy at the house that always lacked at 'club' clubs. People were more willing to acknowledge each other, strangers talking to strangers, strangers more openly dancing with strangers, the DJ was talking to people. I was having a good time.

After twenty minutes of dancing and drinking, I went up to the second level and got a coke and vodka. The DJ seemed friendly so I asked if he could play a Virgin Prunes song. With a happy smile and admitting to being a Prunes fan himself, the DJ put on "Our Love Will Last Forever, Until the Day it Dies ..."

Once the coke and vodka was finished, I went back to dancing. Not too much later, Chaos and Sax came down below to the lower level and started dancing. Soon, they were near me. Bernardo wasn't around. I chose to dance closer to Sax as we enjoyed ourselves for a while but never got that close.

Sax, like before, dressed sexier than Chaos but while dancing kept her distance from people. The two girls let their inhibitions down more than normal, though, and seemed a little drunk. In a moment when Carolina danced further away from me, Chaos crept closer, then stumbled a bit and found herself in my arms.

I thought she'd quickly stand away but instead rested her head against my chest and her arms around me. Both Sax and I were surprised. Chaos felt so nice and warm in my arms. We held each other for several minutes, her arms tightly grasped around my waist, her hands tenderly touching my back as she moaned.

I was turned on intensely as she told me she was comfortable being held by me. I leaned down as her face was turned to mine, her eyes closed, mouth open, vulnerable, tempting. I opened my lips and was about to kiss her when she turned away and told me "not yet."

People dancing began acknowledging the intimacy between us. Some were amused, some smiling, some laughing. Sax seemed a little jealous, occasionally stepping in close to us with a dance move. While I cherished this moment with Chaos, I could tell she was really drunk. She told me she liked me, but she wasn't ready for a relationship. I wasn't thinking of a relationship, I was thinking of a kiss. She felt and looked like a little dark angel in my arms.

Almost fifteen minutes past of holding Chaos in my arms before Sax came and pulled her away. The two girls went somewhere in the house, perhaps to be with some friends. I was disappointed with the abrupt yank by Sax. Even if Chaos was drunk and didn't mean what she said, the tenderness felt good.

Then it was time to find Bernardo. Usually he'd do some dancing when we went out, but apparently not tonight. Where was he? I left the dance area and went on a search. Bernardo was sitting by himself outside on the upper level, next to one of the patios.

It was one of those nights where one guy was having a good time while the other was not. Bernardo looked miserable. It wasn't as if I got any closer to hooking up with anyone, it was just I enjoyed the night more. There were plenty of other nights where I was the self-pitying misanthrope. Tonight, though, that role belonged to Bernardo. He seemed real bad.

Bernardo babied a beer, looking off into nothing, as I sat next to him, inquiring into his state of mind. Bernardo told me about Chaos and Sax, how after he and I split up, he hung out with them for a while. At some point they began to give him the cold shoulder and ignored him. So he left and began talking with some other people.

At the start, Bernardo thought the group was interesting and the conversation worthwhile. Then at some point in the interaction, everyone began acting as if Bernardo didn't exist. No one in the group, girl or guy, treated him with any sort of friendliness. Bernardo's sense of isolation screamed out inwardly. He continued wading through the party, continued to get the feeling no one gave a shit about him, no one gave a shit about anyone.

As the night went on, he became bleaker and bleaker. In his despair, his frustrations with sex came out. He couldn't seem to connect with anyone. What was off about him? What was holding him back? Was he doing something wrong or were people really that cold? Was he deep down gay or bi-sexual or a-sexual? Was he just a frustrated heterosexual with too much Catholic guilt? Or was he simply an awkward, insecure, inexperienced guy? He admitted to me at that moment he felt completely a-sexual, that he just wasn't able to make anything work, on a sexual nor emotional level, with anyone.

As Bernardo was near the bottom of his despair, I sympathized with him and worried. I told him that was exactly how I felt on many occasions. Just sitting there, listening with understanding ears, kept Bernardo from going off the deep end. I could tell. That was enough. There was no false sympathy. Still, Bernardo was furious and stood up.

"Fuck it. Let's go." he shot out after finishing his beer.

"You want to leave the girls behind?" I asked.

"Sure, why not?" Bernardo said in a flat, bitter anger.

"Hey, um ..." I put out with hesitancy, not sure if I should bring up what I was about to. "Did you see what happened between me and Chaos on the dance floor?"

"Yeah."

"She was drunk ..." I said, hoping the intimate moment with Chaos wasn't the main reason for Bernardo's bleakness. "I don't think she knew what she was doing."

"It's alright. If you like her and you think something might happen between you, we can stay." Bernardo said sincerely, though had a pain of jealousy within him, as well.

I looked at Bernardo and waited. What was I going to say? I found myself liking Chaos now after holding her in my arms, but Bernardo was obviously into her, too. And, both her and Sax and everyone else that night shot ice at the poor guy. There was no certainty of anything between me and Chaos, so why let Bernardo down? He was, after all, my friend, and Chaos was a girl I just met. She also wasn't the warmest person in the world.

"No, let's go." I responded.

"You sure?"

"Yeah."

And with that we left the house and walked to Bernardo's car. Chaos and Sax were stranded – with friends – all the way out in Pomona. On the drive back to Los Angeles, Bernardo's mood continued to be black. I watched my friend drive for over an hour at the pit of depression, at times near tears. I asked if I could drive but he wouldn't let me.

The next morning, the phone rang off the hook. Since the phone was closer to Bernardo, in the kitchen, I usually let him answer it. After the sixth series of rings, I got out of bed, walked out of my room, to the kitchen, and answered the phone.

"Hello?" I said with a groggy headache, into the phone. "Oh hey, Chaos ..."

"Fucking hang up on her." Bernardo said while still half asleep in his bed in the living room.

"Yeah ... well, it seemed you two were fine on your own ..." I continued to talk and listen to Chaos on the phone.

"Hang up on her." Bernardo repeated from his bed.

"Uh-huh ... what? Are you sure? We didn't see it ..." I said to the phone.

"Tom ... hang up on her."

"She says she left her purse in your car." I turned to Bernardo.

"I didn't see it."

"Chaos, look," I said, back to the phone receiver. "let me go check Bernardo's car and then I'll call you right back. ... Yeah, right, that's the number we have. I'll call in a couple minutes."

I went to Bernardo's car and found Chaos' purse hidden underneath the front passenger seat. I came back to the apartment and called her, letting her know. About an hour later, she showed up outside the apartment. What seemed like her father was in a car waiting for her as she met me to get her purse.

"That was fucked up what you guys did last night." she said as she finished looking through her purse to make sure everything was there.

"It wasn't as if you two wanted us around."

"You should've fucking told us you were leaving. I thought you were stealing my purse."

"We don't enjoy being treated like chauffeurs, to be honest with you."

"Bernardo was the one driving." she shot me a look, as if in remembrance of the moment we held each other on the dance floor. "Why should you think you're a chauffeur?"

"He's my friend."

"Oh well then." she said.

She continued to have a wall in front of her but at the same time she didn't leave. I couldn't help myself. I loved looking at her and remembering her in my arms.

"Next week there's a show me and Sax are going to." she continued awkwardly, still defensive.

"What kind of music?"

"Mexican ska bands. It's in East L.A."

"Can we go?" I said eagerly, almost forgetting everything that happened up till now.

"I don't know ..." she said, turned off by my eagerness. "I don't think Bernardo would want to, would he?"

"Well, um ..." I said, wishing I hadn't jumped the gun so much. "I can talk to him about it."

"Whatever. If you guys want to go, call me or Sax." she said then turned and went to her car and drove off.

The girls still needed a chauffeur. Chaos' dad could take her some place to get her purse in the morning before work, but not to clubs out in Pomona or East L.A. And there were still no friends who could drive them around like Bernardo or I could.

I went back to the apartment and told Bernardo what happened. He said he didn't want anything to do with the girls. If I wanted to go, I'd have to go alone. Eventually, I persuaded Bernardo to go to the Mexican ska show. Neither of us never had anything to do with ska before and we were curious.

Bernardo realized three things: one, it'd be be worthwhile to check the show out; two, we weren't obligated to Chaos and Sax, and three, the two girls always seemed to know where things were going on. Almost on a weekly basis they knew about some club, show, or party that Bernardo and I would probably like. Being their chauffeurs wasn't that bad when the girls were our party coordinators.

A couple months went by and every other weekend or so the four of us went out. Bernardo and I alternated with our cars chauffeuring and we pursued other girls at the clubs. The four of us were just friends.

Bernardo really didn't seem to mind this as time went on, but I couldn't forget that moment holding Chaos in my arms. While I chatted other girls up, she was still weighing my heart down.

One night before going out, the four of us drank and hung out at our apartment. I got Chaos alone in my bedroom to show her something. While she sat on a chair, I was on the floor and felt her leg up her dress with my hand ... At first, she ignored it. Then she grabbed my hand and pulled it away.

"No, Tom, don't ... I don't want to do anything with you." she said quietly, turning away from me.

I sat still, looking at her with a smile. She didn't smile back. I gazed into her distracted eyes, pondering who the hell she was and why I was so attracted to her.

"Whatever happened to that moment we had on the dance floor?" I finally came out from the silence.

"I still like my ex-boyfriend ... I think we're gonna get back together. Besides, you're too old for me."

"I'm only 23."

"And I'm 18."

"That's only 5 years."

"It seems like a lot, though. Maybe its 'cause you act older, I dunno."

"There's something between us, but I don't know what ..." I said as I came closer and touched her leg gently. "... that night you felt so good in my arms ... and you told me you liked being with me like that, too ... you even told me you couldn't be in a relationship with me, but I never brought it up ... it was on your mind ..."

"It was ... but I don't want to do anything with you ..." she said softly again, not sure what to do. I came up closer to her and tried to kiss her. She then abruptly pushed me away. "Stop, Tom ... let's go back to the living room with the others, 'k?"

I sat on the bedroom floor, quiet, dejected, then followed her into the living room. The two of us acted as if nothing happened. We all went out and had a good time, but I was starting to feel like Bernardo did at the beginning. I had really fallen for Chaos and she was shooting me ice like she did to Bernardo. Sax and Bernardo seemed to get along better because neither took the other that seriously. They teased and joked a lot and that was it.

With Chaos and I, there was this unresolved romantic tension between us. I seemed to get more and more frustrated with her. At times she seemed to leave the door open to me. Other times she shut it firmly in my face.

One night I made a tape of music for Chaos' 19th birthday and the four of us were going out to celebrate. Bernardo and I were drinking, at our apartment, waiting. As the hours passed, we wondered where the girls were. I called Chaos on the phone and, sounding a little drunk, asked where she and Sax were. Chaos point-blank said she didn't want to see me ever again. Sax may hang out with us some day, but as far as she was concerned, she didn't want anything to do with me.

"Fucking cunt!" I yelled after slamming the phone receiver down hard.

"What'd she say?" Bernardo asked with a laugh.

"She doesn't want to see me ever again ... she's a stupid, heartless bitch ... I made this tape of music for her and this is what she does ... out of the blue just tells me 'I don't want to see you ever again'. No fucking feeling behind it either, as if she was reading the ingredients to a cereal box ... the exact same thing Maya told me five months ago ... it's like they can put the fucking breaks on when it's good for them but when you want to do the same? Ohhhh no. You're the fucking villain. You're the evil one, the heart breaker. But for them? They're the innocent ones ... they mean no harm ... fucking bitch ..."

"Maybe you're more upset about Maya than Chaos really. I mean you had a lot more between you and Maya, than with Chaos."

"Yeah, maybe ... still, what a cold bitch to say that ..."

I looked at the tape of music I made for Chaos, and in a volcanic instant, threw the tape to the floor and began smashing it with my feet. Bernardo began laughing hysterically.

"This is what I think of your cold heart, you god damn fucking whore!" I screamed in outrage as I continued to break the tape into tiny pieces with my feet.

"I guess this means we're not celebrating her birthday." Bernardo said as he continued laughing at me.

The two of us ended up just staying at home, drinking and watching a Cassavetes movie. After that night, Bernardo would periodically hang out with Sax, but rarely.

CHAPTER THREE.

THE FRIENDSHIP DRIES UP.

"Fucking punch me!" Bernardo yelled at me in the middle of the street, in the middle of the night, in West Los Angeles.

"Would you cut this shit out? I'm not going to punch you!" I snapped back.

"Punch me! I'm not worth anything, I'm a nobody, a loser, a fucking bum ... hit me!"

"I'm not playing into your little Fight Club fantasy! It's fucking silly and it's gay and it has nothing to do with what happened to you just now!"

"You made me come out here at three in the morning and knock on Sandy's door and then she tells me to go home ... I feel like a piece of shit, man ..."

"You told me she was the love of your life! You couldn't stop talking about her the whole night! Was it wrong for me to tell you to get those feelings off your chest and tell her? Directly, once and for all, that you were in love with her?"

"It was a stupid move and you know it."

"Why?"

"Because it just creeped her out and now she'll avoid me and think I'm a weirdo. At least before we were good friends and I'd see her once in a while. Now I'm a stupid, bumbling fucking idiot to her."

"Well you could've played the good friend and continued being the nice guy, but underneath you'd be torturing yourself and wanting to jump her pants. You wouldn't have been happy like that."

"There's a way to go about making these kinds of things work, and me being drunk tonight and listening to you was stupid."

"At least now she knows."

"She knows I'm a moron."

"She knows your feelings and that you were brave enough to tell her. Some day she might want to jump your pants."

"You don't understand how people think or maybe you do and you don't care. You think she was going to be impressed with me coming out here like this?"

"Sometimes acting like a dashing Romeo shows you have balls." I said with a sarcastic smile, taking a stab at Bernardo's sometimes Mexican machismo.

"That's stupid."

We went back to my car and drove home, continuing our argument in the car. Bernardo felt I wasn't taking him seriously. He thought I saw the night as a joke, that his love for this girl Sandy and her rejection of him, was a joke.

"I take your love for this girl very seriously." I said intently. "It's not my fault she didn't reciprocate. You told me yourself she was cold."

"You know what your problem is? You think everyone should be 'free' and liberated – as if you are – and just respond the way you want them to. Maybe she does like me and maybe she's considered going out with me but ..." Bernardo said while sitting in the front passenger seat, then drifted off, becoming quiet and pensive. "... fuck it ... whatever ... You don't get it or you're just fucking with me."

"I do get it." I said with a frustrated laugh. "I don't know what you want me to say."

"That you fucked up, or you pushed me to fuck up."

"It was just an idea and we were drunk. So what? I thought it was fun."

"It was fun for you because you weren't the one who looked like a jackass. Anyway, forget about it. I don't want to talk about it anymore."

"Okay." I said, then felt sorry. "You do have it, uh, pretty rough with women. Have you ever wondered why?"

"Of course, Tom. What do you think?"

"I mean, it's not as if I'm any better ..."

"But you do get laid."

"Sometimes."

"More than me."

"Well ..." I pondered what I should say, hoping the right words would come to me. Unfortunately, I asked something I shouldn't have, probably. "Do you think you might be gay or bi-sexual?"

"No ... I wouldn't be able to get it up with a guy. Guys don't turn me on." Bernardo replied calmly at first then his brooding tone came back. "Why'd you ask? You think I'm gay?"

"No, that's not what I meant."

"That's disappointing - you asking me that kind of question ..."

"I don't know ... uh ..." I tried to make up the lost ground. "I used to have a friend from film school who, after a few years of knowing him and seeing his frustrations with women, ended up telling me one day he was bi. It didn't bother me and it wouldn't bother me if you were, too. I guess that's what I'm trying to say."

"Yeah, well, I'm not." he responded with a quiet anger.

"I shouldn't've asked. I'm sorry."

“It's just I've had other friends ask me that before. I don't know why. It bums me out that people, my friends especially, might think that of me.”

The rest of the night was dour. I felt guilty over egging Bernardo on to spontaneously knock on that girl's door in the middle of the night, then asked him if he was bi-sexual. Bernardo was depressed the whole night, filled with the regret of exposing himself so awkwardly to the girl, only to be shut down by her with an 'oh, Bernie, be a nice boy and go home.' To top it off, I asked him if he was gay or not.

Consciously or not, Bernardo began to harbor resentment towards me after that night. For me, I didn't care if people thought I was gay or not. But to Bernardo's Catholic Mexican Manhood that was in the dark woods of his subconscious, it was a big deal. And, even after all this time, Bernardo now wasn't sure if he could trust me. A part of him still believed I pushed him to go knock on the girl's door as a joke.

When we went out and got drunk, the condescending jokes Bernardo made on my behalf increased more and more. A few times Bernardo attempted to get me to punch him again, to my annoyance again. Once when my mother and her husband came over for dinner, Bernardo instigated a heated argument with them over a trite topic. Another time Bernardo got into an argument with my dad, Jean, about jealousy.

Bernardo slept in more and more, as well. There was rarely a day he woke up earlier than one in the afternoon. He soon quit his job at the restaurant and moved back with his mother, sister, grandmother, and uncle at the family house in Santa Monica. He was considerate enough to give me a month warning before he left so I could find a replacement roommate.

We continued hanging out, went clubbing, and also began co-writing a screenplay. It was a coming-of-age romantic comedy which, despite hours and hours of meetings, never got past page ten. I was frustrated with Bernardo's slow pace and felt he was falling into the trap so many of my previous friends did: of doing nothing but talk.

I told Bernardo I was tired of that pattern and wanted to make my first feature film. At first I pursued professional actors but after that didn't work out, Bernardo was one of the friends I went to for help. Bernardo obliged but from the beginning was constantly second guessing, testing, and criticizing my choices.

A week into rehearsals, Bernardo quit over the telephone in a mean-spirited conversation. Bernardo told me I was making my movie – like everything I did in life – half-assed, and I spat back that he'd never do anything creative because he was always waiting for others to do the work for him.

One night a few weeks later, we tried to make up by going out to a bar in Silverlake. Like the good old days. We ended up meeting a group of young Asian women who'd just graduated from USC. Initially, the conversation went well. Ten minutes into the interaction, though, Bernardo told the girls the way I met him was through my ex-girlfriend, and that we were both screwing her at the same time. He said while I didn't know it at the time, my girlfriend was a slut, and slept with everybody.

I didn't say anything but I had a tense, strained smile while Bernardo kept making fun of me. In my drunken fury, I took Bernardo outside and asked him why he said that.

"I was just saying something funny." Bernardo said. "It's not my problem you took it the wrong way."

"The wrong way? I don't mind if you slept with my ex but why bring it up like you did, in front of those girls? You never told me before. Why not tell me in private? Why call my ex-girlfriend a slut? You were intentionally throwing shit at me. There was nothing good-humored about it!"

"Your ex was a slut. You're just being overly sensitive, Tom. Chill out."

“So what is this? Revenge for that one night when you went to that one girl and knocked on her door in the middle of the night? Revenge for our entire friendship?”

“What the hell're you talking about? I was just making a joke, you idiot.”

“That was fucked up, you stupid jackass! You think it was funny? Fuck you!” I flipped when he called me an idiot, the tone in his voice full of hatred. I went over the edge, screaming at Bernardo. “You've always egged me on to punch you and you know what? It's time you fucking got it, you little bitch!”

And with that I punched Bernardo squarely in the face. He always wanted Fight Club. Here it was.

“Ow, shit!” Bernardo said as blood came out of his nose and he took a step back.

“Come on, you motherfucker! Since the day I met you you've always fucking taunted me and wanted to fight! Let's go, right here on the sidewalk!”

I went nuts and got into my insane, maniacal, berserk mode and was willing to do anything. People coming out of the club watched the two of us in confusion and curiosity, and one woman laughed.

“Come on, they're laughing at us ...” Bernardo said as he held his bleeding nose.

“I don't give a fuck! I'll throw you into the street for all I care.”

“Tom, come on! Calm down!”

Eventually, I did calm down as I felt the pain in my hand. Bernardo never knew how insane I could get. Sure there were times he saw me go crazy in the past, especially that night at Myagi's, but never had he seen so much hatred. It looked as if I could kill.

Months and months went by and we'd hang out now and then, usually with Gus. While there wasn't an all-out hostility between us, our friendship reverted back to how it was when we first met years ago. We just didn't like each other. One night soon before the U.S. Invasion of Iraq, we got into a verbal fight over the war, with Bernardo being the upper middle class Mexican American supporting Bush. Me, of course, being the peace activist, against the war.

At that point, it was hard to say we were friends at all. Gus convinced me to go over to Bernardo's mother's house and show my film to Bernardo. Bernardo agreed, joking that he wanted to see what half-assed movie I came up with. He had to keep his awkward humor going.

Waiting at the house was a drunk Bernardo, two female cousins who I met before, and Bernardo's fat, gay cousin. I came in with Gus and from the beginning Bernardo kept making off the mark, insulting jokes at me. I threw my own insults at Bernardo and at first it seemed the banter was harmless. Just as the movie started, Bernardo's uncle came into the living room and was making crass comments about the movie.

As his uncle let the verbal crassness fly while the movie played, Bernardo chipped in with demeaning remarks again. At one point, the uncle called the character Maya played a whore. I was steaming the whole time and continued to throw shit back at them. When the film was over, Bernardo stood up arrogantly and said while the movie wasn't 100% horrible, he definitely wouldn't pay to see it.

Bernardo's uncle said he would, to see the "amputated hooker do her fucking" (as he was referring to the opening sex scene between me and Maya). I couldn't keep the tension in the realm of joking anymore. I lit one of my Winchesters and started smoking it, tapping the ashes on the clean carpet.

The uncle and Bernardo told me to put the cigarette out. I refused and told the uncle never to call Maya an amputated prostitute ever, the cock- sucking, motherfucking, no good wetback he was. With that, Bernardo flipped and attacked me. Bernardo and I punched and kicked each other in the living room, with Bernardo's mother screaming, and Gus and the cousins watching. The uncle soon joined in, along with the fat gay cousin, who both held me down while Bernardo kicked me in the head and pulled my hair out.

I began laughing devilishly, almost enjoying the intensely absurd situation, even as I was getting beaten up. Part of my pleasure came in seeing Bernardo so upset. He was crying, screaming expletives over and over again in the highest pitch of outrage. It was ridiculous.

Soon, Bernardo's mother was able to stop the insanity. At some point in the fight, though, she was in tears, screaming at me to stop, even though I was the one being pinned down and kicked in the head! I had to laugh at her, too. The whole thing was a complete circus. Bernardo kept crying and screaming as Gus got me out of the house. Just as we were leaving, Bernardo took the DVD of “Loveincrazy” and broke it, telling me that's what he thought of it. I continued to laugh.

There was obviously no reason for the two of us to ever see each other again. A month later, though, next to a movie theater in Hollywood, I was passing out fliers to a screening of my movie. I walked into a public restroom and just as I went in, I passed Bernardo and his fat gay cousin. Both Bernardo and I turned, but neither of us acknowledged for more than a split second, and kept walking in separate directions.

PART FIVE. GUS.

CHAPTER ONE. CASSAVETES AS A GURU.

Putting together an actor's workshop with a small amount of money, mostly non-committed wannabe actors, and no one in charge, were the first steps Gus, myself, and other friends made towards creating a Cassavetes-like collective that was a bad idea. As I left a taco stand on Vermont and Santa Monica with Gus, it dawned on me the whole thing was doomed from the start.

Gus and I had just met with the only two other people who were consistently showing up every week. It was the four of us that started it. Gus and I told them we weren't doing the workshop anymore. Since Gus was the one paying for the space, it was all over. The guy and girl were friends of both me and Gus, and huge Cassavetes fans. The girl had organized a Cassavetes retrospective at the Laemmle's movie theater in Santa Monica and from that the idea came up to do a workshop.

Cassavetes had done one in 1950's New York, around the time of shooting his first feature film, "Shadows." Why couldn't we? The girl had gotten thirty to forty people who said they would show up.

But this was L.A., the capital of empty promises. Out of the 40 or so "contacts," one guy showed up. The space was part of an artists loft in a sketchy part of downtown. The artist renting the apartment upstairs would occasionally come down to try his hand at acting, smirking at the size of the group.

The one guy who showed up from meeting at the Cassavetes retrospective was a lonely, nerdy, but well meaning, down on his luck actor and filmmaker. The second person who participated was an attractive Asian girl who was a "plant" put there by her boyfriend, the owner of the space and artist loft. The owner was a friend of Gus' and wanted "eyes" to make sure the former drug addict and sometime troublemaker wasn't doing anything too crazy.

The low turn-out was especially a bummer for Gus, who told the two friends his part of the deal was get the space and their end was get the people. Not only did they not get the people but they didn't get any attractive actresses. Gus was looking for his Gena Rowlands. No one in the small group was "bugging out" - as Gus was fond of saying – either.

Everyone was low energy most of the time, uncertain of what to do and self-critical. We were all so critical of not only ourselves but everyone else that no one took any chances. When someone did, they were shut down. The guy and girl who did the retrospective were often tired, tried too hard to be cool, and were usually high from smoking pot. My step-father Frazier even showed up twice, and he was either worn out, or talking about astrology or reincarnation (his second favorite subject).

I tried to "bug out" but didn't trust my own judgments as an actor so I held back too much. Gus didn't quite know how to strike up the energy since he didn't trust his leadership skills. The workshop ended up being a laxadazicle failure.

At the taco stand Gus told the guy and girl he took full responsibility. It was mostly his idea and he had the experience but didn't follow through. I said I also felt I wasn't doing my part. The guy and girl thought Gus and I weren't telling the truth. We were and yet we weren't. We did feel responsible but we also felt the others didn't do their job either. There was no need to tell them, though. All it'd do is hurt their feelings since it'd never work out anyway.

"That was bad." Gus said with a nervous laugh, in the front passenger seat as I drove my car.

"I could tell by the look on their faces they were actually surprised. And disappointed, of course." I replied while driving to Gus' apartment in Silverlake.

"Real disappointed."

"I thought they'd see it coming."

"Maybe they did."

Gus was in his early thirties, stood about 5'8", had a scrawny, thin, rough build, dark hair and eyes on an attractive but "scratchy" face. There was something about him that seemed broken down, worn out and beaten up, despite the spunky energy that would surface now and again with his cigarette ridden New York accent.

He grew up a child of swinging, drug-addicted, separated Jewish parents in '70's Brooklyn. He spent most of the time with his step-mother while his dad was busy partying, and his real mother busy with her nervous breakdown. His step-mother was pretty crazy herself, having a weird, controlling, and slightly sexual battle with the young Gus.

The battle was so intense that at times they got into fistfights, or at least wrestling – kicking, screaming, and flaying their limbs. Gus' half-brother was the favored golden child, pushing the awkward and rebellious Gus out onto the streets most of the time. Being with kids like himself got him into tagging, riding the subways, and sniffing glue.

As he got older, Gus began taking real drugs. Having a certain amount of charm while being a social outcast naturally found him getting into acting. Acting was his call. There he could express himself and be in a land of play and dynamics, opposed to the dreary, depressing, and responsible BLAH of life. He took classes and usually either quit or got kicked out of them not too long after starting.

Gus fell into the counter-culture scene – whatever it was in the '80's and '90's – and befriended New York street hipsters and underground fashion designers. He was never really "one of them," but was appreciated as the troubled funny guy. At least he made people laugh, his friends felt, even if he wasn't as socially slick as they were.

Gus got tired of New York and moved to Los Angeles, to see if he could get his acting career going. His mother had already moved to San Pedro but Gus didn't make the move to see her. They continued to be distant, alienated, even hostile to each other. Perhaps subconsciously, though, he needed to be near her. For however rough and hard-nosed he was, there was definitely the scarred child in him that needed to be taken care of.

I met Gus a few years before the actor's workshop fell apart when I was 19 and he 26, at a movie theater we both worked at in Santa Monica. Gus was doing considerable amounts of speed then, unbeknownst to me. At the time, I wanted Gus to be in my second short film. We tried to work it out, but Gus was too wild and I was too inexperienced to make anything happen.

A couple years went by and we didn't see each other. Gus went to New York, then back to L.A., then traveled with friends to San Francisco and Portland. I worked on the movie zine with my dad and made a couple short films. Then the two of us, along with Bernardo, started hanging out. Initially, it was through our mutual friends – the guy and girl who did the Cassavetes retrospective.

We all bonded through Cassavetes. Cassavetes was our god, our guru. The Godfather of American Independent Cinema was to us and many others more than just a filmmaker. He was a revolutionary, a great and electrifying human being who rebelled against all forms (according to Cassavetes) of pretentiousness – intellectualism, politics, religion, philosophy, sentimentality, materialism, and more. Anything that wreaked of phoniness, formulas, convention, detachment, hipness, any expression of being "mental" or coming from "in your head" was tossed out the window.

Cassavetes himself said he was narrow-minded in his focus. All that mattered was love. Fighting with it, playing with it. A relationship between two people was the center of his universe. The pragmatic interaction of individual to individual, the flux, fight, and pull of the various emotions was the be all and end all. It was revolutionary behavior in action: throw oneself into insecurities, into awkwardness, into the moment. Emotions were gods.

Often, me, Gus, Bernardo, and the others would hang out at somebody's place, get drunk, watch a Cassavetes movie, and talk. When going out we self-consciously attempted to behave in Cassavetes' fashion.

Let loose, have high energy, stay out of one's head. We tried to stay in the pragmatic, physical, and emotional realm as much as possible.

For a group of relatively introverted, awkward, and questioning truth seekers, though, this kind of behavior became forced and rigid. It was the opposite of what we were going for. We were, in the end, still in our heads. It was like spiritualists who say they've killed their ego and yet their egos are still enormous. Since we all understood Cassavetes' ideas, the knowledge was there, but the acting out of the ideas was rarely ever natural. The girl and guy who did the Cassavetes retrospective were the worst. Never was there a moment where they didn't feel the pressure to ask themselves - "what would Cassavetes do?"

At heart, all of us were intellectuals, including Gus, and weren't naturally inclined to "bug out" every minute of the day. But we all, except me (although, I, too, was susceptible at times), were violently against "intellectualism." So there was a problem. By nature, we were incapable of behaving the way we wished. Insecurities arose and people's self-esteem were shot down. "You're not real enough!" "Show us your balls!" "Stop being phony!" And so on and so on. The whole thing became competitive and flat.

But that was part of the problem with Cassavetes' philosophy. Human nature is not built to sustain a consistently high level of energy wherein people were ALWAYS ON, always responding to every given physical and emotional stimuli in every given situation. And even when a person was "on," was it really them? Or were they just behaving like Cassavetes? Despite questions of identity, there was even the problem of, "is it even being truthful?" When one was so anti-mental, one was being anti-something that was naturally a part of them. The mental process worked whether we wanted it to or not.

Whatever the flaws in Cassavetes' philosophy and how we brought it into our lives, there was no doubt there was a valuable, electrifying life force in it, too. Cassavetes got people to be more playful, spontaneous, and more emotionally truthful. The filmmakers' "message" was life affirming without relying on safe and sentimental solutions. The scariest place to go for anyone – human emotions and insecurities – was where Cassavetes explored. There was a daring quality to his life and work, a risk-taking that truly seemed no one else was taking.

This was what excited me, Gus, Bernardo and the others, and what helped us. As we all wanted to make films, Cassavetes got us to take chances we probably wouldn't have taken, in our life or art.

"It's okay to smoke in the car?" Gus asked me as we drove down the street towards Gus' apartment.

"Yeah, go ahead." I replied, even though we both knew we were getting close to Gus' apartment. But when Gus had to smoke, he had to smoke. It was the only drug he allowed himself to still be addicted to.

"Thanks." he said. "How long you been smoking?"

"About four months now."

"Soon after you started working at Circus of Books, right?" he said with a gleeful, odd chuckle. "Selling all that gay porn got you nervous. No, I'm just kidding."

"That and the fact I've been selling cigarettes there, stressing out over Maya since she came back, that whole spending two days in jail for kicking the parking enforcement vehicle in Santa Monica, and then hanging out with you."

"Thanks. Blame it on me." he said with a hurt smile.

Even with a little jab like that, he'd take it personally, although not much. Life was a battle to him, ego against ego, even with friends such as me, who he butted heads with less than most people. I was like a little brother to him.

I dropped Gus off at his apartment then went home. The two of us started hanging out more as both our friendships with the guy and girl from the Cassavetes-like actors workshop began to dissipate. Bernardo was often involved in our outings, even after he left my apartment in

Silverlake.

One night Bernardo came to pick Gus and I up at Gus' apartment. We were going to a couple bars out in Atwater Village, a little area nestled in-between Silverlake and Glendale. Drinking Budweisers with Gus, I'd already arrived when Bernardo showed up outside.

"Gus! Hey, Gus!" Bernardo's strained yell came from outside. It was hard for him to project his voice.

"Yeah, I'll be right down!" Gus jumped off the floor and to his window, yelling down below at Bernardo outside. "Ber-nar-do ... the man from Maine and Spain ..." Gus said to himself quietly as he got his shoes on then opened the door to leave. "Be right back."

As Gus left, I sat on the floor, looking at one of his New York indie street fashion magazines. The bachelor apartment was run down and exhausted. The walls were uncovered red brick that must have had asbestos oozing from the surface. The ceiling had cracks everywhere. The bathroom sink didn't work and the toilet didn't always either.

Added to all that, Gus made it even more chaotic. There was no furniture anywhere, only two worn out mattresses – one in the "room" and one in the walk-in closet next to the bathroom, where Gus slept. There was a filing cabinet jammed with papers, magazines, and socks, a refrigerator, a stove, dirty and clean clothes thrown together all over the floor, mixed with empty cigarette packs, empty bottles filled with cigarette butts, magazines, papers, and other miscellaneous stuff. If he was lucky, some days he could find his keys and wallet within ten minutes.

Soon, Gus and Bernardo came through the front door.

"You guys started drinking already?" Bernardo said with a sarcastic smile.

"Always the observant one, Bernie." Gus replied.

"Drinking half-empty bottles of Bud with cigarette butts in them?"

Bernardo cracked at Gus, still smiling, still pushing his obvious sense of humor.

"Not yet." Gus cracked back. "Have a bottle in the fridge. No cigarette butts, just beer inside."

We ended up finishing the six pack, two bottles each, listening to Cat Power (Gus' choice), Cocteau Twins (Bernardo's), and The Cure (mine), and talking about women. The dynamic between the three of us was different minus the guy and girl from the actors workshop. Less "put your balls on the table" and more joking playfulness. There was a bond through our commonality: we were all single, drinkers, socially a little stiff, outsiders, jokers, and Cassavetes fans.

Soon we left for Atwater in Bernardo's car, listening to Gus' tape of John Frusciante's first solo album, a schizophrenic guitar extravaganza with loopy vocals. The dark music and alcohol we'd been drinking got us dark fellows even darker. But at least we were having fun. This was the first trip to Atwater together.

"What's the name of the bar again?" Bernardo asked while driving over the I-5 freeway bridge into Atwater.

"The Roost." Gus replied.

"The Rooster?" Bernardo said, smiling.

"No, Bernie, the Roost. You're gonna like it. There's a buncha girls like Chan Marshall there, just not as talented."

"So female versions of you?" Bernardo said to Gus, still poking.

"Silverlake girls, Bernie. Los Feliz, Echo Park girls. Girls who went to art school, work at coffee shops, dress hip slickin' cool, grunge, punk, indie-pop, don't shave their armpits, cute faces, thin, some are wannabe actresses, some in wannabe rock bands, some are feminists – the ones who don't shave, so if you see one with a mustache, that one's a feminist – some are lesbians, some are straight, some are bi, some don't like guys named Bernardo ..."

"Or guys whose name rhymes with bus, and sounds like a name for a walrus." Bernardo said, laughing.

"Walrus rhymes with Gus, too." I had to chip in.

"You guys are hysterical." Gus said.

"I am." Bernardo said simply. "I'm not so sure about Tom."

"Well you said a female version of me. I'm not any of the things I just mentioned." Gus said quickly.

"You live in Silverlake, you're an indie rock kind of guy, you're a wannabe actor, a lesbian, and you don't shave your armpits." I said, still chuckling.

"Very funny. I thought it was just Bernie making fun of me tonight." Gus said dourly, poking fun at himself while being irritated with both me and Bernardo.

"I wasn't making fun of you." Bernardo said with a laugh. "I was just making fun of you."

"Ha-ha. God, the humor's bad tonight. Take a right at the next street." Gus said as he took out his cigarettes.

"There it is." I said as I looked at the bar.

"Hey, don't smoke in the car." Bernardo told Gus as he made the right turn.

"I'm not smoking in your mom's car. I was just getting ready. Find parking anywhere." Gus said as he got anxious for nicotine.

Bernardo soon found a spot, and as we got out of the car, Gus immediately lit his Winston cigarette. I decided to follow suit and lit one of my little cigars. Bernardo, the non-smoker, locked his car then followed us.

"What the hell're you smoking, Tom?" Bernardo asked.

"Winchesters. They're little cigars." I replied. "They have a nice flavor and they're two dollars less than normal cigarettes."

"Let me try one. It smells like shit." Bernardo asked as we continued walking to the bar.

"Sure." I handed him a little cigar, then lit it.

"It's disgusting." Bernardo said as he coughed and handed it back to me. I laughed.

"I'll take it." Gus came in. I gave it to him as Gus finished his Winston.

"Smoking is stupid. You'll live 15 years less because of those things." Bernardo said as he continued to cough.

"That's why me and Tom are idiots." Gus said as he puffed on the Winchester as we arrived at the Roost.

The Roost was right on the corner of the street with a residential area right behind it, where we found parking. On the main strip were a couple other bars, a pool hall, a motel across the street, an AMPM, a few restaurants, and a bakery. The area was dead at night except for the bar patrons. Atwater was a spot where Silverlake, Los Feliz, and Echo Park hipsters came to if they were tired of those three neighborhoods. It seemed to be removed from everywhere else. The Roost was a simple, older bar that had a glowing red neon sign. Inside, it was shaped long and rectangular, with a dark glassed "wall" separating the booths to the right and small tables near the bar on the left. At the end was a more open space where the bigger tables were.

Gus, Bernardo, and I walked into the bar and found it packed. All the tables were taken, the bar was full, and people were standing. Bernardo rushed to the bathroom in the back, as he normally did when entering a bar. Gus and I scoped the place out. It was all hipster guys and gals, with a few old school drunks at the bar talking to the middle-aged female Asian bartender.

"There's no where to sit." I said to Gus.

"Let's get a beer and wait for Bernie." Gus responded.

The two of us waded through the crowd to get to the bar and ordered ourselves a Bud each. Bernardo soon arrived next to us, looking refreshed but still with bad breath. Neither Gus nor I had the nerve to mention it to him the whole night. Bernardo ordered a Heineken for himself.

"There's no where to sit." Bernardo said.

"We noticed that." Gus replied dryly.

We ended up squeezing ourselves in at the bar behind a couple at the stools, drinking our beers. As always, we were outsiders. After ordering our third round of beers, a booth opened up on the other side of the wall. We snagged it quickly, then relaxed into the seats.

One hour went by, then two, then three, as we drank more beers, smoked cigarettes, and talked. We never were able to break any walls with the others in the bar. We were cut adrift, pushed to the side, unnoticed. We thought about approaching some girls in another booth, but none of us struck up enough nerve to do it. So we were stuck with each other. At around 1:30am, we decided to leave.

"Next time, we'll go to 'Tiger Lilly's'." Gus said regretfully, as we began walking back to Bernardo's car.

"Is that a Chinese whore house?" Bernardo joked.

"No, it's a bar like the Roost, just up the street here in Atwater." Gus replied.

"Too bad it wasn't a Chinese whore house." Bernardo joked again.

Months passed and the three of us continued going out together, bar hopping, club hopping, and some parties. We had more interactions and more fun than that night at the Roost, chatted some girls up, flirted and so on, but nothing ever really happened. Our nights out on the town had a certain fun to it, but in terms of getting laid, we weren't that successful. It only happened if it was with girls we knew or met on our own time. The L.A. night scene for us wasn't the Land of Opportunity ...

CHAPTER TWO.

MAKING A MOVIE AND BECOMING A PEACE ACTIVIST.

I had to get away from my job at Circus of Books. Sure, I was working on the script to my first feature film, I could walk to the store from home, and the pay was decent for minimum-wage work. But it was hell. It was slimy, degrading, and demeaning most of the time.

I had to sell and rent out gay porn, catalog the tapes, box and wrap them, put them out on the wracks next to leering, gay, scummy, horny customers, watch and make sure "defective" porn was actually defective. The store sold "video head cleaner," or in gay subculture terminology – poppers. They were a chemical in a little bottle which if one were to inhale, would give an intense but short head rush.

The chemical was legal in itself – to clean the heads on video tape – but certainly not meant to be inhaled. Why gay men used it was during ejaculation or receiving anal penetration, a guy would get an extreme high mixed with the orgasm when he took it. The problem with these poppers was that if used on a normal basis, it fucked a person up. Hair would fall out, teeth would fall out, skin would dry up and flake off, and brain cells would disintegrate.

In the six months when I worked at Circus of Book, I saw regulars who, in the beginning, looked perfectly healthy. By the end of the six months, those same guys, after daily purchases, sometimes two or three times a day of "video head cleaner," lost most of their hair, teeth were missing, their skin was flaky and red, and they didn't seem socially all that functional. I was selling the goods to these guys. Of course, these men were probably doing crystal meth at the same time, a big drug in the gay Silverlake scene, which caused the same damages, even more so.

Not only was there the problem of drug use, but one time a customer brought up a photo-book of child pornography. I never knew we had that. Where did it come from? I never saw it on display or on the shelves. I refused to sell the book to the guy. Besides all of this, on a routine basis, customers would come in using the store as a pick-up joint. It was so obvious it was both entertaining and disgusting. Disgusting especially when teenage boys would sell themselves to older men.

So I answered an ad in the LA Weekly from California Workers For Peace and Social Justice – Now! The ad was intriguing - "Get paid to put an end to the Military Industrial Complex!" I responded to several political job ads but C.W.F.P.S.J.-Now! was the only one offering a permanent position. All the other jobs were for the spring or summer only.

I went in for an interview and got the job. It was rare someone didn't at least get a chance. Soon, I started working and quickly got along with everyone at the office. I was excited that I could actually get paid for talking politics. No more gay porn, no more poppers, no more popcorn, no more candy, soda, cleaning movie theaters, selling and tearing tickets, no more distributing real estate fliers and so on.

Both Gus and Bernardo were a-political, so when I got the job and was all happy about it, they didn't care much. After all, Cassavetes was our leader, and Cassavetes thought talking about politics, religion, or philosophy was bullshit. It was too mental.

Bernardo and Gus always knew I was of the liberal political persuasion, and that I'd talk about it now and then. They were just hoping I'd "grow out of it." I tried to explain there was a more human interest in the experience for me and that it wasn't all mental BS.

There was interesting social interaction. Going door to door and talking to hundreds and hundreds of people in a month, one got a wide variety of inter-play and dynamics. And, of course, there were the girls at C.W.F.P.S.J.-Now! There was not only Charlotte, Cassandra, and a few other regular activists working there, but a lot of girls would come and go. The job was a wonderful opportunity to meet women. Gus and Bern agreed, but then asked what kind of women? I smiled in recognition.

Charlotte, Cassandra, and the other women took a liking to me. They trusted me. I was nice, understanding, non-judgmental, and open.

I was a good canvasser, passionate about the ideas, and could inspire people. And I was fun to be around. They hung out with me, invited me to parties, and did other activities with me. Everything but sex (and anything else sexual).

One day I came up with the idea to play a game of basketball. Being the athletic girl she was – in high school spending all her time with soccer – Charlotte jumped on the opportunity. She thought it was a great idea, another opportunity to bond with her male peace activist co-worker. Sharon was the only other person who wanted to join us so it was the three of us and Gus. I had just moved into Gus' apartment, as I couldn't sustain the rent nor find a roommate at my Silverlake apartment, nor was I getting along with Maya at her place.

With my move to Gus' pad, the two of us spent more and more time together. In many ways we became best buddies. I looked up to Gus, being in some weird kind of way a role model to me. So I asked Gus if he wanted to get involved in the pick-up game. He hadn't played basketball in years and was out of shape, but he was curious about meeting Charlotte. I talked about her and everyone else at C.W.F.P.S.J, and mentioned the girl from Minnesota was darn attractive.

I also didn't make it clear whether I was into Charlotte as a friend or more, or if I was looking to hook Gus up with her. The point was kind of moot since Charlotte was involved in a lesbian relationship at the time anyway. It was supposed to be a friendly outing only.

I drove with Gus and picked up Sharon at his mom's house in Hollywood, off La Brea and Melrose. I didn't have a basketball so we searched Sharon's backyard for one. We found an old worn-out ball that smelled of dog urine. It was either that or buy a new one, so we took it.

Sharon and I had been friendly at the office. Months after I was hired and became a field manager, Sharon was hired, and I helped him out a bit. He was a little tentative and shy, not sliding into the role of canvasser that easily. Most of the feminists at the office, including Charlotte, weren't all that eager to help him.

While Sharon and I were friendly, we weren't close pals, either. We just got along, and not much else. It might've been because there was some kind of subconscious understanding we were both attracted to Charlotte.

After Gus and I got Sharon and the basketball, we drove to Venice Beach to pick up Charlotte. She was living at a "commune" and waited for us inside. The building was in a rough area of Venice and seemed like a worn down one story living compound. There was maybe twenty or so rooms, some for two people, some for one. Charlotte stayed in a room for one. Even though the complex was shitty and so was the neighborhood, she still had her dad paying $750 a month for the tiny little room she had.

At this time, I was the closest to Charlotte. Sharon was relatively new at C.W.F.P.S.J and a ways before eventually hooking up with her. Gus and Sharon followed me through the side entrance to the commune. I'd been there before, hanging out with Charlotte several times after work, a couple times smoking pot with her on her bed.

As Gus, Sharon, and I walked down a hallway, Charlotte came out of the restroom, immediately grabbing our attention with her appearance. No matter how she was feeling or what she wore, she was always good at that. In that moment, she was all smiles, happy to see us. She had her green soccer shorts from high school on, a wife beater, and high tops. Simple and plain, but on her body and persona, it glimmered. Her long legs looked great, and her breasts were glorious, held firm by a sports bra.

"Hi ya, guys." she greeted us.

I introduced Charlotte to Gus, then he made a quick crack about not being into politics, which got a snappy reply from her. She then swiftly showed us the commune and her room. She didn't want us taking too good a look around, her room especially. We soon got into my car and went looking for a basketball court.

I called Bernardo on his cell phone to see if he could join us. Bernardo wanted to, but was out in the valley with family. It didn't work out for him to make it in time, even though Bernardo wanted to meet Charlotte just as much as Gus did. It was better Bernardo didn't join us anyway, since it would've given us an odd number of five to play a game of two on two.

I mentioned to Charlotte, Gus, and Sharon a basketball court in Santa Monica not too far from Venice. Parking was easy and there usually weren't a lot of people. They agreed it was a good idea so we went.

On the way there, the silly, drunk adventurer I was, I suggested we stop at a liquor store and get beer and, of course, water. The day had the feel of adventure so the others complied with my impulse. Why not? I could be a rascal leader at times, and anyways, how serious were we going to take this game?

Back in the car with beer in our hands, discreetly already drinking, I drove the car, with Gus in the front passenger seat, Charlotte behind me in the backseat, and Sharon next to her. As always, Charlotte had her childish, "innocent" flirtations going on. She had three single, fairly good looking men in the car with her, going to play basketball. She had shorts on, she was beautiful, and she was fun. We were all attracted to her, and the subtext was there. We knew it but she was taken, by another girl. Still, the dynamic was there. Perhaps some day she'd be single and into men again.

Charlotte and Gus were throwing digs at each other up until we got to the park. She didn't like his remark about not liking politics. The whole time she had her left foot up near my left shoulder on the seat and her legs spread open. She had us. Gus could see her wonderful crotch (with soccer shorts on, of course) while bantering with her. Sharon could see from the side sitting next to her. I couldn't see the sexy, open crotch, but feeling her foot near, my imagination could paint the picture.

Several minutes later we made it to the basketball court, parked the car, and brought the ball, water, and beer with us. Everyone complained about the basketball smelling like dog pee too much so I rubbed it against the grass over and over and over again. There also wasn't enough air in the ball.

I just so happened to have an air pump in the trunk of my car. Charlotte took the pump and put it in-between her legs while she sat on the bench. As she adjusted the needle into the hole of the ball, Gus, Sharon, and I turned to her. Not only did she get us horny with her legs spread wide open, knees up, and chest bent over, but as she pumped the ball it was giving her a hard time and she began moaning and groaning. She was loud and goofy but definitely sexual. She was "innocently" playing around with her sex appeal. We came to help her but she was able to do it herself.

As soon as the ball had enough bounce in it, Charlotte rushed to take the first shot. She missed, then her second shot, then third, and forth.

"Fuck! Stupid ball!" she yelled.

Gus and I chuckled as we drank our beers. Sharon decided to join us and got one from the bag for himself. Charlotte turned and saw us amused at her basketball skills, then smiled back self-deprecatingly.

"Ya know," she said with a fighter's smile. "if we were playing soccer, I'd kick all your guys' asses."

"I'm sure you would." Gus remarked while lighting a cigarette.

"Are you guys smoking and drinking while playing basketball?" she said to me and Gus.

"This is a health-nuts pick-up game, Charlotte." I said with a smile and taking a sip from my beer. "We all smoke and drink beer here."

"Yeah but I don't smoke while doing sports. That's crazy." she replied while eyeing the drinks in the bag. "Can you get me a beer, Sharon?"

Sharon happened to be closest to the beers and got one for her. As we all drank away, and Gus and I smoked, we took turns taking shots at the hoop. None of us were that great, even me, since I used to play for my high school basketball team. I hadn't played in years though.

After a while we got bored with just taking shots so we decided to play two on two. We'd do one game up to eleven, going by one point for each shot made, then switch teams. First it was Charlotte and Sharon against me and Gus, then Gus and Charlotte, then me and Charlotte. All three of us guys liked playing defense on Charlotte, especially when she backed down, doing a post-up move, pushing her ass into us. She was wild, throwing her body into us, bumping, pushing, slapping.

"Hey, it's not a hockey game here!" Gus yelled jokingly at her after she pushed him to get the ball.

Charlotte laughed. She was having fun. I loved getting physical with her. We affectionately bumped into each other, going after the ball and defending, laughing and drinking. When Charlotte and I played together on the same team, we crushed the other guys. Perhaps it was just that Gus and Sharon were so out of sinc with each other. However it was, though, Charlotte's timing with me was just right, each pass connecting, our movements smooth and swift. We seemed to communicate so well physically, knowing where and when the other person would be.

We all began to get worn out from the basketball playing, drinking and smoking. Towards the end, Charlotte lunged after the ball as it went to me. Our previous smooth communication went out the window in this one instance. We banged into each other, her hand striking into my throat, right at my adam's apple.

"Ow, shit!" I exclaimed, holding my throat in pain.

"Oh, fuck, I'm sorry! You okay, Tom?" she said, laughing initially, then becoming concerned.

"God damn ... yeah, I'm alright ..."

"I'm sorry."

"You need to watch where you're going ... you're out of control sometimes ..." I said, slightly ticked off by her carelessness.

"Shit, shit, shit ..." she said with guilt, as she came to comfort me. "I'm so sorry."

"It's okay." I replied as she put her arms around me tenderly, almost motherly. I got all warm inside and turned on by her comforting hug. Afterwards I could tell Gus and Sharon secretly wished she was hugging them instead.

It seemed at this point, I had the best chance out of the three guys to hook up with Charlotte. That is, if she were to break up with her girlfriend and want a man. She seemed the most comfortable with me. Over time though, things changed. Sharon, of course, ended up being the man. Before we all left the basketball court, a thirty something black man played soccer with his six year old son. Charlotte – the social activist she was, never truly out of canvasser mode – went up to the father and son and played soccer with them.

Gus, Sharon, and I watched as eventually she convinced the father to let her give his son soccer lessons. When she came back to her guys, she was all happy to make the personal connection, as if she'd somehow "saved" two citizens. She was a crusader, even on finding a kid to teach soccer to. When I asked her a month later how the lessons were going, she said she was never able to follow up on that.

Back in my car, Charlotte said she needed to get back to the commune to take a shower. I asked Gus and Sharon if they needed to go home. Sharon said he didn't need to be anywhere and Gus was surprised I asked, thinking I wanted to continue hanging out with Charlotte. She wasn't shooing us away, she just needed a shower. And wouldn't it be great to be around her after a shower?

I took Charlotte to the commune so she could wash up as we three guys waited for her to go to the beach. She wanted to go to the Drum

Circle for a bit and see Cassandra, who was there. In a couple hours, Charlotte's girlfriend would be at the commune and we were welcome to hang out then, too.

While waiting for Charlotte, it was obvious Gus and Sharon didn't click too well. They weren't hostile, just not enjoying each other's presence much. Gus could be extroverted, loud, and sarcastic while Sharon was introverted, quiet, and mellow. I was fine with both of them but obviously preferred Gus.

When Charlotte was ready, we walked out of the commune and towards the ocean, which was about ¾ of a mile away. Charlotte put on her hippie dippie clothing, knowing she was about to see Cassandra. Charlotte somehow looked elegant even when trying to look earthy and grungy in her flowery, ratty, torn dress.

On the way to the beach, Gus and I got caught up in a conversation, enabling the silent Sharon to sneak closer to Charlotte. A few minutes later, though, she ran into a Venice Beach guy friend, gave him a hug, and chatted with him for several minutes. It wasn't as if she tried to ignore her men walking with her, but she got so focused on this one guy she forgot about me, Gus, and Sharon. The beach guy was better looking than the three of us, too.

Once she said her goodbyes to the beach guy, she caught up to her three men and explained he was the person who did the tattoo right up above her ass. Lucky guy, I thought to myself, as did Gus and Sharon, I'm sure. I got a harsh, bitter, jealous feeling inside me while watching Charlotte with the cute beach guy. I thought maybe that'd be the guy she'd choose some day, or a guy like him. What chance did I have? Perhaps Charlotte was out of my league, even if she were to break up with her girlfriend and want a man.

The Venice Beach boardwalk soon came up and in the distance on the sand, we could see the Drum Circle. There were about forty or fifty people gathered, mostly locals, street folk, "bohemians," ex-hippies, current hippies, reggae and Rastafarian hipsters, tourists, and more. In the midst of them was Cassandra, dancing with friends to the drum beats.

Charlotte found Cassandra and ran to her, once again leaving me, Gus, and Sharon behind. I waved hello to Cassandra then talked with Gus, while Sharon quietly laid on his back on the sand, watching Charlotte. A while later, Charlotte came to get us guys to join in the dancing. The dancer I was, I happily obliged. I'd wanted to dance with Charlotte for some time now.

I danced to my own beat while remaining somewhat faithful to the drum circle rhythm. I tried to get closer to Charlotte but she kept her distance. She didn't seem all that into her dancing, holding back for some reason. Gus goofed off, doing a silly but stylish Kung Fu kicking and punching dance. Gus was making fun of not only himself but the drum circle, which he felt was pretentious. It was, in a way. It was forced, put on, not authentic, as if the people were dancing all "crazy" because that was how they thought they should be.

I picked up on this, too, but neither Gus nor I said anything. The Minnesota lass, Charlotte, was still enamored with the idea of Venice Beach. We didn't want to burst her bubble. Charlotte turned to Sharon, who was still on his back on the sand, watching everyone. She tried to get him to dance but he wouldn't. I then noticed her look at Sharon differently, as if something about how he was in that moment perked her interest. I became jealous again, got tired of dancing, and walked away.

Gus joined me at the shore, complaining about the drum circle, all the people there, then proceeded to light a cigarette. He noticed I was somewhere else, and asked if I wanted to leave. I replied that I was looking forward to smoking pot with Charlotte.

Not too much later, Gus, Sharon, Charlotte, and I did indeed meet up with Charlotte's girlfriend, Ali, and smoked pot. Things were pretty loose and care-free at the commune. When we all hung out outside in the courtyard area at a table, no one seemed to mind the pot-smoking. Gus, who tried to turn his back on all illegal drugs, even pot, denied the weed, saying it made him paranoid.

As we settled at the table, ordered a pizza, drank more beer, and everyone but Gus smoked pot, we had fun through our conversations. Sharon, though, was almost completely silent. He seemed a little intimidated by Gus, and now, Ali. Ali and Gus were the big talkers, joking around, talking about tagging, music, New York, Los Angeles, and more. They seemed to hit it off, not sexually but personally, while Charlotte and I would occasionally contribute.

While Gus and Ali joked and talked, Gus sat next to Sharon on one side of the table while on the other side was Ali, Charlotte, and myself. Charlotte was in between me and Ali, her back to her girlfriend as Ali massaged her back, hips, ass, and shoulders. I had my legs straddling the bench while facing Charlotte. She leaned forward towards me, her knees up to her chest and her face looking down, lost in thought. The way I had my legs open, I almost felt Charlotte was eyeing my cock. She wasn't that far from my crotch.

As I looked at Charlotte, with Ali behind her, I put a fantasy into my head: Charlotte going down on me while Ali screwed Charlotte doggystyle with a strap-on dildo. Wouldn't that be just great, I thought to myself as I got a hard on. I wondered if Charlotte could see my erection through my pants. Sharon was tense, seeing the physical intimacy between me and Charlotte, Charlotte and Ali, and also not being able to break into Ali and Gus' chat.

Gus, Sharon, and I got up to leave a couple hours later, saying our goodbyes to the lesbian couple. Ali promised Gus she'd hang out some time, and that she wanted to play b-ball next time with us all. Charlotte came to say goodnight to me, and for whatever reason gave me the longest, warmest, tightest hug out of the three guys. I loved it and moaned. Charlotte moaned with me, then said she'd see me at the office tomorrow.

The following week, I got more involved in the pre-production of my film. I still wasn't done with the fourth draft of the script, but it was getting more and more polished, enough to figure out casting, locations, equipment and other logistical needs. If I wasn't working on the script or production notes, I was on the phone, calling people who responded to my ads for cast and crew.

One day, though, I started the letter to my representative Weinckoff in retaliation to the happy card I got in the mail. Gus was sitting on his thin sleeping mat in the closet near the bathroom, smoking, flipping through the LA Weekly, bored. He glanced at me, as I was caught up in writing my letter, while sitting on the futon mattress in the living room. Gus would get irritated with my inward isolation at times, when I seemed "too mental," too "in my head."

"You been working hard on your movie." Gus put out, hoping to engage me a little bit.

"Actually I'm doing a letter to my representative."

"Oh yeah? Your rep in congress?"

"Yup. His name's Weinckoff." I replied as I continued to write.

"What's it about? A letter of protest?" Gus replied condescendingly, slightly annoyed with me, as well. I seemed not wanting to be disturbed. And I was writing something political – 'wasting my time'.

"In a way."

"Is it about Iraq?"

"Not really. I include it but that's not the main focus."

"What is?"

"Human beings."

"That's a pretty big subject. Kinda massive to tackle in a letter to your representative that only his secretary is gonna read, if that."

"Hopefully he'll read it and if not, then someone else."

"And if not, his trash can will."

"It'll be his loss then."

"So what're the specifics in your letter on human beings?"

"Well ..." I said, gathering my thoughts, putting the notepad and pen down. "I got a letter with some silly card from the guy – or his office – a while back, and it pissed me off. I wanted to respond."

"What got you so angry?" Gus said, condescending again.

"You probably wouldn't be interested. It has to do with politics." I responded defensively.

"I see. It's above me."

"I don't think it is."

"Tell me already."

"So representative Weinckoff sent me this card about how strong he is on defense, how much he supports Bush on the War on Terror, the invasion of Iraq, and so on. Then the letter goes into how disturbed he was by Internet porn when his daughter could get into these sleazy websites, and how he plans to wage a war on pornography. He called pornography a social terrorism and said people who deal in pornography are terrorists in that way."

"Maybe they are." Gus said simply.

"Sure." I replied dismissively.

"How do you know? Maybe the guy's onto something."

"What? Stupidity?"

"He's just doing his job. And he's a family man."

"Doing his job? He's not doing his job. He's my representative and he's not doing that."

"What?"

"Representing."

"But he's representing the majority of the people in his district. You're one of many, dude."

"He's not doing that, either."

"Most people aren't like you, Tom."

"Everybody's the same."

"People are paranoid about terrorism, and parents are paranoid about pornography. He's doing his fucking job."

"What do you think're the most important things to people? Love? Relationships? Finding out who they are? Their emotional life? How to deal with the existence they're in? How to deal with their human condition? What's the complexity to their natures and how to better understand that?"

"Those are important and your rep thinks so, too."

"No, he doesn't, and you know he doesn't. You know he's full of shit."

"I don't know the guy."

"Look ... you being a Cassavetes fan -"

"I'm not a fan."

"Stop jerking me around." I said, laughing, frustrated.

"I'm not jerking you around." Gus answered seriously.

"Okay then. Cassavetes is one of your favorite human beings, let alone artists -"

"Yeah, he is. What's your point? He definitely wouldn't be wasting his time writing a letter to a politician."

"Why do we like Cassavetes? Because he confronted people's insecurities and took the time and energy to put it on the screen. Like all true existentialists, he -"

"Don't say that. Those're fightin' words. He wasn't no fucking existentialist!"

"Whatever you want to call him, he understood life was short, and the only real certainty any of us have is this life we're living is worth it. We can't waste it by not confronting it. Life's too precious and torturous to ignore it. Cassavetes did it by throwing himself into emotions, into relationships with people, into fun, play, humor, pragmatism, all that. Some people, I'll just call them existentialists for lack of a better word, do a different kind of confrontation with life, but they're still confronting it head on like Cassavetes did."

"Probably not the people you're thinking of, but okay, keep going."

"And when my representative is telling me what he thinks are the world's greatest concerns, I think he's full of shit. He's running away from his own insecurities, his own troubles, his own doubts, his own failings as an individual and of our society, and focusing – like everyone does – on the War on Terror, the War on pornography, the Stock Market, the Weapons Industry, and so on. What he's basically doing, and what all politicians, the media, and everyone else in authority, and all of us as 'citizens' are complicit in, is distracting the attention away from the important thing: us. A true representative would represent our complicated emotions, our troubled minds and make sure -"

"That's where you lost me. 'Troubled minds' isn't important."

"You can't disconnect yourself from your brain."

"But you can disconnect from your feelings by focusing on your intellect, and the intellect is bullshit. It's just mental masturbation."

"That's where I part from you and Cassavetes. There's nothing wrong with being intellectual and as much as you deny it, you have an intellectual side to you, too."

"If I do, that's the bad side."

"Alright. Anyway, what a representative should put first and foremost on his or her agenda is the human side of things – the emotions or the intellect. Put that on the table and discuss that. A representative should be challenging his people, make them question things, look at themselves, doubt, search ... he should be pushing for a more personal and philosophical way of life. He should be a true leader."

"Maybe he is."

"Now you're just being a troublemaker."

"Tom, you're talking about a politician. It's not their responsibility to do what you're saying, and it's never gonna happen anyway."

"It will if people want it to. If they don't, it won't. Society will continue being about money, about buying things, about possessions, homes, cars, the latest cell-phone, the latest computer, the latest gadget. It'll continue being about social status, ambition, power, fitting into your own little secure corner. It'll continue being about security: being secure from the Devil (making everyone run to Church, Temple, or a Mosque); from terrorists (making everyone run to their governments); from pornography, from being ugly; from whatever. People will continue being safe, boring, ignorant, and enormously destructive in the end."

"If you want to change things, do it as an artist. Politics has always been bullshit and always will be."

"I am doing it as an artist, thats what I'm trying to do with my film. But an artist can only do so much. We still have to play the game because of the context we're in. We have to try to change the context, too."

"And how do we do that?"

"Doing what I'm doing – talking about it, asking for it, 'planting seeds' into people's heads as much as a nobody like me can. Put the human being first, put life itself first, discuss that - "

"A person can do that now, whether or not the 'correct context' is there or not."

"To a degree. But you have to force money and security to take a backseat. Making money, having security has to be a means to another end and not a thing in itself. Money and security has to provide the context of luxury for having the time, space, and energy to be asking the personal and philosophical questions. You know as well as me that there are millions of questions that need to be looked at."

"Tell me some."

"The structure of family, the dynamics of friendship, sex, romance, identities, monogamy, work -"

"Monogamy is a fucking shrine, man."

"So no questioning on that one for you." I said with a sarcastic smile.

"That's fucking right."

"Alright then. Maybe we should just stop there."

I smiled in frustration and amusement as I went back to writing the letter. Gus hated my "snickering" look, put out his cigarette and got up.

"Monogamy's the last vestige of human hope we have." Gus said before going into the bathroom and slamming the door behind him.

For all our shared qualities and views, we had just as many differences. We both despised consumerism, capitalism, corporations, the corporate mentality, 9 to 5 jobs, Hollywood, Hollywood movies, the Hollywood mentality, anything hip, cool, "in", popular, hipsters, the hipster mentality. We even both agreed on what I was just talking about – that the life of the human spirit, people's emotions, insecurities, dreams and desires should take priority over concerns about making money, buying things, war, and security.

But where we diverged was the expression of the human spirit. Gus tended towards a conservative outlook, a looking back, honoring old social values, while emotionally being wild and unconventional. True feeling, true dynamic emotion, was to be in the realm of social norms of the past, things like monogamy, family, marriage, and so on. They were to be held onto, not for the sake of the institutional ideas themselves but that somehow there was an emotional purity by not letting them go.

I felt similar to Gus in that most progressive people challenged or ignored the old ideas as acts of coping out. A lot of liberals thought that by simply turning their backs on conventional ideas like family, monogamy, marriage, religion, patriotism, heterosexuality and other things, it was enough to have a dynamic human spirit. No more emotional nor intellectual work had to be done. One could stop feeling and questioning, since one was already in the "aware" boat. Anyone who believed in the old stuff was simply in the wrong boat.

I broke from Gus by believing that the old social norms got in the way of the human spirit, even if a person was as emotionally dynamic or expressive as Gus or, even, Cassavetes. The old ideas held an individual back from seeing freshness in the new forms. By holding so firm to monogamy, someone like Gus would have to ignore the possibilities of day to day reality. Even when someone was involved in an intense, compatible, electrifying relationship, there was always the situation of having that with someone else – at the same time. And there was nothing wrong with that.

A lot of our diverse views, on monogamy especially, came out of personal reasons, particularly in our fathers. Gus' dad was sleeping around all the time, living the '70's hedonistic lifestyle to a hilt. My dad also didn't stay in a monogamous relationship in the '70's. The difference was that my father was emotionally present with every woman he was with, and cared intensely for me as his son. Gus' dad, through his actions, was indifferent, cold, not very involved in both his relations with Gus or women.

Gus and I got along primarily as creative, compassionate, emotional, and alienated people. We were both outsiders, as was Bernardo. However different Gus and I were, in our politics, philosophy, social values, backgrounds, and demeanors, we were great friends in our interests.

I shared a lot of the pre-production process with Gus, especially the casting. We both joked about the 300 to 400 head shots with resumes I got in the mail, all the Brad Pitt, Matt Damon, Tom Cruise look-a-likes. The first actor to grab my attention, though, was not any of the young guys, but an older actor to play Jack Henry. I showed the head shot to Gus and asked him what he thought. Gus said the guy looked like a cross between Eddie Albert and Boris Karloff.

There was something there, though, Gus said, and maybe I should contact him. I asked if Gus could help by reading with the actor and possibly, in the future, other actors. I would video tape a scene, give them direction, then watch the footage. Gus agreed to help out, so I called the older actor to set up a time to meet.

Gus and I met the actor at a Subway in a strip mall on Olympic and Crescent Heights. I hated the location but had to meet there because it was close to where the actor lived. Immediately, I knew something was wrong. The actor looked nothing like his head shot. There was much less darkness, less wear and tear in the guy. In person, he looked more middle-aged, quainter, and less rough, more squeaky, chirpy, as if he'd just come out of an aerobics class before taking the dog for a walk.

Defensively, the older actor said he was hoping to get a new head shot soon. When we got into the reading and acting out of the scenes, the actor couldn't go two minutes before interrupting, asking questions and making statements such as, "... I don't get this." "This is uncomfortable for to say." "Do I have to say that? I don't like to swear, even once or twice." "I'm a writer normally, not an actor that much." "I don't understand this."

It was a headache and he wouldn't be the final casting headache. Gus got into the scenes pretty well, better than the older actor, by far, of course. Gus was good at reading scenes. After the audition was over, I realized something. Why not cast Gus as one of the brothers? Not only did Gus read so well, but I thought it'd be better to have someone like him acting with the others. He could help create the Cassavetes atmosphere I was going for since he saw acting in the same way. If I had to explain things to the actors, having him there with me would make it easier.

Since Gus' car wasn't working, the brakes almost gone, the starter not always working, the power-steering not functioning 100%, etc., etc. - I drove Gus around to places in town he needed to, if taking the bus was too much of a hassle. A lot of times we worked it out if Gus had to be somewhere - usually giving blood or trying to contact a director he was a driver for in the past - we'd meet actors and do a reading, with me videotaping.

Other times I met with the actors by myself. By the end, I auditioned close to thirty actors, most of them disappointing. The three professional actors I got from the auditioning process were chosen not so much because they were so great, but because they were at least more interesting than all the others.

Once I settled on the cast, I wanted everyone to meet, have pizza and beer at Damiano's – a pizza joint on Fairfax and Beverly. I decided to have Bernardo and Charlotte in the cast, as well. Gus and I picked up Bernardo first at his mom's house in Santa Monica, then the three of us went to the C.W.F.P.S.J.-Now! office and got Charlotte. She was just finishing a meeting with Cassandra and Siango before coming outside.

Sharon was coming and going from the van to the office, not acting very friendly to me, Gus, or Bernardo as we waited outside. I thought maybe Sharon was upset he wasn't chosen to act in the movie, even though I hadn't promised him anything, and only mentioned it once. More likely, it was the fact Charlotte was going with me and the other guys while he wasn't. I noticed Sharon was giving Charlotte more attention at the office recently Soon, Charlotte came outside and jumped into the backseat of my car, sitting next to Bernardo.

"What do you think of Sharon, Tom?" Charlotte asked in her sweet, friendly, maybe overly friendly, tone of voice. There was something vague about her question, and she didn't follow up with more of an explanation. It seemed as if she was testing.

"Well, you seem to know him better than I do these days." I said with a sarcastic smile.

"You are the best person to answer that question, Charlotte." Gus shot out to her, as well. There'd been a few parties where Gus could see the new intimacy between Charlotte and Sharon, and, like me, felt not only jealous but that she could choose better. Like one of us.

"Alright, no worries, fellas. Just askin'." she responded, still bubbly and cute, not showing any signs of being hurt by our sarcasm. Perhaps she knew we'd react that way. Her question was, after all, out of the blue.

At Damiano's, the first actor waited outside, meeting me, Gus, Bernardo, and Charlotte. He was a decent enough fellow before, a little awkward and shy. But now he didn't seem all that happy to see me and the others. As we walked into the restaurant and to a booth, I realized I made a mistake – the place was extremely dark inside. It was lit so low it was hard to see other people's faces even.

Everyone was quiet and reserved, put off by the darkness and the first actor's isolation. My nerves kicked in, not helping to break the ice with everyone. As the other two actors showed up – the older, ex-Vietnam vet, gruff, but funny guy to play Jack Henry, and the guy to play the youngest brother – things didn't improve. I continued to be nervous and stiff.

The older guy tried to break the ice with dirty jokes, which made everyone laugh a little, except Charlotte. She got offended and left the table, saying she had to make a phone call. There was too much testosterone, and one strange, dirty, old man for her. She wanted me to come outside with her but I refused, not wanting to abandon the others.

Perhaps I felt I didn't want to show the others – all men – Charlotte had that much sway over me. Of course, a simple act like that – and many more, over time – would've swayed Charlotte to consider me as a boyfriend. Things like that, putting her first before anyone else, turned her on. But for all of my attraction to Charlotte, at this point in our friendship my desire was much more tame than it came to be later.

When Charlotte came back to the table, she made sure to stay on my side, towards the edge, as opposed to before when she was in-between bad breath Bernardo and the dirty old man. Then to my and the other guys surprise, Charlotte comfortably nestled her head into my lap, curling up like a little girl, bringing her knees to her chest. It almost seemed to me she liked to put her head close to my crotch ...

It was another out of the blue act of Charlotte's, which made everyone unsettled. I loved feeling Charlotte's warm body on me as she moaned quietly a bit to show her comfort being like that. I put my hand on her waist, which she approved by holding my hand. It must've looked like to the others at the table Charlotte and I were lovers. I didn't exactly know what to make of it, but was casual and acted as if nothing was unusual.

It did, though, strike a tenderness into my heart. I wished I could be like that with her all the time. It was heaven, the sweet warmth of it. Was she telling me she was attracted to me by doing that? Or was it a move of friendliness and trust in me? Or a way of bringing attention to her, and making the other guys jealous? Or maybe, she did it as way to show her support for me, in opposition to everyone else's complete lack of enthusiasm. Perhaps all four or none.

The vibe of the pizza meeting didn't improve unfortunately. Even the old man got a little closed off and stopped telling jokes and stories.

Gus was the most shut off out of everyone, putting the hood of the sweater over his head. He didn't say one word the whole time, as if he was embarrassed to be there. I should've called Gus out on his "New York, hooded, streetwise, I'm more real than anyone else here" posturing, but I didn't. I was still too nervous, and acted as if I owed everyone there something.

I made some attempts at loosening things up, asking each of them what they wanted to get out of not only this movie but their careers. All the guys gave short, one or two sentence long, clammed up answers. Charlotte was the most enthusiastic, saying that if she could become famous through acting, she'd use her name recognition to influence people's thinking on social and world issues. She said it in her bubbly, corny way but it was sincere and honest. It was more honorable than what all the guys had to say because she wasn't trying to be cool like they were.

I just couldn't ease things up. There didn't seem to be any chemistry going on. As I went into discussing the next steps for the production, I got a sunken, disappointed feeling in my gut. I lost confidence in myself as a director and was not only disappointed in the professional actors, but my own friends. Gus and Bernardo were like lumps of wood. Out of everyone – my buddies – they were the least enthusiastic, especially Gus.

Gus' sense of creative and personal superiority over me had been in our friendship since the beginning. As I got older and we got to know each other better, Gus gave me more respect, but the underlying feeling of superiority was still there. It was a relatively common dynamic in my friendships, unfortunately. Other friends besides Gus, in the past, were similar in their attitude towards me. Not that I was completely dissed all the time by friends, including Gus, but the undertone was there. It would express itself in moments like the cast meeting at Damiano's.

After the relative disaster with the male actors (yet beautiful tender moment with Charlotte) at Damiano's, I took Charlotte back to the C.W.F.P.S.J office. Sharon was waiting to give her a ride home. Gus and Bernardo wanted to go out for a beer, and since I rarely turned down alcohol, the three of us went to a bar near Bernardo's house on Pico and 28th.

Most of what Gus and Bernardo wanted to talk about wasn't my first feature length movie we were all about to embark on, the characters they were going to play, the story, the ideas, etc. That didn't seem important. The main focus was Charlotte. Was she still a lesbian? Was she going out with Sharon? Was there something going on between her and me? Bernardo said she wasn't all that special, really, that there were a million other girls out there exactly like Charlotte. She also reminded him of a lot of women I got into relationships with (Maya, my first girlfriend, other women): controlling.

Gus described how he'd have sex with Charlotte, talk dirty to her, spank her, grab her ass, have anal sex, do her with her girlfriend Ali in a three way and so on. It made me and Bernardo laugh as we continued drinking beers, playing pool, and joking around. Inside, though, I was empty and frustrated. I could tell my friends didn't take me or my film seriously. Was it because the script was bad? Was it because I didn't seem to know what I was doing? Did I rub them the wrong way? Was I acting arrogant or dismissive of them? Were they jealous of the fact I was making a movie and they weren't? Or jealous of Charlotte possibly liking me and not them?

The first actor to drop out was the old man. He called the night of the first all-cast read-through, and left a message on my answering machine. He said he just didn't feel it. The old man had complained about my script, that the dialogue was too monologue-driven, there wasn't enough quick back and forth banter between the characters. I admitted he was right, and that the dialogue needed to improve. But the script was to be used only as a springboard, a skeletal outline to provide structure. In the month of rehearsals and while shooting the film, there would be intensive rewrites coming from improvisations. That kind of process wasn't okay with the old man. He needed a script that was set in stone and a director that wouldn't call upon him to contribute with dialogue or ideas.

The other two actors had the same concerns but stayed for the first read-through. Because the old man had given such a late notice, I had to find a replacement fast. So I called my step-father Frazier, who agreed and showed up at Bernardo's mom's house. Bernardo said it'd be okay to use the dinning room for the read-through. Everyone showed up, except for Charlotte. She finally called me and said she was on her way. She'd been caught up with something in Westwood with her girlfriend.

I chastised her a bit on the phone and she felt bad for leaving everyone hanging. When I got off the phone, Gus and Bernardo semi-jokingly chastised me. Besides the fact they didn't want Charlotte to leave the production, they also were right in knowing Charlotte needed her director to be as supportive as possible, surrounded by an all-male cast. And they saw me as having a chance to hook up with her some day. I was stubborn, though. My main priority, for better or for worse, was the film.

Soon, Charlotte arrived humbly, apologetically, with the smell of pot on her breath. I could tell when she gave me a hug. The brightness of the dining room helped, along with scripts in front of everyone, as opposed to the darkness of the pizza joint. I soon got everyone started with the reading, each actor for their part, with myself reading the narrative and description. Of course, there was beer on the table, which only me, Gus, Bernardo, and the younger actor partook of. The guy playing the oldest brother seemed offended.

Not too long after beginning, I stopped the reading to critique the older brother actor and Frazier, both for hamming it up too much. I wanted a cold reading, wherein any emotions would come out through the text, once the actors got caught up in the story. I didn't like that they tried to impose emotions on the words, two or three lines into the reading. Frazier was humble about it and responded accordingly. The older brother actor was much more uncomfortable, becoming defensive and uptight. I explained that he didn't have to worry, this was just the first reading, not even a rehearsal. Only several minutes after getting back to the script, the actor interrupted mysteriously, saying he got a phone call.

While the actor was in another room on his cell phone, everyone else waited in the dining room, some using the bathroom, some drinking, some chatting, and, of course, Gus smoked a cigarette outside. When the actor came back, he told me he had to leave because of an emergency. His acting was much better here. The guy just wanted to get the hell out.

Once the guy was gone, I read his part and we proceeded with the reading. I was happy with Gus and Charlotte, liking the chemistry between them, while I was most disappointed in Bernardo, who put close to no interest in the reading, or at least appeared that way. The youngest actor was okay, but not as good as on his audition, and Frazier was just getting used to the script.

When the reading was done, I came up to Charlotte and Gus to give them encouragement. The two shrugged it off, for different reasons. One, for both of them, the last scene between their characters was bitter and the taste was still there. The other reason for the sourness was Gus was ticked off at Charlotte. She didn't respond to him the way he wanted. For Charlotte, she just wanted to get out of there, and go to a party she promised someone from the office she'd go to.

She asked me to take her and so I obliged, asking if it was okay if Gus and Bernardo came. I wanted to be loyal to my friends, and I didn't think Charlotte was interested in me anyway, so why go alone with her? At the party near Sepulveda and National, we went first to get our drinks. There was a group of rowdy young people in the backyard, cut off from the C.W.F.P.S.J people. The peace activists were distinctly alienated by the rowdy, college football group. How did these two crowds merge into one party? Someone must've known both. Gus and Bernardo stayed with the rowdy crowd, while I went back and forth between my C.W.F.P.S.J co-workers and Gus and Bernardo.

A couple weeks before rehearsals were starting, Charlotte told me she had to go up north. The Berkeley office needed her help for a month, so she couldn't be in the movie until she came back. Kristianna had to leave soon after the scheduled shoot, so she wouldn't be available if I bumped the shoot a month later. It was either Kristianna or Charlotte. I chose my cinematographer.

The news bummed Gus, Bernardo, and the younger actor. Gus wasn't all that interested in working with Frazier, who he felt was a dud at the actors workshop we did downtown. He also wasn't too hot about the script. The script ... the script ... the thorn in my side.

"You know what you should, Tom?" Gus said to me at his apartment, as he cooked pasta and spaghetti sauce. I was sitting on the floor, the script in front of me, other papers, as well. I was flustered.

"What's that?" I asked.

"Wait for Charlotte to come back."

"I can't do that."

"'Cause of your cinematographer?"

"Yup."

"Alright ... so who's gonna replace Charlotte?"

"I was thinking of Maya."

"None of the original black girls you interviewed?"

"None of them were right."

"I don't see any chemistry with me and Maya, if she's supposed to be my character's girlfriend. Maybe you should play Colin's part."

"I don't want to act in the film. All my attention should be on directing. ... Look, if you have a problem with the script, the part, the cast dynamic, you know I've told you everything's going to get fleshed out in rehearsals. I wanted to fine-tune only after I knew who was in the final cast."

"You can't fine-tune something that needs a lot of work to start with."

“What exactly do you have a problem with in the script again? Specifically?” I said with frustration, turning my attention away from Gus, to the script and other papers.

“Oh, I see how it is.” Gus said indignantly as he lit a cigarette. He hated how I would get 'dismissive' and act as if Gus 'wasn't important.'

“How is what?”

“You're playing the cool, detached director. Mr. In-Control, keeping me at bay, at a distance ...”

“What're you talking about?”

“You don't want your hands getting dirty, so you're tuning me out. Nice.”

“I'm tuned into you. See? Channel Gus.”

“No, you're not. You're lost in your fucking head again, stuck in these concepts you have about your story. The movie's happening right now but you're not interested in participating. Pay attention and you'll see where the real magic'll happen for your film.”

“This has nothing to do with the film. We can make another movie some day, about you and me, but that's another story.”

“This has everything to do with your 'Loveincrazy' movie. You're acting in it right now.”

“I'm not acting in it, Gus.”

“You better be if you want a good movie. You'll have to be acting with us from behind the camera.”

“Okay, fine, but save this energy for rehearsal.”

“You're not doing any fucking rehearsal until you're ready and you're not ready now.”

“Maybe I should go take those acting classes with that one guy you liked. What was his name?”

“Being a smart ass isn't gonna help you.”

“Why don't you tell me more specifically what's wrong with the script and with what I'm doing.”

“You're not playful enough. You're too stiff.”

“I'm not in a playful mood right now.”

“Alright, man. You want specifics? I'll give you specifics. I don't like my character. He's a schmuck and a jerk and all he says are cynical, snide remarks. His girlfriend's a dummy and has nothing interesting to say. You've got all the characters talking in monologues like it was a Eugene O'Neil play, and each character is a representation of intellectual ideas you have about society. The oldest brother is a repressed, lonely religious guy; my character's a cynical, smart ass business man; the third brother's a moody musician; the youngest brother is a naive, idealistic self-righteous snob; and the father is a cold, detached, insensitive, rich patriarch.”

“Sounds like a good film.” I said with a sarcastic smile.

“It's not, dude, and don't fucking snicker at me like that.”

“Look, I know what you're talking about and I'm open to making some changes. We can work things out but I can't change the whole thing.”

“Dismissive, again.”

“I'm not! What do you want me to do?” I said with a flabbergasted laugh.

“Hey, I know. How about ...” Gus said as he finished cooking the noodles and sauce and made a plate for himself. “You want some of this?”

"No, it's okay."

"You sure? It's fine cooking. My grandfather showed me how to do it."

"Okay, a little bit." I said, getting up and taking the plate Gus made for me. "So what's this idea you were about to say?"

"I don't think you'll like it."

"Just tell me."

Gus went into his idea for my film, detail after detail in a fairly grandiose performance at his apartment. There was something captivating about the way he described the concept, and I wished I had a camera to capture it. Gus "bugged" out, exactly what he wanted to do, in hopes of getting me to do the same, and stay that way while making the film.

But for however captivating Gus' apartment performance was, it was so fantastical and imaginative that it was also completely unrealistic and un-filmmable. The idea involved me playing the director both behind the camera and in front, wherein I'd say something to one of the actors, whisper in their ear without them noticing, or shout at them. Not only that but I was supposed to be a ghost. Perhaps the idea wasn't un-filmmable, but it certainly had nothing to do with "Loveincrazy."

Once Gus finished his creative proposal, he could tell I didn't think too highly of it. I tried to be nice, but eventually Gus gave up. I wondered if Gus really wanted to be in the movie from the beginning.

"You don't want to be in the film, do you?" I finally asked.

"Um ..." Gus said with some condescending relief and embarrassed smile at the same time. "... could you tell?"

"It's too bad but I guess it's not working out for you, is it?" I said with a sarcastic smile, hiding my feeling of rejection. "I don't think you can act in other people's films. You have to direct, as well."

"I don't know about that ... maybe if you were paying me big bucks I'd consider it." Gus said jokingly but with a hint of bitterness. If only I could bug out the way he wanted, Gus felt, he could work with me. Maybe.

"Not going to happen." I replied. "You were mainly doing your friend Tom a favor."

"Now you're making me feel guilty."

"Just telling you the truth."

"We still friends?"

"I guess." I joked.

"You guess?"

"This film does mean a lot to me, Gus."

"Well ... guess it needs to be made ... your way. It is your film."

Gus did care about me as a friend, but just could never see me as an equal, creatively speaking. He felt I was just too inhibited, too serious, too mental. He thought I couldn't bug out, let loose properly, so there wasn't enough chemistry between us. I moved on and finished the film. The cast, story, and everything else ended up being vastly different from when Gus was a part of it.

CHAPTER THREE.

THE ROMANTIC OUTSIDERS.

While I was making "Loveincrazy," Gus ran into his ex-girlfriend at an art store in Hollywood on La Brea. He hadn't seen her in years and she was there with her mom, looking for art equipment. Gus was just walking down the street as the attractive brunette and her mother came out of the store. A rushing spark of love came inside Gus the second he saw Angela. She looked so good and even her mother did, too.

Angela was several years younger than Gus, meeting him when she was still a senior in high school. Of course they didn't meet at school but at a coffee shop Gus worked at. He befriended a lot of the high schoolers who came into the Santa Monica cafe. Angela was one of them, after he came to her defense when another older guy was hitting on her.

Seven years later and Angela's beauty didn't diminish. It actually became fuller, blossoming into mid-twenties womanhood, probably at the peak of her physical sex appeal. This drove Gus nuts instantly, but he played the part of polite ex-boyfriend well. Angela's mother was there after all and even though she liked him, she didn't like the idea of her daughter getting reunited. When Angela broke up with Gus, it sent him down an emotional breakdown, leading him to completely snap. Angela's mom had Gus sent to a mental institution, where he stayed for about 4 months.

But Gus convinced Angela to give him her number right there on La Brea. Of course he called her, leaving a message on her answering machine. He was hoping to get Angela live but knew that was a thin chance. Gus also knew there was a thin chance she'd call back. But she did. She left a short, conflicted message, which Gus played over and over again.

One day when I was having lunch with my dad, Jean, Gus played the message for us. Angela was relatively happy initially, but obviously had reservations about hanging out. Gus wanted to see if either Jean or I could detect interest on her part.

I couldn't tell. She seemed to change her tone back and forth before hanging up. Jean, despite Gus' past arguments with him, reached out in an earnest, compassionate way. Jean asked question after question to find out Gus and his ex's history, what happened, what went wrong, what were the good things, the bad, how he – Gus – changed. Gus appreciated Jean's interest, but was at a remove. It seemed strange to me. Gus was the one who put his personal life on the table for us and wanted our feedback. So, that's what we did. It was odd for him to get defensive.

Perhaps it was because Jean's approach was more psychological and not "emotional." But Jean was trying to get at the truth of the situation, which required knowing about the past. Gus believed one didn't need to know about the past to find the truth. He certainly felt this way when playing the message for me and Jean.

The next day, Gus declared to me at the apartment that whether or not she wanted to get back with him, he was going to do everything in his powers to win Angela back. I asked how he was going to do it and Gus' replied it was meant to happen. He and Angela were meant for each other. Now I could tell whatever inkling Gus had towards seducing Charlotte went out the window. I wasn't sure if I really liked Charlotte in that way yet, but now with Gus not being interested, it made it easier. I didn't want what happened with me and Bernardo (in regards to Chaos) to happen with me and Gus over Charlotte.

Gus called Angela back, of course, and just as likely, she didn't call him in return this time. Gus pined and pined, smoked and smoked, days and weeks went by. He told me it was probably her mother who convinced her not to get involved, or her shrink. According to Gus, Angela was heavily into psycho-therapy. Any description of her relationship with Gus would've been a big "STAY AWAY" to her psychiatrist.

The only outlet for Gus' obsession was to write a screenplay about it. His magnum opus, called simply, "A Boy and a Girl." Gus quickly started the script, writing on a notepad feverishly. He shared the beginning of a previous script with me a year before about the madcap adventures of a British exhibitionist and fake stunt artist. It was based on the director Gus worked for and who emotionally tortured the already tortured Gus. The story was an interesting, sometimes hilarious send-up of the insecure but outrageous filmmaker, who's career was close to if not ruined by his shenanigans. The script was funny but lacked heart and Gus knew it.

From the first twenty pages of "A Boy and a Girl," almost all dialogue, I could tell this was Gus' masterpiece. As much as I might've been inclined to criticize because of Gus' bailing on "Loveincrazy," I couldn't do much of that. Gus had a tendency to be too cute with dialogue, but other than that it was great. There was a lot of depth, insight, and humor in not only the character based on himself, but on Angela's character, and others as well. Gus kept going and going, with a sense of purpose I never saw in him before. Gus remarked a lot of it was being inspired by me doing my movie.

Gus went over and over his relationship and past experiences with Angela to me. In time, I began having admiration for what the two went through as a couple. Whatever things I disagreed with Gus on – Gus' jealousy and possessiveness, the sometimes overly cute banter between them – what I connected on was the purity of the relationship. Both Gus and Angela were searching with all their hearts to make it work. Their relationship was rarely pretentious nor guarded or predictable.

As it often happened, I was subconsciously influenced by my older friend. I looked up to Gus, whether I wanted to admit it or not at the time. Not too long after Gus' obsession with Angela came back to his life, I began to get closer and closer to Charlotte. A month after Gus' love rejuvenated, I fell madly in love with my feminist co-worker. The passion and/or obsession I felt for Charlotte wasn't that different from Gus' for Angela, except, of course, the dynamics were different and so were the expectations. Gus expected to re-unite with Angela while I expected nothing from Charlotte. Gus had a romantic history with Angela, I didn't with Charlotte, so both our expectations were realistic ... relatively.

What was it about Gus which I admired? Most people who knew him had a certain amount of admiration for his spirit, but mostly what he got was bewilderment, ridicule, competition, disgust, lack of trust, or outright resentment. Gus was not a great Leader of men. But I saw something in Gus – similar to what Prince Hall saw in Falstaff – a charming, large, older, humane wit to gravitate to. Gus even joked a few times he was Falstaff to my Prince Hal, and that some day I would turn my back on him in the same way …

Another thing I admired in Gus was his love for Angela. As with everyone, I had an urgent need to feel life. But since there were so few outlets to feel deeply in society, most people turned it off and directed that energy into work, religion, acquiring possessions, social status, doing yoga, studying astrology, or doing other varieties of closed off expression. People needed to find a wall to hide behind the fact they were human. Whatever lunacy, misguidedness, and illusory passion Gus had for Angela, the feelings he had were intense. I knew I, too, needed an outlet. At the time, Charlotte was the object for me.

When I came to Gus' apartment, telling him about my new found love for Charlotte, he wasn't too sure. I'd told him about tons of other girls before, then quickly got over my infatuations. Was this the same? I said it wasn't, since I waited about six weeks and the desire became more intense, not less.

Since Gus didn't respect Sharon, my lust for a taken woman didn't bother him that much, even though Gus was ardently pro-monogamy. Sharon and Charlotte had been officially boyfriend and girlfriend for a couple months by then. Not only was I Gus' friend, but we all started our attraction to Charlotte around the same time. I was actually the first to know Charlotte, the first to have an attraction to her. It was fair game in Gus' mind.

He still thought I was crazy for writing the love letter to Charlotte and told me so. I laughed it off – at this point. Gus decided to take a break from writing "A Boy and a Girl." Sometimes he felt like completely quitting, even burning the two hundred pages he already wrote. Gus was unfortunately like that and knew it. He was awful at finishing things.

But not this time. I pushed Gus to keep going. The script was brilliant so far. Besides, what else was he going to do? Gus wasn't working, still collecting unemployment from his driving job for the insane British director. He was still obsessed about Angela and couldn't find any feasible solution to get back with her. Why not resolve the whole thing in a script, and better yet, a finished film?

Gus went back to his desperate scriptwriting, this time on a laptop his dad in New York bought for him. His father was now a yuppy Manhattanite, by marrying into it. Gus also had a screenwriting program I put on the computer for him. It was serious now. Sometimes he stayed up all night in a fast-paced, non-stop writing fever, only now and then interacting with anyone from the outside world, including me.

Nights when Gus needed a break, he and I went out and got drunk at one bar or another. The Roost, a couple other bars in Atwater, Chinatown bars, sometimes ones in Silverlake, Los Feliz, Echo Park, and once in a while on the west side, or Hollywood. One night we went to a German beer specializing place in Silverlake. I had a lot on my mind that night. Just a few hours before, I'd been fired by Charlotte at the C.W.F.P.S.J. - Now! office. I had to talk to Gus about it.

When I finally told Gus what happened, after several beers, Gus' first reaction was to laugh. It seemed ridiculous, absurd, and while he sincerely felt bad for me, he was also ridiculing me. Once Gus saw the look on my face, though, guilt stabbed at him. His friend was in pain. Still, it wasn't his pain. Why couldn't Gus empathize more? He wanted to in a way, but couldn't. A strain of compassion conflicted with the detachment, as if there were two people inside him.

"What the hell happened?" Gus asked me as we left the Silverlake German bar, both lighting up cigarettes and walking to my car.

I went into the whole story of what went down at the "firing squad." Gus believed as crazy as the militant feminists were at C.W.F.P.S.J, they'd eventually come around and forgive. He thought if I just apologized and admitted I was wrong, they wouldn't really fire me. Gus knew Charlotte and Cassandra had a gentle side. All they needed to hear was my admission of guilt, that I was a bad man, like all men, then they'd let me back into the family.

I felt Gus could be right, but, in the end, what did I do that was really wrong? I didn't want to admit to doing something wrong if I felt, in my heart, I didn't. I would apologize for harming Charlotte, but that there was no intention to do so by expressing my love for her. I wouldn't admit to being wrong for saying I loved her. Gus said that however I decided to do it, after all this time, I'd been close friends with Charlotte and Cassandra. They wouldn't fire me. Maybe some guy they didn't know as well, but certainly not me.

A week later and I was fired. I was shattered, and Gus was surprised. He felt bad for me and could tell I just wasn't the same. Something had been taken away inside me, extinguished and put out ...

A few weeks later, Gus completed his 280 page screenplay. The last week he stayed up all night almost every day, in a frenzy to finish, revising and revising to the bitter end. When it was all done, he was a proud bird, but unsatisfied. It was still just a script. The need to be with Angela was as strong as before, besides the fact screenwriting was just the beginning. Only the first part of the film was done. Shooting the movie, editing it, promoting it, showing it, all that was still left.

This daunted Gus and a trembling fear came over him. Was the script unfilmmable? 280 pages, of which he wouldn't cut, meaning 280 minutes, four and a half hours! A cast of maybe thirty substantial roles, besides the two leads, and scene after scene of emotionally "on" moments. He'd have to get the cast members in tune with what he was all about, having them "bug out" with focus, every step of the way.

Gus had to climb a mountain, but he felt he could do it. Now he knew why I stripped my film down to the bare essentials. One or two locations, only four characters, and 90 minutes long. I suggested he turn

"A Boy and a Girl" into a novel. It was close to one as it was anyway. But Gus refused to go the literary route. He was an actor, first and far most, then a director to give the actors the time and space to do their thing. Writing was third on the list.

And besides, Gus wanted to cast his ex-girlfriend Angela as herself and himself as, well, himself, eight years before. This script was a love letter. He told me he was going to give the 280 pages to her somehow. He had to think of the best way. Fate seemed to intervene. Gus saw an ad in the LA Weekly for a play about surrealism and Buddhism, co-starring ... Angela. This was his opportunity. Or maybe he shouldn't. Was he becoming a stalker?

I said he should go, approach her about his film, then give her the script. Gus said no, then said yes, then said no, then went into ten other things he'd do. He decided he was going to the play, but didn't know what he'd say if he saw her. An idea hit him. Wear a t-shirt that said, "I Love Angela." He could go to some shop in Hollywood that made personalized shirts like that.

Gus got the shirt made, then at the last second changed his mind. It was too nutty, too stalkerish, too much like how he was before. He wanted to show Angela he changed. He was more mellow now. I drove him to the play at the Odyssey theater and dropped him off, even though I wanted to see her, too. I practically knew her, after all this time.

Afterwards, I picked him up. Gus didn't seem that excited. Once the show was done, he saw Angela and her friends. It was awkward. She was reserved, friendly, but cold and distracted. Her lady friends were chatting with her at the same time. She asked Gus if he thought the play was weird enough for him. There was always competition between them. Gus blurted out he finished a script he was planning to direct. She was half-way interested, then said she had to leave with her lady friends. In the car with me, Gus wondered if she became a lesbian. There were hints of it in their relationship.

Gus became bleak over the next few days, but tried not to show it.

It had to come out, though, and one night it did. He got a little money from a commercial he did in the past, and decided to go to a strip club. All the strippers loved him for those few hours. He tossed bills at them like candy, bought them drinks, and bought himself beer after beer. When the strip club closed, he roamed the streets, not wanting to go home to the loneliness of his apartment. I moved out months before. An hour after leaving the strip club, he found an alley and passed out.

A couple days later, Gus told me about his night out, emphasizing how much the strippers loved him and how he entertained them all with his wit and charm. I was amused and unfortunately didn't see the sadness in it. I still saw Gus as an Adventurer of the Spirit. It was somehow Noble.

Gus decided to call Angela yet again, this time telling her he'd leave a copy of his script at a print shop for her. She didn't call back. Weeks went by and the copy remained there. Gus became irritated, bitter, then left a nasty message on her answering machine. I was still sitting courtside, rooting Gus on, but now felt she definitely wasn't going to do Gus' movie, let alone pick up the manuscript.

Gus felt he needed to switch gears. I was caught up intensely in editing my movie. That helped me – to a degree – in not dwelling on what happened with Charlotte. Perhaps thats what Gus needed to do. He hated being dirt poor and nothing going on. He thought why not write a script with me to sell to a Hollywood studio? Gus knew a couple people that might be able to help.

After a little hesitation, I agreed. Hell, I'd like to make some money, too. But would the same thing happen as it did with Bernardo? It wouldn't even get finished? What was the likelihood of selling the script anyhow? Gus promised it would get finished and would sell. He was certain. We brainstormed ideas for a couple weeks, then landed on a story.

The screenplay was a trite sci-fi story where in the future all men were extinct and the world was run, obviously, by women. We were focused and spent hours and hours, days and days, working on it. The process also helped Gus forget about Angela a little bit. As the weeks went on, and as I was still immersed in my editing, I became annoyed with Gus' intensity. I began to see the collaboration as taking too much time away from my own projects. What guarantees were there we'd sell the script? Not any.

After the editing for "Loveincrazy" was done, I was still obsessed about Charlotte. I wanted to know what happened. Why did she do what she did? Over the phone, a while back, she promised to explain things to me. She never did. So one day I went to the C.W.F.P.S.J office to see her and drop off tapes of my movie.

While working on our script, we drove to the Fatburger in Los Feliz for a break. I told Gus I went to my old job's office to give Charlotte the tape of "Loveincrazy." I mentioned how Charlotte reacted the second she saw me at the top of the stairs, through the window of the front office. She froze, then quickly ran away. I could hear her behind the door yelling in a silly, childish, goofy, but also frightened voice,

"Oh shit, it's Thomas!"

Gus laughed at Charlotte's reaction, and at first, so did I. But then I became serious. I complained about Charlotte's behavior, saying that after everything that happened between her and I, after her firing me, after she told me she wanted to explain everything but never did, after the whole fucking mystery of it, I told Gus I felt it was kinda fucked up for her to do that. She owed me more than an "oh shit, it's Thomas!"

Gus replied, "Can you blame her?" I said, yeah, I could, to which he said, me going there like that was kinda stalkerish anyhow. I was struck low. It was just a comment, but as I weighed in the significance of it, the way he said it, so detached, an unbearable resentment swelled up inside me.

I clammed up completely. I didn't say anything as I continued to drive. After all my support for Gus' desires for Angela, in his strange, stalkerish actions, Gus was calling me a freak? I couldn't take it. We parked the car, went into the Fatburger, and ate lunch, not saying a word to each other for a good fifteen minutes.

Without saying anything, once I finished my burger, the volcano inside blew, and I rushed out the door. When I got into those silent, shut off, dark moods, I was another person, animalistic and strange. And once I was in it, I was in it for a while. I walked as fast as I could, with no direction, no particular place to go, just going, going, going, furiously, letting the anger rush through my pores. I didn't want to say anything to Gus because it might get ugly like it did a few times with Bernardo.

I went up a hill, all the way to the top. I was sweating, breathing heavily, and as I got tired, I began to calm down. I was still pissed at Gus. The whole experience at C.W.F.P.S.J was so demeaning, so humiliating, being made to feel like a creep, a misogynist, a freak. The one person – besides my father Jean – who I expected to understand where I was coming from, was Gus. Gus himself was trying to express something deeply important to Angela, and was probably seen by her as a creep. He should be understanding as hell.

Perhaps I overreacted, I thought, and I knew I could be overly sensitive. Still, I wasn't going to back down. I'd walk back and see what Gus had to say. I saw him standing near my car, coolly smoking his cigarette. The way Gus stood there, no vulnerability, with a tough guy smoker pose, I realized I couldn't count on him too much. For all his declarations of wildness, Gus was, in the end, too self-conscious of other people's opinions for me to see him as a true soul brother.

Despite coming to acknowledge this, I decided to apologize. But I couldn't work on the script with Gus anymore. Forget about it. Once I came close enough, Gus apologized to me, surprisingly. He said he understood how rough it was for me after what happened. I, in turn, apologized for my overreaction. In the car back to Gus' place, though, I explained I couldn't work on the script anymore. I didn't want to work on something that wasn't personal, even if there'd be money involved down the road. There was no mention of being irritated with Gus.

Gus was obviously disappointed. A strong feeling of rejection came blowing through him. He should've expected it, I thought, after bailing on my film. Maybe he even thought I was getting revenge, perhaps.

We continued to hang out as friends, get drunk, go to bars, clubs, parties, strip clubs. Wherever we went, we were always outsiders. We never clicked with any one group, ever. We would interact, for sure, mingle, socialize, but always from the outsider angle. Neither of us identified with anyone. We were both emotional and social perfectionists, absolutists. We just couldn't settle for what other people offered us. Other people were too unsatisfying. But we searched, we looked, hoping to find someone, somewhere, who we could identify with. Especially women, so we'd get laid in the process.

All the years of going out, going out, going out, for both Gus and myself, but especially Gus, was taking its toll one Saturday night. Both of us wanted to go out, but where? No more Atwater, no more Chinatown, no more Echo Park, Silverlake, Los Feliz, Hollywood, West Side, etc. Where then? We decided, fuck it, go somewhere nearby Gus' apartment. They hadn't gone to the Los Feliz bars on Virgil in a while. One place had some tasty barbecue wings, which Gus loved. I didn't, but I also didn't mind going.

The bar with the barbecue wings turned out to be overpriced and a dude ranch. Eventually, though, we were able to snatch a table for ourselves at least. We considered going to a strip club, then opted on staying, drinking beer and, for Gus, eating barbecue wings. It was my treat, as I felt bad for ditching on the script a couple weeks before.

"You know, if the script sells and I make some decent dough off it, I'll give you a chunk." Gus said, eating a wing, then wiping his hands with a napkin.

"You don't need to do that. I dropped out. It's your thing now." I said as I drank my fourth Budweiser. The bar was loud from the music and patrons, lots of testosterone, but we could hear each other well enough.

“The idea and outline came from both of us. You'll get your share.”

“It's okay. Don't worry about it. That kind of thing doesn't matter to me.”

“It'd be the right thing to do.”

“How many guys in here you think are writing scripts like you and I were? You know, either by themselves or with someone else, trying to be the next Matt Damon/Ben Affleck writing duo?”

“I don't know and I don't care ...”

“I heard they didn't even write 'Good Will Hunting', that what's his name, the guy who did 'Clerks' -”

“Kevin Smith. The script sucked anyway.”

“It did but that's besides the point. He apparently shadow-wrote for them or something. Makes you wonder, because they haven't written one more script ever again, either together or solo.”

“They're both schmucks.”

“But it's just crazy because all those young wannabe filmmakers, writers, actors out there who look up to those guys, or celebrities like them, they're all chasing after something that didn't really happen. It was probably a sham.”

“Yup.”

I was trying to remind Gus of the Don Quixote-ish nature of running after making money through screenwriting. There wasn't anything more definite about trying to sell a script than making a personal film as a way to make money. Either way was a crap shoot. Gus wanted nothing of it. To him, selling a Hollywood-style script seemed to offer more possibilities to make hard cash.

A deep sadness festered inside Gus as he was bored with me, the bar, himself, his life, everything. He began feeling hopeless, desperate, and started shaking. I noticed and didn't know what was going on.

"You alright?" I asked.

"It's okay. I need a cigarette." Gus said as he got up and left the bar.

I didn't know if I should follow him or not. A minute went by and I realized I had to. I never saw Gus when he "flipped out," basically lost his emotional stability, becoming almost schizophrenic. But I knew Gus had been that way before. There was something wrong with him right now. I went outside and found him standing by himself, looking off into who knows where, smoking. He turned to me and nervously smiled as he put out his trembling hand.

"The shakes." he said, still politely smiling.

Standing next to Gus, I lit one of my Winchesters, smoking along with him. Neither of us said anything. I had an idea of what was happening to him, that it wasn't exactly the cold air. I remembered times when I was in emotional black holes, emptiness, horror, despair, fright, paranoia, everything ... all bleak and hopeless, pointless ... and it would get so bad I shook and shook and shook, uncontrollably, as if I was an epileptic almost. I could see in Gus this must be what was happening to him. But Gus was holding it back as best he could.

"I hate it when this happens." he said, laughing, trying to control himself. "All I fucking want is some magic ..." he continued by opening up completely now. "And all that ever happens is a big letdown. It's like the only way to make it happen is to go nuts ... be a schizo ... like those people R.D. Laing talked about ..." he said with a laugh. "That way you can chase after your own private magic and not worry about it making sense to anyone because you're crazy and everyone just leaves you alone ... my problem is I worry too much about making sense to people ..."

"You can do and say things the way you want and not be concerned with how they respond, and you don't have to be a schizophrenic ...

Besides, that's a subjective label, anyway, 'being schizo' ..."

"I know, Tom. I was the one who introduced you to R.D. Laing, remember?"

"Right ... and I thank you for it."

"You think Cassavetes was really the way he was or it was all a big scam?"

"Well ..." I said, never expecting to hear that from him. "I think he was the real deal. I can't be that way but I think he really was."

"If you can't do it, if most people, if everyone can't do it, then what's the point?"

"I like to think I take what I can from Cassavetes. That's all. I'm doing something different than him."

"It has to be all the way or not at all. There's no point in half-measures."

"There is for me."

"I think it was a big lie ..." he said with a hopeless, nervous laugh. "I don't think what Cassavetes put into his films, all the beauty, all the moments and magic, that just can't happen. At least not anymore. There's no magic in the world." he said, at the pit of his own soul, as a tear went down his face. "I just want you to know, Tom, I think you're a good guy and don't let anyone tell you otherwise. ... I love you, man."

He came up and hugged me tightly, more tears coming from his eyes. I was moved to tears myself. I knew what he was talking about. But there was nothing I could do. There was the feeling in both of us for something more, something inexpressible, as if nothing either of us could do could get us to that point. Were we attracted to each other? Was there the possibility of being lovers? Neither of us felt it, neither of us had the urge, so nothing was said or done. We were just left with the understanding, but the emotional, unfinished, untouchable goal, a place where neither of us would probably ever get.

Gus had to get out of L.A., and an opportunity to go back to New York came up. His father urged him to move in with his granddad and help out with things, along with getting his own life in order. Even though Gus despised the idea of going back to his home town, where the "tyranny of his family" would dominate, the need to leave L.A., be further away from Angela, from the general stagnation of L.A., and make an attempt to get his life more organized, won out. He believed he could deal with his family better now that he was older.

Three months being back in New York, working for some soul-killing jobs his dad got him, dealing with his over-bearing grandfather, and seeing old friends, Gus realized he was wrong. He couldn't deal with New York. I stayed in touch with Gus by e-mail and phone, and Gus thanked me for it. He needed a resemblance of connection and understanding with someone. When I came out there to show "Loveincrazy," we had a good time, Gus liked my movie better on the big screen (more than that night at Bernardo's), and we seemed to bond again with beer and sitting on Brooklyn stools.

There was some spark while in New York for Gus, though, enough for him to stay. Two old friends were considering helping Gus make his film, "A Boy and a Girl." It was promising and Gus even got me to think of moving out to New York. The old ideas of forming an actor's workshop came up, or of some kind of creative partnership with me, Gus, and the two other guys. Then it all started to fall apart. Gus ran into conflicts with his two old friends, both of them not liking his script nor having confidence in him as a director. Then the living situation became impossible with the astronomical costs of living in New York.

Still believing Gus and I could work together on projects, with me doing my second feature film, and Gus "A Boy and a Girl," I convinced him to move back to Los Angeles. I just found a bachelor apartment in the Pico/Union area near Downtown L.A., and while the place wasn't that big, there was space on the floor for him to sleep on.

He liked the idea and wanted to give it another shot to work with me. Over the phone, Gus joked he'd kill me if I dropped out this time. I came back by saying I'd kill Gus if he dropped out. We laughed, though with slightly nervous hesitancy. Gus had been to a mental institution before and well, I was known for violent streaks, as well.

I picked Gus up at the Long Beach airport with some expected excitement. All those years of dashed hopes and unfulfilled collaborations, now was the time something would work out. I could feel it. Gus was just tired from the trip and needed a shower. I finished reading the entire script to “A Boy and a Girl” and loved it.

He read the script for my second feature and liked it, except for a few things. He didn't like how the character based on him was portrayed. Still, the script was an improvement from my first film, he said.

While Gus stayed at my new apartment, we went back and forth, argued and discussed our projects. We just couldn't agree on a lot of things. The excitement for me became frustration more and more. I told him he didn't have to be in my film, but that we should work together on something.

We began working on different ideas for a play, banging around stories and characters, neither of us able to completely satisfy the other. My dad Jean, tried to help by coming up with an idea for a story. Gus didn't want to do it. I didn't want to do Gus' ideas.

Months passed and Gus was still staying on the floor in my apartment, still not paying rent. He was looking for a job, but apparently couldn't find one. Originally, he promised he'd either be out of the apartment in one month or help with the rent. One month turned into two, two turned into three, three turned into four ...

By the fourth month, I had completely given up on the idea of ever collaborating with Gus on anything, even though the lead role in my second feature was written specifically for him. I'd have to find someone else to play Gus. Gus wasn't even doing much for his own movie. He kept talking about Angela, about seeing her pass by in a car while he was on the bus. He kept talking about making his movie, but never took any steps to do it.

What was he doing? Not much. I was constantly wondering and frustrated every time I came home, I'd find Gus sitting around, reading my books, watching videos, listening to music, smoking, writing scenes for another incomplete script, throwing out ideas, telling me stories.

Once the fifth month came along, I began to have serious doubts in my friend. After all those years of looking up to my 'big Cassavetes brother', my Falstaff, now ... he really was turning into the Falstaff that almost asked to be betrayed ...

Gus was also seeming just like my step-father Frazier. The memories of growing up with Frazier's behavior struck me down low. Uninspired, lazy, a big talker, bored, pipe dreams extravaganza, depression, illusions ... staying home all the time, doing nothing, smoking, telling one bullshit story after another ... It was draining ... day in ... day out ... the same thing, over and over again, coming home from work, from anywhere and seeing Gus doing nothing in my apartment.

I tried to help him find a job but to no avail. Gus was just soaking in the free rent. I became tired of him and demanded he leave the apartment in one week. This was in the middle of the fifth month. Gus said he found a job and a place to stay.

Like most of Gus' stories, it was bullshit. He had no job, no place to stay. It was in the middle of one of the rainiest winters in Los Angeles. I felt bad for kicking Gus out into the rain but I had to get rid of him. Otherwise he'd become a permanent leech. The two of us weren't even talking to each other at this point ... I was beyond fed up. How could Gus do this, I felt. There were other friends. Why wouldn't he go to them? As usual, he had excuses. I was the only one he could rely on, and so on and so on ...

Gus had simply reached the end of the line. He was beyond despair. He wouldn't admit it to me nor even himself, but he gave up ... I wondered if he got back into drugs, which kind I didn't know, although, there was crack sold just up the street in the next neighborhood. But Gus didn't have money. At least thats what he said. Whether he had any money or not, it didn't matter. He had to leave the apartment.

When one day Gus came by to get some of his things at the apartment, I saw him and snapped. He was supposed to be gone two weeks before ...

“If I see any of your shit here tomorrow, I'm throwing it out to the fucking street! I don't want to ever see you at this apartment ever again!” I screamed, erupting in frustrated anger.

All the years of our friendship ended in unfulfilled creative hopes and a disintegration of dreams ... Gus did indeed remove all his things from my apartment the next day. That was the last time I saw him, at my apartment or anywhere.

PART SIX. DORIS.

CHAPTER ONE. KEY TO THE PUZZLE.

The minute I finished the final cut of "Loveincrazy," I decided to take a break from my film. It was an intense six months of non-stop editing after all. Two weeks later, I would begin the part I dreaded most of all: post-editing post-production – the "selling" of the movie. This consisted of submitting to film festivals, getting a distributor, publicity, marketing, networking, and more.

Unfortunately, I was alone in this area. I had no co-producer, no manager, no agent, no business partner, no one who was much more savvy at pushing the film than me. I had to get myself back into the canvassing skin, really, get my mindset back to salesman mode. By nature, I was far away from a salesman but my C.W.F.P.S.J experience made me learn how to be one. At least for things I cared about.

For my movie, I cared even more for it than the selling of peace and politics. The selling of "Loveincrazy" should be even easier. The difference, though, was there was a format, a follow-the-steps guide to canvassing. There was no such thing for selling your movie, other than bogus industry "how to" books.

I knew the basics. Find a distributor to show the film in a theater or some other venue, and help my possibilities by getting into film festivals. As a low budget, "maverick," outside the system, guerrilla filmmaker, I hoped to get into as many big ones like Sundance, Cannes, Toronto, etc. as possible, win awards as much as possible, get as many good write-ups by film critics as possible, and thereby lure a decent distributor to pick the movie up. The ultimate outcome would be decent exposure and business for the film and for myself, which would also hopefully lead to future filmmaking gigs and a long career. I could quit my day job for good, do well, and maybe even become famous.

But how to make all those things happen? That was the trick, especially if one was like me: didn't know anyone in film festivals, no one in distribution, no names were attached to the movie, no film critic friends, no friends or family in the business at all. I saw the difficult road ahead, saw the near impossibility to "make it," to succeed, but like Don Quixote, I still went ahead and tilted my lance at the windmills of Hollywood.

The first thing I did was create a press kit of some sorts. I'd seen a few over the the years in various places. There didn't seem to be much in guidelines, other than a cast and credit list, brief synopsis, longer synopsis, press reviews or coverage (if any). Some press kits had pictures from their film, some in color, some in black and white. For me to grab people's attention, I believed I had to have color pictures and a nice layout for the entire thing.

I had access to a decent graphic design computer program, so I could put frames from the movie footage together with cool looking fonts and designs. The first version, though, of this press kit ran almost 30 pages, mostly of the longer story synopsis and pictures. It was way too long, and people, while impressed with the layout, told me so. I cut it down to 10 pages.

Once I had the press kit ready, I researched on-line all the different film festivals. There were hundreds and hundreds of festivals in the United States alone, perhaps thousands and thousands. I found an on-line service that was connected to about 80% of the running fests, where I'd be able to apply on-line to each and every one of them. Once I filled out the forms, off I sent a VHS or DVD copy of "Loveincrazy." Along with that, the press kit and the special edition of the Hollywood Absurd on the movie my dad Jean and I put together. And, of course, the fee, usually around $50 per fest.

What I hoped for most of all was that people would actually watch the movie. There was no way to know for sure. The rejection responses never gave me any sense they saw a second of "Loveincrazy," since the notices were formal, generic e-mails sent to all the rejects, not just me. All the fests thanked me (most not even by my name) but there were thousands of applicants and they were just so sorry they couldn't accept my movie.

But that was the problem. There really were thousands of other young filmmakers like me. How could I stand out? I had to somehow maneuver into a better relation with the people at the fests. I had no idea how to do that. I tried calling all the people who were listed as contacts, but fest after fest gave me the cold shoulder. As charming as I could be at times, I didn't have just the right amount to warm any of them up. As I submitted to one fest after another, month after month I got rejection notice after rejection notice after rejection notice ...

There had to be at least one festival out there that wanted "Loveincrazy." I ran into a few people who could possibly help. Oliver Stone's ex-wife, who gave a VHS copy to her son, who gave it to his dad Oliver, who saw the film and liked it but couldn't help. Stone no longer promoted young filmmakers and he was too busy anyway working on "Alexander." Then there was the low-key and versatile African American director Charles Burnett, who actually watched the movie twice and liked it. But like Stone, he couldn't help. There were also film critics from the LA Times and LA Weekly, who had the same response.

There was also IFP-LA, the "resource center" for all aspiring no-name filmmakers. I became a member after the $80 fee, then paid $180 for the first seminar, in order to "network." The only people there were struggling filmmakers hoping to find the missing ingredient. Hey, just like me. The IFP staff in charge of the seminar were smug, condescending, and completely useless. Well, there were always more seminars, each one costing at least another $180 ...

The unthinkable came next: submit my film to the New York Indie Underground Spirit Film and Video Fest. For years, I knew of the infamous festival. The whole thing was a scam. The submission fee was $300 and then they "accepted" movies after "reviewing" its "excellence." A filmmaker paid the $300 and got into the fest. That was it. Then the people in charge pushed and pushed each filmmaker to reserve a table at the "Distributor's Opening Night Gala." The tables were $2,000 each and up, depending on how much space one wanted.

I fortunately turned the table down. I did show up at the

Hollywood hotel on the night of the opening, seeing all the poor filmmaker souls who got a table ... to show to no distributors, no industry folk, just other filmmakers and their friends and families ... It was a sad sight, although at least my dad Jean met a Japanese artist who would attempt to collaborate with him on a story.

There was no disappointment in my heart. I knew what I was getting into. The cost of the fest - $300 – was cheaper than renting a theater at that time of night – 7:30pm. Also, being under the umbrella of the fest, the DigiBeta projector and the projectionist wasn't extra. That would've been another few hundred dollars.

So it wasn't exactly 100% of a scam. Well, it was, but a scam someone like me could get something out of. I had no other offers. For months, day after day, festivals had all turned me down. I soon started going after distributors, even without festivals attached, since I had none to attach. Mostly I called companies in Los Angeles and New York. I called, faxed, talked with hundreds and hundreds of different distributors. Several promised to show at the screening of "Loveincrazy."

The night of the screening, none of them did. Still, I hustled my butt and got 60 people to show up, mostly people I knew, which in L.A., if one were a nobody, was even hard to do. The New York Indie Underground Spirit Film and Video Fest tried and tried to get me to let them be my distributor. I refused. I knew their deal. There was a cost, at least $1,500, and I knew they'd do nothing but let "Loveincrazy" collect dust on a bookshelf.

A month after the L.A. screening, I went to New York for the East Coast Premiere to find the same result. I did get a small write-up in an underground N.Y. paper, but that was it. Hundreds and hundreds more distributors, all New York based, turned me down. Coming back to L.A., I was bleak ...

What could I do next? As far as "Loveincrazy" was concerned, not much. Perhaps I could make one more attempt at getting distributors and the press interested by doing a midnight screening at the Laemmle's

Sunset-5 or an 11am screening at the Laemmle's Monica 4-plex. I'd have to round up a few hundred dollars for the theater and projector/projectionist, then hustle to get the interest going. I could do it, but would it lead to anything? Without money for publicity, without any recognition from fests, without interest from the press, without anyone from the industry even knowing about it, there wasn't a good chance many people would show ...

Around this time, I ran out of unemployment checks (from C.W.F.P.S.J) and needed a job. I went back to Laemmle theaters, who I worked for years ago. The job allowed me to work on personal projects because of all of the down time, and at least I was around interesting movies. At this job, the Laemmle in Beverly Hills called the Music Hall, was where I met Doris. It was a slow Wednesday night when I saw her frustrated at the literature counter, flipping through the LA Weekly.

"Can I help you, Ma'am?" I asked as I turned to her.

"Well, maybe. I just thought you were playing 'Balzac and the Little Chinese Seamstress' but apparently you're not." Doris said with some aggravation.

"The 7:30 and 10 o'clock show were canceled because of a screening."

"Of course. And tonight's the last night, right?"

"Yeah. Sorry."

Doris appeared to be in her mid 50's, fairly short, about 5'4", dark, long hair, bright, beautiful blue eyes, but a stocky, square build, and uptight, rigid wrinkles in her features. There was a kindness about her, a gentleness that went along with a grace, intelligence, and wit. Under the uptightness in her face lay a harsh resentment, though, an unpleasantness. It was as if she seemed tortured by the inability to control the reality in front of her. This aspect of her reminded me of Cassandra.

At first Doris seemed just another frustrated, angry customer. But when she explained how disappointed she was by not seeing the movie, and I could tell how earnest she was, I realized I should try to help. I looked up the Laemmle reference schedule and found 'Balzac and the ...' playing in Encino. I told her it was there and to make it up to her, I'd call a pass for her. She was delighted by my kindness. We ended up going into both our interests in film before she left. I found out she was a film critic/writer and served on a board for a European film festival. Her job for the fest was to find American films and recommend them to the review panel. A light went on in my head. Doris could be my last ditch hope for "Loveincrazy." As I took her business card for the German film fest, I asked myself – should I do it? Should I use Machiavellian tactics to help my filmmaking career? I could tell she was attracted to me. Hell, I was half her age. If I wanted to, there was an opening for manipulation.

On the way to my apartment – where Gus was lounging around, waiting to argue, or tell a story, or listen to music, or watch a movie – I knew I had to take one last risk for my movie. "Loveincrazy" was, after all, my baby. If I really cared for it, really wanted it to succeed, I should be willing to do anything to make it happen. And anyway, it wasn't as if it was an old man I had to seduce. I could find Doris attractive, mainly through her personality and interests.

Gus recommended I stay away. I didn't have a gigolo nature and besides, who was this woman anyway? It wasn't as if she was Kathleen Kennedy, Steven Spielberg's producer. Gus suggested if I was going to be a gigolo, at least be more discerning with my targets. Gus was probably right, but I felt I had no other options. It wasn't as if Kathleen Kennedy was the one who walked into the theater that night. Nor was I at the beginning of pushing my film. It was an agonizing 18 months since "Loveincrazy" was shot.

After talking with her over the phone a few times, I drove to Doris' apartment in Los Feliz, just off Virgil and Franklin. Her place was on the second floor to an apartment building in a nice neighborhood. The area compiled of well-off Los Feliz hipsters, industry types, and some old folks. Coming into her apartment, I was impressed with how well she kept it. It was cozy, clean, comfortable, spacious, and had culturally classy things and film decorations around.

“Hi, come on in.” Doris said as she greeted me, with a wide, excited smile, then closed the door behind me. “Sorry the place is such a mess.”

“Uh ...” I said a little off-guard as I looked around. “... it looks fine to me. Very nice.”

“I'm just a perfectionist when it comes to house-cleaning.”

“I can tell.”

“You're too kind.” she said as she blushed. She felt like a little school girl again, so excited to have this attractive young man in her apartment. As I would find out, horniness only increased with age for women. “Do you – I mean, would you like something to drink?” she asked nervously as she shuffled around before going into the kitchen.

“Sure.”

She proceeded to fill glasses of white wine for both me and herself, along with bringing out of the oven two delicious Mediterranean appetizers. While we ate, drank, and waited for the main course to cook, she shared some issues of the film magazine she wrote articles for. I shared issues of my “Hollywood Absurd.” The magazine she contributed to was an academic quarterly, with intellectually dense and long articles. Her style of writing fitted into that academic niche, I found.

Doris was of the academic mold, having spent most of her life in and around academia. Born into an upper middle-class Wisconsin Lithuanian American family, she grew up a favorite of her father but the black sheep to the rest of the family. Her mother and her were always at odds, her older brother busy making money, her sister busy being a society lady, and her younger brother busy being a schizophrenic. She was a seeker, so being from a family that saw education only as a means to further social status, she rebelled by pursuing education for its own sake.

In college, Doris fell in love with her drama and philosophy professor. She was spellbound by his charisma, insights, and sex appeal. He was the same age as her father but unlike her dad, he had a provocative mind. He introduced her to the world of theater and philosophy, after all. Ibsen, Shaw, Brecht, Pirandello, Beckett, Chekhov and others for the theater; Marx, Engels, Schopenhauer, Angela Davis, many feminist writers and others for politics and philosophy.

They had a nasty break-up but she stayed in academics and became a teacher herself. It worked out for a while until she became so frustrated with the students and faculty, she quit. Still, through her academic connections, she was able to support herself through free-lance writing, and odd jobs here and there. For the last 15 or so years she was doing this and never returned to teaching. She had a few books of her own she was working on but never got off the ground.

After dinner and still drinking wine, Doris explained to me how the German film fest operated. They were primarily concerned with showcasing non-American independent filmmakers, but sometimes they would have two Americans in a year. Usually, one film from the West Coast – her responsibility – and one from the East Coast – another person in New York's job.

Based on her four or five recommendations, they would choose one. The last couple of years, though, they chose none from her selections for some reason. The way she saw it, as she did for many things, it was because of personal politics. A couple people running the fest had issues with her more than the movies she chose.

The way Doris explained the fest, the way she spoke whenever bringing forth "the industry" or "the business" (film or literature), she got into a different gear. She became forceful, direct, and really, overly so, as if a button was pushed inside her and put her into presentation mode. This, even after several glasses of wine. I felt she must be like that because of years and years in and around cut-throats in the academic, publishing, and film worlds. It was an unconscious trigger which made her stiff and strange in those moments.

By the end of the night, I could tell she was probably going to be supportive. She hadn't seen the movie yet but based on our conversations, the press kit and the Hollywood Absurd zine, she seemed to believe I had an artistic vision. It wasn't only because she wanted to jump my pants, although that was definitely an overwhelming motivating factor.

I was wary of how far I was willing to go. I really only wanted her to help me out if she "got" the movie. I wasn't comfortable with the gigolo role as Gus predicted, and I wasn't sure if our intellectual understanding was a cover for her seduction. But I was seducing, too. One minute charming her, the next taking a step back, checking to see if she was connecting with my head as much as my dick. I was split on the two agendas.

A few days later, Doris called me and said how much she loved "Loveincrazy." She went on for a good 20 minutes over the phone, detail after detail, of why she liked the film. She seemed sincere and if she wasn't, her acting was excellent. In terms of the social, cultural, and political critique my film was making, she was right on the money, for the most part. Doris tended to place situations into categories too much, though, much like my ex-co-workers at C.W.F.P.S.J did. For me, everything didn't come down to Classism, Sexism, Racism, Ageism, and all those other "isms."

The aspect I felt she really missed was the emotional dynamic, the psychological undercurrents of the drama. When I brought up D.H. Lawrence, Cassavetes, or Ozu in our discussions, she didn't respond much to their work. The emotional life was most important to those artists, and not so much for Doris. Still, it was refreshing to hear her praise. No one else besides my father Jean took the time and energy to try and understand the import of "Loveincrazy," whatever its success or failures in communicating that importance.

I was on a relative high. Not only did she like the film, but she promised she'd pick it as her #1 recommendation. I now seemed to have an into one of those god damn festivals. Still, there wasn't complete certainty, as she warned over the phone. The board at the German film fest hadn't picked one of her choices the last few times.

All the years of no return film work, of disappointment after disappointment, now this one hint of hope was so electrifying, so much so that Doris actually became attractive to me. Besides that, she was appealing in her own way, mostly for her kindness and intelligence.

We met again soon over coffee at a Los Feliz cafe, then a movie (she got private screening press invites) and then another time for dinner at her place. By then I finished the German fest application process and sent a video tape off to them. Now it was a matter of waiting, although one thing remained: Doris' letter and list of recommended films. There was a couple others she was writing about besides "Loveincrazy."

I wondered, despite all her adulation, was she only being nice just to have sex with me? Was she really going to recommend another movie more? Was she really the player here and not me? This was running through the back of my mind the whole night as we ate her delicious dinner and drank wine. As time went on, the interaction between us seemed to build towards the obvious - sex.

Once we got to the couch on our fifth glass of wine, we both were pretty drunk and the idea shot into my head: seduce her. Giving Doris that pleasure could very well ensure "Loveincrazy" gets the best possible push by her. I went for it. We started making out on the couch. While she didn't physically arouse me much, she was a good kisser. She was also so in awe of me, so excited by my body and mind, the fact she was enormously turned on rubbed off on me. My cock hardened. My movie was on the line. We fondled each other and soon I was taking off our clothes while kissing her everywhere.

My kissing went to her breasts, then down to her stomach, as I pulled her pants off and soon her panties. I'd never been so up close and personal to a body as old as hers. Her skin wasn't smooth at all, rough from age and had lots of freckles. Her breasts didn't have the fullness of women's breasts I'd made love to before. Her legs were also saggy, wrinkly as I put my hands on them.

Doris' crotch was attractive enough, though. She kept herself clean down there, smelled nice, and didn't allow her pussy hair to overflow out of control. And there was her clit, opening up inches away from my face. She was extremely wet as she moaned and moaned above. I'd never been with a woman who got off so easily.

I leaned forward and began licking her clit and now found out just how wet she was. It tasted as if she actually came already and was ready to cum again. Her juices were flowing. I wasn't sure if I liked how she tasted down there. Her wetness was a little turgid. Still, with the wine soaked in my mouth, it wasn't that bad.

I normally loved going down on women. I enjoyed seeing women get off from such intense pleasure, the view of a woman from that angle, her thighs spread open, her breasts above, her hips nearby, her ass cheeks below the divine crotch area. The way a pussy looked was exciting. The pussy mound with its patch of hair, then the clit, especially when wet, then the hole below. But Doris was not erotic for me, even though she was enormously turned on herself. And now Doris was cumming a second time. She was almost screaming from my licking, kissing, and sucking ...

I kept going and going, until eventually she came a third time in my face. By then my tongue and mouth were worn out. She was in heaven as I rested my head on her thigh. We were like that for a while, me sitting on the floor, my arms on the couch, and my head on her leg, as she lay on her back on the couch. She was wiped out from the pleasure.

We proceeded to her bed, where she began giving me fellatio. Seeing her body next to mine turned me off quite a bit and I lost my erection completely. I just couldn't get aroused by the way she looked. I told her my lost erection was due to the alcohol. She wouldn't take no for an answer. She had to get me hard and give me an orgasm.

She kept going down on me, for a long time, and whatever she was doing felt intensely good. Despite how she looked, I had to admit she was giving a great blow job. Because she was so good at it, I eventually got an erection. As I got harder, she went up and down my shaft faster and faster, until soon, I came. My cum bursted all over her sheets, some going on her face.

Doris was happy. She made me cum. As she lay next to me on the bed, looking at me in post-cum "le petite morte" aftermath, she fell in love. She wanted me as her lover, but wouldn't come out with it. She just kept on saying how amazing I was. I enjoyed it, too, but as I turned to look at her wide, starry eyes and face, I just couldn't get myself to be attracted to her at all.

Gus was right. I wasn't a gigolo. I just couldn't do it, this romanticizing part. Doris, of course, kept going on and on in her romantic mood, kept being in awe. It was too much. I began to feel suffocated by her. I got up and went to the bathroom, apologizing for leaving the bed. I came back 15, 20 minutes later, after having taken a dump. I was hoping her romanticism mellowed, but it didn't. Well, if I was to be a gigolo I had to play the part. I spent the night with her, then left in the morning.

The next couple days I had to figure out what I was going to do with Doris. I didn't want to lead her on but I also didn't want to cut myself completely off. Besides the fact I was hoping she'd help me with my career, I actually cared about her, too. She was a kind soul, treated me well, and I liked her as a friend. We had good conversations on literature, film, art, society, politics, and philosophy. There were few people in Los Angeles like her. My dad Jean was the only other one in my life. Still, unlike Jean, there was an aspect of her connecting with me which was slightly phony. This was because of her lust/obsession for me and simply because that was her nature.

So, what to do? I kept pondering. I decided to continue being friendly like before and even have sex with her again, maybe. No, that wouldn't be good. It would only lead her on. What I definitely didn't want is either confront her directly about my lack of feelings, nor pretend to be as enamored as she was. Unfortunately, I had to be wily, slick, slippery, not something I was particularly good at. We continued hanging out, seeing movies, having dinner or coffee, but not as frequently as before.

She e-mailed me the letter of recommendation to the German film fest about "Loveincrazy," wanting me to know for sure she wasn't full of shit. I appreciated that.

A week later, I got the rejection notice from the German film fest.

It was a nail in my heart. Not only was it the nail after hundreds of other nails, but after all the work I put into this particular application, staying up all night working on it to send off in time to meet their deadline, after all the support Doris gave the film ... it was hard ... the final heartbreak for "Loveincrazy" ...

I became bitter, but continued working on the script for my second feature and thinking of how to be more successful this time. I even considered pushing "Loveincrazy" a bit more, perhaps do another screening. No, it was done, it was dead ... I had to move on, which was hard to do ... After the disappointments of "Loveincrazy," getting fired at C.W.F.P.S.J for falling in love with Charlotte, the disintegration of my friendships with Bernardo, Gus, Kristianna, Benny, and with the breakdown in my love affairs ... it all added up ... bruise after bruise ...

It became harder for me to hide my feelings around Doris. I just wasn't attracted to her, not only physically, but personally. She had a certain insecure uptightness about her, as if she was wound up. She reminded me again of Cassandra and even my mother at times. Doris wasn't comfortable to be her own self ... she was glued to me, stuck to me in this strange need, almost a violence in it ... sometimes when I looked at her, it gave me a shiver ...

I felt bad, as well, that I had used her. And I did. I intentionally seduced her so she could help my film. I tried to excuse myself by saying I never led her on romantically, that what I put forth was a physical and intellectual connection, not a romantic one. But I knew what I was doing, and I could see her being enamored. I knew what I was playing.

Fortunately for me, I was smart enough never to commit myself verbally, never expressed any false feelings of love for her, never put into words things I didn't feel. She couldn't hold me to a love I never expressed.

There was still an anger within her, though. She definitely resented my withdrawal from her, and the fact I played the gigolo, even though I continued to be friends with her. But what she most seemed to resent was my attempts to hook her up with my dad Jean. I felt, why not? They were closer in age, and had similar interests and points of view. Jean and I had a lot in common. It seemed natural for her to hit it off with my father if she liked me.

Doris took a liking to Jean, but only on a friendly and creative level. She admired his mind and his writing, but romantically wanted nothing to do with him. She wanted me. One night after seeing a movie with the two of us, Doris was riding in my car as I drove her home. We talked about the movie and politics, but we were uncomfortable.

"You know, I've been meaning to ask you since I saw your film ..." Doris put out there in almost a menacing, condescending tone of voice. "Just philosophically speaking, do you think there's something morally wrong with incest?"

An anger thrusted harshly into my gut as soon as she threw that zinger. One of the key things "Loveincrazy" dealt with was the molestation of the Colin character by Jack Henry – his father – when Colin was nine years old ... I opened up to Doris about my own experience with childhood molestation ... my step-father Frazier had violently dry-humped me before I kicked him off me when I was nine ... only until I broke off all ties to Frazier did I finally come out into the open with this ... even to Jean and my mother ... it was probably the most personal thing I could let Doris know about me, so soon after I just told Jean and my mother, so soon after putting it into my film, with a quick edit, putting a photograph of me as a nine year old in the midst of the last fight between Jack Henry and Colin ... for Doris to bring up molestation in the way she did ... she was purposely sticking a dagger into me ...

I almost had the urge to punch her right there in the car, the same way I felt when Gus had brought it to me in a similar way once before. It was as if, in both cases, Doris and Gus were trying their hardest to push my buttons and see me snap. With Gus, I sent my own zinger back at him, referring to Gus touching his younger half-brother when he was a teenager. But with Doris, I felt sorry as I looked at her. I had, after all, seduced her with ill-intentions, however much I could justify it.

But that was it for me. I wouldn't see Doris anymore, or at least would keep my distance as much as possible. She crossed the line with that remark in the car. I admitted this to her soon after, and she defended herself by saying it was just a theoretical question introduced to her by a George Bernard Shaw play. However she tried to explain it, she was trying to hurt me, get revenge for the pain I caused her.

Doris tried to stay in touch but I eluded her, not returning phone calls nor e-mails. One day, she caught me at the theater I worked at. I hoped she wasn't going to be my stalker now. I brought up some news that hopefully would send the message: I was becoming a father. She was devastated, but hid it as best she could behind uncontrollable, surprised, uptight laughter ... Doris did get the message and never bothered me again.

PART SEVEN. ARIEL.

CHAPTER ONE. EACH MAN KILLS THE THING HE LOVES.

I loved Gavin Friday. The only other modern musician I liked more was Robert Smith of The Cure. The little known but not completely obscure gothic, romantic, independent Irish singer's music was a delight to me for years. Jean introduced Friday to me a while back when I was first falling in love with Maya. Known mostly for being a life-long friend to Bono of U2, Friday forged a distinctive voice and style of music in his own right. It began when forming the experimental cabaret punk band "The Virgin Prunes" and continued with solo work and movie soundtracks.

Friday's first solo album, "Each Man Kills the Thing He Loves," which came out in 1988, was my favorite, although almost everything he produced was brilliant. The only detraction was the fact he stopped putting out studio albums in 1995, leaving a decade long vacuum. But whatever he did release was an enormous influence on me as an artist and a human being. Unlike Bono, who had millions of admirers, Friday had far fewer, but each one took the music much more personally. It was a piece of them, as it was to me.

One day before going to work, I listened to one Gavin Friday or Virgin Prunes album after another while working on the script to my second feature film. Gus was still living at my place, but couldn't stand Gavin Friday, so he went to Alvarado to get a $2 pack of Marlboro's. On my way to work, I felt Oscar Wilde's lines (from whose poem the Friday song was inspired) sunk down inside me more than before. I had, after all, killed many loves myself and been killed by them.

But I wanted something more. I was tired of the pain. In the last few years I'd been through so much, with Maya, with Charlotte and everyone at C.W.F.P.S.J, with Bernardo, Gus, Doris, Benny, Kristianna, the goth girls, other friends, with family, with lovers. I was 26 and I wanted that simple, fresh uncomplicated love affair with a woman. Could I ever have it? As much as I was a romantic, I was just as much a realist. I knew there was no such thing as an uncomplicated romance. Still, I was sure to find something, someone a lot less complicated than what I'd been through up till now.

In the past, I met several female customers at the movie theater in Santa Monica. A few dates went well, but at the time my heart was entangled with Maya and I held myself back. Maybe I'd meet someone like that, a customer, some nice young lass who was coming to watch a movie. One film we were showing at the movie theater I worked at, the Music Hall, brought in a fair amount of young people.

Since the Music Hall was in Beverly Hills and the parking was horrible, with the only option being expensive parking lots, or if you were lucky, a parking meter after 7pm, the theater wasn't open during the week before 5. After 5pm, you could park in one lot for a flat rate of $3. As the theater wasn't open often, there weren't many people working there. And when someone had to take the weekend off, the busiest time, the general manager needed to find workers from other theaters.

The Laemmle's Fairfax on Beverly and Fairfax was one of them. One Saturday night, I noticed an employee from there filling in to help at the Music Hall. Her name was Ariel. Ariel had that kind of beauty not noticed at first glance, not like Charlotte. But with a closer look, there was more to her beauty than someone like Charlotte. There were layers of beauty within her.

She was twenty years old, Jewish, dirty blond/brownish hair like mine, bright, wide, glowing green eyes, long legs for her 5'5" thin frame and relatively small breasts. Her overall figure, and the way she moved it since she was a dancer, was sensual and desirable even if she wasn't model material. I loved dancers. One of my favorite sexual experiences was with a Russian dancer from St. Petersburg a few years before.

What I liked about Ariel in comparison to Charlotte was a more mature, humble, and deeper nature. Ariel was both very friendly and real in her friendliness. With Charlotte, it felt like a put-on at times. Whatever Ariel gave seemed genuine.

But at first I didn't consider asking Ariel out. I liked her and was attracted to her as we talked, but perhaps there was a voice inside saying, "Don't get eager now, Tom." I didn't put any pressure on myself, so I was more comfortable than usual. This was why, during the shift, she kept coming up to me and talking. She was the one taking steps and I confidently responded. I could be like this in the past, but not often.

"How long have you been at the Fairfax?" I asked Ariel while we cleaned a theater together.

"About three weeks now." she responded while sweeping up popcorn.

"So it's like you almost started."

"Not really. It feels a lot longer. Working at a movie theater, you get to know people pretty quick."

"Yeah, with all the down time. I used to work with a bunch of the Fairfax people at other theaters."

"Really? Like who?"

"Well, your manager is an ex of mine."

"Linda? No way!"

"Yup. Back when I was 19 we both used to work at the theater in Santa Monica."

"I can't see you two going out."

"Me, neither."

"How old are you now?"

"26. And you?"

"I'm turning 21 in a couple weeks."

"Cool."

"Who else did you work with?"

"Some others who were at the Sunset-5 when I was. Josh, Sam, Miranda - "

"Josh? Oh no, you had to work with him? He's so annoying." she said as she laughed.

"He is a cheesy guy." I replied with a smile.

"He thinks he's Jim Morrison or something, some kind of player/poet ... he's so ridiculous."

"Definitely. When I worked with him, he got to be annoying real quick. I felt kind of sorry for him because he would literally fling himself at every girl he saw. He was desperate as hell. He hit on so many women and he'd rarely ever get laid."

"Did he ever show you his 'list'?" she said with a giggle.

"Oh yeah, all the phone numbers he got from women. As much as he may boast, most of them aren't lovers, just girls he knows."

"He's so not attractive or charming, with his tiny, scrawny body, elfish face, and hunched over shoulders."

"And the way he leans forward into people as he's talking to them ... he is silly."

"Pretentious to the core."

"What is he doing now? One week he wanted to be a filmmaker, the next a poet, the next a musician, the next a photographer ..."

"I have no idea."

"I'm sure he asked you out."

"Oh yeah. Shut him down quick."

"So you're not on his list?"

"Nope." she said as we both laughed. Eventually, our laughing died down as we finished cleaning the theater.

We continued talking during the shift, mostly about music, movies, dancing, photography (what she was most passionate about). She started taking pictures seriously as a teenager, at the same time I started taking filmmaking seriously – 14. I loved her simple, intelligent, sensitive, fun humility. There was warmth, depth, experience behind her eyes. There was also pain. I wondered what that was, what kind of pain and from where, then imagined she must see it in my eyes, as well. Pain had a way of conveying itself whether the person wanted it to or not.

At the end of her shift, we shared a cigarette together outside. Ariel wasn't a smoker but would have a cigarette now and then. She was one of a few people who enjoyed my little cigar Winchesters. And she wasn't even a smoker. What she didn't let on to me then was she liked the Winchesters only because I did. Her eyes were fixed on me. She had made some kind of internal choice now.

"Fellini's one of your favorite filmmakers, right?" she asked while taking a friendly step towards me. We had an in-depth discussion on filmmakers earlier.

"Yeah."

"Well they're showing a couple of his movies at the American Cinemateque."

"Which ones?"

"'Amarcord' and two short films."

"Interesting. I never saw 'Amarcord'."

"I just looked at the schedule."

"Which day is it?"

"Thursday. You wanna go? With me, I mean?"

"With you? Yeah." I replied with an uncertain surprise. I wasn't expecting that.

"Are you sure?" she said with a smile, catching my uncertainty.

"No, yeah, definitely." I really did want to go, but being caught off-guard made it seem to her I had doubts. "I'd love to go with you." I said with more confidence this time.

"Okay, cool. Here, let me give you my number." she said as she finished the Winchester and went inside the theater.

I was amazed. Not only did she ask me to join her, but she was also giving me her number without me even asking. I forgot sometimes I was desirable to women, especially after what happened at C.W.F.P.S.J. As she left the theater to go home, she gave a movie postcard to me. On the back of it was her phone number and a note saying, "A night out with Fellini! Call me tomorrow. - Ariel." She was cute and wonderful. I loved it.

As usual, though, my insecurities kicked in. We just met that day, and yes we had some great conversations, and we obviously enjoyed each other's company, but it was only the first day. Was she really into me? If so, why? Did she like me for me? Or, as with many women (and men), was she playing games? Was she coming onto me for other motives?

The outrageous idea even came into my head that my father, Jean, had actually paid her to ask me out. There was an Ariel Jean knew who worked at an Office Depot in the valley. Ariel lived in the valley, and how many girls named Ariel were there? Maybe Jean paid her to do a favor. I was that insecure. After all, despite the fact I'd been in bed with a fair amount of women, and I was attractive, I was by no means a successful player, let alone have girls give me their phone numbers right away.

Then I kicked myself in the head. I had to stop thinking like that, stop swimming around in insecurities. This thing with Ariel was probably a real, legitimate, fresh, simple, spontaneous, beautiful opportunity, exactly what I wanted. I sure as hell shouldn't ruin it.

Because of her openness, I had two directions to go. I could either play it cool, be the opposite of the eager boy I sometimes was, or I could meet her with openness. I had to be careful, though, to not come across as too open, or I would then be the eager school boy. But I certainly didn't want to play the opposite, the semi-interested Mr. Cool. It didn't come naturally to me. Of course, thats what most women were attracted to. Ariel seemed different. Fuck it, I thought, she was just being herself. That's exactly what I should do.

Ariel met me at the Egyptian theater in Hollywood, where the Cinemateque was located. She was there first, sitting on the concrete blocks that surrounded the palm trees. A couple years before the theater was renovated to look how it did back in the '20's. It had the tall Ancient Egyptian walls with hieroglyphs and Egyptian gods in stone at the entrance. The entire large building was designed in the same fashion.

There was something angelic and vulnerable the way Ariel sat there on the stone, waiting. She smiled and stood up to greet me.

“Hi.” she said simply.

“Hey. Have you been waiting long?” I said as I was close to finishing a little cigar.

“No, not at all. I got here a few minutes ago. Hey, can I have a puff on that?”

“Sure.” I said, handing her the rest of the little cigar. “You want one for yourself? There's not much left of that one.”

“It's okay. This is all I want.”

“Have you been here before?”

“This is my first time. I like it.”

“It's definitely nice. I love Ancient Egyptian art and architecture, even if it's a contemporary replica of a '20's Hollywood version of it. The ancient mysticism seeps through somehow.”

“So the original was built around the same time as the Mann Chinese?”

“Yeah, I think so.”

“Shall we go in?”

“Let's.”

“So what'd you do today?” she asked as we walked towards the box office. “By the way, I got our free passes already.”

“Why, thank you, Darling.” I smiled deeply alongside a flippant, old Hollywood accent. I loved her spirit more and more, and I had yet to really know her.

“Not a problem, Sweetheart. My pleasure.” she smiled with a knowledge back at me, to go with her joking old Hollywood accent. We shifted our walking from the box office to the entrance. “So tell me how your day was.” she asked again with her normal tone of voice.

“Well, you know ... darling ...” I started as we got to the front door and our tickets were torn by the door man.

“I know ...” she said teasingly, waiting for me to continue. Now we were inside the theater, which for some reason, the interior design had nothing to do with Ancient Egypt. It looked like an industry screening room. I was always disappointed with this part of the theater.

“Well, it's just with life ...”

“Yeah?”

“Do you ever feel let down by it?”

"What part?"

"Any part."

"Of course."

"I find my imagination, the impulses inside me, shoot out, invisibly, it's an internal thing, maybe an emotional thing, a psychological thing ... and time after time the reality around me doesn't come anywhere near to meeting that sensation. That's what I mean by being let down, the Big Letdown. I think in schizophrenics this is their case, but to the extreme, some purer intentioned than others. For people like me who – hopefully – aren't schizophrenics, it's a romanticism. By nature, I'm a romantic, to always want more than what life has to offer. Or, at least, what the world we've created has to offer."

"Wow, um ..." her breathing almost stopped. What was I talking about, she must've thought to herself. But she liked where I was coming from, although a deep concern suddenly got hold of her. She hoped I didn't see her as a letdown. "So whats that have to do with your day?"

I laughed and so did she. I noticed the look in her eyes, though, the insecurities she was feeling. I could almost read her mind and knew that she must be thinking I was perhaps considering her a letdown of some sort. I hated myself for even saying it. She was the last thing I would consider a letdown. And I chose to talk about being let down by life in front of her, as if in some way insinuating she wasn't what I hoped for? I wished I never said the damn words, not like this, not this soon, without her knowing me better. I tried to reach out to her through my feelings, through the subtext of my words as well as the words themselves, to make it up to her, to make sure she knew my true feelings, to make sure we wouldn't start on the wrong foot.

"It has to do with what happened earlier today, far before tonight, having to do with things I've been dealing with for a while. But I guess I was just talking in more general terms, in our day to day lives, what fills up most of our time, what we try to find some escape from, you know?

It's just when we all ask each other how our day went, I wanted to communicate how I really felt. I could've told you the details of my day, but somehow I could tell you'd be more receptive to what I just said."

"It's interesting ... you're definitely not boring me."

"I'm not?" I asked with some surprise. Whenever I got a little philosophical, I always thought people saw me as boring. This was a nice change.

"Not at all."

"Well ... you know what I said does connect with what happened to me today. I have a friend from New York, his name is Gus, and he's staying at my place. We've been good friends over the years and we've tried time after time to work on films, scripts, plays, and so on, but it never works out. And now he's at my apartment, lounging around, doing nothing, staying at my apartment for free, leeching off me for the past three months, and being a daily reminder of what we would've done creatively, you know? I've had other friends where the same thing happened."

"It sucks when friends let you down. It's happened to me lots of times too. I usually start off friendships with a lot of giving on my part, you know ... Like the moment I meet a person, I just want to open up to them and give them all I have, emotionally speaking. Then friends will see that and then take advantage of me ... I've had boyfriends do the same ... but anyways, enough about me!" she said at the end with a laugh, counteracting her openness with humor, almost using her smile to hide.

"I like it when you talk about yourself."

"I don't. I sound boring and strange to me. I'd much rather hear you talk about things. Say something philosophical."

"Philosophical?"

"Yeah, I can tell your interest perks up when you get deep into thought. I like to watch you when you're like that."

"I like to see you like that too." I smiled back at her.

"No, I'm boring like that!" she laughed.

"No, you're not."

"Just tell me something!"

"Like what?"

"Tell me what you think of human beings ... but keep it short because our Fellini movies are about to start."

"Oh yeah, thats right." I said, forgetting we were there to watch movies. I was so focused on her.

"So what do ya think of 'em?"

"Human beings?"

"Yeah. In our first conversation, at the Music Hall, you said they were the most interesting thing to you."

"They are."

"Why? You seem to get disappointed by them ..."

"I do!" I laughed.

"Then why're they interesting?"

"Sometimes ... even in disappointment humans can be fascinating. When you look at why they are disappointing or why you can feel disappointed by them, that can be fascinating. Then there are times when humans are fascinating because they're really interesting. Like you, like right now being with you and talking to you. This is fascinating."

"I'm not fascinating."

“Yes, you are.”

“Maybe to you, but not to most people. I don't think.” she said, blushing, then tried to hide it. “Or maybe you're not telling me the truth.”

“You could rip my chest open and find a bleeding heart, Ariel.” I said with a warm smile, one of the warmest smiles I ever smiled.

“Wow, um ...” she blushed some more, smiling at both my joking and obvious sincerity. Then the lights in the lobby began blinking off and on, signaling the start of the movie. “Sounds like the movie's starting.” she said with some relief, thanking the timing so she wasn't so vulnerable.

First up on the screen were the two short films by Fellini. The one just coming on was the third segment of a 60's film inspired by Edgar Allen Poe stories, starring Terrence Stamp. Stamp played an English movie star visiting Italy for press interviews and other industry events. As the story progressed, Stamp gets more and more annoyed with the whole experience and gets lost in alcohol, daydreams, and eventually nightmares. I had always wanted to see this film, and now I could, on the big screen and next to Ariel. I loved the decadent, humorous nightmarish vision. Poe, Stamp, and Fellini worked well together. I wished Fellini made a feature out of it.

The second short film was longer but not as good, half of a film, the first half directed by another Italian director. This was the “1/2” of “8 1/2” - Fellini's nod in his autobiographical film to the number of films he made at that point. This second short was about a bureaucratic political activist working for the Catholic church, who went around cartoonishly trying to censor the immorality in Italian cinema and television. It was a good idea but not executed as well as the first short film with Stamp.

Once that was done, it was intermission time. We both agreed the first short film was the better one. Ariel wanted to see more Fellini films. While I watched the shorts, sitting next to her in the dark, I wondered if I should make a move on Ariel. Maybe put my hand on her thigh. But I didn't, I wanted to enjoy the films and be patient. When it was the right time, something would happen.

Intermission was soon over and we went back into the theater. I thought this night was great. Not only was I with Ariel, but I was seeing three Fellini movies I never saw before. "Amarcord" opened with a haunting silent movie homage, where all the main characters boarded a huge cruise ship in 1920's Italy. After the inspired opening, though, the rest of the film was not first-rate Fellini. I asked Ariel if she wanted to leave and she said no, but only if I wanted to. We stayed.

Soon, she leaned back into her chair and discreetly put her hand on mine. Her fingertips glided gently across the back of my hand. I didn't want to move, but I also wanted to respond. First, I rubbed my knee quietly against hers, then brought my other hand to smoothly caress her hand. After a few minutes of this, we turned to look at each other. The nervous tension between made us laugh. She warmly moved her body closer to mine, leaning her head against my shoulder, still holding my hand.

We were like that for a while and it was beautiful. Somehow, it made the movie seem better, too. I wanted to do something else to show my affection, so I turned and kissed her on her resting head. She liked that, brought her face up to meet mine ... and then we kissed sweetly on the lips. Our mouths were tender and loving and excited, that nervous, powerful, unknown, uncertain first kiss.

We kissed and kissed for a while, with my hand feeling her thighs, hers gliding through my dark blond hair, and our tongues beginning to dance. It was getting us both aroused, almost too much. She giggled and stopped, saying we should watch the movie. We did and were able to follow the story after missing several minutes from our first embrace, our first kiss.

Once the credits were done and the theater lights came on, we turned to each other and smiled. We were both bubbly and warm inside. We liked each other, we clicked, and it seemed so obvious. It was that fresh, vulnerable, "high school love" that I wanted, and which I never had ...

"That was nice." she said, still smiling at me. "The movie, I mean." she continued, teasingly.

"And the other part." I smiled back at her.

"I hope that wasn't a let down." she teased.

"No!" I exclaimed dramatically, jokingly. "Not at all." I looked at her with the pleasure of her presence. Thats all I needed. "Except for the first short, the movies were kinda a let down. Not bad, but not as good as I would expect from Fellini. You, on the other hand, Darling ... were anything but a let down ..."

She blushed and laughed lightly, touched and embarrassed. She was truly tickled. We were both tickled.

As I walked Ariel to her car, she opened up more about her past. Her parents separated when she was nine years old, and they had a somewhat combative relationship before and after. Nine years old ... that was an age I tried to forget ... it was the age when my step-father molested me, or at least attempted to. Frazier was wrestling with me, then took me to his bed and began dry-humping me ... I kicked him off with my feet ... it was the age I began to repress things, mostly because of that but also it was the first year away from Los Angeles, away from my biological father, Jean ...

Looking at Ariel, I could tell that age left a scar as well ... her parents divorce, the separation of her two loved ones, the disjointing of the two figures in two different directions, caused the rift in her own nine year old psyche ... She was stuck in the middle, another connection I had with her, me being stuck between my mother and Jean ... She had spent the majority of her time growing up in Woodland Hills with her financially secure mom. Her dad lived in a shoddy apartment in Van Nuys, a far less financially secure area of the valley.

Despite the fact her dad was an unstable alcoholic, she saw him as a poet and loved him. He was rough around the edges but he was sweet to her, too. As she got older she came to like him more and her mother less. When she was growing up with her mom, her dad seemed like a weirdo and her mom the safe, secure, well-off one. Now, she felt her mother was too controlling and uptight, while her dad was less manipulative and a freer spirit.

Soon our walk finished as we arrived at her car. She mentioned, continuing our discussion about her parents, that her father liked Charles Buckowski. I said I always wanted to check his writing out, which made Ariel mention a new documentary on Buckowski was in theaters now. We agreed to see it together.

A couple days later, I was house-sitting for a friend in Venice. I was off from work watching a movie the friend had in the VCR. The movie wasn't interesting so I turned the t.v. off. I decided to call Ariel on her cell phone. She happened to be at home and asked me where I was. I told her I was house-sitting in Venice. She asked if she could see me. I loved her spontaneity and said of course, not realizing she wanted to come over. When I asked where she wanted to meet, being as she lived in the Valley, I was surprised to hear she wanted to see me at the Venice apartment. She'd drive all the way over. She was wonderful.

She drove all the way over the hill from Woodland Hills, meeting me in front of the apartment on a dark Venice street. Standing in front of each other, under a large, brooding tree, we embraced in a fun, passionate kiss. This was what love should be like, I thought. We went through the front gate, then around the side towards the back of the building. It was a house that'd been divided in half, the back apartment where I was, being the smaller. Walking to the back was almost like a quaint forest, with all the big dark bushes and trees. Behind the apartment in the back was another, a small back house turned apartment. In between was a beautiful, tiny garden with a fountain.

She loved it and I was glad she could be with me here, wishing it was my own place. She asked me who's apartment it was, and I said a lesbian friend who lived by herself. I was honest but I wanted emphasize the fact the friend was a lesbian, just in case Ariel had any suspicions it was really my girlfriend. Once inside, I showed Ariel a picture of my friend and the friend's girlfriend. To not be too obvious, I also showed the woman's photographs, being as Ariel was also a photographer. Unlike Ariel, my friend focused on inanimate objects, mostly buildings and not people. Ariel preferred photographing humans, which I preferred, as well.

The apartment was small, a tight one bedroom. It had the feel of a bohemian living pad, with its wooden floors, old walls, stained glass windows, and a moon-roof in the ceiling. Ariel liked it and I made her feel comfortable. I brought out a bottle of red wine and two glasses. We 'clanged' our glasses, smiled, then began drinking the wine.

She sat down on the recliner chair and leaned back, looking at me. I smiled, then sat on the floor in front of her, putting my wine glass down after finishing it. There wasn't much furniture, only the one comfy chair she was in, and a computer desk chair.

"You drink fast." she said with a smirk.

"This stuff's like water to me." I replied jokingly but with a proud boast hidden in there as well.

"Is it now? Not to me." she paused, a crack in her voice in the next question. "Do you drink a lot?"

"Now and then."

A silence came over us for a little while, not an uncomfortable silence, but a testing one. She gave me a glance as if trying to figure me out. She was also wondering if she should ask what she was about to. Like I often did myself, she went ahead on impulse.

"If I hadn't asked you out to see those Fellini movies, would you have asked me out?" she gently but bluntly put out.

Uh-oh. I was caught off-guard. I hesitated, out of nerves and not doubt. I really would've asked her out, maybe not that day, but eventually. I paid the price for showing my cards too early or too much in the past. I was much more cautious these days. After a few seconds of hesitation, I realized I had to say something or really screw up.

"Yes, definitely."

"Why'd you hesitate?"

"You caught me off-guard."

"I'm sorry, I just had to ask you. I don't normally ask guys out. ... I'm not the most experienced of girls, to be honest with you ..."

"Perhaps my hesitation came from the fact that I don't usually have girls asking me out ... I'm kind of shy myself ... I really liked the fact you asked me out, actually. It was important for me to see that, since I'm open like that as well."

"So in the past you've gone on impulse with a girl?"

"Oh yeah ..."

"How did that go?"

"... Usually ... not good. ... I've done it many more times than once."

"It's not a good idea to be impulsive, you think?"

"I think it is utterly important to be that way ... it's just that people don't respond well to it ... I don't know, I guess every situation is different ... timing is important ..."

"Did I come across to you as too eager? I was going on impulse ..."

"I know you were and thats why I loved it ... it just caught me unexpected, out of the blue. It definitely didn't come across as too eager. It was beautiful." I said with the utmost conviction. I wished I could let my soul cry out in open, honest, unhinged vulnerability to her at that moment ... I wished I could somehow make it clear, make her understand with no doubt, no uncertainty, no complications, that I loved her deeply.

"Really?" she said with a shaky voice.

"Yeah ... completely ..."

"Cool ..." she said softly, sweetly. She was moved intensely by me, as if something inside her had been put to rest, calmed, and soothed. "I guess I over analyze things ... I'm sorry ..."

"No, no, not at all ... it's serious, you know ..."

"What?"

"Love ... the life of your feelings ... you can't dismiss it ..."

"... I just wanted to make sure you weren't a player, maybe ..."

"I wouldn't know how to be one."

"Still ..." she said with a sweetly seductive smile as she took off her shoes and put her bare feet on my lap. "... we can play together."

She melted me. I loved her style. I kept telling myself not to get too eager, not to mess this up, not to jump the gun, not to be too romantic. Take one step at a time.

"I'm glad you said that." I said as I gently held her feet with my hands, then leaned my lips down and kissed the tender flesh of her feet.

After we smiled at each other, she looked deeply into my eyes, seriously, a little uncertain. She wanted me but she didn't know what to do. I could tell and knew that this was my cue. I liked playing the more experienced lover role with her.

I rested her bare feet on my lap and looked up, meeting her serious gaze. I began massaging her feet, gliding my fingers from her toes to her ankles, gently gripping the arch along the way. Then I moved up above her ankles, going further and further, inch by inch, underneath her pants, feeling more and more of her calves.

She was a little nervous, but liked it, then asked if she could have more wine. I said sure, got up, poured the wine into her glass, then gave it to her. She drank the entire glass in two gulps, then coughed a bit. I teased her she drank it too fast, which made her smile. She put her feet back to me and I went back to caressing her feet, ankles, and calves. As I was doing this, to my surprise, she slowly began unzipping her pants ... all the while looking at me.

I smiled, my hands coming out from under her pants, and helped her to take the pants off. There was that expectant nervousness as her pants came down and down her hips to her legs, revealing her pink satin panties. We both looked there, as if some great mystery between us was made bare. She leaned back and took her hands off, letting me take the rest off.

I slowly pulled her pants all the way off, then slid my hands up and up her legs, caressing and fondling her thighs especially. She put her hands on mine as I pressed my face against the top of her thighs and kissed her tender skin. A rush came over me.

"Can we go to the bedroom?" she asked.

"Of course."

She stood up with me and before we walked into the bedroom, we embraced in a passionate kiss. We moaned in each other's mouth and didn't want to move, until eventually we went to the bed.

"Your friend doesn't mind us being on her bed?" she asked as she lay her back on the sheets once I pulled the blankets to the side.

"I don't think so ..." I said with a smile as I started taking off my clothes. "She won't even know, really."

“Why not?” she said as she eyed me taking off my shirt. She loved my hairy chest and body. She couldn't wait to see me take off my pants.

“I'll wash the sheets before she gets back.” I replied, still smiling, as I took off my pants, her eyes on my crotch.

Once I was in nothing but my underwear, she decided she should join me and took off her shirt, now wearing only her bra and panties. I leaned down next to her. Oh, how I loved this, she loved this. We looked at each other ... we were in love. This was 'high school love', a simple, unbearable, fulfilled crush, now about to be fulfilled by sex.

“I'm sorry, could I put some music on?” she asked, hoping not to interrupt the moment.

“Of course.”

“I think you'll like it. It's a French band called 'Air'. They're a little like Brian Eno and you like Brian Eno, right?”

“Yeah, definitely. Sounds cool.” I said as she got up from the bed and went into the other room to put the CD on. I was in heaven. She was a beautiful soul and she actually knew who Brian Eno was. And, oh, did I enjoy seeing her as she got up to go to the other room.

Soon, she put the 'Air' CD on the stereo, and came back to bed. It was gentle, warm, spacey music, nice, and slow. She lay next to me, expectantly.

“Do you like it?” she asked.

“Yeah. Never heard them before.”

“They're new, pretty much.” she said as she dug her face into my chest, holding onto me, wrapping her body around mine. She held on as if she didn't want to let go. She wanted to be as close as possible to me. I loved the warmth of her body pressed up tightly against mine.

I could feel her breaths against my chest, light, gentle breaths, her arms wrapped around my back, her knee in between my legs. Her tender thigh gently pressed up against my balls, my hands caressing her back, hips, ass, and legs. She looked up at me innocently and opened her mouth, tilting her head back slightly. I leaned down and tasted her lips with mine ... I loved kissing her lips ... Ariel's lips ... Ariel the Angel ...

She let go slowly and lay on her back, just looking at me with a serious, fond gaze. I looked into her eyes, then turned away from the intensity, looking at her shoulder, her skin, her chest.

"Why won't you look me in the eyes?" she asked simply.

"I do."

"Not for long."

"I don't know."

"Is it easier to look at my body?"

"Sometimes. Sometimes I want to see your soul." I said, smiling as I looked straight into the pupils of her eyes.

She laughed once I looked at her with my smile. There seemed something sweet yet sarcastic about me. Once her laughing quieted down, she turned and hugged me, wrapping her body around me again, taking deep, long breaths.

"I feel comfortable with you." she said.

"Me, too."

"You feel comfortable with yourself?" she asked with a smile.

"No, silly." I said, smiling, and then she began to laugh. "You."

We kissed again and again, our bodies entangled as we rolled around on the bed and the music played from the other room. We stopped kissing as I lay on my back and she was on top of me.

“Do you like being on top?” I asked.

“I prefer you on top.”

She turned to lay on her back, then began taking off her bra ... there were her breasts ... naked before me ... oh, I enjoyed seeing her firm, small, young tits ... they were so delicate, so lush ... She felt vulnerable but she wanted this with me. She trusted me.

“Do you like them?” she said with a smile.

“Very much.”

I caressed her breasts with my fingers, rolling around her nipples, lightly rubbing them. She moaned slightly as she looked at her breasts, then at me. I leaned down and carefully started kissing her shoulders, then chest, then breasts, then nipples, all the while gliding one hand up and down her legs.

“I ...” she started to say, aroused, nervous. “I've never done it before.”

I knew what she meant. She was a virgin. That was okay. I didn't need penetration if she didn't want it.

“We don't have to go all the way.” I consoled.

“Yeah, I'd rather not. Not this time.”

“We can keep our underwear on.”

“Okay. Can I touch your thing, though?” she asked, smiling mischievously.

“By all means.” I smiled back.

She reached down, running her fingers along my body until she touched my underwear. She pulled the elastic top part away from my pelvis, then slowly put her fingers to touch my hard cock. I was stiff and throbbing ... the sexual tension between us was amazing ...

"Nice ..." she said, looking at me while exploring more of my dick.

Her fingers glided over my cock head, then further down, going along my shaft and to my hairy balls. I was loving it. Her fingertips were so soft. I caressed her hair, shoulders, arm, breasts, waist, hips, ass, and legs as she continued to play with my thing. We began kissing with more passion now.

I positioned myself on top of her, my hands above her shoulders, holding my upper body up as I looked down at her. She wrapped her legs around my waist as we pushed our pelvis' into each other.

"Oh ..." she moaned, looking at me as she felt my hard cock pressing up against her pussy through our underwear.

The tension was building and building as we continued to grind and grind, our dry-humping through our underwear becoming faster and more and more intense. Her eyes opened wide, as if some uncertain excited feeling came over her. She was losing control and wanted to kiss me.

"You're good at this, at sex, aren't you?" she asked as she leaned up to me, wanting me, body and soul. "Kiss me as you do that."

I leaned down and kissed her as I continued to grind and roll my cock against her pussy mound and clit. We both moaned in each other's mouth, the grinding getting more and more intense, faster and faster, harder and harder. Our eyes locked, our gaze unable to look away. I had this strong urge to call her my girl, my little girl, so I did. After I said it, something inside her, some feeling, popped. It wasn't a physical 'pop', but an emotional one, her high-pitched 'little girl' moans reflecting our desires.

"Can you cum? I want you to cum ..." she said as she continued moaning in that high voice.

I was ready, I was ready to explode, for a while, but now she said that I didn't hold back anymore. As it got hotter and hotter between us, with me on top of her, I soon came, shooting cum all over my underwear.

“Oh god ...” I said, frozen as I held myself up with my arms, still over her.

“Did you cum?”

“Ohhh yess ... oh, fuck, Ariel ...”

“Lay next to me ...”

I crashed to the bed beside her, in that post-orgasm aftermath glow ... le petite morte ... she smiled as she looked at me.

“ ... In the future I'll make sure you cum, too ...” I said, catching my breath.

“Let's not think about that right now ... it's so beautiful being with you like this.”

“You know ... I want to tell you ...”

“Yeah?”

“You're the best ...” I said, wanting to tell her I loved her ... but I knew I should control myself. “I really like you ... a lot ...”

“Me, too.”

“You like yourself a lot?” I jibbed her with a smile.

“No ...” she responded with a smile and light slap on my butt. “I like you a lot.”

We continued to kiss and fool around on the bed, relishing every personal, sensual moment, listening to the 'Air' CD and others. It was late and I knew not much was open, but we were hungry so we got dressed and walked to the nearby Vons several blocks away. We goofed around on the way to the store, with me giving her a piggy-back ride, kissing, fondling, talking about the Beatles and other bands. She started singing 'Let's Do It On The Road'. I chimed in as I gripped her ass and kissed her.

I wanted her to stay the night. I told her so after we came back to the apartment and finished our food. She wanted to but couldn't, having to drive back home, even though it was already three in the morning. She promised we'd see each other again soon.

"Hey, isn't your 21st birthday coming up?" I asked as I walked her to her car outside.

"Yup, in a few days. This Tuesday. I'm going out with some friends. I'm free Monday night, though."

"Cool, so am I."

"Let's hang out then."

"I'd like to do something special for you."

"You don't have to."

"Turning 21 is a big deal."

"Not really. We can just go see a movie or something."

"As it turns out, my mom's staying at a hotel near the airport. She's out of the area Monday and Tuesday, and she said I could stay there. Why don't you stay with me?"

"Wow, well ... okay. That sounds nice."

"It'll be fun. The ocean's nearby, there's a restaurant in the hotel, a jacuzzi, the room's nice, I'll bring some wine."

"I don't deserve all that. You're too nice to me."

"You don't deserve it? Of course you do."

"Alright." she said as we embraced in a warm, tender kiss before she got into the car and drove off.

I was in love. I was glowing inside, carrying that dream-like, hazy, beautiful passion for Ariel wherever I went the next couple of days. I couldn't wait until Monday. I talked to my dad Jean about my love for Ariel, talked to Gus, as well, telling them both just how special this new love I discovered was. They both could tell by the way I talked how much Ariel meant to me. The freshness, spontaneity, simplicity of my experience with her was exactly what I needed, and so different from past lovers or love interests.

Monday finally came and we agreed to meet at the Fairfax. Ariel didn't want me to pick her up inside the theater, so I waited for her around the corner. She didn't want her co-workers gossiping about the two of us. I understood and agreed. I hated how people in the Laemmle theater chain gossiped so much. The company was infected with gossip whores at every theater.

Before I picked her up, I went to Trader Joe's and got a bouquet of flowers and two bottles of wine, one red, one white. I thought at first maybe it was over-kill but then realized, why not? I felt like doing it and normally I'd never do something like that, so why the hell not?

Once Ariel got into my car, saw the flowers and bottles of wine, my heart sank when I saw the look on her face. She didn't want the flowers and wine. She didn't want the over-kill. It was too much. I died a little death in that moment, like so many times before. Still, it didn't completely demolish our love momentum.

"Wow, thanks." she said half-heartedly. It made her uncomfortable. "That's really nice of you, but you didn't have to get me all this."

"It's good wine. I wasn't sure if you liked red or white so I got both."

I still had the sunken heart and so did she, but I didn't want to give up. I was still manic with my love for her, and decided to continue with my plans for the evening. I'd keep both my disappointment with that first moment and my excitement under control. That way I'd be able to enjoy the later moments more and have her enjoy it, as well. The last thing I wanted to do was ruin this night. I'd die if I did.

"So how're things going?" I asked as I drove the car and she sat next to me.

"Pretty good."

"How's the Fairfax treating you?"

"Not bad. Your ex has been a little weird recently though."

"She doesn't know about us, does she? She'd go around and tell the whole city."

"No, she doesn't, and nobody does."

"That's good. You doing anything with your parents for your birthday?"

"We already did this past weekend."

I kept the conversation light from then on, hoping to take us away from that first sudden disappointment. I didn't want to get too heavy and serious and awkward with her. Not tonight.

Soon we reached the beach near the airport in El Segundo, where no one else was. We were giddier now, having fun again as we ran over the beach towards the ocean. It was brisk and windy, so we put on our jackets, running along the shore, chasing each other, goofing off.

We wore ourselves out from all the playing around and dropped to the sand not too far from the crashing waves. It was beautiful. She sat in front of me, looking at the ocean, her back nestled up against my chest, my legs outlining hers, my arms wrapped around her body, her hands holding onto mine. We recaptured our sweetness, I thought, as we looked out into the ocean and talked. She was comfortable with me again.

Romance was also picking up between us after sitting with our bodies like that for a while. She lay on her back, looking up into my eyes as I rested on my arm, my body over her. We kissed and kissed passionately. Some people walked by and we stopped kissing. I joked I wondered how people would react if the two of us were naked on the beach, making love. She laughed a bit, but with an awkward reservation. I continued making silly remarks, which she continued to not enthusiastically respond to. One joke was that we were like Romeo and Juliet.

It was getting cold and dark, so we got up from our spot on the sand and walked back to the car. On the way, she realized she lost her mother's necklace she was wearing. We looked all over the sand, combing every inch we were on, but it was getting darker and darker and I didn't have a flashlight. It was gone.

“Shit ... I'm sorry.” I apologized.

“It's okay.”

“Was it valuable? Personally or monetarily?”

“Yeah, kinda. It was my mom's for a long time, then she just gave it to me for my 21st birthday.”

I felt like shit. I felt responsible and told her so. She told me not to worry, that there was nothing we could do. It was lost. I said maybe we could come back in the morning and look for it in the daylight. She didn't want to. As we got to the car, I was inwardly bummed out about the necklace. If only I didn't insist on going to the beach, making such a big deal about her birthday, going to the hotel, maybe she'd still have her mom's necklace.

Once at the hotel, she was once again made awkward. The hotel was really nice, not cheap at all. Even if I wasn't paying for it, having her come here was, once again, too much. She became less comfortable with me again, not saying much, withdrawing into an inward silence. I tried to keep things going with chatting and making jokes. It didn't help much, although a little.

Inside the motel room, we sat on the couch and got comfortable. She relaxed more as we began drinking the red wine first. We talked and drank for almost two hours, and by that time finished both bottles of wine. She told me about past boyfriends, past and current friends, high school, college. I told her the whole process of making my movie, the zine I did with my dad Jean, talked about past girlfriends, friends, my troubles at C.W.F.P.S.J. (although I stayed away from the sexual harassment aspect).

We began making out on the couch and because of all the alcohol we were looser but sloppier. We kissed and kissed, then she stopped and looked at me with that innocent but penetrating stare. I asked if she was hungry or if she wanted to go down to the jacuzzi and she said 'no'. She looked at me with her silent look for a while, then said she did want to take a bath, though.

"With me?" I asked.

"Of course."

I smiled as we kissed, then we went into the bedroom. On the bed, we continued kissing as our clothes came off. We were clumsy as we did it, but had fun. When we got to our underwear she stopped.

"I want you to see me completely naked for the first time in the bathtub." she said with a seductive smile.

"That's a nice idea."

"I'll go in and make the bath and when I'm ready, I'll call you."

"Okay." I replied with a happy glow.

"There's just one thing."

“What's that?”

“I want you to tell me what really happened at that peace activist job you had.”

“Why? It wasn't important.” I said as my heart sank low again.

“Come on. I'm gonna get nude for you.”

“So am I.”

“But I want you to get a little nude with that.” she said with her sweet eyes. “Okay?”

“Okay.”

“I'll be ready in a couple minutes.”

Shit, I almost said out loud when she went to the bathroom. I could hear her panties and bra ever so gently fall to the floor, and then water spraying down into the bathtub. What was I going to say? Should I tell her the whole story? Be completely up front with her on what went down between me and Charlotte and everyone else?

How would she take it if I explained all the ugliness? Would she understand? Would she judge me? Would she get freaked out by me? Would I seem a creep to her now? Would she want a 'misogynist', 'woman-hater', 'sexual-harasser' as a boyfriend? I had only a couple minutes to decide what to do. I had no idea what to say if I was going to lie. That was one of my big problems in life – I was a horrible liar. I could never be a con. ... So I chose to tell her the truth.

“I'm ready, sexy man.” she said with her lovely voice, calling from the bathtub.

I got up from the bed and walked into the bathroom, where I saw her in all her naked beauty ... there she was, my angel ... there she was, no underwear, no bra, nothing at all but her soul and her flesh ... her divine skin exposed in hot water, her sweet eyes looking at me with utter expectation ... her breasts, her hips, ass, legs and now, the first time for me to see, her fresh, young, delicious pussy ... underwater ... all waiting for me ...

"You like what you see?" she asked innocently.

"... More than anything in the world ..." I replied, overwhelmed by emotion, near tears. Why did my past have to ruin this moment? It was horrible, heartbreaking, as if there was a sharp, sharp knife twisting around my gut, over and over and over again.

"What's wrong?"

"It's just ... I can't believe how beautiful you are and how precious this moment is ..."

"Come on. Now it's your turn. Take off yours. Lemme see, then come in with me."

I smiled at her as I took off my underwear and let it drop to the ground. She was disappointed I didn't have a hard-on. There was something wrong with me, she could tell. I gave myself away so easily. I stepped into the tub with her, facing her, my back against the opposite end, our legs entangled. Oh, what a delight to be with her like this, I thought. ... Heaven. Then I realized I had to tell her my past ... I had to put that out ...

She put her foot on my limp, soft prick, rubbing it gently, hoping to make me hard. But it didn't work.

"You don't have to tell me what happened at that place." she said, knowing that my sudden sadness must have something to do with the peace activist job.

"Well ... now I do." I responded despondently. "We both know something bad happened. We both know now that if I don't tell you, it'll always be hanging over us ..."

She wished she hadn't asked. She didn't like seeing me with this depression. What could she do? It was too late. I was right. We couldn't retreat now. It would always be a nagging problem in our relationship, that troubled mystery in the back of our minds.

So I told her what happened. The whole story. The entire C.W.F.PS.J melodrama. Like how I often did when opening the doors to my pain, to some painful memory, long ago or recent, the emotions overwhelmed me so much that my body became relaxed, heavy, burdened and unmoving. My eyes would look off into an indefinite place, away from the person I was talking to. I couldn't look at her the whole time we sat in the bathtub as I told the story ... I couldn't look at her once ... not once.

There was no release, no catharsis, when I was done. All I could feel was desolation, as if I destroyed my beautiful romance with her. I obliterated our chance of a great relationship with one stroke of a confession ... I felt the world drop inside me ... she didn't know how to respond. She felt sorry for me but awkward. I seemed so far away, so distant and sad that she didn't know how to reach me.

We got out of the bathtub, let the water drain, and dried ourselves off. I asked if she wanted to go downstairs to eat and she said sure. We didn't talk much as we got dressed and went to the restaurant.

Once downstairs, we found out the restaurant was closed. The bar was still open and served food, so we ordered a pizza. As we waited, I got more and more lost and silent within myself. I began to hate myself, hate life, hate everything ... a bleakness came over me, a sadness, a strange, impenetrable, black, bitter anger ... I didn't want Ariel to see me like this ... it was emotional ugliness ... it was too soon for her to see me like this ... the silence was deadening ... I couldn't snap out of i "I'm sorry ..." I said, unable to look at her, knowing it was all over.

"It's okay ..." she said, concerned but also estranged, put off by my bleak silence.

She tried to cheer me up by rubbing her foot against my leg and looking at me, but it was no use. I was so far gone within myself, like I'd been swallowed up by an emotional black hole. She wasn't so sure she wanted to cross the line and console me. We finished the pizza in silence.

While we went up the elevator, my silent, pensive inner turmoil softened a bit. It was like all the chemicals of angst in my body had been flushed out ... I felt more at ease, free from that depression.

On the third floor, we got out of the elevator and went to the room. I realized she must think I was a psychotic wacko. Our romance was over. I screwed up. I destroyed it all. All the waves of depression had worn themselves out, so instead of feeling an intense sadness again, a strong sensation of giving up came over me. A fixation of the absurdity, the circus merry go-round of pain that could only be laughed at. I smiled painfully to myself as we got to our room's door.

"You don't have to stay ... I ruined this night ... this whole beautiful experience with you ... I can take you home, or to the Fairfax to your car ... wherever you want to go ... I'm sorry ..." I said, looking into her eyes, tears coming down my face, hitting the edge of my strained smile.

I felt like a sad, awkward clown who could just never win, never get the performance right, time after time after time ... always hitting the wrong notes at the wrong times ... always trying to juggle my life, and always dropping the balls to the floor ...

"It's okay ... I'll stay." she said with a warm smile.

I was in shock. I thought she'd want to leave, never see me again, but she insisted on staying, even after I asked her a few times more. So, to my delight, to the pleasure of my soul, we went inside the room, tired from everything that happened that night. We walked to the bedroom, took off our clothes and held each other sweetly, tightly, affectionately kissing, caressing, not wanting to let go, until we fell asleep ...

The next morning, Ariel woke up early and looked at me, not knowing I was barely awake. I could tell she was examining me somehow. I could imagine what must've been running through her mind. Who was this guy, this man she got so close to physically and emotionally in such a short period of time? She never did this with anyone ever before. What was it it about me that made her like this? This vulnerable? Who was I anyway? I was complicated, beyond measure ... a strange beautiful man to her ... but she didn't know me ... I still seemed a stranger ...

What had she gotten into with me? Did she get caught up in my darkness? Did she open up a can of worms with me? She was a dark one herself, although didn't tell me the whole story ... she wondered if she should ... Was I the right guy for her? She had her own problems, would it be too intense to stay involved with me, knowing how I could be? While she circled around inside her head with all these questions, looking at me, she was also attracted to me. She went back to sleep, her arms and legs wrapped around me, her face pressed up against my shoulder.

A couple hours later, I woke up. Seeing her asleep in my arms, my angel, her decision to spend the night after everything that happened, made me believe perhaps we hadn't lost the magic. Perhaps I hadn't completely destroyed it all.

Soon, she woke, yawning, smiling at me. It felt so good to wake up seeing her in my arms. I wished her a Happy Birthday. We kissed and kissed, caressing and holding, becoming more and more aroused. I quickly became hard and she felt it. She lay on her back and spread her legs a bit, inviting me. We still had our underwear on and I asked her if she wanted them off. She said no, that she wanted to do what we did last time, at my friends' apartment.

I positioned myself on top of her, my hands holding myself over her as I grinded my cock against her underwear ... Like before, the tension grew and grew, building and building as I went faster and faster ... and, like before, she wanted to see me cum ... so I did, exploding in my underwear ... As I lay beside her afterwards and we smiled at each other, I wondered out loud just how beautiful it would be if there was penetration.

Eventually, after continuing to fool around in bed for a while, we got up and got dressed. As I drove her back to the Fairfax theater, she remembered she had pictures that were developed. She had to pick them up. I didn't mind and actually wanted to see her photographs.

We drove to a special developing place in Hollywood and got the pictures. She showed photographs she took on a road trip with a friend recently. Some were interesting to me, some weren't. The ones that weren't, I didn't tell her, but she could sense it by looking at me. She was disappointed, even though by the end of the pictures I emphasized how much I liked them and looked forward to more.

The Fairfax wasn't too far away and I dropped her off at her car. We kissed goodbye and I wished her well on her night out with friends. As she said goodbye and went to her car, she seemed a bit withdrawn again. I worried ... what was she thinking? I decided to let it go, excited about seeing her again soon.

A few days passed and Ariel didn't call. Was it nothing? Was she just busy? I picked up the phone at my apartment and called her. She answered and when hearing it was me, she hesitated, retreated ... Her voice was uncertain, shaky ... I asked how her Birthday celebration went and she said well, not going into details at all.

She didn't say much about anything, acting almost scared of me ... I asked what was wrong and she waited, paused, took several breaths, was obviously holding something back until she couldn't anymore ...

"I don't ... I don't think we should see each other anymore ..." she said through the phone.

"What? Why? ... I mean, it's been ..." I began, shattered to the core ... I wanted to tell her I loved her, how much I loved her, how important she was to me ... I didn't want it to end like this, so sudden. "It's only been a couple weeks ... we were just starting ..."

"I know and that's why I want to stop it before we go any further ... I'm sorry, Tom ..."

“Well ...” I continued, then tried to grab onto anything. “... can we still see each other as friends?”

“No, I don't think that's a good idea. I might end up wanting to get back with you.”

“Would that be such a bad idea?”

“Um ... I just can't do it. We went too fast too soon and I'm mostly to blame ... I

woke up next to you that one morning at the hotel room and realized I had no idea who you were ...”

A streak of violence came within me after she said that.

“... We were only 'together' for two weeks ...” I shot out in bitterness.

“It's not only that ...”

“Was it because of that night? ... my black, strange, silent mood ... my past ...?” my anger was overtaken by regret, but the rage still lingered.

“No, not at all, it wasn't that. The reason is ... well, anyway, Tom, we can't see each other anymore because I'm going up to an arts school up north. I'll be starting in a few months.”

“... oh yeah? You didn't tell me that ... if you want to see other people, I'm fine with that ... I just need to continue seeing you ...” I said, tears coming from my eyes now. “I love you, Ariel ...”

“Um, I don't do that ... I only date people monogamously ... I'm really sorry but it's over between you and me ...”

I didn't say anything for a while but she could hear my crying ...

“Tom? ... Are you okay? ... Are you still there?” she said, worried.

“... Yeah ...”

"... I'm sorry to do this to you."

"Me, too ..." I said as a black, sad, bitterness came over me, an anger with all the disappointments, all of them ... and now Ariel ... one after another ... leaving the one with the most hope for last to be crushed ... my heart was fully burned to ashes now ... saving the best for last ... the best for last ... "I've got your underwear ..." I said. "You left them at the hotel room."

"Oh ..." she replied, uncertain, awkward, not knowing what to say.

"I thought about just keeping them to remember our good times together ... but then I realized that would probably make me a creep ..." I said, making her feel like shit. Her heart began to crack as well now. "I'll come and drop them off at the Fairfax when you're working."

"You don't have to do -"

And then I hung up the phone, smashing it against the receiver ... cutting her off in the middle of her sentence. In seconds I broke out into an uncontrollable wave of tears, falling to the floor, shaking and shaking, trembling in deep, apocalyptic sadness, at the horror of life, of losing Ariel ... I cried and cried ... an unbearable pain ... tears after tears ... sobbing like a child ... screaming ... cursing God ... cursing life ... I couldn't take it anymore ... for a second I thought of killing myself ... but I didn't ... I held myself back ... some day I'd meet someone else ... I was scared of death ... and I wanted to live more life, however more death blows I'd be dealt with or bring upon myself ...

The next day, I called the Fairfax and found out from someone else Ariel was working that day. I drove over there before work and went inside the theater. I saw her behind the counter. She saw me, panicked, her eyes quickly turning away, unable to look. I couldn't take the pain, either, and rushed up to the counter.

"Here they are." I said as I dropped the bag containing her underwear on the counter in front of her.

I quickly turned and walked away, hating myself for my bitterness, for my anger towards her. I hated that was how it ended ... I hated that this was how Romeo and Juliet truly ended their romance ... this was how they really killed themselves ... this was how they dealt themselves their suicides ...

PART EIGHT. MAYA.

CHAPTER ONE. THE PASSION DIES OUT.

There's only one person who could make me take a trip to Texas: Maya. Your mother, Daniel. Three times, actually, and only because of her. The first, I helped her and the father of her two kids get there. I drove a large U-haul truck containing most of their things, in the middle of a cold November. Maya and her boyfriend Emmanuel drove the '76 Cadillac with their 3 year old twins, Dinora and Javier. The kids cried and cried most of the time, and the journey was stressful. It was a big decision to move from L.A. to a small town in the middle of Texas. One night Maya broke down in a rain of tears at a motel room in Arizona. Both Emmanuel and I asked her what was wrong but she wouldn't say.

Once at the house, close to the town of Weatherford, I helped them unload their stuff. Then I took a bus back to L.A., which Emmanuel paid for as a thank you for helping out. I had known Maya a couple years, but it was in the last year before her move when we became good friends. Initially, we hated each other, meeting through my ex, who was a friend of Maya's.

Once I started coming by to show Maya how to meditate, we began appreciating each other and got pretty close. I came by every other day to meditate, talk to her about spirituality, or just hang out. I was good with her kids and kind. At that time in my life, I was into an experiential, new age Christian lifestyle. After I cast my beliefs to the side and stopped meditating, we were still good friends.

A few months into our friendship, I realized I'd fallen in love with her. But I didn't tell her. When she told me she was moving to Texas, I tried to persuade her to stay. But she had to get away from Los Angeles, go someplace new, and give her boyfriend a chance. Emmanuel was a hardcore alcoholic and ran into many troubles with Maya's intense personality. He got a good job at a restaurant in Weatherford and wanted to try and make their family unit work.

When I came back to Los Angeles, I was filled with an unbearable heartache. I missed Maya tremendously. She'd become such an integral part of my life, especially after losing my spiritual faith. She was, for a year, the center to my life which before was accustomed to God and meditation as the center ... When God left, after two years of devotion and faith and meditation and Christian living, Maya was there to fill the void ...

We stayed in touch by phone and through letters. Maya quickly began missing all her friends and family in Los Angeles and was often calling and writing people. I wrote and called her the most out of everyone. I was madly in love. The distance between us only intensified my yearning. I was constantly thinking about her, crying for her, drinking more and more alcohol, wallowing in my passionate, lonely, self-absorbed romance with an unavailable mother of two in Texas ...

I saw other women now and then but could never be convincing, could never invest much of myself. I always went back to my love for Maya, always writing letters to her, poems to her, calling her. My second trip to Texas came when my ex-girlfriend and I decided to pay Maya a visit. My ex would tease me and Maya we were having an affair, but only in a joking way. She had no idea how crazy in love with Maya I really was.

The second trip to Texas was fun, despite the ongoing trifling squabbles with my ex. Maya thought our arguing was humorous and poked we should get back together. My ex and I thought that was funny. She and I hated each other, really. During the entire trip, I never let on my love and lust for Maya.

The second time coming back to Los Angeles from Texas, my love for the El Salvadorian beauty only intensified more. I thought maybe by then I'd finally get over her. I couldn't. I decided I had to tell Maya. There was no way I could reasonably hide it anymore. She was surprised when she got my love letter ... or at least she said she was. It seemed pretty obvious. Anyone whose time and energy was spent as much with someone like mine was with Maya smelled of romantic love.

Still, Maya made it clear she was surprised and only wanted me as a friend. She was, after all, living with her boyfriend in Texas and a mother of two. I understood and expected her to say exactly that. I just had to let her know. We continued as close, dear friends, still writing each other, still calling.

A couple months later Maya and her kids came to visit Los Angeles. She was still missing everyone, her friends and family, and especially me, she said .... While in L.A. for the week, she stayed at one person's place or another's. A few nights she and her kids were at my single apartment in Mar Vista, sleeping on my futon mattress while I was on the floor. Maya's kids Dinora and Javier loved me and wanted to be around me a lot of the time. As Maya and I were with each other so much, flirtations between us infiltrated our platonic relationship.

One night, the day before Maya and her kids were going back to Texas, she and I stayed up late and drank wine, while Dinora and Javier were asleep. We talked and talked, quietly, and drank and drank. I crossed the platonic line when I put my hand on her leg. She was drunk so didn't mind it much at first, then pushed my hand away. I looked at her and smiled.

"You know how crazy I am about you ..." I said, drunk enough to open up to her.

"I know you're crazy." she replied with a smile.

"I'm in love with you."

"You need to find a girlfriend and forget about me. We're always going to be friends, nothing more."

"Easier said than done."

"What?"

"Finding another woman. I'm in love with you, Maya, not another girl."

“It's easy for men. You'll get over me quick.”

“That's what you think. Try being a man. We have hearts, too, you know.”

“No you don't.”

“Try being someone who's in love with you ...” I said, smiling at the bluntness of her last remark. “I mean, you're beautiful, Maya, body and soul ...”

“Ssshh. Don't wake up the kids.”

“Shit, I'm sorry.” I said quietly.

“Don't swear. You'll make God angry.” she said with a teasing smile.

“I've already made God angry ... because of you.”

“Me? What did I do? I'm not the devil.”

“I fell in love with you when I showed you how to meditate.”

“So you're blaming me for becoming an atheist?”

“I'm not an atheist, I'm an agnostic. I just stopped wanting to say 'NO' to life.”

“So that's my fault?”

“No, it's mine. Just like it's my fault for falling in love with you ... maybe.” I smiled at her, looking at her legs.

“Shut up. Come on, I'm tired. Let's go to sleep.”

She went to sleep not much later, laying on the edge of the futon near me, while the kids were on the other side. I tried to sleep on the floor, but it wasn't happening. I couldn't take my eyes off Maya. It was a warm night, and she just so happened to leave the blankets off her legs ...

they were shining from bronze, smooth elegance ... a street light coming through the window hit her thighs.

Her legs were inches away from my hand ... all I had to do was reach over and feel. That's all I had to do, or that's all I shouldn't do. To touch or not to touch. ... I went for it ... softly gliding my fingers along her calf ... I loved her legs ... up and up to her thigh ... those legs ... so delicious. I could chomp down on her El Salvadorian flesh.

As I pressed harder on her thigh, I looked at her. She moaned quietly, her eyes still closed. Was she asleep? If she was awake, she pretended to be asleep and didn't remove my hand. It was as if she was telling me, 'you can have me, but I'm going to act as if I didn't know.' That way she wouldn't be 'cheating' on her boyfriend Emmanuel, even though at this point they'd broken up. Emmanuel was considering moving back to Los Angeles while Maya and the kids were staying in Texas. The restaurant he originally went out there to work for closed down after 8 months.

Since Maya made no attempts to stop my hand, I was unbearably horny for her ... maybe I wouldn't penetrate. That was too much like rape. But I would go down on her. It was less evasive of her sleeping space, more gentle obviously. And anyway, for Christ's sake, little Dinora and Javier were right next to us. But I had to have her ... she looked so beautiful ... those legs, that body, the person I knew underneath that body ... so I began to more vigorously but not aggressively, fondle her thighs and calves, running my hands up and down her angelic, long, bronze skin ...

I leaned down and lightly kissed her feet first as I continued to caress her legs. Even her feet were beautiful. I positioned myself directly below instead of to her side, my head at her feet, my hands running up and up her legs, then back down. She moaned, quietly, moving her body a little as if she was getting turned on. She spread her legs open a few inches. I was in heaven, looking at her.

She was wearing high cut, loose shorts, so her hips were showing. I began kissing her ankles, calves, knees, then those luscious thighs, up and up. Her legs opened further and I noticed something. She wasn't wearing any underwear ... the shorts were so loose that I could see the place I wanted most ... her pussy ... there it was ... I could see her pussy hair and even her clit ...

I was going insane with horniness, kissing and kissing all over her legs, then paid more attention to the inside of her thighs. It was tender, so smooth there. She opened her legs further apart, as if inviting me. I whole heartedly welcomed the invitation, looked and noticed she was still pretending to be asleep, then put my face below ...

I pulled the thong part of her shorts to the side, revealing her pussy entirely to me. Not only was her vagina great to look at, she smelled so sweet down there, too. She cleaned herself often and just had a natural good smell. I kissed gently the top of her pussy mound, tasting the hair in my mouth, kissing and kissing until I got to her clit. Her pussy wasn't that big, with cute, pretty, bronze clit lips that were getting more and more moist.

Holding the inside of her thighs in my hands, I leaned my face down and oh so slightly touched her clit lips with the tip of my tongue. I slowly moved my tongue up, then down, going back and forth ... she was loving it, I could tell, by her moans and movements, and oh, was I. I loved licking her pussy ...

I licked and licked and licked, kissed and kissed and kissed, fondling her legs, body and breasts with my hands. I went further into her pussy hole, with my tongue, relishing just how wet she was, going in and out, then going back to licking her clit up and down, then back to going in and out, then back to up and down ... it was wonderful ...

I did this for a long time and we both were enjoying it intensely. The whole time the kids were still asleep. Thank god. Imagine if they saw what I was doing to their mama! Then, as I was licking and sucking her pussy, Maya said something in the middle of her moans. At first, I couldn't tell what she was saying, then after a few times of repeating it, I deciphered her words of ecstasy ...

"Ohhh ... Miranda ..." she said quietly while still moaning.

Miranda? Who was she? Why was she saying a woman's name while I was going down on her? That was kind of an insult. Whoever this woman was wasn't the one giving her this pleasure. I was. I didn't mind if she liked women, although she never even hinted at it, and I didn't mind if she was in love with this other woman. It was just in this given moment, Maya and I were making love, not Maya and Miranda. It turned me off. Maybe she really was asleep and was dreaming about this woman, imagining, wishing it was her who was licking her pussy and not me ...

Then I remembered a Miranda. Oh yes, I thought to myself, as I stopped licking her pussy and sat on the floor next to the bed. Maya was still moving and moaning slightly, but then stopped soon after I was no longer giving her oral. She seemed to be asleep, although she probably wasn't, probably in that half-awake, half-asleep space of the mind. She just didn't want me to see her aware of what happened.

But this woman, this Miranda, I knew who she was. She was from El Salvador, about the same age as Maya, and was also a mother. She was married to an older white guy who had an antique store in Santa Monica. Maya and Miranda had been friends for several years, and I knew Miranda was somewhat of a nymphomaniac. But I had no idea she might be a lesbian or have something going on with Maya, of all people.

While being a joker, a prankster, a sarcastic troublemaker who could play with people's minds, Maya was also very concerned about projecting an image of sexual purity. She'd only been with two men in her life – her first husband and the father of her kids, Emmanuel. No one else. I went further than anyone besides those two.

Maya may have flirted with people, but she would never, ever fool around sexually. She had her boundaries. So what was this secret that popped out in the middle of receiving oral by me? The beautiful licking moment I gave her was in and of itself was quite a dramatic thing for her to do. But what was this moaning for Miranda all about? Was she really into girls? Was Maya a lesbian? Was she in the closet? Did she accept her lesbianism, but just hide it from people out of shame, out of her Catholic guilt? Or maybe she didn't even know herself.

I had no idea what to think of it, nor what to do or say. Should I say anything to her? I was in love with this woman, with Maya, more passionately than anyone ever before ... my soul bled and bled for her so long now, not temperately at all, but to extremes ... I cried for her over and over again so often when she moved to Texas ...

What could I say to her? Whether I wanted to admit to it or not, her saying, "Ohh ... Miranda ... Miranda ..." while going down on her, the first time I was with her sexually, the first time being so intimate with the love of my life ... it broke my heart. It was, in the recess of my subconscious, shattering ... so what the hell could I say? It was still too dramatic for me to bring to the surface ... better to keep it underground, for now. I knew I couldn't keep it there forever.

The next morning, I took Maya and the kids to a Norms diner before going to the Greyhound station downtown. In a couple hours they'd be in a bus riding back to Texas ... In a couple hours Maya would be gone again ... I was overwhelmed with emotion as we ate breakfast. I didn't want to see her leave again and I also was distressed about the night before. I kept hinting at our love-making, but she denied it. The kids didn't understand what we were talking about.

"We didn't do anything." Maya said with irritation.

"Actually ... we did." I responded.

"Must've been in your dreams."

"No, I was quite lucid."

"You're crazy."

"You've said that before."

I hated how she always wanted things so "under the covers," so secretive, so in denial. We made love! God, I loved it! So did she! Why couldn't she admit it happened?

If Maya didn't want to admit she moaned that woman's name, she didn't want to admit she could bi-sexual, fine. For now. That's big stuff. It should be dealt with eventually. But to flat out deny we did anything sexually, at all, pissed me off. It wasn't as if she had to worry about the kids. They didn't understand or have to know. But because the experience was so wonderful (until the end), her denying it ever happened was like denying the beauty of it for me.

"Don't worry, we'll be gone soon, Thomas." she said sarcastically, noticing my dour mood.

"... Why'd you say that?" I replied, hurt low. How could she say that? Be so manipulative? So insensitive? "What're you talking about? You think I want you to leave?"

"Maybe. You don't look happy around us."

"I love you, Maya ..." I said, near tears.

"I'm not sure about that." she said, flinging more shit into my face. Why was she doing this?

"Don't ever question my love." I said as an utter challenge. "I'm just pissed off you won't acknowledge what happened last night."

"What do you want me to say? 'Hey, good fuck there, baby, you know how to go down on women so good, baby.' You want everyone to know?"

"They can't know unless we tell them and there's no need to tell anyone."

"Some day soon it would come out."

She was partially right. She had to protect herself. She had to play the role of momma, play the role of girlfriend to her kid's dad, even if they were splitting up. I understood and apologized, although I wished there was a more glowing warmth coming from her, not this hostility.

We all finished our breakfast and soon I dropped them off at the Greyhound station. With each passing minute, my heart sank and churned, as they readied to leave ... Once we said our goodbyes and I watched them get on to the bus, and they were gone, I went to my car and broke down in a rush of anguished tears, crying and crying ... I couldn't help myself ...

A few months went by and I continued to write to Maya, continued talking to her over the phone. I couldn't stop being in love with her ... Then, it got to be too much ... I wrote a letter to her saying I had to step away for a while ... stop being her friend ... My love for her was too much for me to handle while we kept our platonic friendship going ... I had to allow my passion to cool down ... Perhaps in six months or so I wouldn't be in love with her anymore ... then it'd be easier for me to resume our friendship again.

Maya's response was violent. She sent my letter back, all torn to pieces, with a note, saying, "This is my broken heart ..." ... How could she do this, I felt. Why? Couldn't she tell I had to get over my passion in order to be the friend she wanted? Or, perhaps, she didn't want me to get over my passion, perhaps she wanted me to be in love with her and, when and if she was ever ready, she would come to me in her own lust ...

I eventually believed this must be the case. She wanted me to be romantic with her. Of course, she never admitted to this. She wanted our passion to happen without putting it into words, without holding me or especially her, to it. She could be more in control if it was less out in the open. I believed our troubles wouldn't exist, or these kinds of troubles, if she just came out with it. Verbal communication was vital to a relationship. Then I'd know what she wanted and she knew what I wanted.

It was becoming more obvious to me that Maya believed romance was best experienced without communication, without understanding. It was to be felt and felt only. Both people should just automatically be on the same page. After all, we were in love ... we should know exactly what the other wants just by looking at them ...

As much as I knew how ridiculous this was, I was indeed in love with Maya, I was in the midst with her, I was tangled up in who she was, as she was in me. I had to deal with her. I needed her, wanted her body and soul. Emotional and logical understanding was pushed to the side in favor of passionate desire and lust ... god, did I want her ... she was so beautiful, made me horny for her ... I wanted no one else but her ... no one else ... especially after that night of going down on her, on that lush, divine bronze pussy ...

When I got into a car accident with an old lady on La Brea blvd., a couple months later I got a few thousand dollars from it. After buying a new used car for $2,000, I still had money left over. What to do with it, I asked myself. Go see Maya. I had to. I had to get out of L.A., take a break, and when I came back there was a job waiting, to be working for a filmmaker. Of course, once the job was ready, when I came back, the job wasn't there. The filmmaker flaked.

But before that was my third road trip to Texas. I loved the wide open spaces of being on the road, both literally and in my head. I needed the sensation of freedom traveling gave me. This time I was by myself, not helping Maya move out there, not with my irritating ex-girlfriend. This time I was alone and there was more weight to it. It'd become dramatic and serious now between me and Maya. This trip was to resolve things. Maya had officially broken up with Emmanuel and he had moved back to L.A. She was now alone with her kids in Texas.

Maya didn't know what she wanted to do, stay in Texas, go back to Los Angeles, or move somewhere else. There was the possibility of moving to Chicago. Her oldest sister lived there with her family. She wanted to visit her up there and asked if I wanted to go. Of course I did. Anywhere she went, I had to go, too.

We had a few days before we drove up to Chicago and in that time my lust for Maya grew and grew. The kids were at school during the day while she and I were alone at her house. Most of the time, we just hung out, talked, watched movies, went places, went for walks. But now and then I couldn't hold myself back. In the car, I'd touch her leg and she'd take my hand off. While cooking in the kitchen, I'd come up behind her and try to hold her but she pushed me away. I asked why she didn't want me to do that, now she was single, the kids weren't around, no else would know.

"Because we're friends, god damn it!" she screamed.

I accepted her answer, but it tortured me. I wanted her so much. So I spent a lot of time masturbating in the bathroom, thinking of her.

One night, though, Maya came to me in the living room where I was sleeping. The kids were asleep, it was late. She had just taken a late night shower, like she often did, and walked to me in a bathrobe. I looked at her, wondering what was on her mind. She had in her hand a bottle of wine, then put it on the table in front of me. She went into the kitchen and brought us wine glasses, then sat next to me on the couch.

"Pour us some wine." she ordered.

I did, with a smile. What was she up to, I thought. Maybe this was it. Maybe she was ready to have me, be with me, make love to me. After three glasses of wine each, we did ... It was beautiful ... intense ... glorious. I was ecstatic, filled with the most desire and passion I ever felt ... I was worried when this day were to come, after two years, I might get awkward and not respond the way I wanted ... But I did ... The sexual act was perfect, hours long ...

... a hot oil massage for Maya ... my hands digging into her skin, all over, her shoulders, her back, hips, legs, feet, arm, and ass, caressing, fondling, groping every inch ... then we kissed and kissed and kissed on the mouth, our bodies entangled together in heat ... my mouth on her nipples, sucking and sucking, kissing ... she loved that ... then I went down on her, licking, licking, licking with extreme delight ... sucking ... it was unbearable pleasure for her ... she moaned and moaned ... coming twice ... shaking, trembling, writhing ... the second time she came, she said, though ...

"... Emmanuel ..."

... all the while her legs wrapped around my neck, her fingers going through my hair ... I wasn't Emmanuel, god damn it ... Why did she say that? She kept repeating, over and over, "Emmanuel ... Emmanuel ... Emmanuel ..." It was exactly like that night in Los Angeles of, "Miranda ... Miranda ..."

The second time she came, unknowingly or knowingly, calling her ex-boyfriend's name, she wanted to stop. There would be no penetration. I didn't mind but minded the "... Emmanuel ... Emmanuel ..."

Maya lay there in orgasmic aftermath bliss, while I jacked off on my knees, over her, loving the way she looked, so vulnerable, in such open happiness and peace ... her body turned me on immensely, that beautiful bronze body ... I kept masturbating until I exploded in cum, it going all over her body, her ass and legs and hips and waist ... it was so intense that I collapsed to the floor next to her ...

We fell asleep and maybe an hour or two later woke up. We were horny for each other again. We began with kisses, caresses, our bodies wrapped together, then I went and licked her pussy again ... I loved it and so did she ... before she was about to cum, she wanted my dick ... she wanted penetration ...

She got on top of me, straddling my hips, then lowered her divine pussy down my shaft ... ohhh I loved it ... so tender and wet ... my cock thrusting deep inside her ... we fucked and fucked and fucked with her on top, me sucking her tits and gripping her ass, then me on top of her screwing her missionary, then her on all fours getting fucked by me from behind doggystyle ... it was bliss ... she had to be on top of me again to cum and when she did I came soon after ... it was heaven ...

The next morning, Maya was distressed. She felt guilty for having sex with me ... in the house her kids lived in, the house their father bought, having sex with her friend's ex-boyfriend ... it was all guilt, guilt, guilt ... I just wanted to relish the memories of the night. I didn't want her to carry this shame around with her. When I made advances on her again, she pushed me away. I began drinking all the alcohol in the house ... I wanted her ... more than ever ... I was desperate, so I drank ...

Soon we drove up to Chicago and spent several days with Maya's sister's family. Sometimes I went to the city by myself to explore. Maya preferred to stay with her family in the suburbs. I had to figure out what to do. I was still in love with Maya, in complete lust for her and yet she kept pushing me away, yet not letting go ... it was torture.

I wanted to leave early, visit New Orleans before meeting up with her back in Texas. As I was leaving, I broke down in tears, looking at her. I loved her so much. She must of thought I was crying too much or I seemed ridiculous, because she began laughing at me with her cold, sarcastic smile. I would never forget that ...

I loved New Orleans, even though I got mugged there. It was a silly mugging, by a fairly non-dangerous guy who had no weapons. I followed him out of the French Quarter to look for Absinthe with wormwood, the outlawed ingredient. Of course the guy had no intention of getting it for me, and took the only $20 bill I had in my wallet. I didn't resist and actually started laughing when it happened. I was drunk and thought the whole thing was absurd.

I soon left New Orleans after that, not wanting any more trouble. Before going to Weatherford to see Maya, I stopped for a night in Houston, going to bars, talking to people, walking around. Being on the road, alone, meeting strangers and enjoying myself made me realize something. I didn't have to be so absorbed in my passion for Maya. There were other experiences out there. She didn't have to always be the center of where my heart and mind were. It was better to be open to others as well.

Even so, I was still in love with Maya. I loved her so much that it struck me down hard sometimes. No one ever before had that kind of power over me. Maya really had replaced God for me. I saw her in Weatherford before driving back to Los Angeles. When I left, I broke into tears once again ... I shed so many tears for her, it seemed unending ... She didn't laugh at me this time, but she also didn't respond to me emotionally. She continued to put up her wall in front of her, continued with her protectiveness, her defensive stance of mistrust.

In Los Angeles, I began to tell my family and close friends about my love for Maya, and what was going on between us. I told two friends of mine who Maya did not like nor trust. When she found out I told them she and I were lovers, I crossed the line ... she didn't want our love in the open ... She told me over the phone that was it ... She never wanted to speak to me ever again ... never ...

I was crushed ... obliterated in my heart ... I couldn't take it anymore ... I thought of committing suicide ... end it all ... it was over with Maya, buried deep into the grave ... she was no longer in my life ... was life worth anything without her?

But I couldn't do it. I couldn't take my own life ... my father Jean kept me from leaping over the edge ... simply by reaching out and talking with me ... he saved my life ... Jean got me to see that life was just beginning for me ... there would be many others in the future ... Maya was not my one and only ... there would be someone better than her even ...

Deep within myself as the months passed, I made a decision to not let any passion for anyone become so painful ever again. Not like it did with Maya. It was too much, much too much pain. It wasn't necessary. Eventually, the love, the intense, desperate passion died in me ... left me completely. I was over Maya. I began going out with Bernardo and Gus more around this time, looking for women, seeing life as an adventure and not a painful, constant heartache.

CHAPTER TWO.

MAYA RETURNS.

During the six months of not seeing Maya, I moved into the apartment in Silverlake with Bernardo. Eventually Bernardo moved out and an ex-co-worker at the movie theater in Hollywood moved in. Only a few weeks later and I got a call from Maya. She and her kids were at the Greyhound station downtown. What was she doing there, why was she calling me?

There was a desperation, a tremble, and a shake in her voice I'd never heard before. She asked me if I could pick her and the kids up at the bus station. But what happened? She never wanted to speak to me again. She didn't call or write to me in six months. She made it clear it was all finished between us, friendship or romance. What should I do? Tell her to get lost? I couldn't.

"... I ... I thought you never wanted to see me again ..." I said into the phone. "I mean ..." I continued after waiting to hear a response from her, which she didn't give. "... what're you doing down there? What're you doing in L.A.?"

"Can you pick me up or not?" she responded with her typical quick sharpness, holding back the desperation.

"Maya ..." I said, wanting to laugh and cry at the absurdity of it all.

"All you have to do is say yes or no."

"... Of course I'll pick you up ..."

"We'll wait for you outside, at the entrance."

And then she hung up. Just like that, Maya was back in town. What was happening now, I thought as my heart sank to my stomach. Wasn't I over the drama with Maya? She knew very well I couldn't say "no," couldn't refuse to pick her up. So I drove downtown to the Greyhound station.

Maya and her kids were indeed waiting outside, holding a bunch of bags. They had so many things, it seemed they were visiting for a while. Once they got their bags and themselves in my car, I found out they weren't visiting. They were moving. They still had the house in Weatherford, had lots of things there, still had to make payments on the house. But Maya couldn't take it anymore. Emmanuel had moved back to Los Angeles months before, still paying the bills and so forth, but in other ways had left them stranded. A terrible depression came over her.

Maya was isolated there, out in the middle of hickdom. Some neighbors whom she thought were friends broke into her house and robbed a few items. There was just a bunch of ignorant white trash hicks surrounding her, unfortunately. Now and then there could be interesting or kind people, but there were so few that they might as well not exist. Maya had to get out of Texas. Two years was enough.

Coming back to Los Angeles, though, she had no place to move into, no apartment, no house. She and Emmanuel had been broken up for over a year and there was no chance of staying with him. She had to ask friends and family, not wanting to take advantage of anyone in particular, so she basically jumped from one couch to another.

Seeing Maya again, seeing her in this situation, concerned for her, my love for her came back. But this time, I wasn't in love. The passion was dead. She still appealed to me sexually, tremendously in fact, but there just wasn't the romance in me anymore. She had killed it, I had killed it, it was gone, obliterated.

One day while the kids were with their dad, Maya wanted to go with me to the beach in Santa Monica. She missed the ocean so much and she also hoped something sensual might happen ... I could tell by the look in her eyes, a certain smile, a vulnerability. But Maya would never, ever do the first move. She wouldn't make it all that obvious she wanted sex. A touch of the hand, an obviously insinuating remark – no. By now, though, I could read her. Bringing wine in the middle of the night like back in Texas, or a certain look, a pause, a silence along with a smile, but nothing ever obvious.

Now more than ever, though, she had an aura of horniness, directed right at me. Before, yes she had to resist my desires, because of her situation, but she also didn't need me as much. When I wrote that letter about my needing space to get over her, that was the first time a fear came into her. The second time was after she told me she never wanted to see me again, over the phone, she expected me to call her and call her and call her until she replied. But I didn't. I left her alone. I was gone from her life, for six months. I might move on, I might not need her. Now that she left Texas and was semi-stranded in L.A., that fear intensified, and so, therefore, did her need for me.

Maya was also getting older, now in her mid 30's. Since a teenager, she could get a man anytime she wanted. No problem, with her looks and charm. Now she was a single mother of two. This is the case for the majority of women, Daniel. The heightened fear of death, of aging, of not having the power they once had over men, of their biological clocks ticking, makes women more sexually eager and open. Little wonder that scientists say women's sex drive increases at this age, and really, continues to increase, as I would later find out with Doris.

I couldn't help being attracted to your mother, Daniel ... I may have lost the desperate, romantic passion I once had, but I also didn't lose the physical desire. Nor on the human level, either. We clicked in many ways. We balanced each other out personality-wise. She was the more emotional, me the more intellectual; she the more extroverted, I the introverted. We were both compassionate, both sensitive, both had a dark, sarcastic streak. Walking with Maya on the beach, enjoying her company and the beautiful day, I wanted to talk about our problems of the past. This was one of our excruciating rough edges between us, though – communication ...

"So, Maya ..." I said, looking at her as she looked at the ocean. "... we need to talk about what happened."

"What happened?" she asked, still not looking at me.

"You know what I mean."

“No, I don't.”

“The last time I talked to you, you were pissed at me for telling people about our relationship.”

“We never had a relationship.”

“Well okay, I mean whatever we had between us.”

“Nothing happened between us.”

“... Maya ... we made love.”

She didn't say anything for a while, out of shyness, Catholic repression, guilt, denial, shame, fear of rejection ... one or all of them ...

“You told me six months ago you never wanted to see me again ... I expected you to follow through with that.” I continued.

“I was angry at you.”

“That's obvious.”

“Look, I don't want to talk about this now.”

“Fine.” I said with a quiet, frustrated anger.

Then I calmed down, thinking about her, her fear of vulnerability, all her hang-ups. She was almost like a child. She was really innocent about sex, about relationships even. There was something tender within her rigid expression. Her vulnerability came through her wall at times, perhaps without her knowing it.

As we walked back to my car, I watched her buttocks move with each step. I loved her ass, the way it bounced, the round, full, firm cheeks rubbed up against each other, the curve of her hips. She wore high cut shorts, revealing her long, lush, light brown legs. She knew I liked her in those shorts. That's why she wore them.

When we got back to the car, with Maya in the front passenger seat,

I looked at her legs. She noticed.

"What?" she asked with a sly smile, and an affectedly surprised tone. She was pretending, as she always did, to be unaware of sensuality, as if she was completely innocent of sex. She was a good actor, but I also had known her for a few years and, as said before, picked upon her behaviors. She wanted me to look at her legs.

I smiled at her play-acting. The car wasn't going anywhere, stuck in Lincoln boulevard rush-hour traffic. There was a moments pause, from my smile to the next action. I wondered if I should follow my desires. The sexual drive was no longer attached with romantic longing. It was gone. I also didn't like how there were roadblocks between us. Things weren't clear. She wanted communication hazy. I hated that. But, at the moment, the memories of our sex in the past, the knowledge it could happen again, and the fact she wanted me, won over.

I took my right hand off the steering wheel and gently put it on her thigh. She asked what I was doing and I said feeling her leg, with my nervous, sarcastic smile. She said I was crazy, like she often did, but didn't remove my hand, so I continued caressing the top of her thigh. It felt so good in the palm of my hand, on my fingers. Going up and down her leg got me hornier and I quickly got a hard-on. I had to do something about that.

Suddenly, I took a right turn off Lincoln and onto a narrow, obscure street. I drove into an alley and stopped the car, turning off the engine. I turned to her and smiled.

"What the hell are you doing?" she asked, a little exasperated, hiding an expectation. She knew what I wanted.

"I love your legs."

"Is that all you love?"

"No."

I leaned forward, looking into her eyes, which she didn't like. Eye contact was too intense. I picked up on that so looked down at her breasts, which I liked to see anyway. I moved closer and gently kissed the side of her black hair, then her ears, to the side of her face, all the while still feeling up her legs. She was shy and didn't respond, but allowed me to continue. My lips moved inch by inch closer to her mouth, and as I got there, she didn't move, too shy, afraid of letting go right away.

As my lips touched hers, there was a tenderness and softness, but still the hesitation. She wanted me, but wasn't sure if she could trust me with her vulnerability. Would I take advantage of her soul if she offered it? That's what she always worried about with me. I was younger, might go chasing after younger girls, might leave her hanging. But as like with my concerns about our communication, Maya's fears were overrided by sexual need. Not only did my youth, my eyes, my face, my voice, my body, my smell, my way of making love to her, my similarity to a young man in El Salvador whom she loved and who happened to have Caucasian features like mine ... all these things turned her on tremendously ... she was comfortable enough with me to plunge ahead ...

She made the decision to let go, and opened her mouth and kissed me, feeling the moistness of my lips and tongue. As my hand went in between her thighs, she opened them wider, my hand near her crotch. I kissed her neck, shoulders, then down to her chest. She put her fingers through my hair as my lips touched her breasts. We continued making out and feeling each other up, until another car drove by. We stopped in the midst of our horniness and relaxed.

I suggested we needed to make love, but not in a car, which, in her shy way, she acknowledged. She still didn't want to put it out there in the verbal world we were lovers, even between us. She was afraid of making that clear, crystallizing it away from ambiguous romantic involvement. Whenever I hinted at or made attempts to make love with her at my apartment, she resisted. Not while I had a roommate, the guy from work who moved in after Bernardo left.

So one night when Dinora and Javier were staying with their

grandma, Maya and I went out for dinner and a drink. After we were done with the food, alcohol, and conversations, our sex drive made itself known in the energy between us. It seemed to be on both our minds. But where to go?

A motel came to my mind. Take her to a motel. Why not? I always wanted to make love in a motel room.

"You want to go to a motel?" I asked her in my car, with a smile.

"Why?" she replied.

"To have fun."

"A motel?"

"Where else can we go?"

Maya realized I was right. There was no where else to go. It just seemed shameful, dirty to her, as if we were committing adultery. I was actually more aroused by making love in a motel room. There was something risque about it, shady. Maya made an important, inner decision as I drove the car. She would let go with me ... she trusted me.

She spent a whole lifetime of not trusting men, with rare occasions now and then of opening up emotionally, letting her guard down, but very rarely. From the sexual advances of older men as a little girl, a teenager, an adult – sometimes violent – to the murder of her father at six years old, to the amputation of her right arm by a doctor at nine, to the affair her first husband had with her teenage sister, and many more ... men were often the object of hostility to her.

Experience after experience created a sarcastic, cold wall. It wasn't really her but it was the her of necessity and fear. Years of close intimacy with Dinora and Javier in their childhood innocence, even the years of her trusting friendship with me, opened her to vulnerability like never before. She made the decision in her mind to let go with me when moving back to L.A. But she made the decision fully this time, in full awareness, with me in front of her. It was an actuality now, not just in the imagination.

We drove into the motel drive-way, pulled into a spot, and I went to check in. I said I'd pay for the room, hoping maybe we'd get an hourly rate. The "concierge," an old East Indian man, said no. $60 for the night or not at all.

Once inside the motel room, Maya and I sat on the bed, looking at each other. We laughed. I asked if she wanted a massage. She said sure, if I had the oil, which I did. First, though, she wanted to take a shower, then she'd be ready. As she went into the bathroom and I could hear the hot water spraying her body, I couldn't wait to see her in her wet, fresh, clean naked glory. This was a romantic rendezvous for sure, although something was missing for me. The romance. Try as hard as I could, I just couldn't get myself to fall in love with Maya again.

Ironically, because of this, I was more relaxed than I would've been if I was still madly in love with her as before. When she came out of the shower and into the room in a bathrobe, my nerves were loose. I was more comfortable to be myself than I usually was in a sex situation. My lack of nervousness of course made Maya more comfortable around me, and want me even more. We sat on the bed with an instant of shyness, which was overcome by my leaning into her and placing my hand on her thigh. I wanted to forget the loss of romance inside me, forget everything, in this night of hedonistic motel room pleasure. And God, her light brown skin, black hair, wide, penetrating eyes, the naked body underneath the bathrobe made me want to throw myself on her.

She put her hand through my hair, a fairly aggressive move she normally wouldn't do, bringing me to a kiss. My hand felt up her leg underneath the bathrobe, up onto her hip, relishing the fact there wasn't any underwear there. We kissed and fondled for a while, until Maya stopped and told me she wanted a massage. I said I'd love to, as she took off her bathrobe and quickly laid on her stomach on the bed.

There was her back, her ass, her hips, and legs, waiting for me. I took off my clothes, the excitement bristling inside, of being naked on top of her, of beginning the sex act. I climbed onto her back with the oil, my legs straddling her hips, my balls and hardened cock nestled in-between her ass cheeks. As I began giving an intense, long massage, I was in sexual heaven with her again ...

After the massage, we made unbearably hot love for hours, with me going down on her for what seemed like forever, skyrocketing Maya into sexual bliss, wreathing, shaking, moaning in pleasure, almost crying ... to me on top penetrating, thrusting into her missionary style, her legs wrapped tightly around my waist ... to me getting behind her and slamming into her ass doggystyle until I exploded in cum ... we enjoyed it so much that afterwards it was impossible to say anything as we lay side by side on the motel bed ...

As Maya began to be addicted to our sex, she didn't mind making love at my apartment, as long as my roommate nor the kids were there, of course. Because of this, other opportunities arose for us to make love, a few times a week, actually. As we had sex more and more, we began to find what turned the other on in such a way that it was clockwork. Every move we made had a flow, ease, and smoothness to it. We clicked as lovers. When my roommate moved out, Maya and her kids moved in. Maya and I made love every day. We were addicted to our bodies.

On a personal level we clicked, too. Partially. Politically we saw things in a similar way. We both mistrusted the authorities in government, especially Bush and the Neo-cons, we both felt the War on Terror was a scam, we both were against military and corporate greed and dominance, against the exploitation of the Third World (of which Maya was from – El Salvador), and we both were against politicians in general.

Emotionally and behaviorally speaking we were similar, too. We were both against shallowness, materialism, and consumerism. We both had a distinct hatred for phoniness. There were many instances of phoniness in our lives, coming and going from people we knew or strangers we'd run into. There was the kids' father way of talking when ignoring the fact he didn't spend the day with his kids when he promised to (because he was on a four day drinking binge). Emmanuel didn't do it every week, but usually once a month.

Maya was especially aggravated by Emmanuel's behavior and lies. Not only was he not honest, but whenever he talked about anything, it wasn't very interesting or important. He was always going on about some new job he was applying for, some new apartment he was trying to rent, a new car he was trying to buy, a new cell phone, and so on. He never checked in with the person to see if they actually cared about what he was saying. Emmanuel's mother was worse with her phoniness and duplicity, giving a person a smile, then talking shit about them behind their back, all the while praying to the Virgin Mary.

Whenever Maya and I went out together, to a restaurant, a store, a coffee shop, any public place, we'd often run into many different types of shallowness. Sometimes we'd get into a confrontation with these people. Often these same people would get caught off-guard, since they weren't used to others calling them out on their phoniness.

"Dinora, what do you want?" Maya asked her daughter once while waiting in line at a McDonald's, with me and her son, Javier.

Dinora had a hard time deciding. Meanwhile, a woman who was behind them in line was talking loudly, restless, on her cell phone. The woman wore expensive Gucci sweat pants and top, with the letters, "juicy," on her butt. She carried a large Gucci leather bag, wore a pair of Ughs on her feet and had expensive Gucci sun glasses. She was in her forties and athletic, but her skin was ragged and unhealthy looking.

"So, anyways, my father was always 170 pounds, never any more, usually not much less, and my mother was always around 115 pounds, except for that one year where she ballooned to 130 pounds." the woman yapped loudly into her cell phone behind me and Maya while Dinora was deciding. "So I don't know why my daughter's 140 pounds. I don't get it. Her father isn't fat either, nor were his parents. I don't know where she gets it from." she quickly moved the cell away from her mouth.

"Excuse me, if you're not going to order right away, I'd like to." the woman then said obnoxiously to Maya.

"Well, excuse us but the poor girl can't hear herself think when you're on your cell phone talking about how fat your daughter is." I said with a surge of nervous anger.

"Excuse me but -" the woman began to say before being interrupted by Maya.

"Why don't you fucking go to the next line? It's open." Maya snapped.

"I've never been treated so rudely in my life ..." the woman said in fear, almost trembling. She then moved to the other line in an indignant huff, and proceeded to both order food and talk on her cell at the same time.

A lot of my family also presented roadblocks of phoniness at times. My step-family, Frazier's family, were the worst. I could never tell who the hell they were. Among other things, they wouldn't let me bring up Maya and her kids to an island the family owned in the Great Lakes. They lied to me with bogus excuses. The real reason was Maya and her kids weren't white, and I was the black sheep of the family (if even that, really). They snubbed me, like many times before. Not too much later, after "Loveincrazy" was done, I snubbed back by never speaking to them again.

Even my mother entered into the realm of phoniness in her behavior, thanks to an ingrained insecurity passed down to her by her parents. There was a strange selfishness, mixed with a sweetness, that kept my mom and her side of the family from being real sometimes. "Being real" is such a corny term, I think, but there were many times growing up with my mom and to the present where the lack of "being real" was a problem.

My mother had it in her heart for genuineness but there was something holding her back, too much fear, maybe. I think if she had spent more time living life, going through relationships, searching through her emotions, finding out who she really was, then she wouldn't have that problem. But, like her husband and millions of others in the world, she spent the majority of her time working, working, working, and if not that then in her social life trying to fit in. Since her marriage with her second husband, she also saw me in a different light.

Many times my mother would offer something or other, impulsively giving a hand to help, then often would have doubts, sometimes not following through, or she'd pull back completely. She didn't give whole heartedly. She'd, for example, promise to watch Maya's kids, then not do it. She'd always say she wished she could spend more time with us, then always be on the phone with work or her husband whenever she was with us, or leave early, pretending to be tired or feel sick. Or she'd pay for dinner, buy us lunch, then tell us how expensive it was. It was always awkward because it took away from the fact my mother was a great person in many respects.

Part of her behavior was because she'd been so badly taken advantage of by Frazier. After the divorce, Frazier was getting a lot more money every month from my mother than I ever made at any of my jobs. This, after he already received big chunks of money from the settlement, after 20 years of not working, staying at home, lying about one illness or another, forcing my mom to work all the time and support him. Because of all that, it was difficult for my mother to trust people, not surprisingly.

For some reason, though, her husband, her mom (my grandmother, who was helpful to me while I helped her, too) and her Boeing corporate psychiatrist got her to dislocate that mistrust in a strange direction: at her own son. It must be said that my mom, her husband, and my grandmother all sincerely cared for me. I have no doubt about that. What I suppose I must distinguish to you, Daniel, is the kind of love they have expressed, which can be troubled.

On a subconscious level, despite a genuine love and giving heart, my mother feared me. Somewhere in her mind she thought perhaps I'd either be just like my step-father Frazier and take advantage of her, or like Jean and hurt her. Jean, by the way, refused to help out financially when it came to raising me. That was a scar for my mom, and I never understood why he did that. In recent years, though, Jean has given me as much as he possibly can, often when he had close to no money at all for himself.

My mother's mistrust of me was done, in her feelings and in action, without being overly obvious. It was, after all, a part of American (especially white) family culture to abandon family members, both emotionally and financially. In their minds my mother, her husband, and her mother (and others in their family) believed they actually went against the grain. Their hearts were overflowing with generosity. They just had to be cautious now and again and I had to be self-reliant in the end.

"So, I'm still paying for your health insurance." my mom would say to me, over dinner. "It's about $60 a month, and that's only for disaster coverage."

"Okay, well ..." I replied. "If it's so expensive, then don't pay it."

"No, no I want to. I want to help you out."

"I mean that's kind of pointless insurance anyway."

"Actually, not really. You might need it some day."

"If I wanted to go to the dentist or just do a regular check up, I'd still have to pay a ton of money."

"Well maybe some day you'll have a better job."

Maya's birthday was soon coming up. My mom didn't know yet quite how to respond to Maya's relationship with me, didn't know if we were serious or not yet, if we even were in a relationship. She didn't know if she should commit herself emotionally to the idea of Maya and I being together, because we might not last long as a couple. But my mother wanted to show she cared, so she paid for Helen's expensive birthday dinner.

To show I wasn't taking advantage of my mom, I offered to help pay for half. I hoped she would see what I was doing was simply a polite gesture. Instead, she quickly took me up on the offer, and I paid for half the cost of the entire dinner. Sometimes, I'd think my mom must've thought I made just as much money as she and her husband did. I may not've ever been good at math, but $15,000 a year didn't equal $400,000 a year (my mother and her husband made about $200,000 each).

So Maya and I were united in our hearts because of our antagonism to people's phoniness. Whether it was a woman at McDonald's, Frazier and his family, my mom and her family, or other people we knew, Maya and I felt a bond by not wanting to be like any of them.

Our bond split, though, along with other things, in our relations to my dad, Jean. Both Maya and I loved and respected Jean's 92 year old mother, loved her genuine, innocent, sparky spirit. But with Jean it was different. Maya liked him in way, respected him for taking care of his mother with so much dedication, along with being a loving father and friend to me. But she felt threatened by Jean's attitude about a lot of things. Politically, they were on the same page. Other things they weren't. As she got to know him better, know how close he was to me, she worried Jean might be too much of an influence on me.

"Tell me, Maya, in Nicaragua, do people have access to decent health care there?" Annabelle, Jean's mother, said in her chair in the mobile home living room she and Jean lived in.

We all just got back from my grandma's doctor's visit and a lunch afterwards. I sat next to Maya on the couch opposite Annabelle while Jean was getting his mother's medicine ready.

"Mother, Maya is from El Salvador, not Nicaragua." Jean said from the other room, with a laugh.

"Oh, I'm sorry." Annabelle said with an embarrassed laugh, blush, then smile at Maya.

"It's okay." Maya replied with a smile of her own. "It's better than calling me a Mexican."

"So in El Salvador do they have okay health care?" I asked Maya, not for myself – as I knew there wasn't – but for my grandma, to continue the conversation.

"You know that already." Maya said to me.

"I know I know. I was just asking for my grandma."

"I have a feeling they don't, mother." Jean said as he came into the living room with a glass of water and her medicine, handing both to her.

"Yeah, there's not good health care in my country. If you have a lot of money, then it's not bad." Maya said, about to continue.

"But most people barely have any money at all, right?" Jean asked Maya, slightly interrupting her.

"Right." she replied.

"It's kind of like here in the United States, actually. If a person is rich, then health care is easy to come by. If you're poor it's very difficult. Only in El Salvador it's much worse, I'm sure." Jean continued.

"And if you smoke like Thomas does, it doesn't really matter." Maya switched gears and threw a jab.

"Sure." I smiled at her.

"I mean, what happened to him? Not that long ago Thomas wasn't a smoker." Maya continued, speaking to Jean.

"I think he was stressed about his love-life with you." Jean said with a dark smile to Maya.

"That's right. I started smoking while you were still in Texas, around the time you stopped talking to me." I said, gleefully throwing a jab back at her.

"Don't blame your addiction on me." she responded quickly.

"I'm not ... necessarily." I said ambiguously.

"I think you started smoking because you wanted to be like your friend Gus." she shot back.

"Well, you know, Maya, what they say about smokers." Jean said as he sat in the chair next to his mother, leading Maya on with a playful, sarcastic smile.

"What's that?" she asked.

"They're more inclined to be promiscuous." Jean continued, still smiling.

"Oh Jean ..." Annabelle said with embarrassment. She disliked how her son always brought up 'uncomfortable' subject matter.

"Why?" Maya asked Jean.

"Because by smoking, they're doing a 'high risk' activity, and therefore, more inclined to do other 'high risk' activities – drink alcohol, do drugs, have more than one lover at a time ..." Jean said sarcastically, with seriousness and humor at the same time.

"That might be true." I said with an amused laugh. "Whatever I do, blame it on cigarettes." I continued jokingly.

"I've smoked cigarettes before, and I drink alcohol now and then. I don't sleep around." Maya said with great pride.

"But are you addicted to cigarettes and alcohol?" Jean said, still playful.

"No."

"There you go. You have to be an addict."

"Like me." I said with a smile.

"It's just a theory, there's no way to prove it." Jean said, amused when looking at his mother's embarrassed face.

"Jean, she doesn't want to hear that." Annabelle said seriously.

"I'm sorry, Maya, but you know with me it's hard to not make a joke about most things." Jean said apologetically.

"I don't think you were joking, I think you were serious." Maya replied with a tone that sounded a bit more upset.

"What do you mean?" he said, concerned he hurt her, but also realizing he was just making light of her teasing me.

"You don't believe in one-on-one love." she said.

"Monogamy?" I asked Maya.

"I suppose not." Jean said simply but slowly, with a thoughtful breath taken. "When you've gone through a whole lifetime of experiences, you begin to realize that we're capable of loving more than one person at one time."

"But you felt that when you were young." Maya said.

"Sure. I guess I understood that's how love can work early on." Jean replied.

"That's not love." Maya came back sharply.

"Well, everyone's different. Some people can only love one person at one time, and others can love more." Jean responded softly, not wanting to be antagonistic.

"But you're talking about sex, not love."

"No, I'm talking about love. Love and sex."

"A person is confused if they have to be with more than one person at one time."

"Confused? I don't think so."

"Love is about commitment and loyalty, about being faithful and true. It's not about being selfish."

"Would it not be selfish if the person you loved wanted to be with someone else and you wouldn't let them?"

"If that's what they want, to go around fucking everybody, then I would let them. I can't control them."

"No, but you wouldn't want to be with them anymore."

"Of course not."

"So then you'd be punishing them with ultimatums."

"I wouldn't be punishing them. If that's what they want, then they don't want me."

"Perhaps they still want you and another person."

"Then they're confused and they don't know what they want."

"It's not about being confused," I interjected. "he just said the person wanted you and wanted to be with someone else. The person knows what they want: you and another person."

"Then they're being selfish." she came back quickly, clearly upset. "You can't have everything."

"Apparently not." I said with a laugh.

"That's right, mother fucker." Maya said with indignant, proud anger, then stormed out of the mobile home and to my car in the drive way.

"Oh shit." Jean said, saddened. "I'm sorry, Tom. I really upset her."

"No ... we both did, although I don't know why she reacted like that ... or, I guess I do ... I should go talk to her."

"That's a good idea." Jean said.

I walked out of the mobile home and went to my car, where Maya was crying in the front passenger seat. I hated seeing her in tears, it made my heart feel as if it was being cut up, a knife slicing it open. Especially if I knew I was partly responsible. Monogamy was something we'd talked about since she came back to L.A. Maya had gotten enough of a hint to know I didn't really believe in it. But we never discussed it much, not the way I wished we had. Anything that caused friction between her and I was never dealt with thoroughly.

"I'm sorry, Maya ..." I said as I sat next to her in the driver's seat. She turned away, trying to stop herself from crying. "I didn't mean to hurt you ... and neither did my dad ..."

"You can be so cold ..." she said, still crying. "... and your dad is such an asshole sometimes ..."

"Maya ..." I responded, hurt she called my dad an asshole. Jean wasn't trying to be mean. She just disagreed with us. "... he wasn't trying to be an asshole. He cares about you, and so do I."

"I don't know about that ..." she said, hating the words coming from me – 'care about.' She wanted to hear 'in love with you' from me.

"You just disagree with me and my dad, that's all. There's no animosity between any of us."

"God ... can you hear yourself talk?"

"What do you mean? What's wrong with what I'm saying?"

"You're so fucking detached! 'Disagree'? We're not talking about politics or philosophy, it's love." Maya snapped back, in tears. "There's no emotion in your voice. You're just like your dad – you don't have any feeling in your heart."

"... those are harsh words, Maya ..." I said with a swelling of resentment. "How can you say that? After everything you've been through with me? It's like you don't remember anything or you don't want to ..." I shot back in hurt, defensive anger. She hit a sore spot with me.

"I remember how you used to be ... but that's in the past, that doesn't matter anymore. What counts is the present."

"Well, I am the way I am with you now because of the past and whether you want to see it or not, so are you."

"But before, we couldn't do anything, we couldn't make a relationship between you and I work. Now we can. But now that we can, it's like you don't want to make it work."

"I do, but not with that feeling anymore and not with you as the only one. I just can't do it."

"What the hell are you talking about? You just want to throw fucking daggers at me?"

"Maya ... look, we never talked about things. Whenever I wanted to, you told me to shut up. At every step of the way. I don't do things like that."

"...Just drive us home ..." Maya said, worn out and effectively shutting me up when she didn't know what to say.

I went back into the mobile home to say my goodbyes to my dad and grandma, who were wondering what was going on. I spent another ten minutes or so talking with them, which upset Maya, as she waited in the car. I came back to her in the car and started the engine, then backed out of the drive way. On the way back to my apartment in Silverlake, neither of us said a word. We shut down in silence, the entire 30 miles in slow 101 freeway traffic, not saying anything for a good hour. The only noise was the radio, which I tuned to a classical music station, hoping to calm things.

But things weren't calmed. I thought maybe we had as we got to the apartment and I went to take a shower before going to work. The first words to come out of our mouths was me asking her if she wanted to use the bathroom, to which she replied with a quiet, strained "no." Once I came out of the shower, I was shocked to see what Maya was doing. She was tearing up all the letters I sent to her in Texas into the garbage.

"What the hell's going on?" I yelled while still wearing my bathrobe.

"What does it look like I'm doing?" Maya spat back as she tore up letter after letter by holding one part with her teeth, then ripping it to shreds with her one hand. There were tons and tons of letters, maybe a hundred ...

"Those're the letters I sent to you!"

"I know."

"Don't fucking do that! Those mean something to me and they should mean something to you! I gave them to you for a reason! That's my fucking love you're ripping to shreds!" I screamed at her.

"These are all lies." she said, still tearing letter after letter, then throwing them into the trash.

"Jesus Christ ..." I said in desolation. She might as well be shitting on my face ... Tears began to fall from my eyes as I watched her. "Why're you doing that?"

"All these letters are bullshit, so it belongs in the garbage."

"You think I'm the one who's cold? Take a fucking good look at what you're doing now! I meant every word I wrote in those letters and you're ripping it to shreds!"

"Now you know what it feels like."

"What it feels like?"

“For being cold.”

“I wasn't being cold, you stupid fucking cunt! I'm angry as hell right now but I've never been cold!” I said as I rushed up to her.

“Don't you dare call me that, motherfucker!” she snapped back as she tried to fight me off. I was trying to take the letters away from her. “Get away, you fucker!”

“Those are mine! I gave them to you and if you don't want them anymore, if you want to throw my love away, give them back to me! Give me back my letters!”

“They're lies, not love! Lies! Fucking lies!” she screamed as we fought over the letters, tears coming from her eyes now. “You said you loved me and you don't love me! You want to go around and fuck all the women you want!”

“Is that what you think?” I said, ending the struggle with her, pulling myself away, stepping back, taking heavy breaths. “You think I'm some fucking player?”

“You would be if you knew how. But you don't have the charm to be one.”

“That's right. I don't have the charm, and I don't have the interest. That's not what I'm about.”

“If you want to prove something, go ahead. I don't care. Just don't pretend with me.”

“I've been honest with you from the beginning. Everything I've said I meant. I've never played any games with you. And if you want to talk about honesty, why don't you tell me about Miranda.”

“Miranda?”

“The first time I made love to you, at my apartment in Mar Vista, you moaned her name over and over again.”

"You're so full of shit! I didn't do that!"

"You did! I heard it!"

"You think I'm a lesbian? Is that it? You're fucking stupid." she said with a harsh laugh.

"And if you're ripping up my letters because I don't believe in monogamy, let me remind you that not only was there that one time you called for Miranda while I licked your pussy, but the second time I made love to you, in Texas, you moaned Emmanuel's name. Over and over and over again, the whole time I was going down on you."

"You're such a fucking liar! I never did those things! You're making them up, putting it in your head to justify your own selfishness. Moan Miranda's name? Emmanuel's? That's bullshit."

"I heard what I heard."

"It must've been a ghost in your head."

"The only ghost in me is the love I had for you ..."

That hurt ... for her to hear, and for me to say ...

"... Fuck you."

And with that, Maya put on her jacket, grabbed her purse, and stormed out of the apartment, slamming the door behind her. I stood in trembling, tormented silence by myself, next to my torn letters in the garbage and on the floor ...

I still had to go to work, to my dreaded Circus of Books job. I hated working there, hated this pain between me and Maya. Life was not what it could be. Things worked out in such a way as to defeat the human spirit. Society should propel the heart, not beat it down, again and again. Whether it was a job, a relationship, a friendship, creative goals, whatever it was, conditions were not in place to allow growth to happen. Only degradation. That ad in the LA Weekly for the C.W.F.P.S.J. -

Now job was looking more and more appealing to me. Maybe there I'd find satisfaction ...

I came back to my apartment late at night and found Maya asleep with her kids on the living room floor in sleeping bags. I was glad to see them at least. But what would happen in the morning when Maya was awake? What would we say to each other?

When I woke up in the morning, Maya and the kids were gone. Did she just take them to school or did they leave for good? I noticed their stuff was still there, but in traveling bags. So she'd come back to get those at least, but then where was she planning to go? I had to talk to her and make sure she was okay. I'd wait for her, take a shower, brush my teeth, get ready for the day, and hopefully she'd come back soon.

Just as I finished brushing my teeth, Maya walked into the apartment. She didn't say anything as she placed her purse and things on the kitchen counter. I came out of the bathroom and looked at her, not saying anything until she did.

"We'll be leaving today after I pick up the kids from school." she said, still not looking at me.

"Where're you going?"

"My sister knows someone who's renting a one-bedroom."

"So you're moving there?"

"Yup."

"Where is it?"

"Near Washington and La Brea."

"Is it an okay neighborhood?"

"The same as this one."

"Can I help you with moving?"

“No.”

Then nothing more was said between us for a while. Maya got the rest of her things put away into bags while I worked on the script to “Loveincrazy” at the dinning table. While getting clothes out of the cupboards in the hall between my bedroom and the bathroom, I began to hear Maya crying. ... Shit ... what should I do, I asked myself ... Should I go and talk to her? I wanted to but would it make things worse? Things would be bad whether I talked to her or not, so I decided to go to her ...

She sat in the doorway to my bedroom, in front of the cupboard, unbearable tears falling down her face ... She was shaking, trembling, but her body was limp from emotional wearing down, moving only because of her crying ... It was painful ... For Maya to go through and for me to see ... There was ice in my heart, an unrelenting freeze ... I sat down close to her, my back against the other wall so I faced her. Being as close as I was, I almost couldn't look at her ... It was too much ... I didn't know what to say.

“Why ...” she began to say amidst her tears. “... why did you come to Texas to see me?”

“I fell in love with you ...” I responded, as best I could.

“Why did you fall in love with me ... if it was only for a short time?” she said with so much pain and tears that she spoke as if not wanting to, almost hating the words as they came out of her mouth.

“I was in love with you for three years ... unbearable, horrible, angst-ridden longing and love for you ... It was killing me for a full three years ... it ripped me apart that whole time ... if I kept going on like that I would've died, burned myself up to the complete end ... you telling me you never wanted to talk to me ever again over the phone, then not hearing from you in six months ... in those six months my love for you died ...”

“But it's not that ... you don't even want to be with me anymore.

You can be with me and not feel so much pain ... but you don't want to ..."

"I do want to be with you."

"But not only me."

"No ... I guess not."

"... Why?" she asked, barely able to ask through her sobbing.

"... I don't feel it anymore ... I love you ... but I can't ... be what you want."

"I don't want anything from you ..."

"You do, you want me to love you the way you want to be loved and I'm telling you I can't do that anymore."

"Everything you say is like a knife, almost as if you're doing it on purpose ... like you want to hurt me ..."

"That's the last thing I want to do to you, Maya ..." I said with a defensive, frustrated anger. "I can't pretend to feel something I don't ... I want to be honest with you as much as possible. I don't want to be like most men. Most guys would lie to you, tell you how much they're still in love with you, commit to you, tell you you're their one and only, there's no one else, they never ever have the slightest interest in other women, say they want to get married, have kids, and so on and so on. Meanwhile, they're always looking at other women when they can, and then end up having secret affairs with other women behind your back. And yet they'll still tell you how much they love you and how you're still their one and only, and always will be ... I could never do that to you, Maya ... it's what I mean by not wanting to hurt you ... I want to do the exact opposite. I still love you, but not in the way you want ..."

"I told you I don't want anything from you." she said with sharp anger this time.

"Can't you see that wanting me to have you as my one and only is wanting something from me?"

"You don't understand ... when two people love each other ... it's meant to be just them."

"That's how a lot of people see it. Not everyone."

"That's the way God meant it."

"We don't know what God means. Besides, Maya, I could give you that love you need, but I know myself. I know I look at other women. I know something would happen some day ..."

"But why would you need someone else?"

"I don't think any one person can completely satisfy another. And there's nothing wrong with that."

"I don't satisfy you now but I used to ..."

"You do satisfy me ..."

"Don't lie."

"I'm not ... just not ... I don't know ... I don't know what more I can say ... you know how I feel ..."

Maya's tears kept flowing. She was inches away from me ... but there was nothing to be done. The love she wanted was dead. I had another kind of love, but it wasn't enough for her. She couldn't accept it.

"Sometimes ... I feel like I want to kill myself ..."

A long, thick, sharp dagger stabbed me in my gut ... guilt and anger shot inside me but I couldn't release it. That was the last thing I wanted to hear ... oh, the fear inside me in that moment, Daniel! The horror I felt when I heard her say that! Not that ... not that ...

"Maya ..." I said with tears falling from my eyes. "... don't say that ...

please don't say something as horrible as that ..."

"I mean it ..."

"No, you don't, I know you ..." I said, almost trembling in fear, sadness, and anger. I was angry because she would put that on me. She would put that kind of guilt on me. She would enact her revenge on me that way. I was also afraid. She went to the place I didn't want to see her go ... she was getting swallowed up in a black hole. I felt helpless at seeing her helplessness. "You have your kids. You need them ... they love you, they need you ... and me, Maya ... as much as you may not believe it ... I'm here for you."

"Hold me, please I need you to hold me ..."

I leaned towards her and held her in my arms. She cried and cried, rested her wet, teary face against my neck and shoulder. I could feel all her tears on my skin. She was drenched in sadness. My heart was held back, I couldn't let go, couldn't cry anymore. It was strange. Suddenly my tears stopped falling. The sadness was no longer inside me, not in that way. I felt a strong, strong rush of coldness, of impenetrable ice over taking me, and I couldn't help myself ... this strange feeling dominated me and I could do nothing to stop it ... I could only have a cold, helpless, dry sorrow ...

She clung tighter and tighter, every inch of desperation wanting to be close to me. She moved her body to press up against mine as much as possible. I could sense her depression being intermixed now with lust.

"Why don't you love me?" she asked, her mouth near my ear.

"I do ..."

"Not that way ... make love to me ..."

"Maya ..."

"I want to feel your naked body on mine ... I want to feel your dick inside me ..."

" ... Not like this ... there's too much pain right now ..."

"I want to fuck you ..." she said with a strange sexual anger.

She wouldn't take no for an answer. If she was going to be this vulnerable, she wasn't going to lose. But her sexual presence, her coming on to me like this, turned me off. I felt she was forcing it, pushing it, straining it, manipulating me, twisting my feelings around and around.

She jumped onto me, pressed her tits against my chest, grabbed my neck with her arm and tried to kiss me. Her lips were filled with the frustration and anger of rejection, desperate, hopeless, uncontrollable. She kissed and kissed madly, insanely, trying to get me aroused. It didn't work, I couldn't respond. I was turned off and just felt a horrible, horrible, empty, cold sorrow. She stopped kissing and got off me, sitting in black silence ...

"Maya ... look, I usually want to make love to you ... don't think I don't ... our sex is beautiful ... but right now it isn't ... right now all there is, is pain ..." I said, hoping to reach her with compassion.

"I have to get the kids." she said, turning off the anguish, as if by a switch. "We'll be back later to get our stuff."

She stood up, went to the bathroom sink and washed herself up. She washed and washed over and over, almost like an attempt to wash away her tears and love. She didn't want to love me, not really. I hurt her too much. And for what? But she couldn't help it. I opened her up to a love she was always afraid of. But now she felt stranded by me, even though I was right there, even though I offered a love, a cool love, perhaps. My love could not be the burning obsession of the past, but it could be a consistent dedication and loyalty, nonetheless. Honesty and no faithfulness, but loyalty. I would be there for her as long as she permitted.

A month passed and I started working at C.W.F.P.S.J. - Now! In that month, I was unable to find a roommate, so I had to move out. Maya and I quickly became friendly again in that same month, but also never resolved our problems. It simply wasn't dealt with. Maya didn't want to and I liked to be around her, besides the sexual reasons. I liked her as a person. As we spent more and more time together again, our attraction to each other came to the fore. The problem was the intention and feeling underlying the attraction was very different to each of us. For Maya, of course, it was romance and the desire to get me to settle down. For me, it was the enjoyment of the moment.

I asked her how she felt about the two of us being lovers. She didn't want to call what we did anything at all. Okay for me, but what were the expectations? I knew there had to be some on her part.

"Thomas, how many times do I have to tell you? I don't expect or need anything from you." she would often say defensively to my inquiries.

So I took one step at a time. Don't force anything. I liked being with her, joking with her, talking with her, making love to her. Wait and see. I asked if I could stay at her place until I found an apartment. She said sure and I moved in. We split the rent, which of course was great for both of us. Things were looking good. Maya and I were getting along and having great sex, I just got a new job at C.W.F.P.S.J and I was starting pre-production on "Loveincrazy."

CHAPTER THREE.

THE TRIAL.

One thing that could be said for Maya, she stuck by me through hard times. Sure, there were times she could care less. Once, when I had just gotten into a car accident and asked her to give me a ride home, she said no. Or another time when my car was broken into in her neighborhood, right in front of her apartment building, and she said, "so what?" But for the most part she showed her support through action. If I had car troubles, she'd get a mechanic friend to help out. Six months before I moved into her place near Washington and La Brea, there was one dramatic event where she, along with my day Jean, and my mother and her husband, were there for me.

The day was just two weeks after 9/11, and right after a screening of John Cassavetes' "A Woman Under the Influence." Gena Rowlands and Peter Falk talked to the audience after the show. I was there, along with Gus, Bernardo, and those two friends who organized the screening and did the actor's workshop with me and Gus. It was exciting for all of us, seeing two heroes of ours after watching one of our favorite films.

I got the nerve to ask a question from my seat in the audience, then afterwards in the lobby approached Gena Rowlands. I thanked her for what she and her husband (not the current one at the time obviously, but John, who'd long since been dead), for what they gave humanity. I was nervous and didn't know what to say. She thanked me with a powerful gleam in her eyes. I soon left the movie theater on 2nd st. in Santa Monica, the Laemmle's I used to work for a couple years before. I was on a high as I walked out the door, the exhilaration of meeting Rowlands and Falk running electricity through me.

Maya dropped me off earlier so she could go do errands. I waited for her outside to come back and pick me up. Five minutes passed and I heard the car horn honk. Maya was not too far up the block, pulling up in a red zone. I rushed up to the car as she and her kids got out. They were going to stay in Santa Monica for a while and visit a friend at an antique store, so I'd come back to pick them up later. Maya asked me how the screening went and I said with a rush of happiness that it was amazing. As Maya and the kids went to leave, I turned back to the car.

A parking meter attendant was giving a ticket on my windshield. My heart jumped. The last thing I needed was a $60 parking ticket. I was in credit card debt, my rent check bounced since I had only $24 in my account, which meant I had to pay my bank $20, then another $25 to my landlord (at the Silverlake apartment) for a late fee, plus the actual rent amount of $775. Not only that but my car was having some problems. Even with Maya's mechanic friend cutting costs, it still didn't look good. And all this for a minimum-wage movie theater worker.

My financial stress would not be helped by this ticket. What the hell was this woman doing, I thought. The car was there for thirty seconds. I was going right back to drive it away. I went up to the lady while she began writing out the ticket, first attempting to politely plead my case, saying the car was only there for less than a minute. It didn't matter, she said. There was no stopping in a red zone.

My pleading became more aggravated. Couldn't she see I was about to move? Maya was just dropping off the car to me. There wasn't a single available meter for blocks. Was I supposed to pay $6 for a parking structure for 30 seconds, I asked. The parking enforcer continued to be steely in her intent, blocking me out. She was going to give that damn ticket or all hell would freeze over.

I then became infuriated. I began shouting at her, telling her a $60 ticket wasn't chump change for a poor person like myself. Didn't she realize it wasn't fair at all? A rich person wouldn't care about a $60 ticket. So what? Write a quick check, here ya go. No problem. I made sincere, adamant arguments explaining this dynamic with parking tickets. The woman looked me straight in the eye, ice in there, hatred for me, for making her job difficult, me, an ant, making her importance irritated, for whatever reasons were in her head, and said she really didn't care.

I couldn't take it. Something inside me snapped. Usually, I'd walk this off. For some reason I couldn't do that this time. At first, I thought I could, turning away and going to the driver's seat of my car. Right before opening the door, the woman's parking enforcement little vehicle was standing by. In one swift move, I kicked the vehicle, right near the steering wheel.

Everything that happened next went into a surreal, fast gear. As soon as I kicked the parking vehicle, I heard the lady pick up a walky-talky and speak into it. I didn't hear what she was saying as I got into my car and began driving away. In the distance on the sidewalk, I heard Maya saying, "Drive, drive!" urging me to get going. But soon that was a ridiculous idea.

No more than 10 seconds of driving and I heard a police car siren. Then another and another. Four Santa Monica cop cars skidded to block the road in front of me while three more were behind me. I stopped the car and heard voices telling me to get out of the car. My adrenaline was in high gear and while I was shaking with fear, I was also still running on anger from my confrontation with the parking lady.

I got out of the car, my hands up as a police officer pointed a gun at my chest eight feet away. The cop screamed at me to turn around. As I did, I saw right in front of me was the old movie theater I used to work at, several co-workers I knew, Maya, Dinora, Javier, as well as Bernardo, Gus, and the two other friends. Everyone was there. Humiliation ... The cop told me to get on my knees as he searched my car and two other cops pointed guns at me.

Soon they searched me, as well, in front of everyone on the street. 2nd st. between Arizona and Santa Monica blvd. was blocked off. The cops then began to read me my rights as they cuffed me. I couldn't believe it. What were they arresting me for? Sure I probably shouldn't have kicked the parking vehicle, but it wasn't as if I attacked anyone. They made me sit on the pavement with my hands cuffed behind my back for several long minutes as they checked my records, I guess. Dinora and Javier tried to ask me what was going on but a cop told them to get lost. I felt like spitting at the cop who told the kids that, then held myself in check. I was already in more trouble than I wanted to be.

Not too much later, the cops got me into the back of one of the seven squad cars. A couple of the cops were testing me, asking why I freaked out. I heard “The Doors” on the radio while we were driving in the car. I laughed at the irony of the music in this situation and asked them if they knew who they were listening to. They said of course, insulted, then I said they still needed to do some “Breaking on Through” ... maybe watch the movie and see all the problems Jim Morrison had with cops.

On the way to the Santa Monica police station, I asked what I was being charged for. The driver said “assault.” What? I couldn't believe it. Who did I assault? Certainly not the parking enforcement lady. I kicked her vehicle, not her. The cop didn't want to get into it. Things began entering the realm of Kafka.

At the Santa Monica jail, the cops checked me and several other men into the hotel. Half an hour later, me and the others were all put into one detaining or waiting cell. An hour and a half passed before I could even ask a question to the check-in guy.

“Am I really being charged with assault?” I asked as they brought me out for mug shots and finger prints.

“That's right.” the check-in guy replied with irritation.

“What's the bail, just out of curiosity?” I said with a frustrated laugh.

“$30,000.”

“What?”

“That funny to you?”

$30,000?! I screamed inside my mind. Okay, so they were intent on keeping me. Otherwise the bail would be considerably less. So it was all now a matter of waiting ... but waiting for what and for how long? I had no attorney, no way of finding out what was going on. Were they only keeping me for a night? Two nights? More? Were they going to ship me to L.A. County jail? If so, was I to stay for several weeks before I could even talk to anyone, let alone get a public defender? How did things work? I asked the jailers but they either gave me a dirty look or laughed. I had no clue what the legal process was. Thomas meet Kafka ...

My allowed two phone calls came up. Who to call? I was supposed to work at the Sunset-5 theater that night and the next. Call my roommate and have him tell the manager I couldn't work but not explain the reason. Then call my dad Jean, then he could tell others, especially my mom. I called Jean in the middle of a t.v. show he was watching with his mom Annabelle. Jean laughed when he heard the news, not able to believe what I was saying initially.

I was hurt by his reaction, there's no doubt about that. Jean's laugh seemed cold, not what I'd expect. But the whole thing really was absurd, not expected at all. Jean had spent three years in the Santa Barbara prison between 1969 and 1972, for selling psychedelics. Jean knew arrest and imprisonment well. Probably too well and thus his awkward reaction to my call from jail.

The phone calls didn't last long, as they weren't allowed to be, and then they took me and the other fresh prisoners to our cells. Fortunately, I had a cell to myself, as most people did. There was about seven cells lined up, separated by thin concrete walls, all facing a hallway and windows up high on the hallway wall. Of course, the hallway with windows was on the other side of bars.

In each cell, there was a bunk-bed with two cots on steel frames, no pillows, and no blankets. There was a toilet and a sink, both uncovered, so if the prisoner was peeing, taking a shit, or washing up, anyone walking by in the hall could see. And all the other prisoners could hear you or smell you. All the cells were full, a couple had two prisoners in them. I was glad I had my own cell. At least I didn't have to worry about another person's deal or shadiness.

The sun had set through the prison windows and darkness added a tenseness to the hall. The jailer walked in and began announcing dinner was coming as he checked each cell. Someone asked what was for dinner but the jailer made no response and left. A few minutes later, an old guy in what looked like janitorial clothes came into the hall and robotically dropped tray after tray for each person's cell. The "dinner" consisted of a flat, rotten, bleak conglomeration of fish, cheese, some kind of sour sauce, and soggy pasta. Perhaps it was tuna casserole. To drink, there was Orange Bang! It was all god awful and I couldn't eat it. I was so high strung on nerves and worry that it didn't matter much. I didn't have an appetite.

After the food, I peed but I certainly wasn't going to poop and I hoped no one else would either. Someone taking a shit would stink up the entire hall. Then, once the food was taken away by the same old man, the jailer brought wool blankets for everyone. How nice. But no pillows. Not only were the blankets thin and cold, but I hated wool. It made my skin feel prickly and I used to get rashes from it as a kid.

The night was long and arduous. Around 9 o'clock and the lights in the hall went out. The jailer announced it was bed-time. The cots were stiff, cold, and painful. It was extremely difficult to get any sleep, impossible more than three or four hours at a time. I was wracking my brain with worries. How long was I going to be here? When would I have someone to talk to? Visitors? My parents, Maya? A public defender? Could anyone tell me anything? Apparently not. What were the chances of going to LA County? Assault was serious. I thought it must be a felony, which meant I would go to County. Shit, I wasn't the kind of guy who could survive that place. Six months? A year? It looked bleak ...

But what the hell did they have on me? I didn't even make an attempt at assaulting that parking enforcement woman, let alone actually do it. Maya was a witness. She could testify. There was no assault, no attempted assault. Just me kicking the vehicle. Was assault considered for inanimate objects as well now? Maybe in Santa Monica, who knows? They were Fascists in that town, ever since the Gentrification began in the late '90's.

Still, they couldn't possibly pin assault on me. They were crazy. The problem was I had no idea about anything. All I had was the cold silence of the cell, horrible food, and a nervous, worried, paranoid state of mind. Trying to sleep through the night was a drama onto itself.

The morning came and the same shitty food arrived. Disgusting tuna casserole for breakfast, lunch, and dinner and that horrible Bang! At about 10 o'clock the jailer came and barked it was visiting time. Hey, I thought, finally. I was sure someone must come and see me. My mom, dad, Maya maybe. How many could I see and for how long? The jailer wouldn't even answer while I waited.

10:45 came and the jailer called my name. I got up in excitement and asked who was there. The jailer replied my parents, as I followed him through hallways and doors until eventually coming to the visiting room. As I sat down, looking through the bullet proof pexi-glass wall, I saw my mom and her husband walk through the door on the other side.

They sat down and faced me, my mom with tears in her eyes and her husband concerned as well. My mother was sincerely pained and worried as she asked me how I was. I replied I never felt so high strung, helpless, and confused. I had no idea what was going on or why I was charged with assault. I asked if they knew anything, were able to talk to someone, a detective, a lawyer, some clerk or other. They replied no one was helpful at all and that the detective was confrontational with them.

Maya and the kids were outside, along with my dad Jean. They had to leave and let Jean come in to visit, as there was only five minutes allowed per person. My mother said she loved me and that hopefully things would work out. Maya and others could testify I'd done nothing wrong, certainly didn't assault anyone, so I shouldn't worry about going to LA County.

Jean came in and was near tears as well. He felt awful for me going through this, knowing himself exactly what prison was like. He asked how they were treating me and I replied like a Kafka character. We both laughed a sad, dark laugh. Jean was as compassionate as could be in five minutes, explaining that probably the first person I could talk to would be the detective, then tomorrow right before the arraignment my public defender.

Jean hoped I'd get a fair lawyer and that I should feel okay talking to the detective but not trust him. The guy was an asshole outside in the waiting area when he, my mom, and Maya just wanted to know the details of the case. Maya apparently got indignant and yelled at the detective for being a prick. Jean said she wanted to see me but that they only allowed two visitors per person. She wanted to allow Jean and my mom a chance to see me.

Going back to my cell, I felt refreshed, as much as one could in jail. I still had the Kafkaesque paranoia, but not to the extreme. I didn't have as much icy cold uncertainty and worry because of seeing my mom and dad and knowing Maya was there, too. I could sense the compassion and love from Jean, as if he felt bad for his initial reaction over the phone.

I spent the whole day and that night in my cell, with absolutely nothing but the rotten tuna casserole and Bang! for lunch and dinner, the cranky jailer going back and forth, the noises of the other prisoners and my own state of mind. Most of the time, everyone was quiet. Next door was a young black man and an older black man, talking about each of their situations. The young man was frustrated with himself, since he knew he made a dumb mistake by coming in to check on a warrant while having weed in his socks.

The old black man was homeless and ended up telling the younger man his whole life story, town to town, woman to woman, job to job. Life had worn him down, and he gave an impassioned critique of modern society. He was never able to fit in, find his role, so he became homeless. He, like several others, was arrested for vagrancy. The majority of arrests in Santa Monica were of homeless people.

Later in the day, a young guy down at the end of the hall began to cry. At first, no one seemed to mind. The guy seemed to be crying the tears of everyone there. Ten minutes passed and he was still crying. Then, fifteen, then twenty, twenty-five. It went on and on and got louder and louder. It became extremely annoying. Prisoners began to tell the guy to shut up, grow up, be a man, stop being a bitch. As much as I hated guys being macho, this young guy's crying was whiny and irritating. The guy in the same cell tried to calm the kid down, but to no help. Another guy told the kid to stop crying, that everyone here was going through a rough time themselves. They certainly didn't need to hear him whining.

Eventually, the kid stopped crying. But it seemed to go on forever. Hours and hours passed and silence dominated again. I was left to be in my own head in the cold cell. What got me here? Did I have a problem? I did lose my temper pretty badly sometimes. Maybe this experience was a lesson to control my anger. I sure as hell didn't want to ever go back to prison.

The night was bad, not as bad as the first night, but still excruciating. Waiting after waiting after fucking waiting. Not being able to do anything at all but take two steps forward, turn around, take another two steps, turn around. I could lay on the cot, think about things, try to sleep. That was the limit to my freedom.

Whatever they decided to do, I thought, they couldn't steal my mind away. They could lock me up for however long they wanted, but they couldn't do that. My dad had taught me that. Jean had to learn that for real, spending three years of his life locked up. The mind was the one area no one could ever penetrate to take freedom away. Only if one allowed it. Outside in society, of course, I reminded myself how people were indeed locked up in their minds. I just had to look at the jailer passing by to recognize that. It was important to have an existential sense of humor. Jean had also taught me that.

The next morning, the detective was available to speak with the prisoners if anyone wanted to. I did. I wanted to know what they were in the process of doing. The jailer took me to another room where the detective asked how it was in prison for six months, after beating my wife up in San Jose. What? I was thrown off. I asked him what the hell he was talking about. I'd never been married, never even visited San Jose, never been arrested or in prison a day in my life before now.

The detective insisted I tell the truth. I laughed at him and told him to go back and look at my records. They have everything on me, finger prints, identification, etc. The detective asked me if I was Thomas Thorpe. Of course, I said, but he must be talking about another Thomas Thorpe. The detective then left in a huff, either sincerely bothered by my ridicule of their legal ineptness, or continuing with his act, as he probably was. I'm sure he knew very well that I was not the same Thomas Thorpe who already spent time in jail for beating up his wife in San Jose. He just threw that at me for intimidation purposes. Still, it was pretty humorous to me and my sarcastic laughter has a way of bothering people. He was probably sincere in his irritation.

Back in my cell, I realized it must not be ineptness but some kind of strange psychological bullying tactic to make the prisoners afraid and uncertain. In the cell next to me, I could hear the young black man complaining to the older black man that they were doing similar things with him. The detective was insistent that he had a record of things he didn't do, how they were charging him with intent to sell instead of just possession, and so on.

This legal tactic of bullying prisoners with untrue "facts" was confirmed when I went with eleven other prisoners to our arraignments. It took an hour just to get us all from one building to the next until we arrived, chained together, in a waiting cell. Another hour passed of waiting, with everyone silent and worried. I looked at the men, the lower class "dregs" of society for the most part, but looking at their faces, their expressions were the same as mine. The details of what was running through their minds were different, of course, but as far as the feelings were concerned, it was exactly the same: helpless. We were all numbers to the mercy of the judicial system.

The public defenders then came to the hall on the other side of the bars, carrying folders, papers, and so forth. The first two attorneys were cold and demeaning. The guys barked at the prisoners they were supposedly defending, berating them, scolding them, being harsh for no apparent reason other than they hated their jobs and looked forward to the day when they'd be prosecutors. They also did that trick of telling their defendants about things on their records that wasn't true, which made the prisoners have an unstable state of mind, and thus more likely to accept anything. These two public defenders had no interest other than getting their defendants to accept the charges.

I witnessed this for a good 45 minutes, one guy after another, and panicked I might be one of these attorney's defendants. I felt like I might tell these guys to go fuck themselves if they didn't want to defend me.

Then the third public defender came and it was a woman. She came into the hall in a rush, flustered to have to deal with these cases in such a hurry. She probably had to deal with tons of different defendants. Me and the others in our waiting cell were just the ones at the stage of arraignment. She announced my name and talked to me about my case. I could tell she actually cared as she went into how she wanted to get the city to drop the charges. I was utterly grateful to have gotten her.

The woman said the assault charge was dropped – yes! - and that they were now trying to get me on attempted vandalism. She explained that looking in the legal books, she found no basis for attempted vandalism. Since no damage was done to the parking enforcement vehicle, there was no vandalism. If a person doesn't commit real vandalism, and since there is no way of determining an attempt or not, the charge was ridiculous.

She felt they had nothing on me. It was up to me if I wanted to pursue a jury trial or accept the charge. The punishment was six months probation and 12 hours of anger management. I asked if she could try to persuade the judge to drop the charges but if not I'd rather accept the charges and get the hell out of jail.

She understood and said she could at least be able to make sure the charges were expunged, or even completely eliminated from my record.

It wouldn't be anywhere, as if it didn't happen. That sounded good. Soon, we prisoners were led into the courtroom, chained up, and walked in line to our seats. There wasn't many people attending the arraignment, but my mother, her husband, Jean, and Maya were there. The sight of seeing me chained together with the other men shocked them.

The arraignment went as I expected. The judge was cold and heartless, the DA/prosecutor was a gentrified lawyer prick and the two male public defenders were still assholes. My public defender made a passionate case for me. There was no legal basis for the charges. It didn't matter to the judge. She was intent on protecting the dignity of Santa Monica parking enforcement property and this young man - me – needed to be taught a lesson.

The prosecutor was ridiculous. In his case against me, he stated that the parking enforcement woman was so afraid of me, I shocked her so much with my actions, she was so rattled that she thought of quitting her job. He said it was clear I was a professional in martial arts training, being as my kick to her vehicle almost knocked it over! Maya, Jean, my mom, and her husband all laughed out loud at the prosecutor. He really was ridiculous. I smiled. The judge, though, would have nothing to do with laughter, telling them to be quiet.

As much as the judge wanted to "get" me, all that could really be done was 6 months probation and anger management. The public defender won out by getting the charge completely dropped from my record as long as I did nothing illegal in the next six months and attended 12 hours of an anger management class. And then, it was done.

A black man and myself were released from jail about an hour later, on the side of the Santa Monica courthouse. We both had deep smiles on and wished each other well. Neither of us knew anything about the other, but we knew exactly how we both felt. We were free men again. I met my mom, her husband, Jean, and Maya outside the courthouse and never felt so good in my life. I never felt so liberated, never appreciated the sky, the air, the ability to move around, to choose what I wanted to do, so much.

Jean looked at me and knew what I was going through, noticing the wide smile on my face. He joked I should try leaving prison after three years of being inside. My mother was crying in happiness. Maya was glad to see me, her young lover. My mother's husband was happy. I hugged them all tightly, warmly, tears coming from my eyes and breathing the Santa Monica air.

After that day, for several weeks, I was unable to let go of my feelings of appreciation. Everything I did, everywhere I went, I loved my freedom. I was comforted by my loved ones support. Their being there for me was vital. Who knows, perhaps if it wasn't for them, I would've been like that other young guy in the cell, crying and crying away.

I realized just how much Maya cared for me. Sure, a cynical side to me could say she had her own motives to be supportive. She did it to prove her love, to convince me she was the one for me and that I should settle down with her. This could be applied to my parents , as well, each one wanting to prove their love to me, or in their case, my mom and dad trying to outdo the other.

But I knew that this simply wasn't true. Maya loved me, and especially Jean and my mom. My parents were sincere in their love. Maya was supportive simply because she was in love with me. If one wanted to dissect the human condition, as I did, sure, one could find selfish motivations. That was to be found in everyone, myself included.

The point was realizing the situation. The dominant motivation in Maya's, Jean's, and my mother's support of me was compassionate love. I could not deny Maya's sense of loyalty and consistency. She was there while others took flight. All of my other friends – Gus, Bernardo, others – didn't care much at all.

Besides seeing Maya's real love for me during my time in jail, there was a lesson to learn from the experience. Not only did I have a problem with anger in itself, but it was a weakness on my part in relation to others ... uncontrollable anger like I've had at times is something which I hope you will not have, Daniel.

My temper has gotten me into too much trouble, too much pain ... the sudden flash of anger that has come inside me and which I have unleashed has enabled people to use it against me time and again ... losing my temper, losing control, is a weakness because it gives others the opportunity to pull the carpet from under your feet in sly ways ...

Both my impulse for anger and for any other instinctive emotion, such as expressing love, or some kind of honesty within me, more times than not has been an opening for others to attack ... they saw it as a way to get back at me ... so beware, Daniel, of your temper and other impulsive emotions ... beware of what it will get you into ... and how it can be the lethal weapon used against you ...

CHAPTER FOUR.

THE FLUX OF LOVE.

When I moved out of my Silverlake apartment and into Maya's one bedroom near Washington and La Brea, our relationship was under uncertain definitions (as if it was ever clearly defined). We had our blow-up at my apartment where she ripped up my love letters and threw them in the trash. The other time when she broke down in tears on the floor in anguish, mentioning even suicide. Things had calmed down since then but there were no resolutions. I still felt the same way, and so did she. I wanted to be with her, but couldn't promise faithfulness. She wanted to be with me, but only if I was faithful. Maya herself pushed it in that direction, refusing to come out with whether she wanted to define it as a relationship. There was an understanding my move-in was only temporary.

I began my job at C.W.F.P.S.J.-Now! at the same time as my move in to Maya's place. I was excited about the work, fascinated by the different possibilities. Perhaps, besides being a filmmaker, this could be my career, a peace activist. Finally a job that made a difference. I worked from 2 to 10pm, so I arrived to Maya's apartment late at night, after the kids were asleep. Often when I came home, I'd be hungry and Maya would make me something to eat. Because of the schedule, I usually ate food around 4pm. Typical dinner time for most people was when we canvassers knocked on their doors.

So I was hungry after work and Maya liked to cook for me. One night I came home with some C.W.F.P.S.J literature, looking at it while sitting at the kitchen table. Maya was in the kitchen, making me eggs with avocado, El Salvadorian cheese, tortillas, tomatoes, and cucumbers on the side.

"You should check some of this stuff out ... it's pretty interesting." I said, while reading the papers and newsletter. Maya didn't respond. "A lot of what they're saying is right on ... billions and billions of dollars spent on nuclear weapons or systems that don't work ... the Star Wars program, which Reagan introduced in the '80's to have some insane thing in space shoot a laser at a nuclear missile coming to the U.S., which has never no where near been proven to work and yet congress continues to give billions of dollars in funding to it ..." I kept going as Maya still had her back to me and didn't say anything. "And now the military wants these bunker busters and anti-ballistic missiles, both of which have nuclear tips on them. The second of impact, the tips explode and send radioactive fall-out everywhere. The bunker busters don't go into the bunkers underground, but explode after two feet into the ground. And these costs billions and billions of dollars ..." I continued as Maya remained silent and seemed oblivious. "Not only is C.W.F.P.S.J trying to get the public aware that their tax dollars are being used for these stupid things, but we're telling people about arms trafficking, how the U.S. is making huge profits from selling weapons to dictators all over the world ... to showing how if our country wasn't spending hundreds of billions of dollars on defense, we'd have the money for free health care for everyone, we could help dramatically eliminate poverty and hunger in the Third World ... these are really important issues ..."

But Maya still didn't respond as she gave me my food. I knew she must've been hearing me. We were a few feet away from each other. Was I being too preachy? Maybe I was rambling about politics too much. That might be it. Maybe I should try to involve her in the conversation more, I thought.

"Do the kids like their new school?" I asked.

"Yeah." she replied as she went to washing dishes.

"How do you think they're adjusting after moving back from Texas?"

"Okay."

"It's probably a little hard for them."

"They seem fine."

"It's probably hard for you, too."

"I'm okay."

"Have you thought about what you want to do now you're in LA? Go back to school, find a job?"

"I think I'll start working at J.C. Penny soon."

"You still have the dream of opening your own restaurant?"

"Yeah, maybe."

I was frustrated with the conversation. Maya never once looked at me nor showed any interest. I tried again to involve her. I didn't like her so obsessed in her kitchen duties. I didn't want to be living with a house wife.

"Hey, why don't you let me do that?" I said as I walked up to her.

"No, sit down. Don't worry."

"I don't mind."

"I don't want you to. Go back to eating."

"No, it's okay, I'm done. Let me help you."

"Thomas ..." she said, finally turning to me, but in utter irritation. "Please."

"Okay then." I said dejectedly as I sat back down, wondering what to say next. "Don't you think we all spend too much time working, at a job or at home, and not enough energy is spent on stimulating the mind? We get worn out then watch t.v., or we go and buy things. A society of workers and consumers and t.v. watchers, keeping the machine going ... with vacations now and then if one can afford it ..." I said and still not getting a response from her. "I mean, what's the point of this locomotive we all keep pushing? We go to school, learn information, one level to the next, get a job, start a family, join a religion, buy a house, buy a car, maybe two, maybe three, go on vacations, again if one can afford it (which we can't), go back to work, then get dissatisfied with it all, hit a mid-life crisis, get a divorce, see our kids graduate from college, then get married again, continue to work, buy a new house, buy a new car or two, go on vacations, go back to work, go to church on Sundays, go back to work, then retire. The we sit on our asses at home and do nothing, watch t.v., play golf, then our wife or husband dies, we're alone, our kids are going through a mid-life crisis and don't care about us, then we die ... I mean, what do you think about all that?"

"Well, that's life." she finally responded.

"That's it?"

"There's love."

"I know there's love but love isn't everything."

"It should be."

"It can't be."

"That's what you think."

"There's more to life than love, so we should be the same way."

"You're selfish person, though."

"Why am I a selfish person?"

"Because you are."

"You're so nice to me."

"Well, Thomas," she said, frustrated with me. "I don't know what you're talking about."

"I just like to question things. I guess you're right in a way. To question is to want something more, and that's selfish I suppose. That's why I couldn't believe in that spirituality anymore, the meditation and stuff when you first met me. There were too many unresolved things about the human condition that spirituality couldn't deal with. No religion can – Christianity, Judaism, Islam, Buddhism, Hinduism, New Age beliefs, etc., etc. If life could be looked at for what it is, if we could be looked at for what we are, no strings attached, we'd all be living in a more honest world. The nature of existence is harsh enough as it is, yet we seem to want to make it even harsher. I think human beings are afraid to challenge themselves in that way, to strip themselves, even though in the end it'd bring about less pain for us."

"Maybe you're afraid."

"Of what?"

"Of committing yourself to the world, to religion, society, family, friends. It's like you don't want the responsibility."

"Responsibility? That's all I care about, an honest responsibility to life, to my life, to yours. And to society? What do you think I'm doing at my new job?"

"At that job you're not really doing anything to help people."

"That's the whole point of the job! It's definitely helping people more than selling popcorn or gay porno."

"All you do is talk politics to people, but you're not actually doing anything, just talking."

"Look, Maya, you know me. Politics is just a means to an end, only an aspect of changing things. And as far as commitment goes, I'm committed to you, your kids, my family, and my friends."

"You won't commit yourself as a man."

"What does that mean?"

"You know what I mean."

"I won't commit myself to you, as a boyfriend or a husband? Is that what a man is to you? Someone who does what you want them to?"

"I won't say anything more."

"Always bringing me down, Maya ..."

"You bring yourself down. You're just like other men, the exact same way. You think you're different but you're the same. You try to sound intelligent but you make no sense, and what you're really thinking about is fucking women. I see you when we go out and go places. You have to look at every ass that passes by."

"I do, huh? I'll have to watch myself the next time we go out somewhere and see if I do that."

"At least with other men they don't pretend to be intelligent like you and just do their job, be a good father, work, and shut up."

"Well, if that's the case, what the hell're you doing hanging around me?" I said with a hurt, strained, sarcastic laugh.

"I don't know." she replied, irritated by my sarcasm.

"If I bore you or you don't understand what I'm talking about most of the time, go find another man."

"I don't want to. I've told you thousands of times I don't need a man in my life."

"Go find a woman then."

"Fuck you." Maya said and walked out of the kitchen in a huff.

And that was the end of the conversation. She went to the bathroom to wash up, then went to sleep.

The next morning, I woke up from the couch in the living room I slept on every night. The kids were up, eating cereal and watching morning cartoons. It was early, 7:30 in the morning. I hated the early morning, and always woke up sore from sleeping on that couch. In the kitchen, Emmanuel sat at the table, eating breakfast Maya had made. She was still on the kitchen working on things.

As I sat up, groggy and sore, I waved to Emmanuel and said good morning to him and the kids. The kids said good morning but their eyes were glued to the t.v. Emmanuel said good morning and asked how I was doing, but in an automatic sort of way, as if he wasn't really interested. He sat quietly in the kitchen, eating, not saying anything to Maya or the kids.

Maya came out of the kitchen and into the bedroom, not saying anything to anyone. I sat on the couch for a good fifteen minutes and no one said anything. Was this what Maya wanted? Silence? No interaction? God, I thought, I hated that. Sure, I liked to be quiet and to myself a lot of the time. But not as much as Maya seemed to, and in those moments of silence, what was going on? Often, if it wasn't doing house work, or bills, it was watching t.v. The silent times I enjoyed I was either working on something creative, reading, or thinking about non-work related things.

I asked Maya several questions as I got up from the couch, pretty mundane and not very sophisticated topics, and she never answered. I hated that about her, too. It was kinda rude. It's like she just tuned people out whenever she wanted to. When she wanted to talk, it was different. Her feelings were hurt if I did what she did – ignore her. Soon the kids had to go to school and their dad took them.

Maya and I were alone in the apartment and there was only silence. Oh well, I thought, what could I do? That's the way she wanted it. I went into the bathroom, took a shower, and brushed my teeth. When I came out and put my clothes on, Maya was doing laundry. She was always doing housework. I wanted to help her so she wasn't always doing it, but she wouldn't let me. The only thing I could do was take out the trash.

The one thing we seemed to connect on was sex. The high from working at C.W.F.P.S.J, going door to door and raising money for peace, made me still up when I came to Maya's place at night. Seeing Maya, usually showing her legs in high cut shorts, turned me on. I was horny for those legs and body. Usually I'd sit next to her on the couch while she watched her Mexican soap operas and I touched her.

She always played as if she didn't want sex, but eventually after enough foreplay and touching, she let her guard down and was into it. She liked when I went down on her pussy, or when she was on top of me while I sucked her nipples, or when I fucked her doggystyle. Our love-making was normally intense and very satisfying for both of us. It was hard to break up with someone when the sex was so good.

Of course, Maya wanted to believe what brought us together was more than sex. Since the romanticism was gone from my heart, and our personalities weren't always clicking, she had to resort to a romanticization of the past. She didn't really love the present Thomas, but the me of years before. She hung on in the hopes that some day I'd revert to my old Prince Valiant self. She also wanted to stay with me because of her fanatical insistence on a "one and only." If it didn't work out with me, then no one else would do, either.

The thing was, I insisted to her that the old me wasn't really the person she romanticized about. It was only an idea she had in her head, a dream, a fantasy, a creation of her own desires, not a reality. One night after work, I wanted to come home and tell her I was moving out. Gus was offering his apartment to stay at, until I could get a place of my own. But when I got to Maya's apartment, she was arguing intensely in Spanish on the phone. It seemed as if she was fighting with Emmanuel. Some bad Spanish words were used viciously and I knew what they meant. I decided not to bother Maya that night.

Over the next few days, Maya began to block out Emmanuel. He was on another drinking binge and she was fed up. I felt she was beginning to insinuate, by wanting me around Dinora and Javier more and more, to have me replace Emmanuel as their "daddy." I loved the kids immensely and had spent a great deal of time watching them grow up. They were great kids and I liked being a guide and a role model for them.

But I didn't want to be their father. I didn't want to do that to them nor Emmanuel. It wasn't the right thing to do, psychologically speaking, to displace the real, legitimate father. I would be there for the kids, but as a friend only. I had too many demons from my own experience with a step-father. Emotional displacement and confusion existed when father displacement happened to me.

It became apparent at this time Maya was partially using me as a tool or weapon in her battle with Emmanuel. Sure, Emmanuel was selfish and not very interesting, not to mention a horrible alcoholic. But Maya often pushed his buttons, forcing him to drink as his only way to deal with her. The stress level was too high. It was a vicious cycle. She screamed and cursed at him for drinking, which made him drink more.

I didn't want to get caught up in that. So I left Maya's apartment and moved into Gus' place. I hung out with Gus and Bernardo more and more, got caught up in making "Loveincrazy," met Kristianna, Kurt and Cindy, hung out with my C.W.F.P.S.J co-workers, I worked hard. I saw Maya very little those months after leaving her apartment.

As the cast for my movie fell apart, with Charlotte forced to drop out because of C.W.F.P.S.J work upstate, I had to find a replacement. All the actresses I interviewed for the role before I chose Charlotte didn't interest me. So who to find? I thought of Maya. I hadn't spoken to her much recently. Now that I was acting in the film, perhaps it was a good idea to cast her as my character's girlfriend. Because of our history, the chemistry and tension would be there.

I went to the J.C Penny she worked at in the Fox Hills mall. She was in the men's suit department, organizing clothes on display. When I came up to her, she was caught off-guard. There was that child-like vulnerability in her eyes which always got me. She didn't have her wall up in those moments and I liked that. So much that it brought back a degree of my romance for her. The largeness, the warmth of her heart could be seen when she let her guard down.

At first, I expected Maya to turn me down for the movie. After all, everyone else was shooting me down with NO's. She also wasn't exactly given good reason to help me out since I left her as a boyfriend. But she surprised me and accepted the offer. She knew how important the movie was for me. She could see the passion in my eyes. I explained to her that her role wouldn't be that large, either, so it wouldn't be too time consuming.

She wasn't so sure about acting but I told her not to worry. I'd help her. The thing I was concerned about was the sex scene. Would she be comfortable doing it?

The first day of the shoot came and I wanted to shoot the sex scene first. I asked Maya if she still was okay to do it. She said sure. Wow, I thought. What commitment. I was beginning to think she was more comfortable doing the sex scene than I was. I told her we'd film it with no one else in the room but her and I and the camera. We could also have several swigs of whiskey.

Maya turned out to be a dedicated actress. She always showed up on time, for the most part, and tried hard with her acting. Like Benny, she was a natural. After the first couple of weeks of rehearsals, she got comfortable acting in front of the camera. I was pleased with her performance. She was good in the scenes with me and had a terrific improvisational scene of playing darts with Benny.

By the end of the shoot and during the wrap party, though, I could tell she was getting jealous of Kristianna's closeness with me. Kristianna and I seemed to click in ways Maya wasn't able to with me. She also didn't like the attention Cindy gave me. But mostly it was Kristianna who bothered Maya even though Kristianna tried to be friendly with her.

Maya was always a religious person, whether she admitted to it or not. She was a natural born (or psychologically institutionalized by her culture) Catholic. But now she seemed to push her Catholicism more out into the open. She made Dinora and Javier go to catechism school, she began going to church every Sunday, she watched Catholic t.v. programs, and listened to Catholic radio shows. It irritated me. Religion was such a hindrance and an annoyance. I loved Maya and knew she had intelligence. Why was she becoming more religious? I sensed it was kind of an internal message she was sending me. She knew I hated religion.

"So what's this church you go to like?" I asked her one day while driving her to pick up the kids from the catechism class.

"It's good." she replied simply, in another silent mood of hers.

"Well, obviously you think it's good or you wouldn't be going there. But what is it you like about it? Is the priest interesting? Does he give good sermons? How's the congregation?"

"Look, Thomas, I don't want to argue with you. I like the church and that's it."

"I wasn't trying to argue with you."

"I know what you think of religion. You hate God."

"I don't hate God!" I burst into laughter. "It's impossible for me to hate God since I have no idea what God is, nor do I think anyone does. If God exists, I don't think It gives a shit if I hate It or not. It would be beyond my petty human feelings or ideas."

"You are petty."

"I was just trying to ask you about your new church. You seem to be more interested in religion these days."

"I don't like talking with you because you're always attacking me. You're just like your dad."

"I don't attack you!"

"Yes you do."

“I can't ask you questions or involve you in an intellectual conversation?”

“No because you just make fun of me.”

“I don't!” I said with a frustrated smile.

“Just look at yourself right now. You have a fucking cynical, sarcastic smile when you want to talk about 'deep things.' You don't take people seriously when you talk with them. Everyone thinks that about you, you know.”

“Ohhh, the whole wide world!” I said with a laugh, purposefully sarcastic.

“See, there you go.”

“Well, except for my dad.”

“That's because you just copy him. His attitude, the way he looks at things. You even talk the same way as he does, and walk the same way.”

“Like father, like son.”

“It's like you can't think for yourself.”

“Guess that means Dinora will be just like you and Javier will be just like his dad.”

“Fuck you.” Maya said with anger, knowing I was implying that Javier would end up an alcoholic like Emmanuel.

Maya and I were constantly at odds like that and I was constantly looking at other women. She hated every time my eyes wandered to a woman's ass as they walked by. She told me I should go fuck those women if I liked their asses so much. I said maybe I would. She responded by saying if I did, then forget about having sex with her. I should get lost. So I did.

This was when I started to fall in love with Charlotte. I was on a down from finishing the shoot of "Loveincrazy." The excitement of the production was over and the work of editing all the footage was ahead of me. I was getting burnt out working at C.W.F.P.S.J, burnt out on politics, burnt out on the people I canvassed, burnt out with my co-workers' P.C. attitudes. I was disappointed that things just never clicked with Maya besides the sex. Personal demons of mine were brought to the surface from exploring them while making "Loveincrazy." Charlotte was a Kind Light at this time. Something about her shown through to me.

Then of course a month later she fired me. My experience at C.W.F.P.S.J ended in a bleak explosion. I couldn't tell Maya the reason why I was fired, not yet. We hadn't been in a sexual relationship for several months, but still I wanted to take delicate steps. It wasn't just a sexual attraction to Charlotte, I'd fallen in love with her. Maya would be deeply hurt to know the passion I once had for her was being thrown at another woman. Especially at a woman who fired me for it.

A few weeks later and Maya found out. Benny was the one who told her. Maya was angry and upset at me but hid it well. Instead she ridiculed and put me down. She continually insisted I only fell in love with unavailable women to prove something and feel sorry for myself. If there was a challenge in trying to get an unavailable woman, I fell more in love with her. With my love for Charlotte, Maya believed I was only feeling that way to "try and win the prize (Charlotte)" from her boyfriend. It was as if my love was a competition. I would retaliate by letting Maya know how much I wanted to fuck Charlotte, how great the conversations I had with her were ... I was spiteful, we both were ...

Maya and I were now used to saying hurtful things to each other, somehow remaining friends after my getting fired at C.W.F.P.S.J. She realized that as much as I hurt her and she didn't understand me, I was essentially a kind and real person. I wasn't phony with her. A lack of phoniness usually trumps occasional cruelty. It did in our case. My kindness was often expressed through my actions. I'd do things to help her, help her kids, spend time with them all. What she hated and liked about me the most was my honesty. Other people would say one thing then do another, friends would come and go, while I was still there for her. And whether she wanted to admit to it or not, she was still in love with me.

The memories of our sex always lingered in the back of our minds. It was hard to forget how good it was. I would be with other women and find it not nearly as satisfying as it was with Maya. We knew how to please each other in bed. Maya had plenty of other men come onto her and she dated a few, but never did she go all the way with them. They just didn't do it for her the way I did. A lot of the men might've been even better lovers than me, but they didn't make her feel as comfortable to be herself as I did. And there was always that lingering Catholic guilt. She didn't want to be considered “loose.”

So Maya and I got back together again. We broke up and got back over and over, maybe seven or eight times. We couldn't live without each other, we couldn't live with each other. One of Maya's favorite songs was U2's “With or Without You,” and I could see why. Maya became closer with my mother, with Jean (but more with Jean's mom, Annabelle), with my mom's grandmother. Probably on a subconscious level, Maya knew that by becoming friends with my family, she'd be more permanently involved in my life. Jean warned me about this and I knew. I could see that but didn't mind.

Maya's love-making with me continued to be pleasurable, even though she had insecurities that I didn't like her getting fat. She wasn't really overweight, I thought. That was never a problem for me. Sure I preferred her thinner, but that was not the reoccurring problem in our relationship. It was our lack of communication and divergent ways of seeing things. She assumed it was her weight, even though I continually told her the real reasons.

One day after great sex in the afternoon while the kids were at school, I was in the bathroom washing up. Maya walked in to use the toilet. We were both naked and were always comfortable being naked together after the sex was over.

“There's something important I have to tell you ...” she said while sitting on the toilet.

"Yeah?" I responded, wondering what was on her mind.

"I ... I want to have another baby ..." she said with some difficulty. I was taken aback and didn't know what to say. "... before I get too old ... I'm only a few years away from 40 and they say you shouldn't have kids after 40 ... so, anyways, I know how you are and I know you have a lot of dreams and you want to make your movies and all that ... and I know you want to have your freedom so I wouldn't want to take all that away from you ... I'll take the baby with me to Mexico and maybe you could come visit us when you could but you wouldn't be responsible for the baby ..."

"So you're saying you want to have a baby with me?" I asked, still in shock, and just wanting to make it clear. She didn't come out with it directly that she wanted to have a baby with me, as if she was too afraid to say it.

"But you wouldn't have to be involved as a father."

"This is big stuff, Maya ... If we were to have a baby together, I'd want to be involved as the baby's father. That would be very, very important to me ... extremely important ..."

And that was as much as we said about having a baby. There was partial, vague understanding. It wasn't clear but there was the acknowledgment. We continued to have unprotected sex with me cumming inside her. In the past, I'd pull out right before cumming. I knew that was never a reliable way of preventing impregnation. A part of me felt perhaps I couldn't get her pregnant. I told Jean in the past how there were times I came inside Maya and other women but didn't impregnate them. Maybe I was infertile. Jean told me it might be a good idea to check it out, though unlikely, reminding me it depended on the time of month for the woman.

So there was a non-verbal understanding between Maya and I we were trying for a baby. The problem with not verbalizing anything was that both our intentions weren't clear. Did she want to have the baby but not want me involved? She didn't say. Did I want the baby and be the father figure, but not want to be in a relationship with Maya? I didn't say. Mostly why neither of us verbalized exactly what we wanted was neither of us knew 100%. Part of Maya wanted to have the baby and get married to me. Part of me liked the idea of being in a relationship with her. Part of both of us wanted the opposite.

I gave the situation huge weight. Maya's question hit me hard with the significance for days. Should I have a baby with her? Should I have a child at all? I considered it before, felt I would be best ready for it in my late thirties, and with someone else other than Maya. A woman who I was more compatible with, where the understanding was better, the love was stronger, healthier, and less conflicted. A woman who I'd see as my partner in life.

But was such an ideal possible? Sure I wasn't that old but I'd seen enough that what I really wanted, my idea of what a family should be, with a woman closer to my own identity, was hard to come by. I knew a relationship with Maya would ultimately not work out. It just couldn't happen. But Maya as a mother reached heights of wonder for me. She could be an amazing mother, truly amazing, real in her love. While she had problems, obvious problems even as a mother, the part I admired about her motherhood was so strong, it outweighed the bad. She was the kind of mother I wanted for my child. The deficiencies she had were in areas where I was strong. What the child didn't get from her, it'd get from me. The contrasts in our races and cultures was another dynamic. Our child would not only get both our personalities, but both our worlds, as well.

One night Maya and I went to have dinner with a friend of hers. It was Miranda and her older, white husband. I had seen Miranda since Maya moaned her name years ago while I was going down on her. I never brought up that intimate situation to Miranda, but occasionally I'd tease Maya about it when we got into fights. Maya would tease back by saying I was attracted to Miranda, which was true. I'd throw back at her maybe we should do a three-way with Miranda.

While eating dinner and drinking wine, Miranda opened up about having lesbian feelings, and actually had a Persian lady-friend at this time. Amidst everyone's talking – because we'd been drinking and joking around, everyone was fairly loud – I heard it slip out of Miranda's mouth that she was disappointed Maya was no longer a lesbian. I knew what I heard, but didn't respond. It seemed Maya and Miranda's husband didn't hear it and Miranda said nothing more about it. What the hell was that, I thought to myself then. It plagued me for the rest of the night. Maybe Maya really was a closet lesbian or bi-sexual.

Back at Maya's apartment, with the kids at their dad's, Maya and I made love. It was good, as usual, although I was holding back more than I normally did. What Miranda said earlier that night about Maya being a lesbian in the past bothered me. After we finished having sex, we lay naked together on the bed.

"There's something that's been bothering me tonight ..." I said. "... it was something Miranda said. I heard her say she was disappointed you were no longer a lesbian."

"Are you going to go talking about that again? Jesus Christ ..." she snapped, as she got up from the bed and put her clothes on.

"Maya, I heard what she said."

"You're so full of shit."

"I'm not lying to you. She said it. What the hell was that? Did you used to be a lesbian or something?"

"Fuck you." she said then went into the bathroom, slamming the door behind her.

Days past and we never talked about lesbianism at all. I was frustrated with Maya. She was hiding something. Not only did it bother me she wasn't being honest about this secret of hers, but she also shut down so often. Whenever I was around her, there was this same old wall in front of her, pushing me away ...

A depression began to hit me hard. Everything in life was so rotten, so despairing. Nothing fulfilled me. Everything seemed a disappointment. I reached a point of zero, of emptiness. I'd felt emptiness and pain before, but not this harrowing, bleak futility. Everything in life seemed to go nowhere else but desolation. It all added up. The failure of my movie, "Loveincrazy," my failure to get any sort of recognition or success as a filmmaker. The failure of my friendships with Bernardo, Gus, Benny, and others. The problems with my step-family, the failure of feeling truly connected to my mother. The friends I liked, Kurt and Cindy, left town. The failure to have a creative, professional or perhaps even a romantic relationship with Kristianna. The failures in romance with women in general, with Ariel, Charlotte, other women from C.W.F.P.S.J., Chaos, Sax, Doris even, and others. The tragedy at C.W.F.P.S.J. The failure between Maya and myself to understand each other ... it went on and on and on ... blow after blow after blow ...

I didn't know what to do. Suicide had crossed my mind ... but I knew I wasn't completely cut adrift from other people and the world around me ... my dad Jean was there and understood. Despite his support and understanding the weight of my sadness was still strong and I drank more and more ... alcohol was more a staple in my diet than ever before. I masturbated to porn more and more, started going to on-line porn sites. There were sites where you could talk dirty to other people on-line or over the phone. You could even hook up with them in person, which I did. I met a few women and was dissatisfied. As I was jacking off to a porno magazine one day, I thought of something. While I always tuned out the guys who were fucking the women in the pictures, I tried this time to see if I could cum while looking at the men.

At first, it was difficult for me to get aroused. Then, after several minutes of effort, I got hard again and came. Afterwards, I asked myself if I was gay or bi-sexual ... was I? I was never attracted to men. I could be attracted to a man's personality but not their body. But this time I came while looking at a naked man, looking at his cock and I tried it again. I'd jack off to the women and the men sometimes or just the men. Sometimes in bed I'd slide a finger up my asshole while masturbating, imagining a cock was fucking me.

Like any time in my adult life, when some kind of personal revelation came to me, I felt the need to deal with it and not repress it. Perhaps even bring it out in the open with others. I did it before when telling Maya I needed to see other women. I did it before when I finally told my family and friends that Frazier, my step-father, had molested me when I was nine. I realized how much psychological harm there was in repression. All the damage done to me from not telling anyone my father figure at the time, Frazier, had molested me was enormous. 17 years of bottling it up, from the ages of 9 to 26. It had screwed me up in ways not always seen. Most noticeably, though, was my volcanic, unexpected anger, and my lack of trust in people.

So I knew I shouldn't repress these homosexual feelings. The problem was that it was only in porn could I get turned on by men. Out in the real world, I looked at men but couldn't find them attractive. Women still turned me on so I knew I must be bi-sexual. Or was I even that? To have an attraction to the same sex meant wanting to have sex with them. There were no men I could find any desire to be with sexually. It actually turned me off when I thought of it, looking at a real guy and imagining what it would be like.

After having sex with Maya one night, I thought if I should tell her what I'd been going through in the last week. Then it dawned on me. Maybe if I told her I might be gay or bi-sexual, perhaps she'd stop desiring me. Another part of me simply wanted to get it off my chest. I wanted to have an open conversation about attraction to the same sex. It still bothered me Maya's possible lesbianism and how she denied it. Maybe if I was open about my own feelings, she'd open up more to me about hers.

When I told her, though, she got sick, rushed to the bathroom, and threw up. She couldn't believe what I said. The man she was in love with all these years was a fagot? I couldn't help responding with a sarcastic laugh to her harshness, saying I still wanted to make love to women, too, but the idea of a cock going up my asshole turned me on.

She began to cry what sounded like phony tears while she threw up in the bathroom. Whether or not I was really gay, I hated how this was the way she dealt with intimate, difficult, personal things – running away. Funny, I thought at the time, since she always said I was the one afraid to confront responsibility. She couldn't face her own complexity. She was afraid of that kind of responsibility.

I told my family and friends about my homosexual feelings and everyone else was more understanding than Maya. It just scared her, disgusted her. A month passed, though, and I could no longer get a hard-on looking at naked men in porno magazines. I tried again and again, but could never get aroused. Men in public continued to not attract me, either. It was as if the homosexual lust was no longer in my system.

The sexual drive for other men was gone completely, even though when I told people that, I also said I wouldn't deny it'd ever come back again. I wasn't particularly interested in making love with a man, but I never knew. Maybe it would happen some day, maybe it wouldn't. Either way, I didn't want to force it. I explained this to Maya and she thought I was crazy. Secretly, she was happy, so she could allow herself to still be in love with me. It would be an impossibility if I was bi-sexual.

Then Maya found out she was pregnant ... Yes, she knew we were having unprotected sex, knew we were conscious of the possibility, and deep down she wanted to have a child. But she was still caught off-guard and didn't know what to do.

At first, she thought of not telling me. She'd run away to Mexico with Dinora, Javier, and the unborn baby (you, Daniel), leaving both fathers behind. Neither of us deserved fatherhood to her, so screw me and Emmanuel. She actually considered this. But something inside her told her she couldn't do that. Despite all the disappointment she felt she'd been dealt by both Emmanuel and myself, despite the fact she wasn't in a relationship with either of us, she couldn't take the kids away from us. Despite all the pain I caused her, despite how horrible I was in my own mind to her at times, she had to let me know.

On a sunny Sunday afternoon while driving to San Pedro to visit my grandma, Maya popped it out. Sitting on the passenger seat while I drove the car on the 110, she told me the news. She thought I'd be upset, perhaps tell her to have an abortion, or that I wanted nothing to do with the baby. But I was ecstatic, uplifted with a surprised joy. There was going to be a new being in this world, half me, half Maya. I was happy beyond words. This was not what she expected.

This threw her plans off a bit. First was the idea not to tell and split to Mexico. Once she realized she couldn't do that, she half hoped I'd get angry, get into a fight with her and not want the child, thereby making her flight to Mexico easier on her conscience. I'd be a jerk, easier to say "screw him" to. It'd also fit into her idealization, romantization of the old Thomas, the one she really loved, the one that was in love with her. She'd find it's form in the unshaped image of our child. With me out of the picture, it was neat and tidy to do.

But now it was messy, as it always was. I was utterly happy to have a child with her. Was I wanting to settle down, though, get married, and raise a family together? That's what she wanted most of all. But she knew that would be hard to get from me. She was so afraid of my answer so she never asked. That was why she half hoped I'd not want the child. Of course, she didn't get either option. I wanted the baby but didn't make it clear I wanted to be with her. There was uncertainty amidst the joy for both of us. At my grandmother's house we told her the news.

It was a happy shock, but a shock nonetheless, to my grandmother. This was never discussed with anyone. Maya and I ourselves had only that one conversation in the bathroom. The old lady liked Maya and of course her grandson, so was happy about the news, even though, like everyone else, she had uncertainties. Everyone knew of our troubles. Would I marry Maya? I said certainly not. Having a baby was beautiful enough.

Maya began to accept marriage was out of the question with me, but she hoped a committed relationship might not be. I was so excited about the baby, I became more and more attracted to Maya. We had a product of our glorious love-making inside her. All our past problems seemed to be unimportant compared to this unknown being we created.

I began to consider monogamy, though never verbally, especially not to Maya. With the announcement of the pregnancy, it was a consideration. I did love Maya after all. Two heroes of mine – D.H. Lawrence and James Joyce – had wives/life-long lovers, who weren't actually compatible with them. Both women were even quite like Maya: earthy, emotional, more pragmatic than their men, and not exactly outwardly in awe of their genius.

Maybe I could be the same way with Maya. Like Lawrence and Joyce did, I'd probably have an affair now and then. Maya most likely would find out and we'd have fights over and over again about possession and jealousy, like we always did. In the end, though, I would come back to Maya. I then would be like my grandfathers – my mom's dad and my father's dad – in having secret affairs. I wouldn't be like my dad Jean and be open and honest. I'd been honest up until now, but perhaps I could change.

So I moved in with Maya. It made sense financially, even though there wasn't room for me in the one-bedroom apartment. Eventually we'd find a larger place. It seemed to make sense. But I didn't commit to Maya in a monogamous relationship. I never told her so. We made love and I moved in, sure, but I never told her I was going to commit to her as a faithful boyfriend once and for all. Maya assumed I was committing myself, though never asked to know for sure. She was afraid of the answer and I was afraid to make myself clear.

The idea of trying the monogamous thing wasn't such a far-fetched idea at first. Having the baby could make me love Maya more, look past the problems. One week past, then two, then a third, and I began to realize why we had problems in the past. It was the same old story. So little understanding. We got into fights because she mistook something I said then I mistook something she said. I wanted to discuss things, she didn't. I really don't think, even now as I write this to you, Daniel, that either of was right or wrong in an ultimate sense. What worked for your mother was just different than what worked for me.

Maya's continual clamming up really got to me, though. I'd come home and she'd be completely shut off. I'd ask her a question and she wouldn't respond. I'd ask again, and again she wouldn't say anything. She tuned me out altogether. She did the same thing with Emmanuel and he just accepted it and got drunk. She'd give him a hard time, yell at him, and he'd get drunk. Alcohol made Emmanuel deal with her silence and screaming.

I was different, even though I could be drunk, as well. I reacted to Maya. If she wanted to boss me around, test me, push my buttons, I came back with hurtful words and push her buttons back. “Why do you hate me so much?” she asked many times, assuming the role of martyr and victim. If not that question, then she'd come back with “That's just the way I am. I'm a bitch, live with it.” It was always simplification. Black or white, one or the other. Victim or bitch.

I knew I was no victim, either. I'd often be argumentative with her, sharp, sarcastic, cruel. If she threw a zinger at me, I wouldn't forgive her. I was no Christian. I'd throw a zinger back. It was near impossible for me to turn the other cheek. For a little while, but not for long. By the third week, I couldn't take it anymore. I realized it was smart for us to live together financially speaking, to cut rental costs, so I wouldn't move out. I'd tell her that while I'd take on the full responsibility of being a father, I wanted to make it clear I was going to have my sexual freedom.

I didn't know how to tell her, so I wrote her a letter, trying to be as kind about it as possible. She read it and broke into tears. Another blow to her heart by me. How could I do this, she thought, then asked me out loud. After everything. Well, “fuck you,” she said. If I didn't want her and her only, I had to move out. I tried to persuade her that we'd save money living together. I'd also never bring a woman over to the apartment. It didn't matter. The relationship between her and I was just as important as our child, she felt. I didn't. The baby was beyond the importance of idealizing monogamy. She just couldn't accept my being around her in the apartment and not able to have me as her one and only possession.

So as soon as I moved in with Maya, I moved out. Only one month later. Fortunately, the apartment I had before was still available. I moved back in. There was some dark laugh behind all this.

I tried to stay on good terms with Maya but it was difficult. I knew what I'd done, the kind of person I was, was not wrong. Was the problem in other people, in Maya? No. I knew it was complicated, especially when I looked at the whole story, knew where Maya was coming from, knew where I was coming from.

The problem was more in society, in the Majority Opinions, to which, in many ways, despite her individualism, the part of her I like, the part of her which made me want to have a child with her ... despite that, Maya still clings to many ideas which get in the way of her own life, ideas which are the accepted norm, the cruel accepted norm of our lives ....

There is no context for people to understand each other, Daniel. There are no avenues for human insecurities to express themselves in the open ... no genuine avenues ... that's why I'm writing this manuscript, this confession, my life story, to you ... this is an attempt to give you a genuine avenue of expression ... an understanding of my life and of what you will face in your life, in your own way ...

I'll explain to you later how I came about to write this manuscript you have in your hands ... what propelled me to do it ... and to perhaps talk about your mother more, since she is the only person in this story I'm still involved with in some way ... all the others have disappeared. Perhaps your mother and I are meant for each other ... it may seem strange, but perhaps we are meant to be life partners ... probably not in the way she imagines ... as different as we are, as much as we may want to rip each others throat apart at times ... But before I say anything more about your mother, Daniel, I need to tell you about my experiences at C.W.F.P.S.J.

PART NINE. CHARLOTTE.

CHAPTER ONE. MOVING INTO THE MOVEMENT.

My relationship with politics has always been moody. I could be completely passionate about it or completely antagonistic to it. I could love politics or hate it, depending on where I was in my life or who I was with. If I was with someone who was a-political, I could be adamantly for a cause. If I was with someone who was overly political, I tended to be against politics. Whatever I felt about politics, it was genuine. I was sincere in my optimism and cynicism. If I was anti-politics, it was usually because I was fed up with the hypocrisy and ineffectualness of it. If I was all for politics, I wanted to believe true change could happen through it.

My tendency to be a loner, an outsider, kept me from joining political groups through most of my youth. Even as a teenager the need to be an individual, to be alone, conflicted with a desire to be with others, to make a difference in the world. At my high school in Seattle, I joined a human rights group after some hesitation. Something about groups sent a red flag to me. But the teacher who organized the group was intelligent and filled with conviction.

The group got connected with an Amnesty International outreach office in Seattle. One of the big issues of the day – the early '90's – was the genocide happening in a small island off Indonesia, called East Timor. It was a horrible event. Hundreds of thousands of East Timorese people massacred. The government of Indonesia, lead by President Jukartu, had been waging an all-out genocide on the people of East Timor since the '70's. The United States and every other country did nothing about it. In fact, for geo-economic reasons, the great "liberal" President Bill Clinton backed the Indonesian government with millions of dollars in aid during his two terms.

While I didn't stay with the human rights group since I didn't connect with the people involved, the experience still opened my eyes. Now and again I'd help pass out fliers or help with an event, but I spent more time with filmmaking as a teenager. After being introduced to the human rights group, I was aware of Third World neglect or outright exploitation by the First World countries. The First World – the U.S., Europe, Japan, and others – was no longer such a nice place. Sure, to live in (and even that only in a way), but at what cost? My mother and step-father Frazier were die-hard Democrats. I was raised to believe the problem lay with Republicans only. But now it was obvious it went deeper than that. Clinton's support of a government waging genocide was an obvious example, or his support of NAFTA, or his pro-deregulation stance in general. He was capable of making destructive decisions just as badly as a Republican President could have.

The problem lay in the nature of not only the United States' but other First World nation's Capitalist "Democracies." Liberal or conservative, it didn't matter. The assumption of the rights of Capitalistic Imperialism over the weaker Third World was in both parties. When, as a teenager, I came home and told my mother and Frazier, they felt I was a little too "radical," too far to the left. When I showed them the facts of the genocide in East Timor and Clinton's support of the country who was committing the genocide (Indonesia), they made excuses. Their great Democrat President had to play the game of geo-politics: Indonesia was one of the few Muslim nations who the US was friendly with; Indonesia was our biggest business partner in Southeast Asia, etc., etc.

Even as I stayed away from political groups through finishing high school in Switzerland, to getting into my religious phase once moving back to Los Angeles, to my underground zine on movies, to filmmaking - politics still existed within my philosophy. I'd engage people to question their political leaders, to question the nature of their government. Politics always played a part, somewhere. That initial opening of my awareness to the realities of politics – the genocide in East Timor – was always with me. For the most part, though, politics was never my main preoccupation, not enough for me to take action..

Then 9/11 happened. The Third World came slamming into America's living rooms. Why was this happening to us, many Americans asked. Why would someone fly an airplane into the side of a skyscraper?

As the days and weeks passed, Al Qaeda and Osama Bin Laden became household names, but few realized the answer was in this evil-doer's rationalization for 9/11.

As fanatical, destructive, and misguided as Bin Laden was, there was some truth to his words. What he said was that Al Qaeda wanted the United States out of Arab lands. The U.S. had no business being there. That stance was essentially legitimate and understandable. But the second aspect to Al Qaeda was much messier - getting Israel out of the Middle East, as well. However many destructive decisions Israel made over the years, it was much harder to make a case to eliminate Israel altogether. More moderate Arab political entities pushed for more moderate changes in regards to Israel. Unfortunately, those groups were either ignored by the West or criticized by their extremist Arab counterparts.

Al Qaeda and other Arab political forces had a more clear-cut argument against the United States, though. The U.S., Britain, and other Western countries had no right to be involved in the Middle East except as respectful and fair business partners. There was nothing fair nor respectful about American economic interests for decades (nor Britain for even a longer period of time), whether it was with Iran, Saudi Arabia, or Iraq. Thus, what the C.I.A. calls happened: "Blowback."

9/11, though, was never even considered to be "blowback" by Americans, whether it was the news media, politicians, or even the public. If someone ever brought up 9/11 in that way (these were the days before Michael Moore's public war with the Bush administration), they were labeled Un-American and scrutinized immediately. Our history was supposedly uncheckered with any such corruption. Both my dad Jean and myself realized the United States was on the verge of becoming a scary place. Self-censorship was a disease after 9/11. Everyone was afraid to speak their minds. Jean knew from studying history in college that when people censored themselves, and trusted their leaders more, Fascism entered the arena. It's always easier to control people's minds when they allow themselves to be controlled.

Jean began writing political letters to the editor and op-ed pieces to newspapers and magazines around the country. He'd often get published, although many were censored. His "harsh" controversial pieces were never accepted, though, understandably. I was also inspired to get more involved with politics after 9/11. For both Jean and I, 9/11 was a reminder of just what can happen when the Third World strikes back. It was important for us, politically conscious citizens, to insure our government acts more responsibly. We wanted to act as a means to prevent more 9/11's from happening, and to repair the damages done to the Third World. Jean inspired me and I inspired him. Conversations between us about politics energized each other to act politically. That's when I saw the ad for C.W.F.P.S.J. The timing was perfect. I had to get away from my Circus of Books job, as well as do something meaningful with politics.

"Yeah, hi, is this California Workers For Peace and Social Justice?" I asked over the phone, almost tired from saying their entire name, not even finishing it with the 'Now!' part.

"Uh yeah ..." Siango's voice came through my phone receiver, with a quiet hesitation. "What can I do for ya?" he continued with an odd, reserved, yet quiet kindness.

"I'm responding to your ad in the LA Weekly. About the job?" I said with uncertainty, not really knowing what to expect.

"Okay ... do you know much about us?" he said, talking slowly still.

"Not really. I checked your website out and it looked interesting." I was now believing this guy must be a pot-head. Was everybody there hippie-dippie?

"Would you like to come down for an interview?"

"Sure."

I set up a time for the interview and had no idea what to expect. I thought about Siango's voice and realized that I must come across in a similar way over the phone or in person. I had that same slow, slightly monotonous, ironical, sarcastic tone sometimes. Well, I wasn't going to meet Siango for an interview but a young woman, anyway.

C.W.F.P.S.J. - Now!'s office was in Culver City just off La Cienega and Pico. As I parked my car around the corner in a residential neighborhood, I noticed up in the window where their office must be. There were all kinds of political posters in the window, ranging from their own organization to ones of Gandhi, Martin Luther King, Jr., Malcolm X, feminist activists such as June Jordan, Maya Angelou, and others. There were posters with quotes such as, “No New Nukes,” “People Power Vs. Corporate Greed,” “Vote,” “Give Peace a Chance.” All these posters were in their four windows. Ok, I thought, this should be interesting.

Maybe I'd be involved in some kind of 21st Century underground Peace Movement, get involved with a group of radicals. Maybe this was a new stage in my life, a more politically involved stage. Maybe I'd get into something that'd make some real change happen. What would the people be like? Would they be really militant? Fanatical? Have no sense of humor, no irony, no complexity? Or would they be really interesting? Would they be a bunch of kids trying to duplicate the hippies of the 60's or would they have a newer, fresher vibe about them? What would the job actually be like? I was, after all, going in for a job interview.

All these questions ran through my mind as I walked up the steps to the office, putting out my cigarette at the garbage can. What about my smoking? Would they not let me smoke around them? Would they force me to quit? I imagined most modern day peaceniks wouldn't like my smoking, a sign I supported the big tobacco companies.

Down the hall on the second floor, I walked to the office and knocked on the door. The young woman opened and invited me in. She was in her mid-twenties like I was at this time, she had a buzz cut, casual clothes, and military boots on. She smiled politely but seemed distracted. No one else was in the office as she worked on papers, saying I could sit down. She explained she wasn't working with C.W.F.P.S.J anymore, that this interview was the last thing she had to do as a Field Manager.

She was cordial yet busy, finishing up paperwork as she asked me questions. The interview was informal and loose, not very detail-orientated. She just wanted to get a sense of what I was like, see if I was "normal" (sometimes they'd get people who were a little deranged). She also wanted to see how much I knew about politics, what were my interests, how I saw the job. Being as I was a filmmaker, we talked about movies, introducing social commentary along the way. I wanted to convey my political and social awareness.

Since I liked to talk about things of this nature a fair amount – anything intellectually stimulating – I talked her for a while. She enjoyed the conversation herself, but mentioned that the interview was longer than most and she didn't have much time (where she had to go she didn't say). She explained the job briefly and said one of the key things is brevity. Fitting interactions into short periods of time was vital to a political organizer.

I understood and went on my way, planning to come back the following week for the training day. Till then, I continued to wonder what my comrades would be like. I still hadn't met anyone I'd be working with. On my training day I arrived at the office at the scheduled time, 2pm. Inside the office were seven people, all busy working at desks or putting things together. The office was as it was when I came the week before for my interview.

Like the window I saw from the outside, there were political posters everywhere. There were three desks, each in a corner (the fourth corner where the door was), with papers and folders scattered all over the desks. There was a large table in the middle of the room, with chairs surrounding it and more papers, folders, boxes on the top. There was a couch against the side wall underneath a window, facing the wall on the opposite side of the room a chalkboard with writing on it. The room was pretty small, made tighter by everything in it and the busy movement of everyone.

I was a little intimidated entering the room. I didn't know what to expect from these people or the job. Here I was, in a political activist environment, throwing myself into it. Everyone seemed to know exactly what they were doing, like they were on a mission, a mission to save the world. I felt so fresh, so uncertain, outside of this activist bubble. So these were peace activists, I thought to myself.

There was Charlotte working at the large table, wearing a wife beater and jeans, tying her hair back. She seemed to be naturally more feminine than what she was trying to be. Cassandra was working at her desk, the largest one to the left. The desk to her right was Siango's, where he was talking to someone on the phone. He looked up and acknowledged my presence in the room while still talking on the phone. At first no one else registered the fact I was there.

The four others in the room were two young women and two young men. One guy was about 19 or 20, tall, overweight, and didn't seem much of a political activist, more like a nice, witty pizza delivery guy. The other guy was an athletic Scottish hipster living in L.A. He worked there because his American girlfriend thought being a peace activist would be cool. One woman was a bit older and seemed very reserved, holding her folder close to her chest in a weird, nervous silence.

The other woman was Katrina. She, along with Charlotte, grabbed my attention the most. She wore white baggy pants, a colorful t-shirt, and white sneakers. Her short, wild hair was bleached blond, which matched her light skin complexion. She had wide, big blue eyes, a cute face, and a relatively small body. I thought she might be a punk rock girl, because of her appearance and demeanor. She did a little dance while immersed in paperwork.

There was something appealing to me about Katrina, a vulnerability that Maya had, one which seemed to hide behind a strong exterior. Katrina had a more approachable air than Charlotte or Cassandra did. Charlotte had a shut-off, "I'm busy" or "I'm serious" coldness, and a body which was so gorgeous it seemed unattainable.

Eventually, everyone began to open themselves a bit more to me once I said hello. It was odd to me how many of them just turned on some kind of social switch. Before they were so focused, cold, professional, and then suddenly now they were the epitome of bubbliness.

"Why, hello, you must be Thomas!" Cassandra said as she turned to me, letting out a big, warm, loud smile.

"That I am." I replied.

"Hey Thomas! Welcome to California Workers For Peace and Social Justice, buddy!" Charlotte said, her body language still detached, focused on her work, but her tone of voice loud, fuzzy, bubbly.

"How's it going, Thomas?" Katrina asked, also with a loud warmth but still working.

"Pretty good." I responded, still adjusting to the environment.

I was a little thrown back by the quick turn of tone by these three young women. Their friendliness wasn't exactly phony, but was more coming out of the nature of a busy canvasser. They were all testing a bit, too. So many people came and went with this job that they didn't give much until they could tell I was serious. And I was a man.

"Take a seat at the table. I'm about to give my first briefing. I'm so excited!" Charlotte said, putting away folders into a box. She came across as the most outgoing out of everyone, an odd mixture of coldness and bubbliness. Cassandra was more low-key, and Katrina was more in her head at the moment.

I sat at the table and soon Charlotte got in front of everyone else as we sat down to listen to her briefing. I was still adjusting. No one introduced me to how things worked or anything. They just jumped into what they normally did. Everyone said their names at the beginning of Charlotte's briefing, as if this was an AA meeting. There was a seriousness in the air as this happened, a little too much self-importance, I thought. Oh well, the people seemed interesting enough.

Charlotte's briefing came across to me as some kind of Self-Help Motivational class. She cheered people on as they worked on the techniques of canvassing, on their "rap." The rap was the pitch they gave to people at the door when trying to get financial and political support. Everyone in the room was high energy, especially Charlotte, and at first I felt it was forced.

An hour later and the briefing was done. Charlotte was excited about her first one as Cassandra and Katrina congratulated her. There was a lot of "team support" between the three of them. They were definitely gun-ho about this. Charlotte quickly gave a clip-board with the organization's literature to me, saying she'd be the person I would follow and watch for my first training day, called the Observation day. All I had to do was be near her while she went door to door, watching how she worked the people at each house. If I liked what I saw from the job, I could give it a shot.

Before going to the neighborhood to canvass, it was time to get food. Everyone – except Siango and Cassandra, who stayed to continue doing office work since she was the Canvass director and he the assistant canvass director – went into a van and drove down La Cienega blvd. to Venice blvd. This was Charlotte's first week as a field manager, replacing the woman who interviewed me. She was a little nervous but hid it behind her bubbly excitement or cold detachment, depending on the moment. But Charlotte wasn't the only one with an odd behavior.

The mood within the group in the van would shift quite a bit. One minute, there'd be complete silence, the next an outgoing, energized bubbliness. Either way, no one seemed relaxed, no one seemed comfortable to be themselves, as if they were constantly on guard, on defense. There was stress in the air, a vibe of uptightness. For the most part, they were friendly to me. Perhaps everyone was just a little stressed because they all knew they had to raise money this night and do well at it. Or perhaps there was something else.

Since we were canvassing in Culver City, southwest from the office, we went to a Noah's Bagels on Venice and Robertson. Everyone did their own thing, got their own food or looked at their folders. Charlotte sat by herself as she ate a bagel sandwich. She was in one of her silent, serious moods as I decided to sit opposite her at the table. Despite her momentary coldness, she seemed so beautiful to me, so beautiful that I felt never able to obtain an intimacy with that beauty of hers. There seemed to be a wall in front of her. It was a different wall than Maya's, more aloof, firmer. Charlotte's vulnerability could at times be more apparent, but at the same time more under control.

Seeing the wall as I sat with her made me want to engage. I asked her questions about the job, how long she'd been working with the organization, where she was from. I detected an accent. She was from Minnesota. She was still rigid as she asked what sign I was. A Leo, I responded, although, I continued, I didn't believe in astrology. She did and said she was a Scorpio. I said I had a Scorpio Moon, which was the sign for one's emotions. She replied, still with the serious wall, that I must be an intense person like her then, and that other people don't always understand our kind of intensity.

Neither of us felt like we were flirting, since we weren't really. She certainly wasn't. We were just chatting, still not very open, getting to know each other as co-workers. She was, after all, going to show me how the job was, and a little nervous, although she didn't want me to know. She wanted everyone to see her confidence as a new field manager. Going back to the van, we drove to the first pair's drop-off spot. Two people would work three or four blocks, one person on one side. The next pair would go to another area to do the same. At the first drop, the field manager would organize everyone to do a “dynamo,” a canvassing exercise each person participated in. It was a way to get the activist juices flowing.

Charlotte stumbled a bit as she led the dynamo, but soon had Katrina help her. Fifteen minutes later, we were on our ways. Katrina and the younger guy went first, then the Scottish guy dropped off Charlotte and me as he went to go by himself.

Charlotte sat with me on the curb in a middle-class residential neighborhood south of Culver blvd. At first, she was a little put off by how close I sat next to her, then she was comfortable once she got the vibe I didn't mean anything by it. She surprised me by bringing out a pack of Camel Lights and lighting a cigarette.

"I didn't know you smoked." I said with a smile.

"Yup. With this job you kinda have to. Do you?"

"Sure do." I said as I lit a Winchester.

"Are you nervous?" she asked as we smoked together.

"Yeah."

"Me, too." she said with a sudden drop of her guard. She felt a bit comfortable with me, though still tried to figure me out.

"You hide it well." I told her.

"What about you? You seem okay."

"I guess I'm excited about the job mostly, so I'm running on an expectant adrenaline."

"That's cool."

"You have to know that where I'm coming from is years of minimum-wage jobs where I sold popcorn, swept popcorn from the floor, sold tickets for movies, or went to real estate offices dropping off fliers into agents mailboxes. Or I rented videos to people or sold magazines or worked for production companies that treated me like a slave. This is the first job where I actually care about what I'm doing – selling Peace to people, telling them information that interests me. And I'm really curious to go out and meet the American public. That should be interesting."

"Cool." she responded simply, a bit moved by my speech. "Alrighty, buddy, let's go to work and meet that American public, or at least the

Culver City public."

We went down the block and to the first house. No one was inside so she just left a flier at the door. If no one answered the door, we were supposed to leave the organization's literature. In the beginning, not many doors opened, since most people hadn't come home from work yet. These houses were called "callbacks," since we'd go back later in the evening. Soon, we started talking to people at the door. I loved the way Charlotte chatted with people, with her high, nasal Minnesota accent, and fuzzy bubbliness. Normally, I hated bubbliness, but I liked it in her because she had intelligence and something genuine behind it.

Charlotte was appealing to me. She was physically gorgeous, with a long, lean body and legs, beautiful curves, a perfect ass, great tits, and an elegant face. But it was her quirkiness that did it for me. She shifted moods so quickly and out of no where, to go along with a sensitive intelligence and dark sense of humor. I was just picking up on her humor now that we went door to door. Before she was so serious. One person we met was an old lady who didn't want to give us money but let us use her bathroom. Before leaving, the old lady told us a dirty joke. Outside, Charlotte and I bursted into laughter.

A few hours into canvassing, there was a possibility of attraction between us. It was very tentative, though. Neither of us went anywhere with it. She did ask me if I had a girlfriend, to which I replied no (I'd broken up with Maya recently, sort of). I asked if she had a boyfriend and she said no. The doors were almost open, but she held back. Why she suddenly seemed withdrawn, she didn't explain and I didn't push for an answer. She did open up to me more than she usually did with men, she said, and told me about a couple past boyfriends. One, in high school, killed himself over her. Another was a much older man whom she lived with and after they broke up, he began stalking her.

Needless to say, she had intense experiences with men. I was grateful for her opening up so much on the first day meeting me. Out of sensitivity, I didn't inquire into more details. It was horrible, in both cases. Probably unbearably painful for the high school boyfriend tragedy, then scary when it came to the old guy. She then said how much she missed her best friend, wish she could hang out with her even now. I asked about her friend but didn't ask if they were lesbian lovers nor did she admit they were. She just said they were close.

The end of the night came and Charlotte asked me if I liked the job. I did and she said she would recommend me to Cassandra and Siango. She enjoyed my company and felt I was good interacting with people. I was intelligent and friendly, she said. We even had fun together. One part of Charlotte just liked to cut loose and enjoy herself. Another part would get uptight and riddled with political and feminist responsibility. I seemed to make her more comfortable with herself. But she had a girlfriend. I pretty much figured this out but didn't know why she didn't tell me. Perhaps she felt I'd judge her. Her discovery of bi-sexuality was fairly recent.

The next night Charlotte and I canvassed together again, this time I went and knocked on doors by myself. Cassandra and Siango figured it'd be a good way to start me off by working with Charlotte again, since we got along well. I noticed she dressed differently this day, wearing a white flowing skirt and making herself much more feminine overall.

While canvassing, occasionally we checked in with each other. Charlotte was frustrated, not raising much money. I was excited, fresh from my new job high, and I got a new member for $40. She said they must like me here, then went into how a girl up in the Berkeley office raised $200 a night easily, and how kick-ass she was. It wasn't true, though, as the girl raised $1,000 one night (in a questionable interaction with an older male donor), but normally raised $70 per night.

We went back to work, going up a hill to the wealthier houses. We didn't get much luck. Then, as I was talking to an old German man about resisting coming tides of fascism (overt winking by me to Germany in the conversation), I heard Charlotte yelling back up the street.

"Thomas! Thomas! Help! Help!" she screamed.

I turned and ran as fast as I could up the street towards Charlotte. I soon got to where she was and saw what was happening. She was crying next to a door of one house as an old drunk guy walked up to her, yelling expletives. Another man opened the door she was near, yelling at her.

"You fucking stupid bitch! You can't run away from me! I used to be a Marine! Don't you dare insult me or my country! Fucking cunt!" the old drunk screamed at Charlotte.

"What did you do to him?" the other man yelled at Charlotte as she backed away from both of them.

"What did I do? What're you talking about? He's coming to attack me!" she yelled in complete fear and defiance, as well.

"What the hell's going on here?" I yelled at the two men. When my adrenaline was running, I wasn't exactly a hero, but I could get nuts. And seeing these jack-offs acting as horrible as they were got me running full-steam with intense anger. "Get the fuck away from her!" I screamed as I ran up to them.

"This has nothing to do with you!" the second man said.

"Excuse me, asshole, but we work together!" I yelled back as Charlotte ran to me. She was relieved as hell to see me. "You need to get the fuck away from her! Whatever she may have said to your dumb asses doesn't give you the right to fucking attack her!"

"Who the hell're you, buddy?" the old drunk man said as he came up to me in a violent huff. "You're not a fucking peacenik, too, are ya?!"

"That's why we're here, you senile piece of shit!" I replied in my continued rage.

"Why I outta punch you in the face!" the old man said, getting close to me and ready to take a swing.

"If you do, you'll be spending the night in jail for assault. I don't think you'd like that." I said, stopping the old man in his tracks, staring him down in a Gandhi-like moment. I figured a strong will of non-violent defiance would be best, especially since I was working for a peace organization. The old man huffed and puffed, then backed down.

“That's it, I'm calling the cops on you two.” the second man said as he got his cell phone out.

“You're calling the cops on us? We should be calling the cops on you, asshole!” Charlotte yelled as she stood near me.

At the entrance to the next house up, an old lady came out to see what was going on, then fell to the ground. The old man turned and saw his wife had fallen.

“Lucille! Lucille, I told you to stay in the god damn house!” the old man said as he rushed up to his fallen wife.

The sight of the old lady falling – and not badly, not hurting herself – and the drunk old Marine running up to her made me and Charlotte laugh. This whole situation was insanely absurd.

“I'm calling the cops right now. I'd stay here if I was you.” the old man's neighbor, the second man, said.

“What the hell you think the cops are gonna do?” I asked the man. “We have a permit to do what we're doing out here and we're not the ones attacking anybody! That old fart was the one who wanted to attack us!”

“Forget it, Tom. The guy's a stupid jerk. Let's just sit here and wait.” Charlotte said as she pulled me with her to the curb.

“These people are fucking morons.” I said as I sat next to her.

She explained the whole story, how the old man at first thought she was from some pro-military conservative group, then when he found out who she was really working for, he got all pissy. They got into an argument and for some reason the old man went off his rocker. She tried to get away, hoping the old man's neighbor would let her in to protect her, but instead what I saw ended up happening. The neighbor did the opposite. She told me she didn't know what would've happened to her if I didn't show up. The neighbor guy was saying the old man should've beaten her up when she was asking for help.

The police eventually showed up and of course couldn't do anything to Charlotte nor myself, since we didn't do anything wrong. But since it being the neighborhood it was – fairly upper-class – the cops asked if we could go down the hill to canvass another neighborhood. By law, Charlotte and I didn't have to, but we didn't want anymore trouble that night.

As we walked down the hill, Charlotte said she needed to stop and relax. She was still understandably shaken up over the whole thing. We sat side by side as she nestled her head onto my shoulder and I rubbed her back warmly. We felt so good comforting each other and talked about what happened. We couldn't believe it. It was insane. We had to laugh. As comfortable as we were with each other, there still seemed to be something holding us back.

Back at the C.W.F.P.S.J office, we told Cassandra and Siango what happened. As much as Cassandra and Siango were concerned about us, they also, playing their Canvass Directors roles, wanted us to think how we could've avoided the blow-up. They especially focused on Charlotte having to be more in control from the beginning, not letting the confrontation escalate. I could tell Charlotte wanted to defend her helplessness more but didn't. It was understood that canvassers were in complete control of their night. Free will was not to be questioned. I said something in Charlotte's defense but Cassandra and Siango gave me a silent look. Okay then.

Right then, Charlotte's "close friend," Ali, rushed into the room. She quickly consoled Charlotte in her arms tenderly, telling her everything was going to be alright. When she called Charlotte "baby," I knew. Ali's appearance was pretty butch, as well. They were lovers. I caught myself being jealous when I saw how more affectionately Charlotte held Ali than when she held me earlier that night. Charlotte was truly unattainable.

After that night, Charlotte and I became good friends, as did Katrina and Cassandra with me. They admired my peaceful yet strong standing up for Charlotte that night. I was quickly becoming like a brother to them. All three women were involved with other women, so the platonic trust was there with me. Even after knowing they were unavailable, I showed I still liked them as friends. Despite being sincere about that, I was also secretly disappointed they were lesbians. This was especially true with Charlotte, since she seemed to almost open the doors to me those first two nights.

One day while eating at an Ethiopian restaurant on Fairfax, I told them about Maya, that she was my girlfriend. I was sitting near Charlotte, Katrina, and Cassandra. Katrina almost defensively began talking about her girlfriend, while Charlotte was quiet, almost still embarrassed about being a lesbian. Perhaps she also felt bad about not being up front with me in the beginning, not resolving if she was actually attracted to me or not.

Cassandra diverted the attention to me, asking why I never mentioned my girlfriend (Maya) before. I said it was because Maya and I just got back together, which was true. Also, I said I was never asked. Cassandra seemed to hint that she thought it was maybe because I wanted to flirt with the women at C.W.F.P.S.J, although she didn't come and actually say this, nor did she show much displeasure with me, really.

I quickly got comfortable rapping people at doors and began raising a fair amount of money. Pretty quickly, I made staff, no longer being only a "trainee." Everything was going well. I was good at my job, I liked it, I felt we were making a difference, and I enjoyed the company of my co-workers. I never thought I'd get along with feminists or political die-hards, but everyone appeared to have dimension and humanity to them. We were almost like a family.

CHAPTER TWO.

POLITICAL PASSION.

The second month into working for C.W.F.P.S.J, Cassandra wanted me to become a field manager. She felt I was ready and they needed someone for the position. She was impressed with how I interacted with people at the door. To her, she told me, I was personable, engaging, and even inspiring at times. She could tell I had a lot of conviction working for C.W.F.P.S.J. In her recommendation to the Berkeley people above her in the organization, she lauded me with praises galore. I was surprised at her.

One guy who worked at the L.A. Canvass for a bit told me he thought Cassandra had a crush on me. I said if she did, she hid it well. I felt she just liked me as a co-worker and friend. I joked by telling the guy I had become a Lez-Hag, since Cassandra, Katrina, and Charlotte took a liking to me, and I to them. The guy jokingly warned that one of those lesbians might want dick some day, perhaps mine. I said with a smile that wouldn't bother me.

It was possible, I started to think. I began hanging out with all three women fairly often. Cassandra liked to go out for a drink at a bar with me, not get too drunk – she still had to be the In-control Boss – as we talked about the exploitation of the Third World, Third World debt cancellation, the need for a viable third party in the U.S., and other issues.

Katrina couldn't join me for a drink since she was a recovering addict apparently. She did play pool with me while drinking coffee and also talking about world events. Katrina was very helpful for guiding me as a canvasser, as well. We worked many hours together, going over and over techniques she learned. Katrina was the best fund raiser in the house, raking in money week after week.

Charlotte was the one who spent the most time with me, though, simply because she was the most outgoing and was the most comfortable with men, (despite her moments of the complete opposite). Out of the three women, she got me to have the most fun, even though I liked to be with Cassandra and Katrina, too. Charlotte was just a freer spirit. I played basketball with her, drove her home and smoked pot with her in her room, went to the beach with her. And she wanted to be in my movie. Once she found out I was casting, she jumped on me and asked if there was a role for her. The only female part was for a black woman. But she was so eager, I knew I'd like her presence during the shoot (she might even be a good actress), and the actresses I interviewed didn't cut it, so I said okay to Charlotte.

On the night after work I gave her the script, I drove her home to her commune in Venice. She invited me to smoke pot with her. I couldn't say no and enjoyed the couple times before I'd done it with her. We talked about my movie, talked about C.W.F.P.S.J, talked about our co-workers, made the same complaints: Cassandra could be too non-verbal and too proud; Siango could be too anal and too unemotional; Katrina could be too whiny and too self-righteous.

Charlotte opened up a bit more and told me about how she'd been molested by her dad's friend when she was 12 years old. I had blocked out my own molestation experience with my step-father Frazier that I didn't even think of telling Charlotte. She then went into her family, how her sister was in and out of mental institutions and her younger brother was playing the bohemian in Spain with their dad's stock market money. There was no mention of her mom for some reason. I didn't go there and ask.

“Do you get along with your dad?” I did ask her that as we both sat on her bed in the tight bedroom she had at the commune. We weren't super cosy, as we had our backs against different walls.

“Oh yeah. I love him. He's the best dad in the world.” she said with sweet conviction, although with a little too much sweetness.

“That's cool. I have a good relationship with my dad, my real dad, as well.” I said as I took a puff from the pipe, then handed it to her.

"How about your mom?" she asked as she took the pipe, then inhaled.

"Good, in that we love each other very much. She's been a cool mom. But she and I don't have as much in common as I do with my dad."

"That's the same for me. I would love to be just like my dad."

"So you wanna be a stockbroker, too?" I said teasingly with a smile.

"No, silly." she said, smiling back at me. "He's good to people, he's a peacemaker, you know? He doesn't like hurting other people. That's the way I'd like to be."

"Cool. So, does he know you're involved in a relationship with another woman?"

"No ... not yet ..." she said quietly.

"No? Why not? You've been with Ali for several months now, right?"

"Yeah, but ... I dunno ... I guess I've been afraid of how he's gonna react ..."

"It sounds as if he loves you."

"He does."

"So he'll accept you if you tell him."

"I think so, too. He's coming into town next month."

"You'll tell him then?"

"No, actually, I was gonna do it over the phone in the next couple of days. I've been thinking I should tell him soon."

"I think you should, too. It's a beautiful, natural thing, either way, to be in love ..."

"Yeah ..."

"Whether it's someone of the opposite or the same sex."

"How about you?"

"Me?"

"Have you ever been with a man?"

"Nope."

"Never kissed a guy or ever wondered what it'd be like?"

"No. Men don't turn me on." I said honestly. This was almost two years before I had the week long questioning of my sexuality. "I'm for what you've talked about with me a few times, though."

"What was that?"

"Androgynizing men and women. Making men more feminine and women more masculine. I think it'd make communication between men and women better if we all became more like the opposite sex."

"Right on, dude." she said with utter cuteness, smiling with a deep gaze into my eyes. She could be such a charmer. I wanted to lean over and kiss her sweet lips ... but I didn't and she didn't give encouraging signs ...

"Hey, have I shown you my new tattoo?" she asked, breaking the silence, and showing her forearm to me.

"No, what is it?" I said as I looked at her arm.

"The moon. Isn't it cool?"

"Yeah. Can I touch it?"

"Sure, but be careful. I just had it done."

"Okay, I'll be gentle."

I wanted to touch more than just her tattoo. Part of me felt if I got closer to her to touch the tattoo, perhaps the vibe between us would become more intimate and something would happen. Instead, as I touched the tattoo, a small piece of it flaked off.

"Oh, shit, I'm sorry." I said, feeling like a dumb ass.

"It's okay, Tom." she said, but not really meaning it. I messed up her tattoo!

"It came off so easily."

"That's why I said be careful."

That pretty much ruined any chance I had at making a move on Charlotte. Her girlfriend was out of town for the week so I thought perhaps tonight would be the best opportunity I'd ever have. After talking for a while longer, I got tired and told her, hoping she'd invite me to stay the night with her.

"It's a long drive to Gus' in Silverlake." I told her.

"You want me to call a taxi? You could get your car tomorrow."

"No, that's okay, I can't afford that. Is there any chance I could stay here for the night?"

"No, no, buddy, can't do that. I know you don't mean anything by it, but I don't want anybody at the commune thinking something was going on between you and me. It'd get back to Ali."

"It would?"

"Yup."

"Okay then ..."

"Have you ever thought about moving into the commune?"

“Well, sure, but how much is the rent?”

“It's like $750 for something like what I have. Then you and I could car-pool and hang out even more.”

“Yeah, that'd be cool ...” I said, a little confused by her. She seemed to push me away, then leave the door open. Why did she ask me if I wanted to move into the commune? Was she insinuating something? Or maybe she wasn't at all, maybe she simply saw me as a friend and only a friend. Maybe she wanted to have a guy buddy around all the time, who knows. But anyway, the rent was too expensive for me. I knew for Charlotte it was nothing. Daddy paid for everything with his stock-broker wallet. “Unfortunately, I can't afford that.” I continued.

“Oh ...” she said in disappointment, just as much that money was an issue for me as the fact I wouldn't be able to move in.

“I know it doesn't seem like a lot of money, but for me it is.”

“That's too bad. So how're you getting home tonight?” she asked, suddenly getting short with me.

“I'll drive. It'll be okay.”

She saw me to my car outside and made sure I was awake enough. I said goodnight, hoped she'd like the “Loveincrazy” script, then gave her a hug. As we had our arms around each other, I leaned my lips towards hers. She turned slightly away as there was an awkward silence between us. I then landed my lips on her cheek as she said goodbye. I waited to read her, but she quickly turned away, and went back inside the commune.

During that week, Charlotte was a little withdrawn from me. I missed her usual attention and was bothered when she told me she hadn't started reading the script. Everyone at the office wondered about her and I, whether there was something going on between us. When it was noticeable Charlotte had withdrawn from me, there was a hidden glee in Cassandra, Katrina, and some other girls working there. Sharon had just started working a few weeks before.

Sharon wasn't so sure about the job at first, but I helped him along, gave him guidance and confidence, more than the others did. I hung out with him a bit, once with Gus and Bernardo at Sharon's family barbecue. Like me, Sharon wasn't used to the political activist lifestyle, so he gravitated at first to me and the non-feminist women working there. There was one girl who was Ecuadorian American, but looked more European Spanish, and who was extremely beautiful. She took a liking to Sharon and me, but more to Sharon, to be honest. I could tell she felt like the others in believing there was something going on between me and Charlotte.

Like Bernardo couldn't decide between Chaos or Sax, I couldn't decide which woman at the job I liked most. Well, Charlotte, but she was recently pushing me away. I liked Katrina, Cassandra, the Ecuadorian girl, and a couple others. Every night I came home after work to Gus' apartment and told him I was in love with a new girl. One night Katrina, another night Cassandra, another night, another girl. Gus laughed.

It was summer time and the canvassing office had been making tons of money. We had about 14 people canvassing at the time and everyone was doing well. The people up in Berkeley were impressed. They never thought there was much possibility in Los Angeles. After 9/11, things had changed, though. The whole world became more political, even a jaded, cynical place like L.A.

Cassandra was proud of leading this canvassing office and having people working for her that were so inspired. We all had conviction and passion – her, Siango, Charlotte, Katrina, me, and now others, including Sharon, who got the canvassing bug, too. It seemed the only way to go from there was up. We were on a roll. After having canvassed for almost 8 years, though, Cassandra knew this high wouldn't last. Canvassing had its ups and downs, and summer time was always good. It was just this up was better than past ones. Anti-Bush sentiment was starting to grow in the summer of 2002.

I began to think C.W.F.P.S.J was really where it was at. We were making a difference. We were influencing policies. We were specific in our attack. We went to the constituents of representatives in congress. We were a powerful movement, a force to be reckoned with. I found a political outlet that actually did something. We were reaching the people and got them to influence their representatives. We even went to the representatives themselves as some of the Berkeley people did lobbying visits. We could threaten the politicians with all the thousands and thousands of members we had.

Charlotte had become the second assistant canvass director, since the office was doing so well, the workload expanded, too. One day, Charlotte realized she hadn't worked with me in a while. We'd gotten relatively close again as she read the script and participated in a few rehearsals. There were some things she didn't like about her part, so I told her we could work together to make the changes. We hung out a few times at a couple parties, but she wanted to canvass with me. It'd been at least a month.

The office was canvassing in Silverlake for a couple weeks. Charlotte and I dropped everyone else off before driving the van to a wealthy neighborhood near the man-made lake in Silverlake. As we got our clipboards and folders ready, I noticed Charlotte provocatively bent over, into the van from outside so her ass was sticking straight at me. Ohh, what a lovely sight, I thought to myself, getting an instant hard-on. She was so much fun.

But I still wasn't sure about Charlotte. She did these flirtatious behavioral things before, like sticking her ass out, but at the same time she made it clear she didn't like guys coming onto her. There were so many instances she went to me, complaining about one guy or another, hitting on her aggressively or even touching her. I was there to console her, one of the few men she felt comfortable to do that with. The problem, I felt, was she sent mixed signals to men. She could be a tease, as she was now, bending over and and showing me her ass for a good three minutes while she scrambled through the folders.

Was I to take her flirtations differently than other men? Did she tease me because she actually liked me? Or, as she was with other men, just "expressing herself" and didn't mean anything by it? In fact, maybe she was more sexually teasing with her body around me because she trusted me not to do anything.

Whatever Charlotte's intentions, they weren't clear. As we finished putting all our stuff together and locking up the van, I made the decision that as much as I was turned on by her, I wouldn't make a move. It was too risky. I didn't want to make her uncomfortable if, indeed, she didn't mean anything by her ass in my face. I liked this job too much to cross the "professional line" and show interest in her. And she was, after all, at this point, still involved with her girlfriend Ali.

So while Charlotte was all warm and bubbly with me, and I had fun, too, I held myself back. She sat at a small staircase nearby, telling me to sit next to her. There was an awkward moment when I chose to sit at a step below her and not on the same one. I noticed a split second of disappointment on her face when I did that. Oops, I thought. Maybe she did want to flirt with me and go somewhere with it. Who knows?

We went into our folders to study the turf and members. In each folder was a map of the area, along with membership cards with information on members we went to renew and get more money from. As we sat on the steps and talked about what we were going to do, there was hesitation in our voices, as if we both picked up on something. But we were afraid, we were shy.

Both of us needed to make money that night to make up for the last couple days. We found one member and Charlotte was surprised. She knew the guy, he was a friend of Cassandra's. For some reason, she wanted to make it clear she thought the guy and Cassandra would some day get married. Okay, I thought, as Charlotte looked at me. I felt perhaps she said that to see how I'd react, to see if perhaps I liked Cassandra.

As we canvassed the area, Charlotte wanted to stay as near me as much as possible, constantly checking in with me. She said maybe if the guy Cassandra knew gave us a lot of money we could stop canvassing early and hang out. That sounded good to me. It seemed she liked me but didn't know what to do to get it across. She was afraid to say anything or do anything. Maybe I didn't like her, she thought perhaps.

I did, but I also didn't know what to do or say. I also was afraid maybe she didn't like me. Like I often did when I was attracted to a woman, I got stiff and nervous. The nerves weren't horribly noticeable, but I definitely wasn't as charming as I could be if I was with a woman I wasn't attracted to. I kept telling myself to loosen up but I couldn't. Sure, we had fun joking around, but it was a little forced on both our parts. In one moment, she told me to pop a zit on her back. I couldn't at first, telling her I used to have bad acne when I was younger.

She urged me to pop the pimple. I thought maybe she was wanting me to as a way to break the ice between us. So I went up to her – she wore a dress that exposed most of her back – and worked on popping her zit. Soon, the pimple burst, squirting its juice at me. We both laughed. But that was it, nothing else happened. I thought maybe she wasn't interested in me, that maybe she was just being goofy and friendly flirty. Maybe she just didn't know herself and wanted to see what I would do.

As the night went on and we didn't make enough money to quit early, I didn't do anything more than be friendly and joke around with her. Maybe we couldn't make it work. Maybe we didn't have the chemistry. It just seemed a part of us wanted it to work, though.

As the week went on, I noticed Charlotte spent more time with Sharon. The very next day after she canvassed with me, she did with Sharon. After we all finished canvassing that night, I noticed the two of them seemed closer, more intimate. They made a lot of money that night, compared to the previous night when Charlotte was with me. I started to think Charlotte was testing the waters with her male co-workers. So did that mean she gave me the first crack at it, and I messed up? Was Sharon more successful with her? It looked like it.

I then began to feel it was for the best. Charlotte annoyed me some times. Her cuteness could be irritating and so could her feminist political correctness. She was also a little snobby, coming from a wealthy Minnesota family. I could never connect with rich people. Charlotte was a phony, I thought. I realize now that a part of her really was a snobby rich Daddy's girl with an annoying feminist agenda. But it was also more than that. I felt snubbed, passed up. If she was interested in me, why didn't she make it clearer? There was that time at her commune apartment where I attempted to kiss her on her lips. Wasn't it clear on my part? Perhaps not. Perhaps she felt she did make it clear to me that night of canvassing together, and I didn't react quickly enough. So she moved on to the next contestant, Sharon. But what about her girlfriend Ali?

During a party thrown at a friend of Cassandra's in Echo Park, I found out what happened between Charlotte and Ali. I went with Gus and Bernardo and we discovered the party was a happening thing. There were tons of people, lots of room in the house to move from one conversation to the next and lots of alcohol. Charlotte was to show up with her dad and everyone from C.W.F.P.S.J could finally meet her much cherished father.

She arrived shining brightly in a white dress with her dad in tow. She was so beautiful. Bernardo and Gus were enamored with her as well, telling me not to let her leave the cast for my film. As she saw me, she gave me a warm hug and introduced her dad. As soon as I began chatting with them, Charlotte whisked her father away to meet more people. I was one of many.

Sharon, on the other hand, was not. Charlotte was looking for him at the party and when she found him, she was noticeably excited to introduce him to her dad. Alright, I thought, give up and move on. As I went through the house and chatted different girls up, there was a pain in my heart. I couldn't forget Charlotte's snub.

While driving Gus and Bernardo home, I found out what happened to Charlotte's girlfriend. They broke up. Gus said he overheard a conversation Charlotte had with someone and told them she broke up with her. Sharon was nearby and Gus noticed his eyes light up. Gus was pissed off Charlotte could be so interested in a shlub like Sharon. There was nothing going on with the guy, he was as exciting as a wall. I said that's why Charlotte wanted him. He wasn't a threat.

At work, things started to change. Everyone was getting along for the most part, there were two new hires that I got along with. One, was Max, who I thought was good to mix up the dynamic at the office, bring a more urban, street-wise, earthy, non-p.c. vibe there. The second guy was a tall, intelligent, humble thirty-something Topanga Canyon bohemian, the strangely named (but interestingly, for me, named after the Egyptian god) Thoth. He was actually someone I had canvassed in Topanga Canyon and got him to write four letters. He didn't have enough cash to join as a member, as he didn't have a job at the time. I recommended he work at C.W.F.P.S.J, which he went ahead and applied for.

The changes that weren't so good had nothing to do with my co-workers. It was the organization itself. Another canvasser from the LA office had asked one of the people from the political strategy department a question. It was about the lobbying visits C.W.F.P.S.J claimed to make. The guy just wanted to know how the visits went during the summer recess. The person I asked said they didn't do any lobbying visits. That wasn't something they really did.

Wait a second, I said to the co-worker who was telling me this. "Not something they really did"? But wasn't that an integral part to the whole process C.W.F.P.S.J did to apply pressure on representatives? To actually lobby them? Visit them? Show them all the support the organization had through its members and say,

"Hey, all these people – your constituents – want you to vote on legislation a certain way. Stop voting for more funding on new nuclear weapons. Stop voting for other insane, wasteful military programs. If you don't, you may pay for it come election time."

That's what I was telling people at doors all over Los Angeles for months. Saying that convinced tons of people to become members. It made C.W.F.P.S.J sound like it had political weight on a grassroots level. Enough to make a difference. Enough to back up claims we actually influenced legislation.

So how did C.W.F.P.S.J make a difference? How did we use the "political weight" we had? And actually, I was told also, the 40,000 members in California was closer to 10,000, maybe 15,000. Not even half of what I was telling people? Apparently. That was the threatening weight. The money was put mainly towards keeping the organization going. Paying for over-head, the literature, fliers, postcards, the newsletter that came out once a year (instead of quarterly as promised), for employee's low wages, for the occasional newspaper ad, and of course, the money to pay the people on the board, the people who made all the decisions for the organization. How much did they get paid I had to wonder. The only thing C.W.F.P.S.J could claim to do was inform people on the issues and get them to write or phone their representatives. That was it.

But that was not what we were telling people. We told people we made quarterly lobbying visits, ones that made a difference, too. Representatives knew of the organization and was influenced by our work, some actually feeling threatened. In Sacramento and D.C. everyone apparently knew C.W.F.P.S.J and took us seriously, certainly as much as Amnesty International, Green Peace, or the Sierra Club.

That just wasn't true. I was lying to people about the political pull the organization had without even knowing it. I felt like I'd been had. I'd been conned. I hated lying to people like that, especially since I invested my own feelings into the work. I believed in what I was doing, heart and soul.

A big wave of disappointment came over me. Maybe my co-worker had gotten it all wrong. I had to make sure. I called the political strategy department up in Berkeley and talked the guy who told my co-worker. After ten minutes of slippery B.S., by the end of the phone conversation the guy basically admitted it was true. I sensed a disillusionment on his part, as well. That was it. My anger grew. I didn't tell anyone else at the office, but I wanted to. Over the next few days, my fund raising dropped. I explained to Cassandra I was just in a temporary funk.

That Friday night everyone but me and Katrina went up to Berkeley. There was a state conference up there where numerous peace groups were going to meet. I had to do something with Maya over the weekend, and Katrina had to move her stuff into her girlfriend's place. The two of us decided to do a night's worth of canvassing in Venice. We went to separate areas and met back at the office.

"How'd you do?" Katrina asked me as she came into the office on her bicycle. She rode it the whole night, going from one members house to another, just doing renewals.

"Not bad. Two new members and one renewal. $120. The first time this week I made quota." I replied as I finished paperwork at the table. "How was your night?"

"Okay. $200 for two renewals." she said, putting her bike against the wall, then sitting down at the table, breathing heavily.

"Tired?"

"I haven't ridden my bicycle in a fucking long time."

"Yeah, I'm out of shape myself. I mean, not to say you're out of shape."

"You're funny, Tom." she giggled at me. "Oh, I shoulda got more money out those two. It's like, okay, just $20 bucks more and you're renewing at our standard membership rate. $120. But no, they had to stay at $100. I didn't feel like re-polling them a third time."

"You make canvassing sound so easy."

"It doesn't feel easy."

“You're so smooth about it, though. I mean, you really helped me when I first started.”

“No, I didn't. Did I?” she asked, blushing.

“Yeah, definitely.”

“Look at me, I'm blushing!” she laughed in embarrassment.

“Did I do that?”

“I'm sorry.” she said as she collected herself.

“It's okay. I think you've made me blush before.”

“Really? When?”

“I don't remember exactly when, but I know it happened. Actually, I think every time you or Charlotte or Cassandra would give me a scalp massage. Oh, I loved those.”

“You liked that?” she laughed, touched, but also ever so slightly bothered I mentioned Charlotte and Cassandra's scalp massages, as well.

“You're good at them.” I said, making sure this time not to include Charlotte or Cassandra. I couldn't admit being turned on by Charlotte's the most.

“Thanks.” she said awkwardly, then shot me this intense, almost seductive look. I almost felt what she really wanted to do was walk over to me and give me a scalp massage right then and there. But she couldn't. She was held back. She thought maybe it'd be wrong. Being alone with me in the office was different than when everyone else scampered around. “Hey, what're you doing after work? Which I guess is right now.”

“I don't have any plans. I was thinking about getting a drink with Gus, that friend of mine you and I hung out with in Atwater.”

“Oh, I remember him.” she said, laughing.

"I still feel bad about that night."

"It wasn't your fault. Your friend was the jerk, not you."

"I actually thought you two would get along since you both used to be taggers."

"That guy was so wrong. But hey, if you've made plans with him, you should go."

"I didn't make plans yet actually. Why, did you want to hang out?"

"Well, only if you did. I thought maybe catching a movie would be nice before spending the whole weekend moving my shit to my girlfriend's place."

"Let's go see a movie then."

After finishing the paperwork, we went to our cars and drove off. Katrina had to go to her old apartment in Silverlake to take a shower. I would meet her at the movie theater a little later. I wondered if I should tell her what I found out, spill the beans about what C.W.F.P.S.J wasn't doing. Was it a good idea to not only tell her but anyone else? Did she or anyone else already know? Was it really no big deal? It was to me. A little lie here or there was okay. But a flat-out duplicity about the nature of our work irked me intensely.

If I didn't care about the job, didn't see it as that important, didn't see it as making a difference, didn't invest my own personal emotions into C.W.F.P.S.J, didn't see the work any different than dropping off real estate fliers, selling popcorn, or renting videos, then the lie would be no big deal. So what? It was a job like any other. But it wasn't. It was my first job with meaning. C.W.F.P.S.J required you to believe and invest in what you were doing. Seeing how passionate Katrina was about the work, I knew she must not know the secret. She couldn't have. Could Charlotte know? Anyone else? Probably not. Possibly Cassandra did. She was such a secretive, closed-off person herself. I felt it might not be a good idea to approach Cassandra, Siango, nor even Charlotte first.

They were upper-level management. Katrina was a field manager like me.

As Katrina and I watched “The Good Girl” at the Sunset-5 movie theater in Hollywood, I decided not to tell her that night. I wanted to get a sense of her better, see if she was the best person to tell. Despite her sometimes fanatical feminism, she had a vulnerability, openness, and sense of humor that appealed to me on a personal level. She seemed to like and trust me, as well.

There was a slight awkwardness between us, as if the possibility of attraction put us on our toes. She was an outspoken lesbian, with a girlfriend who made it clear Katrina was hers. Unlike Charlotte and Cassandra, she made it clear she wasn't bi-sexual. She only liked women. But she dropped hints of being otherwise.

Once, during a briefing at the office about sexism, she declared everyone in the world was bi-sexual, then laughed ambiguously. She was a bit more affectionate with me than other men. The night she hung out with Gus and I, afterwards, Gus told me she was definitely into me. She did say that same night, every now and then she needed dick.

As much as she may have wanted me and dropped hints of her desires, Katrina was like Charlotte in making it clear she also didn't like male sexual aggression. It was the same situation with Katrina as it was with Charlotte. I may be attracted to them both and both may have even reciprocated, but the chance of their not responding positively was a heavy cloud. It was too risky. I felt I could have misread them both. If I had and they became uncomfortable with my overtures, then the work environment would change for the worse. I might even lose my job for making come-ons to lesbian co-workers.

So as we sat side by side watching the Jennifer Anniston indie vehicle, “The Good Girl,” I did nothing but watch the film. If only Katrina would make the first move, if she really did like me in that way. If only Charlotte had made a move before, as well. With women like them, I thought, it was best for them to be the aggressors.

Either one of them could take a come-on in the wrong way, get defensive and ruin the friendship. So how did it work with Charlotte and Sharon? What did Sharon do to win her? Anything? Perhaps not, seeing as Sharon was a passive guy. Perhaps Charlotte just chose him and made the first move. What might've appealed to her was his lack of male sexuality.

As the movie finished and Katrina and I left the theater, I decided to go the friend route with her. Expect nothing more. She was, after all, a self-declared lesbian. If she wanted me for sex, she'd have to make the move. We talked about the movie as we walked to our cars, both of us surprised at the quality. It wasn't a bad movie at all, and Jennifer Anniston was pretty good. There was even a bit of social criticism in the story, appropriately (as Katrina was a feminist) about the roles women are forced to play in small town America.

We hung out some more as we met up with Katrina's girlfriend at a non-alcoholic "bar" on Sunset blvd. The coffee shop bar was owned and run by a group of recovering addicts and all the customers were the same. I didn't mind the fact they didn't have alcohol, drinking coffee and playing pool with Katrina and her girlfriend.

Katrina's girlfriend was on-guard and shy around me. Katrina was obviously the extrovert in the relationship. Her girlfriend sent the vibe to me she was a bit jealous of my friendship with Katrina. She didn't trust me behind her polite smiles. Katrina had a blast, though, enjoying the attention both her girlfriend and I gave her as we played pool.

The next week Katrina and I canvassed together in Burbank. I decided I would tell her about the big, recent C.W.F.P.S.J disappointment. She deserved to know. The co-worker who brought it up to me was no longer working with the organization, and he said he told no one else but me. As Katrina and I were dropped off at our spot and began going over our folders, I thought now was better than later, after an evening of canvassing.

"No way!" she said with shock, as she often did when surprised by something.

“It's true.” I replied, having the strange satisfaction of letting someone in on a secret, to go along with the regret of bringing that same person the disappointment.

“That can't be.”

“It is. I found out for myself by asking them.”

“You asked them and they told you?!” she said with her flabbergasted laugh.

“Yup. Whats his name from the political program admitted to it in a roundabout way at first, trying to minimize it by saying we were still a grassroots lobby who lobbied, that sit-in meetings, one-on-one or with other groups, weren't that important.”

“Whether or not he thinks they're important is fucking besides the point. We've been going around telling people something that isn't true. That's messed up.”

“I know. At the end of the conversation, it was kinda weird, when he just flat-out said they didn't do sit-in visits, as if I detected a disappointment in his voice or something.”

“I mean ... I can't believe this!” she said, standing up with a frustrated laugh. “Then why did they tell us they did sit-in visits?”

“That's what I asked him, and he said he doesn't remember ever specifying that was something the organization did.”

“What? I've been saying it for like six months now. It's a big part of my rap.”

“Mine, too.”

“So is it Cassandra who's been telling us this lie?”

“I don't know who to blame because I swear I heard Rick, and the political program, including whats his name who I talked to on the phone, tell us to say we did sit-in lobbying visits."

"I swear the same. And we only have 10,000 members? We don't even have half of what we've been telling people?"

"That's right. Maybe 15,000."

"This is so not cool. I've put all my blood, sweat, and tears into this job and now I find out it's been bullshit? This is not a little white lie, it's a big fat one."

"What do you think we should?"

"I don't know ..."

We chose to continue canvassing that night, though with a half-assed sense of focus. How could we try hard? Katrina was especially walking around with a defeated air. She had just found out. I'd been sitting with it for over a week. Getting this canvassing job had helped me fight off an already strong feeling of cynicism about politics. Now with this news, I had to re-evaluate my political pessimism. Perhaps Cassavetes was right. Perhaps politics was in the end a lot of hot air.

I began to think I should stop investing so much of myself into C.W.F.P.S.J. I was getting closer to production for "Loveincrazy." Filmmaking was where it was at for me. Art not politics was the true way. I'd continue working at C.W.F.P.S.J until they let me go or I found something better. It still was better than flipping burgers. The end of the canvassing night came and Katrina and I met up. The depression she was carrying around for a few hours seemed to dissipate.

"Hey, are you familiar with petitions?" she asked with her usual friendly, warm, canvasser, salesperson smile. She was herself again.

"Kinda. Not really."

Katrina then went into an idea she just thought of. Rather than accept the b.s., lies, and duplicity of what we found out, move on and lose interest in our work, she told me there was another option. We could write a petition. We would approach our fellow staff, but not anyone else. Not Cassandra, not Siango, not Charlotte even. We would put into words our grievances and direct them to the top – the president of C.W.F.P.S.J. We'd go over everyone else's heads. It was a dangerous move, something we could get fired for. But it was worth it. I liked the idea. I didn't want to give up on my political integrity just yet. Katrina was right – if we were truly seeking justice in our job, the organization itself should be doing the right thing, as well.

Katrina and I thought about who to go to first. One reason we decided not to go to the canvass directors, especially Cassandra, was that it wouldn't get anything done. Cassandra would stop the petition in its tracks and that would be that. She'd proven to be someone you couldn't go talk to about things of this nature, or any other. I found Cassandra to be similar to Maya in that way: they both shut people out. They didn't seem to like communication, or if they did, only on their terms. Maya was actually much better than Cassandra in this regard. It made sense to not even bother with Cassandra.

It was important for Cassandra to keep the L.A. Canvass successful and one of the ways she felt this was to be done was to shut down openness. The office had to have a closed-off, distrustful, mysterious air. She didn't trust anyone, not even her fellow feminists like Charlotte and Katrina. Even they butted heads with Cassandra's controlled ego. She felt the need to have favorites and those were people who didn't question her authority. In the beginning, I was a favorite of hers. I was so excited about the job, I didn't question much about C.W.F.P.S.J at first.

As I was more comfortable to be myself at the office, Cassandra trusted me less. One time, there was a woman who worked one day canvassing with us, then quit. She was a practicing Wicca witch, a cranky, annoying, mean-spirited, fat, ex-phone sex operator. A couple days later, I made fun of this woman while everyone was doing paperwork at the office. After my joking around, I noticed no one was laughing. There was an overly obvious, uncomfortable silence. Rick, the Berkeley head canvass director was in town, and eventually mentioned to me that Cassandra was a practicing Wicca witch herself. I couldn't help but find Cassandra's hurt feelings by my jests on witchcraft to be a little ridiculous. I didn't know Cassandra was a witch, and the woman I was making fun of was horrendously obnoxious. It wasn't as if I liked to make fun of people mean-spiritedly, unless they were mean-spirited themselves like that lady was. It didn't matter. I offended Cassandra. I should have known better. One doesn't make fun of anyone unless people like Rick make fun of them first.

Siango and Charlotte probably couldn't be trusted with the petition, either. I thought at the time they most likely would tell Cassandra, as they were more interested in saving their own behinds. Cassandra would be motivated by self-interest to protect her job. How would it look to Berkeley if there was so much dissent in her office? Why would Siango and Charlotte be different? The way to go was get support from the co-workers at Katrina's and my level.

There were a couple women working at that time who were having difficulties dealing with Cassandra and the job in general. I suggested to Katrina they'd be good to approach first about the petition. So was Max and Thoth. They, too, seemed dissatisfied with aspects to the job. Pretty much everyone on staff at the L.A. Canvass was approachable, except Sharon. Because of his relationship with Charlotte, a new found friendship with Cassandra, and his own desire to move up the C.W.F.P.S.J ladder, he couldn't be trusted. Katrina and I agreed on that. Sharon was too slippery.

Katrina and I told people the news individually, sometimes together, sometimes separately, and usually after work. They were sworn to secrecy. Everyone agreed, as everyone was pissed off to discover the reality of their job. It wasn't only Katrina and I who invested ourselves. Everyone else did, too. We all felt let down in the same way, a feeling of being conned and taken advantage of. Everyone we approached wanted to sign the petition. First, of course, the petition had to be written.

For the sake of clarity, Katrina and I would be co-authors, and anyone who wanted to support it could sign on the last page. Katrina met with me several times before and after work in that one week. We had to finish the petition before the C.W.F.P.S.J President came to the L.A. Canvass the following week. He didn't visit L.A. that often, so we had to take advantage of the timing. We would read the petition out loud in front of him and everyone else at the office.

The primary grievances of the petition were the lies about lobbying visits and the number of actual members the organization had. If canvassers were expected to talk to the public on how much political clout C.W.F.P.S.J had, then we had to back it up with facts. For someone like myself, I didn't like lying to people to get their money or support. Cause or no cause, shadiness was not up my alley. In fact, it somehow seemed worse with a cause. That's where the duplicity was really disquieting.

Because of Katrina's communist idealogical leanings and background in union work, she introduced worker grievances as well. As field managers, Katrina's and mine hours far exceeded the eight hour work day. The normal hours were 2pm to 10pm. We both would often come in early at 1pm to train a staff person, then stay late, sometimes after midnight, to finish paperwork. An 11 hour day was not uncommon at all. Since the organization paid a daily and not an hourly wage, there would be no over-time pay. The organization apparently didn't break the law since as a non-profit they could cut those kinds of corners. But there was no compensation in any way for those extra hours. Cassandra shot the steely cold eye at me or Katrina for any time we ever complained. How dare we want to slow the movement down with talk of too many hours and no pay?

There were other things, as well. There were no official slots of time for breaks. If there was a long distance to travel to a neighborhood like Burbank, everyone got their food and ran to the drop-off spots. We had five minutes to eat. In the LA Weekly ad C.W.F.P.S.J put out, it said the job included medical benefits. As soon as one was hired, it was made clear only for field managers and above, which wasn't clarified in the ad. Besides that, it took three months after becoming field managers for Katrina and I to get the medical. And what was that? A lame program which would cost almost $200 a month!

Then there was the personal politics at the office. Again, it came down to Cassandra playing favorites. It was amazing to see the discrepancy between people's opportunities to continue working. If a person who Cassandra didn't like was having a difficult time, then low and behold, they'd usually get cut loose pretty quick. If a person she did like was also having a difficult time, weeks would pass for them to get second, third, four, five chances. The rules for everything in Cassandra's workplace were so ill-defined, so vague and ambiguous, that she could make decisions on a whim. It was much easier to control that kind of environment since no one knew what to expect.

Soon, Katrina and I finished the petition and presented it to our co-workers for review. We wanted everyone to have some input. We all met after work a few times, going over the content, issue after issue. Then at some point, Sharon was introduced into the petition. Katrina and I didn't like it. One co-worker accidentally opened their big mouth, so of course he wanted to see what it was all about. Fortunately or not, he came to the last meeting. The very next day, the C.W.F.P.S.J President would be at our office.

Sharon appeared uncomfortable with the petition, saying that yes it may all be true, but the job was just a job and a cool one at that. He didn't like Katrina's nor my tendency to rock the boat. Despite his reservations, Sharon said he wouldn't tell Cassandra, nor even Charlotte, who was up in the Bay helping the Berkeley office.

One thing I admitted to myself, even at the time, was part of my desire to do the petition was driven by personal resentment. Right before the petition idea came up, Charlotte had told me she couldn't be in "Loveincrazy" until after her trip upstate. That couldn't happen because of Kristianna's schedule. I had to pick my cinematographer over Charlotte. But the odd thing about Charlotte's trip was that it was so out of the blue. There was no talk about it before, and not only that but someone else could have gone upstate, like Siango. He even admitted to me he was available to do so. But Cassandra specifically wanted

Charlotte to go. I resented Cassandra's demand of Charlotte to go when she knew very well it would mess up my filming schedule. It was obvious Cassandra was doing it on purpose. She wanted it known Cassandra's role as Charlotte's boss was more important than me being Charlotte's director. I was fine with that, but for her to go to the extent of fucking things up for me was malicious.

At the end of the last meeting for the petition, everyone but Sharon signed it. While Katrina and I hung out, going over last minute details, we got a call from one of the others that scared us. The person said Sharon told them he leaked the petition to Cassandra. Katrina quickly called Sharon to find out. He laughed, saying he was just joking. But because of Sharon's generally insincere tone of voice, it was hard to tell. Perhaps he was lying, and really did tell Cassandra. We'd find out the next day, perhaps.

Katrina and I were nervous as we walked up the steps to the office in the afternoon. Down the hall, we saw the C.W.F.P.S.J President going into the LA canvass room. Inside, everyone was there except of course Charlotte. All the co-workers who signed the petition looked at me and Katrina expectantly. Neither Cassandra nor Siango said anything. If they knew of the petition, they were silent. Katrina had the copies of the petition in her hands. She was shaking from nerves when she turned to me as we sat at the table.

“Maybe we should wait for Charlotte?” she whispered to me.

This caught me off-guard. Was she having second thoughts? She continued to look at me, waiting for a response. Why wait for Charlotte? Did she think maybe she'd be supportive of us, and if so, it'd help our case to have an assistant canvas director on our side? I knew we couldn't wait anymore, though. The President of the organization was there. We had to take advantage of this opportunity. Doing it right then would be dramatic and grab everyone's attention and might actually make something happen.

“No, let's do it.” I quietly told Katrina.

She smiled back, thankful for my gutsiness, even though I was scared as much as she was. She stood up.

"Okay, everyone, we have something important to say right now." she said, nervous. "Thomas is going to read out something and we'd like you all to listen. Here are some extra copies." she continued as she handed copies of the petition to Cassandra, Siango, and the C.W.F.P.S.J President, then quickly sat back down.

I went ahead and read the petition out loud, as planned. I was forceful, focused, dead serious, and extremely nervous. My hands were shaking while my voice trembled and cracked. Everyone was intently listening.

About ten minutes later and I was done. An utterly uncomfortable silence. Everyone was waiting for the President's reaction. As much as this was way out of the blue for him – it seemed he wasn't told beforehand – he was pretty quick on his feet. All the years of canvassing shown forth. He didn't react with noticeable anger nor hostility. He talked about how when he was working for the organization in Washington D.C., he'd done a petition himself. The guy was slick. He eased everyone down and released the tension, then at the end quickly (really, dismissively) said petitions shouldn't be done in this manner. It was too out in the open, too dramatic. It should've been addressed to Cassandra, being the LA Canvass Director, and not to him.

In front of everyone, he shifted any blame to Cassandra, to Rick in Berkeley, or to the political program. He didn't understand why canvassers were saying things that weren't true. Whether or not he was being honest about this, no one knew. Like Cassandra, he also seemed to thrive on an ambiguous environment. There was no accountability. Who was really responsible? Who wasn't? It was never clarified. Perhaps Cassandra, perhaps Rick, perhaps the political program. No one came out and said anything.

All the worker-related grievances should be dealt with by Cassandra, the President said. I interjected that the non-pay of over-time, all the hours and hours that I worked for free basically, was something over Cassandra's head, it seemed. The President responded by saying I wasn't working for free. The wages were done by the day, not the hour, and being a non-profit, C.W.F.P.S.J were allowed to do that. After that, the President said no more time should be discussed about the petition. If Katrina or I or anyone else wanted to talk more about it, we'd have to schedule times to meet him privately.

After the President's briefing, everyone in the office was uncomfortable. Cassandra didn't say anything, shutting off into silence as she usually did. Siango didn't say anything, feeling left out, but also uncertain. A part of Siango seemed to wish we had included him in the petition. Apparently, he agreed with most of what I said. At the same time he didn't want to rock the boat. Not in that way. It was too explicit.

Outside on the landing, the other co-workers, except Sharon, secretly congratulated Katrina and I. There was a rush, an excitement of having given voice to our discontent. Whatever happened from now we were all glad to be a part of the petition. Katrina gave me a long, warm hug. She felt so close to me. We worked together on something important. I was one of the few men she really admired, she said, one of the few she could really trust. She gave me a look of deep affection.

Later that night after work, almost everyone who signed the petition met up for coffee at a place on Fairfax, north of Beverly. We celebrated, still on a high. We talked about what would happen next, conjecturing on this and that. It was possible something might be done on the grievances. Perhaps the organization would end up being more active, more honest. Soon, Katrina's girlfriend arrived and joined in the celebration. The two of them couldn't stop kissing. I realized there was no chance for me and Katrina to be intimate in that way. We would be good friends. As the night went on, people left. I had to do something early the next morning, so I got up to leave. Katrina was disappointed. She wanted me to stay. She wanted me to be with her the whole night. She rushed up to me and gave me a tight hug. Our bodies felt so good together ... but I had to leave.

As soon as Charlotte came back down to LA after a month's absence, Cassandra made me go up to Berkeley. While she said she wanted me to get familiar with certain duties - as I may some day get promoted - she really was continuing with her game-playing. She suspected Charlotte might support the petition, so she wanted me away from her as well as away from Katrina. Any means to dissipate solidarity between the three of us was a good idea, for her and for the organization.

During my trip up to the Bay, I was put into the keeping of one of the Berkeley field managers. It was a young woman who spent most of her time with Charlotte when she was up there. It seemed Charlotte and her had been talking about me. The girl not only knew things about me, but seemed to take a liking to me. I loved the Bay area. San Francisco was especially appealing. Such a beautiful, romantic, interesting city, I thought. I relished every moment and wanted to go back some day soon.

Every night after work, the girl and I hung out. She had a boyfriend, and admitted she thought Charlotte had a crush on her. The girl did seem a lot like Charlotte's ex, Ali, with a deep voice, and tall, skinny, lanky body. While the Berkeley girl and I flirted and had fun together, nothing happened. For some reason, on my last day, she wouldn't speak to me. The previous night we got pretty drunk together and I don't remember everything we did or said to each other.

Back in Los Angeles, Charlotte jumped on me and gave me a lovely, long hug. Oh, she felt good, and I guess I really did miss her. She seemed sincerely happy to see me, as well. Katrina was nearby and felt insecure, as if she couldn't match Charlotte's energy nor looks. Men wanted women like Charlotte, not her, she seemed to think at that moment. Katrina turned and walked down the hall as Charlotte and I talked. Away from everyone else, Katrina quietly called her girlfriend on her cell phone.

Charlotte took me by the arm and brought me to a corner of the landing. She wanted to speak privately.

“Are you pissed off at me for doing the petition?” I asked with a smile. At this point I had no idea.

“No! Not at all. I wished you and Katrina would've waited for me! I'm all for it.”

“Really?” I said with genuine surprise.

“Yeah.”

“I guess we should've waited then. I didn't think you'd like the idea...”

“Why?”

“I figured you wouldn't wanna rock the boat.”

“You don't trust me, Tommy?” she said with a cute, warm look into my eyes. She could kill me with her looks.

“Of course I do. It's just ...”

“Anyways, I wanted to talk to you about something else. Whats her name up in Berkeley, the one you hung out with a lot ...” she said, as if hiding the fact she liked the girl. “She told me over the phone you told her I was having sex with Sharon while I was still going out with Ali.”

“What?” I reacted flabbergasted. “I didn't tell her that. She's lying to you.”

“You didn't?”

“Not at all. I wouldn't say something like that. You know me, Charlotte.”

“I do.” she said with a sweet smile, as if she was already convinced I was telling the truth.

“The only thing I said was she reminded me of Ali. Then she said that made sense, since she felt you had a crush on her.”

“She said what?” she was caught off guard, and switched gears in her mood, getting uncomfortable. “She's so full of shit.” she began walking away, as if hiding something. “Don't know where she got that from.”

“That's what she said. She was a strange one.”

“Well, anyways, Tommy boy, that's all I wanted to talk about. Let's go back to the office.”

As I walked with Charlotte back to the office, Katrina suddenly ran up to us in excitement, a big smile on her face.

“Hey, you guys, I got the job up in Berkeley! I'm gonna be an Assistant Canvass Director!”

CHAPTER THREE.

THE DOWNWARD SPIRAL INTO LOVE FOR A FEMINIST.

I had always been a little uncomfortable with the militant feminist attitude at C.W.F.P.S.J. I'd never spent a great deal of time with outspoken feminists before, so I didn't want to judge. Sure, I was familiar with feminism, liked some of the ideas, had female friends who considered themselves one, but never was I in an environment like C.W.F.P.S.J. I wanted to give die-hard feminists a shot.

For the die-hards at the office – Cassandra, Katrina, and Charlotte – they tended to meet men like me half-way. They didn't want to come on too strong. Once they saw my sensitivity the first week of getting to know me, they chose the friendly route. I wasn't a macho man, wasn't defensive nor judgmental, so they chose not to be stand-offish with me as they would with other men.

There was another aspect. Due to the nature of canvassing, with it's salesperson conditioning, Cassandra, Katrina, and Charlotte were converters as well as militants. They were so used to going after anyone for money, that the acquisition of male feminists carried over in the same way. They were Crusaders. Any male could be a feminist, especially an open-mined guy like myself. Besides that, through the hours, days, weeks, months of working closely with me, hanging out socially, getting to know me well, the typical feminist barriers that usually would be up, were down.

There was another gray area in this dynamic, which I touched on earlier. I liked Charlotte, Katrina, and even Cassandra, so whenever they came across as too militant, I didn't criticize. And visa versa. Since the three of them liked me as a friend in return (and perhaps more), they toned down their preachiness around me. On both sides of the equation, self-checking was going on. They weren't too sure of how supportive I was of feminism, and I wasn't so sure just how militant they actually were. That would soon change.

C.W.F.P.S.J wanted all their canvassing offices to have monthly or bi-monthly "dialogues." These were one to two hour long sessions at the office in which a subject matter was dealt with in a "non-judgmental" environment. For scheduling and other reasons, there'd been only one dialogue session since I started working and it was pretty harmless and not involved.

What the sessions were called appealed to me – dialogues. I liked to dialogue with people myself. That was one of the things I enjoyed about canvassing, going door to door and interacting with people. Open communication was of the utmost importance in life. So when I heard Katrina was facilitating a dialogue as one of her last tasks before moving up to Berkeley, I was looking forward to it.

As I sat down on the couch next to Max, I watched Katrina write on the chalkboard. Everyone else sat down as she finished writing. Once she was done, the words gave me a slightly queasy feeling. She made a chart, in which on the top, portions were titled with: "Classism," "Sexism," "Racism," "Ageism," and some other ism. Elsewhere on the board she had written: "White Male Superiority is a Thing of the Past – Time is Needed for a New Power to Take Place! Women and Minorities Unite!" I told myself not to worry. This was Katrina, after all. She was cool, we were so close while doing the petition, she was so trusting of me, so down to earth and humane. She wouldn't make this a Femi-Nazi indoctrination seminar.

But then she began to speak. Her tone of voice was angrier than usual, nervous, strict. The whole time she never looked at me in the eyes, seemingly trying to shut me out as an individual. It was odd. She spoke down to all the men and the pretty Ecuadorian girl. Katrina talked harshly behind a ridiculing, laughing anger, not even having the warmth to patronize. That was what Cassandra and Charlotte did to men, sometimes – patronize. That was below Katrina, at least now it had become that way.

Katrina asked questions as if her fellow canvassers were stupid, even to me. I was surprised. She made one blanket statement after another.

"If you are a white, straight male in today's society, then you have a good life ahead of you. 50% more likely than anyone else to get good grades in school, get accepted by the best Universities, get the best job offers, get better wages, get raises, and so forth. You're also less likely to get pulled over by the cops!" Katrina said the last line with a laugh. I looked at her intently, knowing she knew I'd been arrested. I told her the whole insane story. Then she continued, seemingly catching my glance, "And even if you do get arrested and you're a straight, white male, and even if you're poor, the judicial system will make sure you get the best public defender, and the minorities will get the worst public defender."

Ouch. She was out to kill. God, I hated her in this moment. What a cunt, I thought to myself. She was throwing unnecessary daggers at me. Katrina kept going for a good hour like this. She continued to ask questions then tried to make people's (all the men and the cute Ecuadorian girl) answers sound stupid.

"So, Thomas," she said still not looking at me directly. "as a filmmaker, how more likely am I to get the role in your movie if I was a pretty white girl who gave you blow jobs than if I was an ugly, black lesbian who didn't? Hypothetically. And of course I'm speaking to you if you were some hot-shot Hollywood director, which, obviously, you're not."

She just wouldn't stop with this zinger fest. Was this a shot at me for casting Charlotte in my film and not any of the black women? Well, I certainly didn't get a blow job from Charlotte, and she ended up not in the movie, anyway. My first impulse was to jokingly say, "Well, it depends on how good the blow job was." But the dead serious looks on everyone's faces told me not to do that. That would be horrendous in this environment.

"If you want me to be me in that situation, you know very well I'm only interested in casting the best actress." I said to Katrina as sincerely as possible, with a quick glance at both Charlotte and Cassandra. They knew I wanted Charlotte in my movie.

“Well, I'm not so sure about that, Tommy!” Katrina replied with a laugh. “I think if we were to catch you in a locker room with your buddies like Gus and that other guy, you might say something different.” she continued with a condescending glee.

“You have a rather low opinion of me, Katrina.” I said to her with both seriousness and a sarcastic smile.

“Not to single you out, Tom, but most guys would be like that. It's just another example of how the system works. Men have been so indoctrinated to see women as sex objects that in almost every situation where women put their body forward, they'll get ahead of the self-respecting, qualified woman. For us as peace activists, we have to make sure that not only must there be justice in our government, there must be justice in all aspects of our lives.”

The whole room went into applause after Katrina's flourishing speech. Only Max and myself gave lukewarm applause, and we only clapped because we had to. I didn't understand why she went on like that. Simplifying things to fit her agenda was one thing, but to directly throw at me hostility, after all the months of bonding as co-workers and friends, after working on the petition together, it seemed strange. I wasn't her enemy.

Katrina knew who I was. She knew I believed in equality between men and women, that I saw the injustice done by white males throughout history, that there were indeed still injustice being wrought on the earth by white males. But Katrina wanted more, she wanted to make it clear the others and I needed more work to do. She had the answers, we didn't; she had the clue, we didn't; she was leading the cause, we needed to catch up. Or perhaps she believed it wasn't so much about me catching up. Perhaps it was about fighting me and straight white males like me, rich or poor, to the death. It was War.

After Katrina was finished with her speech, the actual “dialogue” part of the dialogue began. Max questioned Katrina's positions on a number of things in her speech. Being the outspoken person he was, he couldn't hold back his opinions anymore. After all, this was a dialogue. There was supposed to be free, uninhibited non-judgmental communication going on. Max should be able to say what he wanted. He wasn't trying to be offensive. But less than a few minutes of his explaining how power can go both ways, depending on the situation, he was attacked. Katrina was the most vicious, but Cassandra and Charlotte jumped in on the attack, as well. It got so heated that Katrina even went out-right racist and insulted him. She said he couldn't understand power dynamics from a woman's perspective since he "was an uneducated, straight black man from Inglewood who only cared about 'Baby got back'."

Whoa, I thought to myself at the time. That was not only a low-blow, but completely the kind of behavior Katrina was supposed to be criticizing! The argument between Katrina and Max got even more heated, as obviously Max got his feelings hurt and lashed back at her, saying she was a spoiled, obnoxious, muffin lover. It was bad. Cassandra, Charlotte, and Siango tried to calm the situation, but it was difficult. Katrina soon began to cry and left the room. Siango and Cassandra went to console Katrina while Charlotte berated Max. Somehow the insult made against him wasn't mentioned. He was the bad guy.

I didn't like this, but I held my tongue. I wanted to play it safe, at least this time, and until things calmed down. Was Katrina always like this but I never realized? Was Charlotte and Cassandra as well? I knew there was an element of this behavior before, but never so extreme, so simple-minded and insensitive, so dogmatic. It was never so cultish, so much like a religion. Had things changed? Did they want to stop being "nice girls"? Perhaps. Perhaps Katrina was flinging hostility for other reasons. Maybe she started flinging mud at me during her speech because she was feeling rejected by me in some way. Now that she was moving up to Berkeley, she wanted to make me pay. And more than likely, this animosity towards straight males had deeper origins, as well.

Katrina soon moved to Berkeley with her girlfriend and started her new Assistant Canvass Director position. The others and I wished her well, exchanging e-mails and all that. I sent a couple short messages but she never replied. That was that then. She did stay in touch with Charlotte and Cassandra, though.

To make up for Dialogues missed before, another one soon came up in the LA canvass. This time, Siango would facilitate the men and Cassandra the women. Siango took all the guys outside while the women stayed in the office. This dialogue was fairly simple. Both Siango and Cassandra had a box of small papers. On each paper was a sexual offense against women, going from rape to whistling.

Siango would ask the male group to rate each offense from 1 (least harmful) to 10 (most harmful). Cassandra would do the same with the women. Once all the papers/offenses had been rated, the two groups would meet in the office and discuss the conclusions we made. Kurt and Cindy had just joined C.W.F.P.S.J and were subjected to this. No wonder they quickly got turned off by the job.

Kurt had a passing interest in the dialogue, though. He had an ex-girlfriend who was a small town pseudo-feminist. Cindy, though, despised feminism. Once Cassandra took out the papers and asked the women to rate each offense, Cindy laughed when all the women rated every offense as 9 – except rape, which got a 10. Whistling and sexual flirtations was a 9?

“That's insane. You can't put sexual flirtations that high. It's right next to rape!” Cindy said with a loud laugh. She told me about this afterwards. “I mean, how're guys supposed to hit on women?”

“Maybe they shouldn't hit on them.” Charlotte said coldly.

“Okay, well, how're they supposed to convince a girl to sleep with them?” Cindy replied.

“What's wrong with the woman making the decision?” Cassandra said.

“Uh, okay, but you're not getting what I said. If a guy likes a girl, what's he supposed to do to let her know he does?”

Cassandra, Charlotte, nor any of the other women answered Cindy. They just shut down, dismissed her with a quick silence, then moved on.

Outside, all of us men rated rape as a 10, then all the others of varying degrees. Siango was a little upset we didn't rate the other offenses higher but understood. He picked up on my displeasure with the whole proceedings, noting a couple criticizing remarks I made on this dialogue. When Siango told the guys that these dialogues were part of a social de-programming - techniques to un-learn negative patterns of behavior - I said this felt more like systematic programming. It wasn't un-learning, it was enforcement. Siango was a bit frustrated with me, but then had to wrap it up and go into the office with us.

Once us men walked into the office, the women's ratings were put on the chalkboard. All the girls – except Cindy, who sat uncomfortably quiet – gave silent, defensive, expectant looks. Charlotte especially wanted to see how her boyfriend Sharon responded. He apparently hadn't proven his undying support of feminism yet. Max wasn't there that day and Katrina was in Berkeley, so Cassandra and Siango looked forward to a non-confrontational dialogue.

I was disturbed when I saw all the offenses besides rape at 9, right up close to the 10 of rape. It was almost as if the women were minimizing rape without their knowing it. When Siango put on the chalkboard the men's ratings, the women were shocked to see so many offenses so lowly rated.

"I'm sorry, but rape is serious as hell, and these other things aren't even close." I blurted out after the women's criticisms of the men's ratings.

"How can you say that, Tom?" Charlotte said, turning to me in surprise. She didn't expect me to be critical.

"What do you mean 'how can you say that'? Is rape not serious?" I replied with irritation.

"That's not what Charlotte meant. She was asking how can you minimize these other offenses?" Cassandra said solemnly.

“'Whistling?' 'Cat-calling?' Sexual flirtations?' 'Sexual jokes?' We're talking about verbal things, with no inference of violence at all. Rape is not only physical, but violent. There's a vast difference.” I continued.

“Any objectification of women is a form of degradation. It still is destructive, just not in obvious ways. You may have a hard time understanding, since you're a man. You don't have to go through the daily objectification of your body that we do.” Charlotte said to me as if reading from a textbook.

“That's right, I don't. But I go through other things that you as women don't have to. Every one of us has to fight against one form of objectification or another.”

“As a white straight male?” Cassandra said with a laugh. Part of her tried to lighten it up and a part of her was ridiculing me.

“Believe it or not, Cassandra, yes. Hey, look, you and Charlotte know me pretty well. You've worked with me for several months now. You can see from my actions I'm no sexist pig. I'm not saying these other offenses are harmless. Not at all. But a 9? That high? I think we should be more reasonable, shouldn't we?”

“Any of these so-called harmless offenses -” Cassandra began to say.

“I didn't say they were harmless!” I interrupted, with a frustrated laugh.

“Excuse me, Thomas,” Cassandra continued with a short, cold tone of voice. “but what I was about to say was that you're not getting our point. Sexual objectification of any kind is destructive. It all plays into the systematic degradation of women. We are dealing with powerful social stigmas, centuries and centuries of patterns of behavior. The submission of women is everywhere, meaning it's all connected. You have a hard time seeing it, but rape is not far from cat-calling. There is more than one way to rape a woman.”

"What?" I said, not believing what she said.

What was this all about? Something clicked in my head. The Women's Retreat took place only a couple weeks ago. There must've been some discussion of how the women wanted to make the organization more militantly feminist. I remember Cindy even mentioning something like that. That's why Cassandra, Charlotte, and Katrina, as hard-core as they may have been before, after the Retreat, they became even more so.

"Statistics have shown that a man who obsessively cat-calls after women or obsessively hits on them has a good chance of crossing the line and raping a woman." Cassandra said, like Charlotte before, speaking as if from a text-book she recently read.

"It's the facts, dude." Charlotte said to me.

"It seems to me you're hanging onto a lot of our Puritanical conditioning, if you want to talk about centuries of conditioning." I said to Cassandra and Charlotte.

"What do you mean by that?" Cassandra said with her put-on air of intellectual questioning.

"America was founded by Puritans, essentially, yes? No one liked them over in Europe because of their fickle religion, so they came here. American culture and the American mentality is deeply rooted in Puritanism. The Women's Movement that eventually got the right for women to vote in this country was motivated by a highly puritanical, a-sexual group of women. They planted the seed of a-sexuality in American feminism, and you can see it today. Haven't you noticed American feminists have a particularly Puritanical streak to them, meaning, they don't like sex?" I said.

The whole time I was talking, I felt the rage burning against me from the looks I got. Cindy laughed, then was shut down by stares.

"Be careful not to make blanket statements about things you don't know, Thomas." Cassandra said.

"Okay then. I agree blanket statements are uncalled for." I shot Cassandra a harsh look, making sure she got my acknowledgment in rebuttal to her feminist blanket statements. "So why don't I give you an example. You know who Simone De Bouvoir was?"

"No. Who was he?" Cassandra said, honestly thinking I was referring to a man.

"She," I said with a smile. "was one of the most famous feminists of the 20th Century and she didn't have your puritanism, maybe because she was French. She was all for sex. She and her life-long partner Jean-Paul Sartre had numerous lovers and I'm sure they made a sex joke now and then, maybe even a dirty one. Jean-Paul might've even whistled at a woman or two."

Cassandra was put off by my reply. She felt threatened. She didn't like her authority being questioned like this, so out in the open. She didn't like being shut down in front of everyone, made to look like a fool in front of everyone. She especially didn't like being upstaged during a dialogue. Charlotte was also put off by my "defiance" but also gave me a quick, odd, affectionate look. It seemed like a part of her admired me for what I did, standing up to Cassandra like that. I know the two women, as much as they were comrades for the Cause, had their disagreements.

Siango tried to stop the debating, for he felt I was taking everyone off-track. He hated so-called divertimentos. We were all there to discuss the particulars of the dialogue, not get sidetracked on Puritanism. Of course, he was such a literalist that he didn't see the "debate" between me and Cassandra as exactly what the dialogue should be used for. Siango officially ended the debate by asking the pretty Ecuadorian girl how she felt about the ratings.

I finished shooting "Loveincrazy" a week later. The excitement of the production was over. C.W.F.P.S.J was not only losing its enjoyment for me, but its purpose. Nothing about the petition was ever discussed again. The grievances were never dealt with. The organization continued on in the same way. The militant political correctness was suffocating. I didn't see what C.W.F.P.S.J was doing as all that important anymore. It was obvious we weren't making much of a difference. Perhaps we were, but there was no way to know. Claims were made on influencing politicians but there was no proof, no facts to show. The only claims the organization could honestly make were that we existed; we had 10,000, maybe 15,000 members statewide; we provided info through literature and an ad now and then, and that's it.

That wasn't enough for me. This "great and powerful" grassroots lobby I worked for lost its appeal. Not only that, but the American public I canvassed was also a big letdown. Very rarely I met someone interesting. Most of the time I ran up against walls of ignorance, blandness, shallowness, triteness, or outright hatred and hostility. I began to drink alcohol more around this time, come to work late, was disinterested in the briefings and dynamics, and didn't raise much money canvassing.

Charlotte, Cassandra, and Siango began to notice. The hiring of Kurt and Cindy seemed to re-stimulate me but when their interest began to lag, so did mine. It was obvious I was burnt out on C.W.F.P.S.J. They'd all seen me go through a few dramas with Maya now and then, stress about my film, but this time it seemed different. The problem was the job itself.

However much they were at odds with my "stubbornness" against feminist ideology, Charlotte, Cassandra, and Siango wanted to help me get out of my rut. They had, after all, spent a great deal of time with me as co-workers and friends in a seven month period. And I'd been an integral part of the LA canvass success that year.

As usual, Charlotte was the best at reaching out. One day, there was a dynamic before canvassing in Echo Park in which Charlotte wanted to have everyone get in a circle and lock arms. Each person would take a turn telling the person opposite what they thought was special about them. It was corny and cheesy as many of Charlotte's ideas were, but somehow it worked. Charlotte could make corniness work for her. Her bubbliness initially rubbed me the wrong way, though. I was in a bad mood. That wouldn't stop her. She decided to make me her new project.

"So ..." Charlotte said as she looked up at me. I was her opposite person, which she did on purpose. She gave me the most amazing, penetrating, knowing, beautiful, alluring smile ... I was melted instantly as she looked at me with her gleaming gorgeousness. "... my buddy Tommy-boy ..." she laughed warmly, as did I. There was something exciting about the energy between us, a fun electricity that made us laugh. As much as I loved it, I knew she did this with everyone. Still, I loved it. "... I am completely blown away by you ..." 'Blown away'? I was getting hot. Sharon then became noticeably uncomfortable, his body stiffening, his nerves tightening, as he watched Charlotte and I. "... Since I met you I've loved your intelligence, your compassion, your sincerity, your passion, your commitment to the organization, your ability to stimulate and inspire others, your friendship with me ... I could go on but I'll stop there."

Sharon became more and more uncomfortable with Charlotte's praise of me. He knew and so did the others that it was just part of the dynamic, that everyone had to do it. But Charlotte was heartfelt and really seemed to enjoy giving the praise. Sharon was jealous and suspicious, although, as always, never expressed it in an obvious way. It was always subterranean for him. Charlotte was always such a flirt, with me, with others. And now, it seemed she went overboard. Sharon couldn't help but let his insecurities seep out.

A night came when one of the co-workers was leaving the office. She was a 30-something, humble, kind lesbian that just needed to move on. Canvassing was too stressful. The office decided to take her out to a lesbian bar in West Hollywood. It was fun and everyone chatted and drank. Charlotte ended up sitting in between Sharon and I in the booth, drinking beer after beer. I could tell how much she enjoyed being in between us.

As I talked with Charlotte, I couldn't help but get turned on by her.

There was an air of flirting between us that made Sharon a bit quiet, then he turned and talked to someone else. Charlotte got up and took me by the arm, as she often did, and went to the bar with me. The lesbian bartender obviously liked Charlotte. Who wouldn't? She was so beautiful and charming.

Both Charlotte and I playfully flirted with the bartender, then went back to the booth. Sharon was involved in a conversation still, so Charlotte turned to me and paid me exclusive attention. As we drank more, our talking turned into goofing off. We began to hand wrestle, grasping the others hands and pushing against each other, laughing and yelling. Everyone looked at us with a look of "what're you doing?" It seemed like there was an odd tension between Charlotte and I in the moment, which put others outside, at a remove from our goofiness.

Then there was a mild argument between Sharon and someone else about political correctness. I jokingly interrupted (but with conviction), by saying I hoped the world will never be run by the P.C. Police. Cassandra was, of course, uncomfortable, as was Siango, but lo and behold Charlotte surprised me by leaning into me, yelling "Right on, Brother!", laughing, then high-fiving me. She could be so much fun. Everyone not only thought our goofiness was annoying, but that there was some slight offensiveness to what Charlotte and I were doing.

And it didn't stop. As we all left the bar, Charlotte teased me, egging me on as I chased her down the street. Soon, I caught her. She laughed as she tried to get away. I grabbed her, then picked her up off the ground. She wrapped her legs around my waist, hoisting herself further up, put her mouth near my ear, and began making moaning noises. I was so drunk that I didn't catch it at first. Then I realized she was moaning into my ear, with a definite sexual quality to the noise. What was she doing? Was she moaning because she was turned on or was she goofing off? Whatever the reason, I was intensely aroused. Her making that noise into my ear, feeling her breath, feeling her legs wrapped around me, her body on mine ... It made me so horny I lost concentration and lost my balance, making us both fall to the pavement. We sat on the sidewalk for a while, laughing, catching our breath. Soon, the others caught up to us. Charlotte left with Sharon, then I went to my car and drove home.

I began to realize – I was incredibly attracted to Charlotte. Was I all this time and didn't know it? There were several moments where I knew I was, definitely, but things always seemed to stop anything from happening. Well, I couldn't do anything now anyway. Before, Ali was her girlfriend, and now, Sharon was her boyfriend. Not only was she unavailable, but her boyfriend was our co-worker. I already sensed a bit of jealousy coming from Sharon. Best not to go there and upset the workplace.

At the office, Charlotte and I continued to be friendly, but we never overtly flirted. Outside of work, there were other instances where the flirtations came more to the surface. There was a party at a co-worker's house where Charlotte and I drank and talked off and on. She was with Sharon so it wasn't constant, but the goofing off continued to come up. After several drinks and walking around the house, running into Charlotte, it began to sink in heavily – I was really into her.

Someone took a picture of several of the LA canvassers. Charlotte pulled me next to her to pose. I couldn't help myself and as we stood with our arms around each other in a friendly way, my hand glided down from her back to her ass. It felt so good, I loved her ass. God, I wish I could feel the skin on her ass, grip her cheeks with my hands, spread them apart, and eat her ass out! I was sure she'd pull my hand away. But she didn't. She let my hand stay there.

As I was leaving the party, I went to say goodbye to Charlotte and the others. She was up at the top of the staircase smiling down at me. I smiled back. As she said she'd see me at the office the next day, being a little drunk, she moved her body seductively. She caught my eyes looking at her body, then she opened her legs, putting her knee against the railing. It was another move of hers which I didn't know her intentions. Wasn't she goofy, bubbly, and flirty with everyone?

Another night came up a week later. Charlotte, Cassandra, and I were all finishing paperwork at the office. Everyone else left already. Sharon went somewhere with his brothers. Charlotte said she wanted to go out dancing with me. Cassandra of course was included but she kept saying the two of us could go without her. Charlotte was uncomfortable with that and eventually persuaded her to go, too.

The three of us went first to a club in Santa Monica off Lincoln blvd. While I went to get money at a nearby ATM, Charlotte and Cassandra tried to convince the bouncer to let them in. There was a private party going on inside. The girls thought they could use their persuasive, seductive canvassing skills. Once I came back, I found them in disappointment. They couldn't get in.

We got back into my car and decided to go to a bar near Kantor's on Fairfax. Tuesday nights there was a dance club at the bar. On the way, Charlotte wanted to listen to my Gavin Friday tape. It was the "Shag Tobacco" album. Typically, when I shared Friday's music with people, they didn't care much for it. His voice was strange and the music too moody. But Charlotte instantly dug it. I was surprised. I didn't expect her to be the kind of person to like Gavin Friday. Sure, the two of us would goof off and Karaoke sing Pearl Jam or U2 songs in the van while going to canvass. But that was Pearl Jam and U2, this was Gavin Friday. She was a classic rock and hip-hop fan. Friday's music was new and interesting to her somehow. She especially loved "You, Me, and World War Three," wanting it played again and again. She told me for her birthday if I made a tape of my favorite music, she'd love it.

We soon arrived at the bar and the place was packed. Not only was there a lot of people but there wasn't much room. It was fairly long, but narrow, with booths to the left, a small dance floor to the right and the bar in the back. Cassandra, Charlotte, and I walked in together then went to the bar to get drinks. After sitting at a booth for a few minutes, Charlotte wanted to get up and dance. Cassandra and I followed.

Charlotte's style of dancing had a hip-hop, R+B flow to it, not especially dynamic or interesting, but because it was her, it was fun and charming. Cassandra had a strange way of dancing where she'd kick out in front of her. I tried to be fair and give them both dancing attention, but Cassandra kept kicking, forcing me to stay away. So, I chose to dance near Charlotte most of the time. During one song, we began hitting our hips together, then our butts. We laughed and did it for a while. I loved her full, firm hips and ass, and it felt so good banging into her. I fantasized what it must be like to do her doggystyle as I bumped into her again and again.

Later in the night, Soft Cell's "Where Did Our Love Go?" came on. I loved Soft Cell. Charlotte was getting tired and came up to me closer. She wrapped her arms around me, then leaned her head on my shoulder. I was in heaven having her with me on the dance floor like that. We danced slowly together as she started quietly singing along to the song, her mouth near my ear, "Oh baby, baby, where did our love go? Don't you leave me, don't you leave me no more ... Oh baby, baby, where did our love go? Where did our love go?" Where did our love go? Why weren't we lovers? Why didn't it happen? Oh, I almost couldn't take it, dancing with her like that, her singing into my ear tenderly ...

As Charlotte's birthday came up, I began to make a tape of music for her, then got her a Rolling Stones t-shirt. At the office, she announced there'd be a birthday party for her at Cassandra's place – where she was staying for a month – and everyone was invited. I drove out to the Mount Washington apartment and found Cassandra's pad to be pretty nice.

The apartment was more like a house. It was a house, actually, with a third of the building sanctioned off as another apartment for someone else. The rest belonged to Cassandra – a kitchen, a large living room, two bedrooms upstairs, two bathrooms, a back porch, a front patio and a large front lawn. Not bad.

Everyone from the LA C.W.F.P.S.J office showed up for Charlotte's birthday celebration, along with other people. I even brought Gus, who didn't forget Charlotte. The two of us got her a birthday card and some flowers. I had also brought the tape of music and Rolling Stones t-shirt. Gus made fun of the t-shirt while noticing I had become more into

Charlotte. This was before I told Gus I'd fallen in love with her.

Gus and I waited for Charlotte to come downstairs. She was busy with getting ready apparently, according to Sharon, who came down to tell. Gus had to leave, so I took him back to his apartment. On the way, we talked about how much we disliked Sharon. We really couldn't believe how Charlotte went for him. I wanted to go back, so I drove to Mt. Washington again. It wasn't that far from Silverlake, especially since Charlotte was there.

Back at the party, everybody but Siango – who came and left like Gus – was in the midst of getting drunk or getting high. I had to catch up. As I got a beer from the fridge, I heard Charlotte call my name.

"Tom!" she said in excitement as she rushed down the stairs. I turned around and got tackled by one of her warm, long hugs. "I'm so happy you're here!" she said as she gave me a deep look straight into my eyes after the hug.

"So am I, Birthday Girl." I replied with a smile. "You look great."

"Thanks." she said, blushing. "Hey, you wanna come upstairs with me?"

"Of course."

Charlotte took me upstairs to the room she was staying at. No one else was there. I gave her the flowers, card, t-shirt, and tape of music. She blushed again, then took out a baggy of weed and a pipe.

"It's been a while since we smoked out together." I said as I sat opposite her on the floor.

"I know. That's why I want to with ya now, Tommy-boy." she said as she finished putting the weed into the pipe, lit it, then began smoking.

"You had a good birthday so far?"

"Yup." she said as she handed the pipe and lighter to me.

"Everybody's been so nice. That's always one of the advantages of birthdays: it gives people an excuse to be nice to one person for a day."

"That's true." I said after taking a puff, then handing the pipe back to her.

"You know, Tom?"

"What?"

"One of the things that's gotta happen when the Revolution takes places is kindness."

"Kindness?"

"Kindness and understanding. Love, really. Things can't change without those things."

"No, they can't."

"It's like that song we listened to in your car the other day."

"'You, Me, and World War Three'?"

"Yeah, that one! I loved that song."

"I didn't think you'd like Gavin Friday."

"Why?"

"I thought the music would be too dark for you."

"I'm a lot like you, Tom, more than you think probably."

"An existentialist?"

"Yup, a Feminist Existentialist."

"Like Simone de Bouvoir?" I said with a smile. She caught my reference to the Dialogue we had at the office.

“And you can be my Jean-Paul Sartre!” she said as we both laughed.

“No, seriously though, I'm starting to realize that, too.”

“What?”

“I've gone in and out of closeness with you, but now I realize from the beginning how much I liked you as a person.”

“Cool.” she said, blushing once again. Alcohol and pot seemed to get her to do that a lot. “I liked you from the beginning, too, Tommy. We're good buddies. Hey, speaking of which, I have an idea for a movie, and I was wondering if you could help me write and make it. Of course, if you wanted to. The story's about male/female relationships and I want to deal with the adrodgynation of the sexes.”

“Sounds interesting. I'd love to work with you on it.”

“Really? Cool! We'd make a great team.”

Just at that moment, Sharon came through the door. When he saw me and Charlotte sitting on the floor opposite each other, smoking pot, he froze. Sharon felt awkward, even though there wasn't physical closeness between Charlotte and I.

“Am I interrupting something?” he said with a slight unease.

“No, not at all, baby. Me and Tommy were just talking about my movie we might make together some day.” she replied smoothly, bubbly.

“Oh, cool.” he said, not altogether comfortable with her answer. He didn't like the idea of her and I working on a project together, I could tell. “Well, there's some people who want to see you downstairs.”

“Okie-dokie. Come on, Tom, let's go.” she said as she got up from the floor.

Charlotte was busy with various people the whole night. I couldn't stop thinking about her as I drank, talked with others, and danced.

Charlotte did join me on the dance floor at one point. We loved to dance together. She tried to get Sharon to join us but he didn't like dancing, so she stopped and went with him elsewhere. Late in the evening, after a number of drinks, I got tired and went to sleep on one of the couches.

The next morning, despite drifts of a hangover, I woke up with a glowing, warm feeling in my gut. It was as if I had just come from a nice place in my subconscious. I couldn't remember any dreams, but the feeling was connected to Charlotte. She must have entered my dreams and now stayed with me as I awoke. I couldn't kid myself anymore. I was in love with her.

Looking around Cassandra's house, I quickly realized no one was there. It was 10am. I slept in quite a bit. There was a note on the living room table from Charlotte and Cassandra, letting me know they left and if I could lock the front door when I left. As I closed and locked the door behind me, walked to my car, that rush of love didn't leave. It hung there inside, clinging to me, despite all the reservations I had in my head. We weren't really compatible, were we? Charlotte wasn't as similar to me as she said last night, was she? She was a die-hard feminist, she could be snobby, she could be annoyingly bubbly, she could be shallow, superficial, and simple-minded.

Charlotte could also be the opposite of all those things, as well, though. Besides the obvious physical beauty, I was also attracted to her open, thoughtful, and inquiring side. And then there was that ability she had to zone in on me. I could feel her energy zeroing in and zapping me. I knew of no other woman who did that except Maya, years ago.

That week, the office began canvassing Long Beach. The year before, the LA office did well. The expectations were high. We should raise even more money this time, since we had more people and the nucleus had become more experienced. I hadn't spent much time in Long Beach in my life. I was curious about the area. It seemed interesting, with its moist, gritty air, casual vibe, and quaint, diverse neighborhoods.

On the first day, everyone went to a Mexican fast food joint. It was popular the year before with the office. Some of the people working there were apparently fun, but this year they were gone. And the prices apparently went up. Oh well. We stayed and had lunch. While everyone ate, I noticed Charlotte became quiet, shut off from everyone else. She got into one of her dark moods.

I'd seen her do this before, where she became disconnected and depressed. She got up from the table and went outside without saying a word. Some of the others laughed at her. That bugged me. I shot an evil eye at the girls who laughed, then looked to Sharon to see if he'd go console his girlfriend. He did nothing, so I took it upon myself to follow Charlotte outside.

She was sitting at a table outside by herself, lost in melancholy while looking at a canvassing folder. I came up close, kneeling in front of her.

"You okay?" I asked, putting my hand on her shoulder.

"Yeah ..." she responded despondently, her head low.

"Are you sure?"

"Well, not really, I guess ..."

"What's wrong?"

"I don't know ... I guess I let people get to me when I shouldn't. It's just I'm trying to help everybody and every time I reach out to those two girls, they fucking ridicule me and put me down. Normally, you know, I'd have tougher skin, but it's like I see Sharon and he's talking with them, almost as if he's in on the joke on me, too, laughing at me ... I don't know what to do because I feel if I say something, it'd make me look like a jerk or something ... I just feel real insecure, I guess ..."

"How about don't even bother reaching out to those girls? You tried and they made fun of you, so why bother trying again?"

"But I'm supposed to be a leader, Tom. I'm supposed to help

them."

"You are a leader, which means you don't have to hold them by the hand when they're biting yours."

"I guess you're right, I just don't want to cause any rifts in the canvass, ya know? Especially since it seems Sharon's on their side ..."

"Look at it this way: you're not the cause of a rift, they are."

"Sometimes I feel I'm not cut out to be an Assistant Canvass Director ... Maybe I'm not good at what I do, not like Katrina or Cassandra are."

"Actually, I think you're better at leading people than they are."

"You're just saying that to make me feel better."

"No, I mean it." I looked at her in the eyes, intently.

"Really?" she responded as she turned to look me back in the eyes. My face made her light up. She suddenly began to glow.

"Yeah. You've inspired me more than they have. You reach out to people more openly, more sincerely. Cassandra and Katrina are more closed off, more guarded. They can turn people who're with them against them with their stand-offishness."

"You really think that, Tom?" she said in a sweet, warm voice, looking at me with unbearable tenderness.

"Completely ..." I said, her look and voice making me almost cry. I was on the verge.

I loved this woman, loved her vulnerability in this moment, loved her strength in that nakedness, in that courage to be naked, loved that within her which was so lacking in the world around us ... loved her utterly ... I wanted to take her into my arms ... take her away, away from C.W.F.P.S.J, from Long Beach, from the world we knew, the people we knew ... take her somewhere where we could make this nakedness a real thing and not only a glimmering moment ...

"There're so many things you could do in life ..." I continued. "... if you wanted to make that movie, you could and I'll help you. If you wanted to run for a political office, like we've talked about, kick out that Weinckoff guy, who's both our rep in congress, you could. You have the intelligence, the inspiration, and feeling to go far, Charlotte ..."

"Tommy ..." she said with a crack in her voice.

"Yeah?"

"Are you being honest? Do you really mean this?"

"Yes ... with all my heart ..."

" ... you really mean it, don't you?" she said, near tears herself.

"I do ... I love you, you know ..." I responded, holding back my tears. I was getting overwhelmed with emotion.

Charlotte stood up and quickly embraced me as I stood up, as well. We held each other for a long time, several minutes ... We both felt so good in each other's arms ... I loved it ... being with her like that ... I didn't want to let go ... she didn't seem to want to either ... The others eventually began to stare at us from inside the restaurant, wondering what was going on.

"Thank you ..." Charlotte whispered into my ear.

Soon, the others came outside, making Charlotte and I break our hold. Sharon looked at us stiffly. I invited him to join in hugging and consoling Charlotte, but he turned and walked away. Siango asked if everything was okay. Charlotte said yes, then went to Sharon in the van. I was still overwhelmed with the feeling I just went through as I followed Siango to the other van.

That night, I had a horrible canvassing experience. I couldn't raise any money, couldn't even get anyone to write one single letter, nor take any literature. Several people yelled at me to fuck off and slammed the door in my face. That was normal but that night it happened much more than usual. I felt like a human punching bag.

Back at the office, Charlotte thanked me for supporting her earlier. It apparently helped, since she raised $220. She asked how my night went and I explained the bleakness. It was bad and I felt like shit. She said she felt sorry, that maybe I took her bad energy. I told her not to feel guilty, to which she quickly turned to Sharon and tuned me out. Ouch, that hurt, I thought at the time. Why was she so giddy with Sharon? He gave her the cold shoulder when she needed him earlier, and now she was giving me the cold shoulder? I was the one who reached out to her and I was the one feeling low now. It reminded me how quickly Charlotte could go from hot to cold. And then I thought about the simple fact Sharon was her boyfriend, and a jealous boyfriend at that.

As Charlotte gave Sharon attention, playing around and kissing him, I noticed something odd. She made Sharon sit on her lap as she sat on a chair. He obeyed her passively, uncomfortably, then she began to dry hump his butt in a goofy, childish way. What the hell was she doing? She moaned with cartoonish noises. Sharon caught me watching, then quickly stood up, awkward and upset. Charlotte laughed at him.

“Why do you always do shit like that?” Sharon quietly yelled at her, so as not to attract too much attention, then swiftly left the office. Charlotte kept laughing. I minded my own business.

We all continued to canvass Long Beach and I continued to do horribly. I just couldn't connect with the Long Beach people. Everyone else was doing fine. With each night of fund raising failure, I became more unsure of myself, more insecure. I got into a few arguments. People kept telling me to get lost. It seemed like I was Long Beach's punching bag. I tried to think of ways to help myself. Go door to door with low expectations to calm my nerves. That didn't work. Drink lots of coffee to get myself pumped up and excited. That didn't work, and neither did other things.

One day I was scheduled to give a briefing at the Mexican restaurant we went to for lunch. I was given the freedom to talk about whatever I wanted for the briefing. Excellent. Perhaps this would help me. I began to write a short essay on the nature of political and metaphysical rebellion, much like Albert Camus did with "The Rebel," one of my favorite philosophical works. I charted the development of modern rebellion in historical and philosophical terms starting from the French Revolution, again, like "The Rebel."

I wanted to not only give myself a sense of purpose and context for why I was working at C.W.F.P.S.J, why I cared at all for politics, but also to the others. In the essay, I dealt with the major changes in modern thought. With the French Revolution, I dealt with the Regicides and Deicides of the times. It was the end of an era. God and the King were killed. What replaced it was Commerce. The business class took over, Industry took over, much more than any notions of Democracy, Equality, or Freedom.

From that point on, and especially with the Industrial Revolution, Money as the New God was the driving force for the European nations. The mechanics of money dominated any discussions of what was important. Communism, seen by its advocates as a reaction to Capitalism, was a product of the Industrial mindset, as well. Every other change, every other movement, situation, and action that occurred up until the present were events sprung forth from the mechanized, Industrial context.

I concluded the briefing by saying as peace activists, it was vital to not stop at rebelling against the greed of the powerful and wealthy in the established government. Not to define rebellion against specifics such as Republican, Democrat, male, female, race, class, sexuality, and so forth. An activist had to want to go all the way and rebel against the very nature of Industry. The mindset of Commerce had to be changed. Economic and social justice for all was only the beginning towards a culture of better human understanding. As Commerce replaced God,

Human Beings had to replace Commerce. It was a big idea, obviously, but an idea that had to start at some point.

Once I was done, I breathed heavily in relief. It felt good to verbalize concretely my beliefs to the others. While reading my essay, I gave copies to everyone to read while I spoke. I wondered how they all felt about what I said. Looking at their faces, I was disappointed. They were disinterested and bored, even Kurt and Cindy.

I supposed it was a little too intellectual for my young friends. Siango actually listened intently and questioned me. He didn't agree with me on most of what I said, but at least he showed the respect of paying attention. Then to my surprise, I found out Charlotte really dug it. She zoned in on me the whole time I was speaking and listened to every word. She was impressed and a bit turned on by my intellect it seemed. Once people left to go to the vans, she told me so, saying also that I seemed to speak to something which she thought of herself.

"Really?" I asked her, my heart jumping, excited by this mental connection.

"Yeah. I've studied history myself and what you talked about makes sense. I like your ideas a lot."

"That's so cool you think that." I replied, like a happy little school boy. Her understanding me intellectually made me love her even more. "For a while I thought I was boring everyone."

"Maybe you were for everybody else, but not for me." she said, giving me a deep, almost seductive look. "Come on, buddy, let's go canvass. We should talk about this some other time. You need to make money tonight."

"Speaking of Commerce and Industry ..." I said with a smile at her. She caught it and smiled back.

As I canvassed that night, I did do better. Not great, but better. All I could think about was Charlotte. Her presence was stuck inside of me.

I thought about how perhaps she could be my wife some day even ... she might be my soul mate. I could see us having our differences, arguing, but underlying it would be an understanding, a connection. We would grow, go through phases and all the while be partners in the midst of this madness called life ... we could anchor each other and from there, inquire and search ...

The only problem was she was involved in a serious relationship with Sharon. They just moved into an apartment together in Venice. Despite whatever problems they might have, they both seemed seriously committed to each other. With Sharon's jealousies, it was obvious they didn't have an open relationship. Right? Maybe I'd ask Sharon. One night I canvassed with him, still in Long Beach. There was a slight tension between us, an unease, but I wanted to make it clear I had no bad feelings towards him.

Sharon loosened up once seeing this in me, remembering the days when we were friendlier. Towards the end of the night, I asked him how his relationship with Charlotte was going. He replied by saying it was okay, that they were adapting to each other. Out of pure curiosity, I asked if they had an open relationship. He was caught off-guard, wasn't visibly upset, then said no, they were definitely not in an "open" relationship. He seemed to despise the words as they left his mouth.

As the days past, I hoped my romantic feelings for Charlotte would lesson, even disappear. It did the opposite. I became more and more in love with her. The passion and lust grew within me as I shut down to control it. As I repressed my feelings for Charlotte more and more, the more I became emotionally unstable. I was closed off from the others at the office, moody, quiet, detached. I snapped at people I canvassed. When I wasn't at work, I would sometimes break down and cry, trembling in nervous, painful, wrenching angst. I wanted her so badly. It was eating me up. Whenever I saw or talked with Charlotte, it was as if I was under a spell. I felt completely helpless, swallowed up in a black hole of unattainable love.

For weeks, I was lost in my head. I didn't know what to do. One night I canvassed with Cassandra. While taking a break, she noticed I was shaking.

"Are you okay?" Cassandra asked uncertainly, but also patronizingly.

"... not really, but I'll be fine ... I'm not quite sure what's happening to me ... ever since we came to Long Beach, I've been feeling strange ..." I replied, stuttering as I continued shaking.

"You want to take a break from canvassing?"

"No ... I can canvass ... I just need to calm myself down ..."

"Is something upsetting you?"

"In a way, yeah, but I can't talk about it now ..."

"Maybe you should tell somebody something."

"What do you mean?" I said with surprise. She seemed to say that with a knowledge about my love for Charlotte.

"I don't know. Just get it off your chest. If you're not comfortable telling me, tell someone else. Anyway, you want to just meet at the end of the night on this corner?"

"At nine?"

"Yeah."

"Okay."

Cassandra moved onto the next block, a bit cold as she wanted to get away from me as quickly as possible, it seemed. I stayed on the corner for a while, waiting for my shaking to stop. Eventually it did as I got up and walked, but I was still troubled the rest of the night.

I had to talk with someone about my passion for Charlotte and the only person I could really trust was my father Jean. Jean was always there for me in that way. We went over the details, the circumstances of the situation, of my feelings. Jean hadn't seen me like this, so in love, so obsessed and torn up about it, since the days when I was fervently in love with Maya. He knew this was serious. Like the situation with Maya, Charlotte was unavailable. I had to not expect anything.

Jean didn't want to persuade me to stop feeling the way I did, though. It was important to value the emotions and not stamp them out. The problem with the feelings was what to do with them? Did Charlotte and I have a good enough friendship where she'd be okay to tell her? I thought we did at the time ... she displayed an understanding and trust few people had with me.

I decided that was it then. I had to tell Charlotte how I felt about her. I wouldn't expect anything in return. I just had to get it off my chest. She continually told me me how close we were. Perhaps she'd even respond to my feelings. Maybe not while she was dating Sharon, but some day in the future. One of the things that bothered me was I felt like I never had a chance with her. I'd never known her single. As soon as she dumped her girlfriend, she jumped in with Sharon. By letting her know how I felt about her, if and when she broke up with Sharon, she would know I was there ... It seemed reasonable to tell her and I knew how much it would help in a cathartic way. I'd release all that romantic angst, push it out into the open, out of my system. Perhaps, afterwards, I'd stop loving her, too ...

I set to writing a letter. I didn't think there'd be the time and space to tell everything I needed to say verbally. We were always around other people at work, and outside work she was always with Sharon. A letter also seemed a good way to clarify myself as much as possible, root out any misunderstandings. After two days of writing, I finished it. The timing worked out well when I found out the next night, I'd be canvassing with Charlotte in the Pacific Palisades hills. We were all done with Long Beach.

Charlotte was assigned to canvass with me to help out. For the whole three weeks in Long Beach, I did poorly. I was still in a rut as a fund raiser and everyone noticed something was wrong with me. Cassandra and Siango felt Charlotte could reach out to me the best. She'd done so in the past.

As Charlotte and I were dropped off in the dark, wealthy hills of the Pacific Palisades, I had the letter in my pocket. Should I give it to her? Maybe it was a bad idea. Maybe she'd react badly. But then I'd be stuck with the feelings, stuck with no resolution. And even if my passion cooled, I'd live the rest of my life never knowing if perhaps she felt the same way. I'd never know unless I tried. I decided to go for it.

Before we started canvassing, I gave her the letter and told her if she could read it when she had time alone. Perhaps after work so she could give it her full attention. She said sure, placed it in her jacket pocket, and didn't seem put off or awkward, not asking me what it was about. We went ahead and canvassed, the first hour separately, then later we'd meet to do houses together.

When we met up, neither of us were doing very well. The people were angry, rich snobs who wanted nothing to do with peace activists. We went to one house together and rang the doorbell. A father and his son answered the door, apparently interrupted from a hockey game. The father and son chose not to shoo us away however, and involved us with questions of their own.

At first, it seemed the father and son were harmlessly curious about the organization. Twenty minutes later, though, Charlotte and I realized they were fucking with us. They then began to berate Charlotte for some reason, initiating an argument. I joined in the argument, with Charlotte and I yelling back and forth with the dad and son. All that nervous energy in expectation of Charlotte reading my letter came shooting out.

Suddenly, I snapped. I couldn't stand this arrogant, snide, Pacific Palisades posh family anymore. I blew up at them, cursing and yelling in outrage at their socially acceptable contempt for human beings. I hated how they treated Charlotte, belittled her, shot her down, misogynistically wanting to "put her in her place." I told them to shove their reactionary, women-hating trips up their asses.

"I'm a fucking Democrat, asshole! A liberal! I'm not reactionary!" the father screamed back at me.

"It's the Democrats that'll send this country into Fascism, buddy!" I screamed back.

"What the hell're you talking about, you maniac?!" the son yelled at me.

"Thomas, calm down!" Charlotte said while trying to push me away.

"The Democrats, you idiot, have no fucking back bone! They're a bunch of rats just like the Republicans! They're lack of independence, their 'Hail, Hitler!' salute to Bush will be the reason why this country goes into Fascism!" I continued while Charlotte held me back.

"Don't you dare say that!" the father said with a shudder of contempt.

"We're Jewish, you prick!" the son yelled at me.

"Oh yeah? Well I'm sorry but everyone can't always be concerned about not stepping on your god damn toes! Fucking get over it, and stop using your plight in the same victimized, manipulative way that I always fucking hear! Your people aren't the only ones who fucking suffered! The Jews aren't the only ones who went through a genocide, you're not the only ones who were put down! Where were the Jews during the Genocide in East Timor? Where were the Jews during the Genocide in Rwanda? Fucking get over your own plight and see everything for the whole god damn human picture that it is!"

"Thomas, get out of here!" Charlotte screamed at me.

Soon, I did leave as she stayed to calm down the situation. She didn't want this getting back to the C.W.F.P.S.J. office. It'd be bad news for her and I. She apologized to the family for my behavior. Through her charm, she was able to cool down the father and son, primarily by telling them I was a nut case with an anger problem and that her boyfriend was Jewish.

Half a block away, I sat on the curb, trying to soothe my rage. I hated blowing up, hated losing control like that, hated having my buttons pushed so easily. It always left me with a sour taste. A few minutes later, Charlotte joined me on the curb. She berated me for losing my temper and I felt like shit, apologizing as I lay on my back on the sidewalk, my hands covering my face in shame.

Seeing me in turmoil, knowing I felt bad for what I did, she couldn't help but feel compassion. She said she understood why I got angry, since the father and son were such pricks. She hated them, too. She asked if she could read the letter now, while I cooled off. Uh-oh. This was it. Sure, I said. She walked across the street to where there was a streetlight and began reading the letter. I didn't move, just laid there on the concrete, looking up at the dark sky, waiting.

Fifteen minutes later, she came back. She must've re-read it a few times. I looked up at her as she walked towards me and I noticed she'd been crying.

"I ... I'm really flattered, Tommy ..." she said nervously, emotionally, as she sat next to me on the curb. "I had no idea you felt this way ..."

"... I had to tell you ... I couldn't hold it inside any more ..." the emotions overwhelming ... she now knew ...

I couldn't move, I couldn't even look at her, but I did have the impulse to hold her hand. She accepted and our fingers locked tightly. Neither of us could say anything for a while. We were absorbed in silence until,

"It's a beautiful letter ..." she said cautiously.

"Thank you ..." I replied with a shake in my voice.

"I mean, it's really dense, there's so much to it ... you express so much to me ... it's so heavy and well, you ... I just ... I just don't know how to respond to it, to the letter, to you ..."

"I don't know what to say right now, either ..."

"I mean ..."

"... Yeah?"

We were frozen. We were both overwhelmed and uncertain, at a complete loss of what to say or do. We continued to hold hands. We were out in the abyss, drifting in our emotions, especially me, but perhaps just as much for her, if not more ... this was new to her ... I'd been swimming in this for a while now ...I wanted to say the right thing, do the right thing. I didn't want to screw this up.

"You know, Tommy, how I feel about you ... I like you only as a friend." she said carefully, letting go of my hand. "Nothing could happen between you and I. I'm with Sharon. We're serious about each other."

"I know ... that's why I wanted you to know I don't expect anything from you ... You don't have to do anything."

"But ... I really had no idea you loved me in this way ... I wish you had told me before ..."

"... I ... I do, too ..." I began to say, the weight of her words hitting me. What was she saying by wishing I told this to her earlier? Did she mean that if I told her earlier on, before she got together with Sharon, that she would've wanted to be with me? Was she admitting to this? I couldn't tell. Then, a streak of defiance came within me. I never felt there was the opportunity, although I suppose now wasn't a real opportunity, either. "It's just I felt like I never had a chance with you. When I met you, you were with Ali. As soon as you broke up with her, you got together with Sharon. There was never an opportunity to tell you."

"Just to let me know, though ... you know?" she said, with conflicted motivations it seemed. I could see her almost crying out two different things at once: one, she never wanted me, and two, she wished I tried harder to win her over in the past. "I mean ... not so I, um ... not for us to, you know ... I don't know what I'm saying ..."

"I'm sorry to do this to you ..."

"No. Don't say that. It's okay. You should get this off your chest ... I see how important it is to you ... and, really, I'm flattered you feel so strongly about me ..."

"You don't think it was a bad idea ... to tell you?"

"No, not at all. We were wondering what was bothering you recently and now ... now I know ... But are you sure ... are you sure you really feel what you say you do in this letter?"

"Yes. Completely." I said as I sat up.

"How long have you felt this way?"

"I don't know ... perhaps since the first day I met you."

"Really? All this time? Eight months?"

"Maybe ... I don't think it came on strong, though ... I didn't realize it ... until about a month ago ... It's just ... "

"... Yeah?" She said uncertainly.

"I guess it's been ... it's been a whole lifetime of looking for something, in another person, some kind of understanding, a sensitivity, a kindness, an intuition ... something where I could see a person had that light inside, that they weren't dead inside, that they hadn't given up life, that they hadn't resorted to shallowness, that they were deeply disturbed by life, that they had an unshakable sweetness, a purity that no one, nothing in life could rip away ..." I said with tears streaming down my face, an overwhelming passion screaming out of me. "Just person after person after person of finding nothing, nothing going on inside, like they turned the switch off, decided it was game over, shut down, yet kept going with smiles over the closed door, kept pushing along for no good reason, they kicked out the purity, kicked out the understanding and put their ignorance on a fucking pedestal ...the whole world swallows people up ... never lets them breath ..." I continued, covered in tears, trembling in emotion and heartache. This was a life-long pain, the life-long pain of us all. I was laying myself completely bare, letting Charlotte see my soul, letting her see me in all my desperation and yearning. I never let anyone see me like this, so completely and utterly naked. I was in a black pit and the heavens were shining at the same time. I was engulfed. It was volcanic and Charlotte didn't know what to do. "... and with you ... I thought ... I thought maybe I found someone who could see what I was looking for, someone who didn't want to kill the purity, inside themselves or in other people ... I thought you'd understand, because recently you've shown me you understand, that we are, indeed, the same kind of creatures ..."

"I do understand, Tommy ..." she said, tears falling from her eyes. She was so overwhelmed, hit by a freight train ...

"... in this last month ..." I continued. "I realized just how much I loved you, in so many ways ... and my love for you is free, as free as I can make it, as giving as I can make it ... I don't want to hold you down, I don't want to hold you to anything, to any expectations ... I'm not doing this to get something from you in return ... and I don't expect to get anything from you ... you don't have to feel the same way as I do ... you don't need to reciprocate ... my love for you is so strong and so non-possessive that if some day you were to get married and you told me, the day before your wedding, that you wanted to spend the night with me, make love to me only that one time, I would do it ... whatever you gave to me, I'd accept it ... all that I ask is that you understand ... that's all I need is understanding ... nothing more ... there's so little understanding in the world, it beats me down ... I'm sure it beats everyone down ... day after day ... day in, day out ...again and again ... I guess that's why I reached out to you ... I needed someone to understand ...that's all ... nothing more ..."

We spent a good hour on the curb together. I felt it was one of the most beautiful moments I ever shared with anyone in my life ... there seemed to be a true connection between us ... Life rarely ever gave two people an opportunity like this to happen. We got up from the curb and I asked her if she was okay. She said yes. We came to an understanding that we would remain good friends and co-workers, nothing more. We shared a beautiful experience together this night, and from now on our friendship would be even stronger after this.

As the canvassing finished, right before Siango picked us up in the van, I asked Charlotte if we should tell anyone. She said, no, we shouldn't tell a soul. No one at all. I agreed. No one else would understand.

Driving back to the office in Culver City, Charlotte and I sat next to each other in the van. We were still recovering emotionally from before, but we talked and joked around. It seemed we were comfortable and at ease, as if we had released all the tension in all the world earlier that night. Before going to the office, the two of us wanted to get a bite to eat at Benito's down the street. We talked about a movie she saw recently that was about friendship. As we waited for our burritos, she rested her elbows on the counter and stuck her behind out. She noticed me looking at her ass as I stood behind her, and she wasn't bothered.

The rest of the week, my canvassing still sucked. It seemed I continued to run into people who wanted to use me as a punching bag. The abuse I got at the doors was relentless. I seriously thought about quitting C.W.F.P.S.J. The only thing I enjoyed working there was being around Charlotte. Our continued close friendship kept me from saying "screw it" to the job.

Exactly a week from the day I gave Charlotte the letter, I canvassed the Pico/Robertson area and had one of the best canvassing nights ever. Not so much money-wise, but in the interactions with the people. I met three people who became members and lifted my spirits from the never-ending canvassing desolation I'd gone through before. It was great. I was on a high emotionally as I got back to the office.

I told Siango about my night and he was sincerely happy for me. He then apologized and said he had some bad news.

"What is it?" I asked while we sat privately in the other office. Charlotte and Sharon were the only two left in the main office, across the hall, behind the closed doors.

"It's Charlotte ..." Siango said with a concerned look on his face.

"Yeah?"

"She's come to me and Cassandra with something ... Cassandra was hoping to be here to talk about this with you, as well, but the timing was bad since she needed to be up in the Bay ... so it's just me ..."

"Okay ..." I said, wondering what it could be. I really had no idea.

And then Siango, as gently as he could, hit me with the news. Charlotte went to Cassandra and him, and told them about that night ... She told them that I had blown up at some "mild-mannered" family, then I gave her a love letter, I began to shake and tremble and cry and scream, then told her I wanted to have sex with her ...

I never felt so horrible in my life ...

Never had I frozen so coldly in one flash ... in one moment of complete and utter coldness ...

Never had I felt such bitterness ...

I was crushed ... the good feeling I got from the night of canvassing, meeting those three people and being inspired by them ... that was obliterated in ten seconds of impenetrable ice ...

I couldn't believe what I was hearing from Siango. Was this really happening? Did Charlotte really do this? He then went into how she was uncomfortable working with me, that she felt I was ogling her body almost every second, that she didn't know how to act around me, that she never felt so uncomfortable in a workplace before ...

Charlotte killed me in that moment ... I had never been hurt by another person so much before ... I was shattered ... I could feel the knife in my back, lodged deeply, and going in deeper and deeper ...

But why did she do this? Why did she go and tell them all these lies? What did I do to her to make her do this? I reached out to her in so vulnerable and open a way, how could she betray me like this? Where the hell was she coming from? I couldn't understand it at all. I was furious with her. I never felt so much resentment towards another human being, ever ...

Siango said Charlotte was in the other room wanting to speak to me. I said no. I couldn't look at her right now. I didn't want to talk to her with so much anger. I knew it would get ugly.

I could talk to her in a couple days, when I calmed down, but not now. Siango refused, saying I had to deal with Charlotte right now. The situation had to be resolved, it couldn't wait any longer, the office needed to move ahead. I eventually accepted, burying my head down on the table, waiting for more torture to take place ... These fucking peace activists, I thought, they're sadistic!

Charlotte soon came in and froze once seeing me. Her heart cracked a bit looking at me. She could tell she hurt me, hurt me painfully. I was in shambles. She slowly came up to me and began to caress my hair and scalp. Siango became uncomfortable, not knowing what to make of it. He thought Charlotte was uncomfortable with me. She even apologized to me in her quiet, sweet voice. She seemed to feel horrible.

And then she suddenly changed. Once Siango said we should start talking about that night, she turned away from me and sat stiffly in a chair. Siango asked Charlotte to explain what was wrong, then she defensively said that I was the person who needed to explain myself. Siango said it seemed I wasn't at a place emotionally to do that at the moment. She should be the one to start it off since she was the one making the complaints anyway. Charlotte got ticked off at Siango and felt he was putting her on the spot.

Charlotte became even more defensive and uptight, going into her femi-Nazi mode. She took out my letter and dissected the parts which made her uncomfortable, saying that I continuously objectified her body, continuously implied having sex with her, and continuously made misogynistic remarks about her. ... I was stunned ... How could she do this? How could she shit on me like this? Me, a misogynist? What about the "mild mannered" Pacific Palisades father and son and the way they treated her? What about my coming to her defense?

She went on and on about how creepy my letter was and even began calling me a creep, a psycho, and a misogynist. She threw my letter to the floor in disgust. When I heard her do this, when I heard the papers falling to the floor, I lifted my head up and shouted at her, asking her how she could find my letter sexist and misogynistic. Where in the hell did she find anything I said to be negative in any fucking way? How? I was furious, raging at the fact she could see my love for her in this way, after everything! Was she insane? Did she have a split personality, I asked her? She was perfectly fine the night I gave her the letter.

She picked the letter up and began to dissect it again, insinuating I was stupid as well as a misogynistic creep for not listening to her the first time she dissected my creepy letter. We argued and shouted, and Siango tried to calm us down, but to no avail. Charlotte and I hated each other with a passion in that moment.

In the midst of the argument, I told Charlotte she was projecting other men onto me, that I did nothing wrong to her. When she looked at me now, she wasn't seeing me, the Thomas she knew, she was seeing all the other men who made her uncomfortable with their sexual advances. She became silent, shot me the look of death, and yelled "You're fired, Thomas!", then got up and left the room. Outside in the hall could be heard Charlotte and Sharon's voices and footsteps as they ran down the hall to the staircase.

I couldn't believe it. I couldn't believe Charlotte acted in this way.

Siango assured me that I wouldn't be fired. He didn't think Charlotte really meant it, being as she and I were in a heated argument. He also said that Charlotte couldn't technically fire me like that. Probably tomorrow she would calm down and feel bad about what happened, and we could talk about the situation in a more professional and respectable manner. If I wrote Charlotte a note apologizing to her, Siango thought she would become more reasonable. I agreed and left the note in her box at the office.

For now, though, Siango said, I should wait and not come to work for a while. Cassandra and Rick up in Berkeley had to deal with this before any final decision could be made. I accepted and went home.

I waited and waited until finally, three days later, Cassandra called me over the phone. First, she said ambiguously, she thought the letter I wrote to Charlotte was beautiful ... what? So was she going to be supportive of me? Not in the least. I didn't know why she said the letter was beautiful because she then became a tyrant. I thought perhaps, because of hints I got in the past, perhaps she would've wanted to receive the love letter ... perhaps she would've reciprocated. Then I reminded myself of how she was, how even more uptight she was than Charlotte. No, she said the letter was beautiful to catch me off-guard, to throw me off. That petition was still on her mind ...

Cassandra acted like a cop, phony and condescending. She tried to push me, bully me into admitting I did something wrong. She kept going and going at me like a bull. She wouldn't give up, but I wouldn't either. I told her over and over again I did nothing wrong. She tried to manipulate me with clever feminist guilt trips about all the sexual abuse women have gone throughout history, century after century. I asked her if I was being punished not for my own actions but for the guilt of all the males of history. She didn't respond.

This went on for two weeks, with Cassandra calling me and trying to get me to admit I was in the wrong. I just wouldn't do it, no matter how relentless she was. After the two weeks passed, a horrible, wrenching two weeks of waiting and waiting and waiting and waiting, Cassandra wanted to meet me at the Cuban restaurant Versailles, across the street from the office. She would give me the final verdict.

Cassandra waited until the food arrived to tell me. She supported Charlotte's decision to have me fired. For sexual harassment. I couldn't eat the food. I sat at the table in silence. I really thought they'd be reasonable, I thought that, in the end, we'd all resolve this like mature human beings. We were, after all, peace activists. But no. "Justice" prevailed over understanding. As I looked into Cassandra's cold eyes, I knew that these people, these "good people" who fought the good fight, who courageously stood up to the insane destructiveness of the Bush administration, these peace activists couldn't change the world. Their ignorance, like the ignorance of everyone, of our entire society, was their death ... my death was the pain from their ignorance ...

As time passed, my love for Charlotte, which turned into furious anger and heartbreaking disappointment, then became obsessive curiosity. It couldn't end like that. Could it? I had to know what really happened. Something was missing. That night I gave her the letter, I knew, I knew in the deepest part of my heart, she understood. Didn't she? She didn't feel threatened by me then. She connected with me and knew where I was coming from. I could see it in her eyes. It wasn't just the words she said.

Something must've happened after that night and during that following week. But what? Did someone tell her something? Was someone influencing her? Was it Cassandra? Katrina? Sharon? Did she really go and tell Siango and Cassandra and Sharon, after promising me she wouldn't tell a soul? Was she lying to me that whole night, just so I wouldn't get angry? Or, as she often did, did she change her mind later, perhaps after an argument with Sharon? Or perhaps she didn't want to admit to her own feelings about me? Did she love me, and felt threatened by that love? Was it too intense for her, so she became scared? I had absolutely no idea whatsoever ... I was completely and utterly in the dark ...

Some time later, I called the office to try and get Cassandra and

Siango to sign a letter of recommendation. Charlotte picked up the phone ... we were both uncomfortable ... I said I realized she probably didn't want to speak to me so I needed to speak to Cassandra. Charlotte felt bad and said that she actually wanted to talk to me. She missed me. What? "She missed me"? I couldn't believe what I was hearing. She was either full of shit, or I really was missing something.

Charlotte said no one else was in the office so she felt comfortable talking to me. Huh? She then went on to talk with me over the phone for twenty minutes! I was caught off-guard as hell. She talked to me like nothing happened, like we were the close friends we once were. She read a cheesy poem to me, to try and inspire me, I suppose. She said she was sorry for what she did, but that she was backed into a corner. "Backed into a corner"? What did she mean, I asked. She couldn't explain then and now, but that some day soon when she had the chance, she would. She wanted to have coffee with me and explain everything for two or three hours. She said she needed that much time to go over everything ...

I waited and waited and never got Charlotte's phone call. Months passed, and nothing. I called her and e-mailed her several times but never got a reply. I was still left in the dark ... What the hell happened? The whole time Siango tried to persuade me to stand up to Charlotte, Cassandra, Rick, and the whole organization. I had a case to take their asses to court if I wanted to. They fired me without probable cause.

I went to the A.C.L.U., and they told me they couldn't take the case. Siango said I could still try to find a lawyer but I refused. I just couldn't do it. Whatever legal action I took, it wouldn't only hurt C.W.F.P.S.J but Charlotte as well. I didn't want to hurt her unless I knew for sure she was completely responsible for what she did. Based on that night I was with her when I gave the letter, and based on her wanting to tell me what happened, I wasn't convinced she was to blame whole-heartedly. There was something else, someone else. I believed in revenge, but not until I wrought that revenge on the right people.

The U.S. Invasion of Iraq was approaching and the Peace Movement around the world was enormous. Cities everywhere were having protests and demonstrations in vast numbers of people. London had one million people, New York about half a million, San Francisco around the same. Even Los Angeles, the most jaded of all cities, had a huge protest. I went.

There were thousands and thousands of people packed on the streets around Hollywood and Vine. As I waded through the crowd, a rush came over me. It was such a high to see so many people take to the street like this. As I got closer to Hollywood blvd., I heard a woman's voice yell my name over and over again. Who the hell could this be, I thought.

It was Charlotte.

It was estimated there were 100,000 people at the protest that day. Out of all those people, I see her ... She ran up to me, wanting to hug me, but stopped herself. She had Sharon in tow. Sharon froze once seeing me. He didn't look at me once.

“Isn't this awesome?!” Charlotte yelled to me in excitement, over the noise of the crowd.

“Yeah, it's great!” I yelled back. It was so good to see her, even after everything ...

“You by yourself here?!” she asked.

“Yeah! You here with work?!”

“Yup!” she said, looking at me with a sweet smile. It was as if we could only pay attention to each other, despite the fact Sharon was right there, and thousands of other people were screaming and yelling around us. “It's good to see you!” she said, her eyes still locked on me.

“Out of all these people, I run into you!” I said, hinting at the strange coincidence. I was insinuating we still had things to resolve.

“I know, it's strange!” she said with a smile. “I'll catch ya later!” she said as she continued wading through the crowd with Sharon. “Have fun!"

A few steps away, Charlotte turned back to me. I turned to her expecting her to wave goodbye, then leave quickly. But her eyes locked on me again. She wouldn't move. She gave me the most mysterious smile I ever saw ... for a good ten seconds ... it seemed like forever ... then she walked away ...

What was behind that smile? Why did she do that? What was she trying to communicate? Was she laughing at me? Ridiculing me? Was she telling me that she loved me, was in love with me, despite everything, all this time? I never found out. We never had that two or three hour conversation where she explained everything ... Up until this very day, I've wondered what happened, called her, e-mailed her, came by the office, asked others ... but never did I get any answers ...

EPILOGUE.

THE MANUSCRIPT.

I've come to the end of this part of my life, Daniel, the part in which leads up to your birth, these last few years ... Everything I wrote about in this manuscript, this personal history of mine, is a precursor to your existence ...

I suppose you're wondering why I decided to write this manuscript, what were my intentions, what motivated me to put my life to paper for you to read. I'm also hoping that by the time you get to this, you might understand why I wrote this all down ... once you've lived enough life, once you've accumulated enough experiences, you begin to realize the true nature of life ... the nature of the society we live in ... you begin to realize just how much is wasted ... life can be so much more ... so much more ...

... I chose to write down the undercurrents of my life, the emotions for lack of a better word, since those are the things which we live with ... our emotional lives are what creates so much else ... it's the essence of who we are, it's what we live with day after day ... always value that part of your life, always stay in touch with it ... even if the rest of the world has cut it off ... If you're strong enough within yourself, to confront one's life head-on, to take a look at your life, at the people you knew, you loved and hated, to take a good look at the world we live in, the society we're forced to function in, everything ... all that we're dealt with ... to take it all on, with as much honesty as one can possibly hope to have, that's what's worth living for ... even if it kills you ...

Something specific motivated me to write my personal history down, as well ... About a month ago, a week before I started writing this manuscript, I went to visit my father, Jean, in the valley at his mobile home. Like we do now and then, he gave me a Tarot card reading. He'd been taught by an old Hungarian friend years ago how to do the Tarot. While neither my father nor I ever literally believed in it - neither of us believed in anything superstitious like that, really - despite both of our skepticism, we saw the Tarot as an interesting psychological thing to do. It was important to read it metaphorically, not literally, and to use it to your psychological purpose - to help you.

This one time, the main card, the first one Jean put down, was the card of Death ... it caught us both by surprise. We both froze for a second. We made attempts at understanding what it could mean, look at all the emotional "deaths" I'd gone through the last few years. It made sense to look at it in this way, since, as you can tell now from this manuscript, I did indeed go through a number of emotional deaths ...

But afterwards, the Death card hung inside my gut. I had this strange feeling about it. It scared me. I started to think possibly I would die soon ... All the psychological deaths surmounted within me, so much so that I began to think it would eventually lead to my literal death ... I didn't tell Jean, I didn't tell anyone I felt this way ... I didn't want to scare anyone. I kept it to myself and decided, just in case, just in case I do die, however it might happen, I had to put something to paper for you, Daniel ...

In case I do in end up dying, I don't want to leave you with nothing, no knowledge of who I was, coming from my own lips ... no insight into who I was as a person, warts and all, no knowledge of my emotional life, the most important aspect to who we all are ... I believe you have the right to know who your father was, if I do end up dying ... This is why I've been writing, like a madman, hours and hours of writing each day, obsessively putting my life down to paper for you ... I want you to know who I was ... why things happened the way it did ... and perhaps, in the process, help you with your own life ...

But hopefully, my fears of my own death are simply the fears of superstitions, as I believe they are. However it will be, I realize now how important it is that I did write this down, my personal history ... I didn't just let it all go, become forgotten like so much of our lives end up ... washed away with Time ...

And today, Daniel, I have some interesting news. As I write this to you, I received in the mail something very strange ... I received a letter from Charlotte ...

She says in her letter that she moved to Minnesota with Sharon, that they tried to make it work there, then he moved back to L.A soon after they broke up. She stayed in Minnesota for a year, but felt unfulfilled. She decided to come back to L.A., attempt to get into another progressive organization, not C.W.F.P.S.J. She says she's done with them. Most importantly of all, she says in this letter, she wants to see me ...

She says she wants to meet me at a beach in between Malibu and Santa Monica. Apparently, according to her, we hung out there once, a day we were to go canvassing in Malibu. I honestly don't remember being on a beach in Malibu with her, but I guess we did. The other odd thing is that she wants to meet in the middle of the night. Why, I'm not so sure. It'll be god damn cold out there! Oh well, she did talk about being on the beach in the middle of the night, one time in the past. When she did, it seemed she was insinuating something romantic ... perhaps this is what she wants ...

A part of me is saying, “No!” Another part of me is saying, “Why not?” I don't know ... This could be my opportunity ... to resolve the past with her ... to find some answers ... and perhaps consummate a romance with her ...

I've decided to go ... to see what happens. I've always been a curious person, Daniel. That's the nature of one who looks into things, and I'm sure you'll be the same.

So, the next time I write to you, I will have found out what happened with Charlotte on the cold beach, in the middle of the night. I'll let you know whether I experienced romantic bliss and understanding, or, once again, felt the incessant, uncompromising ... death of life …

I just want to wish you my love, before I go see her ... and know, however bleak life may be, it is beautiful … pain or bliss, there is beauty there worth living for …

This manuscript, my life, has been for you, Daniel ... for you ...

Love,

Your Father,

Thomas.

Made in the USA
Middletown, DE
11 January 2022